The

NETAHS

DOWN *in the* VALLEY

BOOK TWO

LISA KANIUT COBB

PRAISE FOR

THE NETAHS
DOWN IN THE VALLEY

"I loved this sequel to *The Netahs: Into the Wilderness*...! I was completely wrapped up in the fantasy world, and was rooting for Josh and his Netah community, all animal shape-shifters but with very relatable t(w)een problems. The story picks up where the first left off, with Josh now deep into the Netah community and trying to find his place as a half-human. Add the complication of his outlaw Netah father and we have Josh torn in different directions, all while trying to figure out who he is as a halfling. I can see kid readers strongly identifying with Josh all while getting lost in the Netah world. The plot moves quickly, which had me forget about time as I read.

This series is one I'll be recommending for younger YA readers, which can be hard to find books for. **Perfect for fans of Rick Riordan books and the Netflix series *Sweet Tooth*, The Netahs series is going to appeal to reluctant and avid readers alike. Highly recommend it!**"

—Fleur Bradley, award-winning author
of *Midnight at the Barclay Hotel*
and *Daybreak on Raven Island*

An incredibly intriguing coming-of-age story, The Netah's, Down in the Valley, book 2, focuses on the continuing journey of Josh as he navigates his way through the exciting world of the Netahs; shifters who can change between human and animal form. Josh joins a Netah Elk village that accepts him as he learns about life in Netah society and about his volatile family history. My favorite thing about this book is that Josh doesn't take everything at face value. Like every preteen he questions boundaries while struggling with his emotions. The story moves at a good pace with fresh world-building. I almost believed that if I hiked out into the mountains of Colorado, I could possibly stumble upon something fantastic.

I feel like this story would be super great for pre-teens, as they can experience the wilderness through the eyes of local wildlife and a modern teen. I can't wait to see what happens in book 3!

—Katherine Aman, International
Teaching Professional,
Cercedilla, Spain

Lisa Cobb's sequel, *The Netahs, Down in the Valley*, sweeps readers into a world that seamlessly blends humanity with wildlife. The Netahs' gift of transforming from their human to their animal form requires them to exist in a secret society. When Josh is discovered as half-Netah, he's swept away from everything he knows and forced into a new life, the Netah way of life. With beautiful imagery and a dynamic cast of characters, this enchanting tale explores the meaning of family, belonging, and change. After reading this book, I will not look at an elk, a fox, or a skunk without considering bigger possibilities and other ways of being.

—Jessica Speer, Award-winning author of
BFF or NRF (Not Really Friends),
Middle School - Safety Goggles Advised,
and *The Phone Book*

 FriesenPress

One Printers Way
Altona, MB R0G 0B0
Canada

www.friesenpress.com

Special thanks to editor, Jen McClorey and designer,
Teresita Hernandez-Quesada

ISBN
978-1-03-917464-1 (Hardcover)
978-1-03-917463-4 (Paperback)
978-1-03-917465-8 (eBook)

1. YOUNG ADULT FICTION, LEGENDS, MYTHS, FABLES

Distributed to the trade by The Ingram Book Company

TABLE OF CONTENTS

For you, Dad. One of the good guys.

CHAPTER 1

Killing Time

Tension left his shoulders as Josh walked into the aspen grove, breathing in their slightly soapy scent as he remembered the long days it had taken him to learn how to turn into an elk. No one knew how a Netah halfling like him transformed. He had to figure it out while his new Netah friends kept an eye on him. They helped by jumping out from behind trees, which made him panic and transform. When the bear crashed through the woods on a collision course, or a rock slide rushed towards him, Josh shifted into an elk, but inducing fear was unsustainable. There had to be a better way to transform. After a lot of trial and error, he'd learned to think about the scent of aspens to transform into an elk, or hamburger juices dribbling down his chin to become a human.

That was months ago. Since then, he'd learned to transform at will, proven he would protect the Netah's secrets, and helped solve a health crisis among a community of Netah littles. The council had met, asked what he wanted, and told him to wait while they decided. After that, his friend Fern left for a long overdue family visit, but not before she wrapped her arms around Josh and nuzzled his neck. They'd been through a lot together. Before he could say anything like "thanks," she transformed into a fox and skipped away into the woods. His last glimpse of the white tip of her bushy red tail caught his breath and made the day seem suddenly a little colder.

Josh now lived in the vast wilderness of Colorado's mountains. His human parents could never know the secret of his escape, the day his Netah side manifested. Josh panicked when antlers poked through his hoodie in the middle of the crowded high school halls. A large senior whisked him out of school and transformed into a bear as he led them across suburban yards towards the foothills. Josh's body continued to change, shredding his clothes as he ran. His transforming brain became befuddled, he couldn't work his mouth into words, his flight or fight instincts took over as he followed the bear, unsure why, just knowing it was necessary. His torn clothing supported the rumor that he'd been attacked by a bear that had been seen in the neighborhoods.

George, the Netah bear, had also left once his assignment to look after Josh was finished. Josh waited with his remaining Netah friend, Rose, the skunk, while the Netah High Council decided his fate. Rose thought they might as well start walking towards the biggest Netah elk community she knew about, assuming he would be allowed to join them for the winter.

Josh tasted the decaying leaves of autumn in the cold mountain air. He paused at a stream trickling through the brown and crunchy grasses at his feet. He'd forgotten his passenger, who nearly toppled off his back when he lowered his head for a drink. Rose had fallen asleep across his back. She dug her tiny claws into his hide and held tight as his head dipped to the water. Josh asked, "There's no chance those were Netahs who snuck up on us this morning?"

"None. I smelled them." Rose sniffed with disdain, as she slid to the ground. "They were merely humans. Why?"

"Oh, nothing." Josh sighed at the irony of a human who could transform into a skunk, who didn't like the smell of humans who could not transform at all.

"We've only been out here for a couple of days, Josh. Hold on a minute." Rose hopped behind a bush and reappeared moments later. Josh was still a little embarrassed when the Netahs in their animal forms took care of nature's call right in front of him, and he appreciated Rose's sensitivity to that. Josh had a sudden flashback to when Rose had posed as a foster child in his human home. He was very glad she'd pretended to be old enough to be out of diapers! When Rose reappeared, she said, "You are a very unusual case. There are many different opinions about what should be done about you."

"Done? Why, because I only learned how to transform into my animal at puberty? Or because I'm a halfling?" Josh knew both of those made him unusual, but he was getting very tired of being treated like an alien. Josh demanded, "There must be other elk Netahs like me. Why can't I go live with them?" Josh hoped the council would allow this. It was the best-case scenario for his future.

"Hey, you know it's a matter of Netah security," Rose reminded him. "We have lived in secret for millennia. It's how we've survived. Besides, the council doesn't know you like I do. They don't know what a stand-up guy you are."

"Even more so, now that I have four legs, right?" Josh appreciated his elk form: the fur, the four legs, the ability to eat whatever he could forage, all made living in the wilderness easy.

Rose snorted.

"I understand about security," Josh continued, as they wandered aimlessly through the aspens. "But, I mean, how long do they need to decide what to do with me?"

"What, am I boring you?" Rose scoffed. "Humans are not good at waiting. It's something you'll get better at as you spend more time in your elk form. Netah are very patient."

"Well, there's something to look forward to," Josh said.

"Come on," Rose said, having looked around from the top of a boulder. "I know just what you need." She led Josh deeper into the woods.

Leaves carpeted the ground with a range of colors from damp brown to crispy black. The clear mountain air warmed as the sun rose. Josh stepped around the low junipers that carpeted the ground as Rose disappeared in the underbrush. "Hey, I'm hungry. Mind if we stop for a snack?" Josh called after her.

"Yeah, I'm hungry, too," Rose responded. Josh followed her voice. She said, "Found them. Come here. Lesson number one in what elk eat in the cold months." She stood like a dog pointing next to a straggly bush topped with dark red berries.

"What's this?" Josh asked. He bit off a berry and chewed. The sweet pods filled with crunchy seeds made his eyes grow wide until he grimaced at the tart aftertaste.

Rose laughed at his expressions, then stepped out of the way so he could eat more. "I think those are called rose hips," she said. "Also, you can fill up on those grasses." She pointed with her nose at the dried meadow full of seed heads that blew in the wind on the edge of the aspen grove.

"Whatever." Josh didn't care what they were called, he just wanted to eat every last one of these berries that reminded him of sweet/tart candies at Halloween.

Rose searched for her own treats near a small stream. She was full long before Josh could fill his stomach, so she curled up in the sun for a nap.

Still hungry, Josh found a seed head that looked like it used to be a flower. *This could use some salt.* Josh chewed his way through different grasses. Josh was still learning what he could eat, identifying foods by their tan tassels, small dark seed clusters, or soft as baby hair seeds that tickled the inside of his mouth. He took a nice cold drink from the stream. Finally, he wandered back to where he'd seen Rose curl up for her nap.

She looked so comfortable, that Josh couldn't bear to disturb her and decided he could rest for a while, too. Rose napped in a dense stand of pines that blocked the wind. Josh would practice being patient.

He couldn't settle down, though, because his mind raced with questions. *Where is the valley full of Netah elk that Rose said she'd take me to? Will they like me? Where is my birth father? Patience, breathe, wait. Grrrr!* Eventually his eyelids grew heavy.

Josh dreamt he could see his human parents in a cave behind a waterfall. He tried jumping through it, but his elk hooves slid down the wet rocks and he fell into a deep pool. He knew he was dreaming so he made himself surface and swim to the shore. His parents seemed even farther away. He tried to call them, and his throat grew sore from bugling. He couldn't get out a single human word.

Then a flock of ravens arrived. He knew they were Netahs, but they pretended they were just birds and wouldn't talk to him. Then a big, brawny bear walked up. Josh thought it was his old friend George, but George wouldn't help, either. A soundless scream filled Josh's throat when he suddenly woke up, his chest heaving and heart aching.

"Sorry," Rose said. "I think it's not cool to wake someone when they're dreaming, but you seemed very upset. I couldn't watch you anymore. You okay?"

Josh took a few moments to get his bearings. He wore his warm elk fur as he lay in the well of a tall pine. His black nose dripped from the cold. The sun shone at about three o'clock in the sky and it was cold.

Josh got his bearings as his breathing evened out. "Yeah, I'm fine. Bad dream, that's all. How was your nap?"

Rose stood and shook out her fur. "Fine," she said. "I've been awake for a while. I figured you needed your beauty sleep. Come on, I'm hungry again."

"Surprise, surprise!" Josh laughed.

They might have walked thirty minutes or ten. He couldn't check his watch or phone. Elk didn't have pockets or wrists, and there were no charging stations in the wilderness. Josh tried to get used to that, but he wasn't happy about it.

His thoughts returning to what little he knew about his birth father, Josh asked, "Do Netahs have jails?"

"Yes, but they're problematic," Rose answered with a little snort.

"Yeah, how so?" Josh said.

"Well," Rose mused. "For instance, one time my uncle stole a whole bushel of apples. He was just a kid, and what a stomachache he got. My grandpa tried house arrest, but my uncle just dug himself out and ran away."

"Huh, so it's mostly symbolic?" Josh asked, slightly distracted by the scents of Christmas wafting off the firs they passed.

"Each Netah animal community has to take responsibility for their own. They have to decide the consequences. Aberrant behavior is against our better instincts, so it's rare, but it's often dealt with swiftly and sometimes permanently."

"You mean death?" He froze, horrified.

"Depends on the group and the leaders. Some are harsh; some more forgiving. Often servitude is the punishment. The loss of our freedom is one of our worst fears."

"Are you talking about slavery?" His impression of the Netah community was getting darker by the minute.

"No." She hesitated and thought about it a moment. "It's more like community service. It's not imposed because of race or species, but for rehabilitation. There are very clear behavior modification goals, and the service is only for a limited time. The goal is to return individuals to their communities."

Suddenly wondering just how old Rose was, based on her ease in discussing things like behavior modification, Josh asked, "Did your uncle ever come back?"

"Sure."

"Did he have to do service?"

"Absolutely. He was put in charge of harvesting the rest of the apples that year. He never did have much of a taste for apples after that." Rose grinned at the thought. "An apple sounds good right about now," she mused.

They entered a stand of tall lodgepole pines. Josh asked, "So, you don't use animals as servants, what about as property? Do you treat all animals the same or only animals that are Netahs?" Josh didn't have much information about how Netahs lived with each other. Heck, he just learned he was a Netah himself, or at least a halfling. The night before, she explained that the laws for their society were similar to North America's, and explained that Netahs had helped write the American bill of rights. He was most interested in their idea of criminal justice, because he'd been told his birth father was an outlaw. He wanted to know his father's punishment for being with Josh's human mother, which, Josh had learned, was strictly forbidden.

"We're talking about Netahs." Rose interrupted his thoughts. "Animals are our brothers and deserve our respect and their own spaces. They just don't talk."

Josh noticed how easily Rose could disappear into the shadows as they walked. "So, do Netahs hunt?"

"Well, sure. There are Netah omnivores and vegetarians, just like among humans."

Josh laughed. "So Netah bears might keep their own pond full of trout? Or lynxes could keep a pigeon coop?" He watched Rose for a reaction. She ignored him. "I'll bet Netah wolves keep herds of deer."

Rose snorted, but kept moving. "Sure, if we were fat and lazy, but where's the fun in that? We hunt as we've always done, part sport, part grocery shopping. No money required, just some good old-fashioned healthy outdoor exercise."

"Darn," Josh teased. "I liked the image of lynxes and pigeons." He studied the low, dark clouds overhead and thought he smelled snow coming.

"What do you think would happen if humans stumbled upon such a setup?" Rose had led them across an open meadow and over a hill where she paused, her black-and-white fur fluffy to ward off the cold.

"Good point," Josh admitted, catching up with her. "That would raise a whole lot of questions. Although couldn't the Netahs just turn into humans to avoid suspicion?" Speaking of humans, Josh saw no signs of human activity in the valley like roads or buildings, and realized they had hiked into a very remote area. He squinted into the bitter wind, and he rolled his shoulders, appreciating the extra thick ruff of fur keeping him cozy and warm.

Rose huffed. "Again, lazy."

Josh let that go, her opinion clear. As he followed her downhill, his thoughts returned to what they had been talking about before he'd gone off on this tangent, the proverbial crime and punishment. A nagging question popped back up. "I'm just going to say it. Where is my Netah father?"

"Um . . ."

"Aha! You do know where he is!" Josh's heart raced at this unexpected development.

"Yes," Rose answered. "He is in a facility, serving his time."

"Like doing community service?" Josh had a picture in his mind of his father in a steamy laundry room, folding sheets and towels.

"Oh, he's working all right," Rose said.

"Like on a chain gang?" *Come on, spill it! The suspense is killing me!*

"I believe he's in an agricultural facility, growing winter vegetables for the herd."

Josh didn't think that sounded too bad. "Is it near the community in Wyoming?" he asked.

"Yes. How did you know?"

"It's the only Netah elk herd you ever mentioned, and I assumed that's where you are leading me."

"Hmm, sometimes you are too smart for your own good." Rose swished her striped tail in annoyance. "Which brings us to the council meeting," she continued. "They will ask what you want to do. How will you answer?"

"I already told them I wanted to live with my own kind," Josh reminded her. She'd been there at the last council circle, with Lorna the lynx presiding and thanking him for his help taking care of the Netah littles. She'd asked him what he wanted in return, and he'd made it clear. Lorna said the council had to discuss it, before the circle of animals dissolved into the woods.

"Yes, but you don't really have your own kind, do you? You're a halfling."

Josh sighed. "Thanks for reminding me." He lowered his head to munch on some grasses at his feet. Rose seemed distracted.

Josh didn't need to eat so much as stall for time to think. His heart ached when he thought of his human family and his nightmare. *Do I want to go back to them?* Yes, of course. He missed his dad's stupid dad jokes and watching Avalanche games together, and his mom's hugs and casseroles, and amazement at his ability to polish off those casseroles. Was that because he was part elk? Josh had felt like their favorite person on the planet. Who wouldn't miss that?

Could I go back? Well, he'd been told that was a hard no. He didn't want to be banished like his father. *Or do I? Would that mean I could return to my human family?* He lifted his head and pursed his lips, unable to hold back a loud burp and a cloud of breath into the chilly air. Thunder rumbled overhead. The mild days of autumn would soon be over and a thunder snowstorm was building.

Rose said, "Hey, listen, I'm sorry if I hurt your feelings. I'm trying to prepare you for the council's perspective."

"I get it. I'm one of you, but not. Plus, they're cautious with me, because of my criminal dad."

"Right. I think they would prefer that you have no contact with him."

"But he's locked up, right?"

"That's the idea, but there have been some mysterious problems." Rose screwed up her face. "I probably shouldn't have said that."

"Mysterious problems? Are you trying to avoid my questions, or just don't know?"

"Um, I don't know, it's just rumors."

"Rumors about what? Come on, you're my friend. Don't leave me hanging like this!"

"I'm sorry, Josh. All I know is he's a technological genius, and the council is suspicious about something technical that's been going wrong. They blame him, but he's locked up, so I don't know how that can be. Like I said, mysterious."

"Right." Josh took a long breath and let it go slowly. He didn't want to badger Rose. She didn't deserve that. He'd let it go for now. "Where does that leave me?"

"Between a rock and a hard place." Rose gave him a wide grin, showing off her pointy little teeth. "I understand your frustration and wish I could say more."

Josh scanned the woods for signs of movement and heard the song of a chickadee. "Does the council expect us to wait here for their decision?"

"Nah, that's why we're heading to that big Netah elk community I told you about. We might as well head in that direction so you have a shorter trip when they finally agree to let you go there. Don't worry, they'll be able to find us. Leave it to Crawley. She always seems to know where you are." Rose blended into the shadows and Josh had to concentrate to keep track of her, even though he really wanted to search the skies for Crawley, his raven friend. As questions about the future hovered unanswered over their heads, they topped a hill, a little out of breath. The land continued to rise and the clouds grew darker. Josh saw a haze over distant peaks where it was already snowing.

Suddenly, a group of small animals appeared out of nowhere and assembled in front of the two travelers. The group included several beavers, picas, some magpies, and a chipmunk, but none of the littles he'd met before.

Josh had been to several council meetings before, and they were always presided over by a lynx named Lorna. She was nowhere in sight. Josh overheard angry whispers like: "Who does he think he is?" "What a stupid animal, he nearly stepped on Chief Godfrey!" "I told you we couldn't trust him; I don't care what the others say."

Josh fought to keep his smile from turning into a smirk, and said, "Can I help you?"

The beaver lifted his chin and coughed, while the others huddled and kept their distance.

"Ah, yes, young man, or rather," he hesitated and looked for help from the others. "What did we decide to call him?"

"Belk," the pica squeaked.

"Belk?" Josh asked.

"Yes, it is short for boy elk. Clever, right?" The beaver grinned.

"Couldn't you just call me Josh?" he asked.

"Um, well, I suppose." Slightly defeated, the beaver gathered himself and said, "As you wish, young Josh, allow me to introduce myself. I am Chief Godfrey the Elder."

"Pleasure to meet you." Josh grinned.

"Impertinent belk!" Godfrey spluttered and puffed up his chest even more. "Silence!" he bellowed, although his large front teeth made it sound more like "thilenth."

"Sorry, I . . ."

Godfrey interrupted. "I . . . We are here to tell you to go away. There is no place for you among us. We do not trust you; we do not want you here, we do not even like you a little. You are a nuisance and a threat to our whole society, and we will not tolerate your presence any longer." A chorus of cheers erupted from the huddle.

"Uh, hmm. Is that an official council order?" Josh asked, detecting an odd cadence to the guy's delivery. It didn't help Josh take him seriously. He noticed Rose had kept quiet, and that no one answered his question. He concluded that this delegation was not official, as Chief Godfrey attempted to stare Josh down. Still, it was hard to be intimidated by a beaver who spoke like a Dr. Seuss character.

"It's official, obviously," Godfrey insisted. "Where you go is no concern of ours, belk," he sneered. "You have disrupted our preparations for far too long. It is time for you to go." Godfrey glanced at the others, who nodded hopefully.

"Preparations for what?" Josh asked, oddly curious.

"The winter, of course. We have to gather food, insulate our homes, fortify our defenses. Have you no brains at all in that ugly head?"

Josh transformed instantly into a human and towered over the beaver. "There's no need to be insulting." He heard the others gasp. Apparently, Chief Godfrey did not usually meet with resistance.

Josh glanced around at the assembled animals. He kept his voice even and his tone reasonable. "I'm sorry you feel that way and that I interrupted your preparations. Look, guys, I had no control over my birth or what I am. I am trying hard to fit in and meet your standards. Give me a chance."

Josh waited as Chief Godfrey huddled with the others. Murmurs rolled through the group, some angry, some conciliatory.

"Okay then," Josh said. "If you'll excuse me, I have an appointment." With that he transformed back into an elk and stepped over a couple of chirping picas and around an angry magpie.

Rose caught up moments later and they walked along in silence for a little while.

"That was fun," Josh finally said with a chuckle.

"You handled them well." Rose giggled.

"Did you see that coming? And if so, couldn't you give me a heads-up?"

"Well, I suspected something like this would happen," Rose admitted. "Don't worry, they do not, as you suspected, represent the council."

"They wanted me to believe they were a council, though, right?"

"Right, and you reacted perfectly. Your manners won some of them over. Keep it up, and you'll be fine when we meet the real deal again. Consider it a practice round."

Josh laughed and shook his head, befuddled. "Maybe they weren't thinking straight because winter is coming and they need to hibernate or something, but how would it help for me to just go away? I mean, that wouldn't exactly guarantee I would keep the Netah's secrets. Were they just stupid?"

Rose snorted, "You're right. It wouldn't solve anything. They were angry about being distracted from winter prep, sure, but I think it was more fear of the unknown, meaning fear of you. Fear does weird things to people."

Rose and Josh walked in silence for the rest of the afternoon, aiming for the mountain pass, where he'd noticed it was snowing earlier. They reached the snow, which was already deep enough to slow Josh down, and very difficult for Rose. Josh invited her to jump onto his back again and he carried her over the pass. He squinted into the blowing snow and leaned against the bitter wind. "Hold on tight, I'm going to get through this as fast as I can," he told Rose as he picked up his pace and galloped into sunshine on the other side of the mountain.

CHAPTER 2

An Invitation

J osh quickened his pace as he left the snowy heights behind him and the clouds raced overhead. "It has to be at least twenty degrees warmer here," he observed.

"Change of altitude can do that, but yes, I feel it, too," Rose sighed as they settled into a spot in the shelter of some large boulders for a rest. They both watched a black dot approach.

Josh said, "Is that Crawley? Looks like the council found us, just like you said."

Crawley, as she banked into a turn, called out with a loud *caw*, and landed at their feet. She transformed into a girl and said, "The council has reached an agreement. We are gathering just over that outcrop ahead of you. Please follow me."

Her businesslike manner surprised Josh. He also noticed her clothes. She didn't wear the Goth style she had worn at school. He remembered that style was part of her disguise to look like a high school girl. She still wore all black: a sleek, formfitting ski onesie with sturdy boots. Did that portend a gloomy message? He really wished girls didn't expect a guy to read their moods by their clothes. Josh didn't speak that language. Still, he followed the girl with trepidation.

The council was a circle of various animals standing in a small clearing. Josh's heart skipped a beat when he saw his old friends there, including Fern the fox, George the bear, and Lorna the lynx. It felt like a family reunion. Everyone was in their animal forms, so he remained in his as he watched Crawley transform back into a raven and take up a position in a tree above the clearing.

Lorna said, "You have received the council's provisional acceptance to our community. Full acceptance can be achieved within a year. Do you understand?"

"I understand 'provisional,' yes." Josh raised one eyebrow. "How do I get full acceptance?"

Lorna hesitated, so his friend Crawley swooped down to stand next to her. With a nod from Lorna, she explained in a friendly tone. "You must live among a Netah elk community and learn their ways, fit in, follow their rules, and stay out of trouble."

Josh wanted to laugh at that last bit, but pressed his lips together instead and settled for a nod. The look he exchanged with Crawley made it clear they both knew that was a joke. Crawley flew back to her perch.

"Good." Lorna took over. "What do you wish from us? We will reward you for service rendered during the littles crisis."

"Service?" Josh needed to double-check that's what she meant. Lorna's slight lisp had distorted the word. She nodded. "Uh, hmm . . ." Josh knew she referred to the little Netahs who had become sick and couldn't completely transform from humans to their animal forms. He shifted on his hip, where he had taken a bullet. That seemed like so long ago, even though it had only been a few months. *What do I want? I already told you!* "I want to live among other Netah elk," he said.

"Agreed," Lorna replied. "We think you should join a local herd. There is a need for bachelors in our North Park community."

"A need? Why, is it dangerous?"

"No, but we would prefer not to go into details. You must trust that your safety and future among the Netahs are our first priority."

Josh considered this while he studied the faces of his friends in the circle. They seemed to be avoiding his eyes. "Okay fine," he said uncertainly.

Lorna nodded and looked over her shoulder. "Hesta, you may approach."

Josh watched an enormous elk emerge from the woods with its head raised, like a guy wearing reading glasses. "Hello, Josh. I am Hesta, chief of the North Park Netahs. We are happy to host you in our valley. It can be harsh at times, but we eat well. We will teach you our ways."

"Nice to meet you, Hesta," Josh said. "Um . . . I am honored to accept."

Hesta chuckled and Josh returned the smile, which reminded him of his human father's. He would jump through hoops for another dose of that approval. He glanced at his friends again.

"We are not formal, Josh," Hesta said quietly. "We do not require signatures or contracts. We take your word as bond." Hesta paused. "Do you wish to say anything to your friends before we depart?"

"Oh, um, sure. Yeah. Thanks," Josh said. His friends stepped towards him. Fern got there first and circled his front legs, brushing them with her fur in a kind of caress. "Take care of yourself, you big lug," she said quietly. Then she sat down near his head, which he had dropped to hear her. Her eyes were brimming with tears.

Josh gently licked one off her cheek and said, "Thanks for everything, Fern. I'll never forget you."

"You'd better not forget me," she said, wiping at her face with her paw. "I'll see you this summer. Behave!" She pouted coquettishly and turned away with a swish of her tail.

George stood on his hind legs and draped his arm over Josh's shoulders. "Try to stay out of trouble, will ya? I'll see you in the summertime." He dropped back down to all fours and lumbered into the forest.

Crawley swooped in to stand where Fern had been. "You won't see me, but I'll see you. You need me, just bugle. Take care of yourself." Her military tone and stance belied the fact that she was his friend, and briefly his girlfriend, even if they had been pretending. She hopped over to one of his front legs and leaned against him in a kind of hug, then took to the sky, banking over the trees and out of sight.

Finally, Rose approached. "Hey, big brother, don't worry about a thing." She referred to her brief stint as a foster child in his human parent's home. It was their little inside joke. "You're going to be just fine. I'll miss you." She returned to the circle. Josh figured maybe she didn't want an elk kiss like Fern got.

Just then a shot rang out nearby. The Netahs scattered into the surrounding landscape.

Hunters? Josh bolted after Hesta, who'd raced through the woods away from the sound. Hesta ran in a crazy zigzag pattern which Josh copied, assuming it was to avoid making an easy target. Josh's pulse pounded in his ears, as terror morphed into fear of losing sight of Hesta. Eventually, Hesta slowed and paused long enough to release a gush of urine. Josh's jaw dropped as he panted for breath. Moments later Hesta resumed his pace and Josh followed, grinning to himself. *Duh! No bathroom required!*

Hesta slowed to a trot and Josh caught up. "Um, excuse me, Mr. Hesta, but is this hunting season? I mean, that was a gunshot, right?"

Hesta slowed to a walk. "Yes, that was probably a hunter. He wasn't close, and he is now at least a mile behind us."

"Oh, how can you be so sure?"

"The direction of the sound, mostly," Hesta said. "Have you heard further shots? No, me neither. We are safe."

"How do you know there aren't others out here?"

"I traveled through here only an hour ago, I would have smelled them."

Josh just met this elk, and didn't know if he could trust him yet. However, he had no choice. He was out here alone with the guy. His breath came in short gasps as he thought, *this could be the end of it all!* His head could become a trophy on someone's wall. He had to trust Hesta.

Hesta must have sensed the change in Josh. With a calm and reassuring voice, he said, "We have many miles before we rest. Are you ready to pick up our speed?"

"Definitely." Josh had actually been looking forward to settling down for the evening, but the snow and cold would probably make that uncomfortable.

"Try to keep up!" Hesta called over his shoulder as he took off in a trot and then transitioned into a full gallop along the tree line.

Josh's heart soared as he got a taste of the power and endurance in his elk body. He reveled at the scents of dried grasses, pines, and sweet aspens. Seeing his old friends had lifted his mood, especially knowing he'd see them again. The clean mountain air seemed rich with oxygen. With the council's decision behind him, provisional or not, the future felt bright.

Suddenly, Hesta stopped and froze. Josh mimicked him, puzzled. "False alarm," Hesta laughed before he started off again. One time he veered into the trees. Josh followed and watched as Hesta created a pile of what looked like Milk Duds. *Not milk, elk duds!* Josh studied the area. *I wonder why he chose this spot. I have so much to learn!* With a shrug, Josh deposited his own pile before they resumed their travels. *Fertilizer!* He giggled silently. *Very mature!*

Eventually, Josh's stomach growled. Hesta noticed, slowing. "Hungry?"

"Yeah, I guess so," Josh laughed.

"Hang in there, we're headed for a feast," Hesta said.

"Awesome. I love being an elk!" he exclaimed, then shot a glance at Hesta when he realized he'd said it out loud.

"It has its advantages," Hesta called back. "Come on, race me!" He got a good head start before Josh reacted and raced after him.

They passed two deer, who immediately spooked and a small group of pronghorns, who completely ignored the racing elk. They crossed open rangeland along the side of a valley, that appeared to end a short distance in front of them.

A dark mass rose in the distance, difficult to discern in the fading light of evening. Closer inspection revealed a rickety old barn leaning precariously downhill. Hesta slowed and Josh caught up, saying, "What's up?"

"That barn is full of hay, stored for the winter. It's our own private buffet line." Hesta looked around.

"You don't have to worry about the rancher who put it there?"

"Well sure, but his dog always barks if they're close."

Josh studied the barn, convinced it would blow over in a tiny wind. "You sure it's safe?"

"Yes."

The sides of the barn were dark, weathered boards put up centuries ago. Josh watched Hesta poke his nose through an opening and yank out some hay. Josh found his own opening and chewed happily, thinking it might be the closest thing he'd get to home-baked bread in his new life.

Suddenly, both elk stopped and leapt back several yards when one of the roof timbers creaked ominously. When the noises subsided, Josh had lost his appetite, but Hesta kept eating. Moments later an avalanche of hay poured out of an opening overhead as a barn owl swooped out and disappeared into the night.

Hesta struggled to stay upright as the hay buried him. He tried to swim above it; his eyes rimmed in white. He couldn't even back out of the pile. Josh pawed away at the hay with his hooves. It didn't help. He transformed into a boy and used his hands to shovel the hay away. Soon, Hesta wriggled to freedom. He shook himself and walked slowly away. Josh transformed back into an elk and followed him.

"You okay?" Josh asked.

"Yeah, thanks. That was quick thinking back there. I'm a little embarrassed I didn't see that coming. Let's get out of here. We don't want to draw attention to ourselves." He walked away slowly. Josh wondered if he had injured himself after all, but kept quiet, sensing the man's embarrassment.

The end of the valley was a high pass that led to yet another valley. No further signs of humans appeared for miles. Josh remembered the gunshot. He scanned the woods for hunter's orange, but didn't see any in the dark woods.

"Are you worried about hunters?" Josh just wanted to make sure.

"No, that was months ago."

"Except for the hunter near the council meeting?"

"Hmm, true, an obvious rule-breaker. However, have you noticed how remote this area is? We're safe here. Besides, we'll be home soon."

"Good to know." They walked, digesting. "Hesta, you mind if I ask you some questions? I have like a zillion."

Hesta cocked his head. "Sure, but I don't have a zillion answers!"

Josh liked that. "Okay, for starters. Do you have kids?"

"Sure, my wife and I have a brand-new son and a daughter."

"Do they still live with you?"

"Hmm? Oh, sure. I see where this is going. You're wondering what life will be like among Netah elk."

"Yes, that's . . . that's right."

"Don't worry, we're not that different from humans. We live in houses, sleep in beds, work jobs, have families, and follow the golden rule."

"Huh, I never once saw my Netah friends enter one of their homes. We slept outside and I guess I thought that was the norm. Oh, wait, no. George did lead me to a cave my first night. That didn't go very well."

"Yes, well, I assume that's because you couldn't change. They must have figured it was easier to remain in their animal forms." Hesta nodded thoughtfully. "Any other pressing question?"

"When did Netahs first transform?" Josh had heard that "pressing question'" part.

Hesta hesitated before answering, "Where to begin?"

The cloudy evening had turned into a night so dark that Josh could barely see.

"I know just the thing," Hesta said. "I'll tell you one of our origin stories."

"Awesome," Josh said, as he moved closer to Hesta, not wanting to miss a word as they walked through the light snow powdering the frozen prairie.

Hesta told this story:

> In the beginning, there were people and animals, and they all got along very well. The people took care of the animals when they were injured or sick. The animals taught the people where to find good foods like berries, nuts, and fish. The people were grateful to their older brothers for teaching them how to live in the world. The makers were very proud of the people and animals and decided to give them a gift. The people could turn into animals, and animals could transform into humans. They called themselves Netahs.

Some people liked the idea, some didn't. The animals had the same reaction.

Two separate societies formed on that day. The ones who didn't choose to change in the beginning were never able to do it later, and they became angry and jealous. This led to wars. People and animals attacked Netahs, those who could transform. The makers were very upset that their gift had created such problems, but were unable to make things right. The makers watched to see what would happen.

The Netahs separated themselves from the others and made their own communities. Wars still happened when the Netah villages were discovered. The makers gave the Netahs another gift to help them. They took away the Netah's scent so they could hide more easily.

Josh waited a beat, and realizing the story was over, said, "Huh, cool!"

They walked in silence, as Josh considered other wild animals in the area. There were very few wolves in Colorado, so far, anyway. Colorado did have bears and mountain lions, though. A bear might sneak up on them, unless they were all hibernating by now, hopefully. He wondered if Netah bears hibernated, and remembered his friend George had still been awake enough to see him off. A mountain lion, on the other hand, would hunt at night in the fall and the winter. He recalled his previous encounter: the claws, the weight of the animal. The scent was unforgettable; he'd recognize it if one came close.

Suddenly, an unfamiliar scent filled his nostrils. Josh froze when he caught the sight of movement near the ground. The dark form of the animal flattened to the ground, while twitching its hind legs. The animal continued with its odd movements and then suddenly disappeared.

"What was that?" Josh asked Hesta, as they walked away.

"A badger."

"It didn't seem afraid of us. What was it doing?" Josh asked.

"She was digging an escape hole with her back legs, and then she used it."

"Is she still there? I can't smell her anymore."

"No, she's long gone. It's feeding time for badgers, and we surprised her. They usually have multiple escape holes within their territory. She's probably down the tunnels and far away by now."

"Hmm, cool." Josh pictured that in his mind, his legs on autopilot. The only other pressing question was about his birth father, but Josh didn't want to spoil the mood. If Hesta didn't bring it up, he wouldn't, either. A pale band of peach light spread across the sky over one side of the valley. Josh listened to the wind gusting through the trees, as the first cheeps of a sparrow sounded nearby.

Josh decided they were heading north as the sun rose over his right shoulder. The landscape had changed from tall pine-covered mountains topped with snow to dry grassy plains only lightly dusted with snow. They climbed and descended rolling hills. He wondered how Hesta found his way in a land so empty. He squinted into the steady wind.

CHAPTER 3

The Valley

The snow glowed pink as the sun rose higher in the sky. A pungent scent assaulted them as they topped another low hill. Josh tried to avoid breathing in too deeply as he studied the small herd of animals only a few yards away.

"Don't get your hopes up, Josh," Hesta laughed. "We don't want to spook those lady elk. Keep your head down and follow my lead." They circled the animals, who barked at each other in warning, as they moved into a tighter cluster. Their blank stares told Josh these were merely elk.

"They have calves," Hesta observed. "We want them to remain calm. Don't mess with the local wildlife!" Hesta chuckled at his little joke.

Right, 'cuz we're not wildlife, we're Netahs! Josh smirked at the distinction.

With the herd well behind them, Josh asked, "Wait, how did you know they were elk, not Netahs?"

Hesta squinted at Josh. "Couldn't you tell?"

"Nope."

"You smelled them, didn't you? Netahs don't smell, remember?"

Josh rolled his eyes. "So that part of the story was true?"

"All of it was true. Another way to tell the difference is, Netahs will talk to you."

"So, if my pickup line doesn't work and all I get is a blank stare, it's not that she's not interested, but that she doesn't understand words?" Josh grinned.

Hesta nodded. "Not only that, our females don't wait to be approached. They're more liberated than that. If they like you, you'll know."

"Really? Human girls prefer to play hard to get."

"Ah, yes, we have a few like that, too. You'll see. We're almost there." Hesta picked up the pace again towards what looked like the edge of the world as the sun nearly blinded them on the horizon.

Josh slowed, letting caution rule as he paused next to Hesta on the edge of a mesa. A broad valley surrounded by layers of mountains filled the horizon, while a ribbon of river wound through stands of gnarly cottonwoods, all frosted white. The sky seemed immense, and now blown clear of clouds, a richer, deeper blue than he'd ever seen. The sun sparkled off small ponds, and Josh decided the song about "purple mountains majesty" must have been written about a place like this.

Tiny figures moved down in the valley, but they were not ants. They were elk. "Is this it?" Josh said. "This is your home?"

"Yes, and we arrived at a beautiful hour of the morning."

"How many of you live here?" Josh stood in awe as Hesta proudly surveyed his home.

"One hundred and three, last count. We figure we can support maybe another fifty before our environment gets stressed. We are careful to keep our valley healthy with a variety of other animals that make their own kinds of contributions." Josh remembered the elk duds and thought "contributions" was a nice euphemism for it.

"Other animals?" he asked. "You mean other kinds of Netahs?"

"Oh, sure, and regular animals, but we keep mostly to ourselves. We try to be good neighbors, though."

Josh had never considered this. *What other kinds of animals would share this habitat?* "You mean like predators?"

"Of course. It keeps us fit and on our toes. Mostly we have to deal with a mountain lion who considers our valley hers. She and her cubs are wary of us and mostly leave us alone. It's her suitors who cause us most trouble. But that's the way of things." Hesta looked out over his valley like a king inspecting his kingdom.

"Huh. All those elk are Netahs?" Josh asked.

"Yes. Can you see any signs of humans?"

There were multiple trails down the side of the hill, but they didn't look like hiking trails people would use, more like deer or cattle trails that ended in clumps of rabbit brush or willow stands. It all looked so natural, except for the shine off a dark line in the distance.

"Is that a road, that dark line, or a river?" Josh asked, indicating the direction with his nose.

"Oh, right, yeah, that's a road. It runs along the edge of our lands, marks the border. I forgot about that."

"Okay, so, no, other than that." Josh took in the vast valley. "How much of this belongs to the Netahs? Is it on a map? Like marked as Bureau of Land Management or something?"

"This entire valley is ours. As for maps and stuff, that's above my pay grade. There are others who deal with protecting our secrecy."

Josh could tell Hesta was not going to elaborate on that. He couldn't help wondering how they'd avoid satellite images from space, and drones that could find them with heat signatures. He squeezed in one last question. "Do you stay elk all the time?"

Hesta snorted. "No, why would we? What would be the advantage of being a Netah then?"

Josh felt stupid. "Sorry, I know I have a lot to learn."

"Don't worry about it, it'll take time. Come on, my family is waiting for me." Hesta bounded down the side of the mesa. As Josh followed, a deep sadness overcame him as he remembered his own parents. He tried to shake it off by pasting a smile on his face. Two adults with a calf watched them approach. Josh couldn't tell the males from the females, because none of them had antlers. He assumed the guys had shed antlers in the fall. *Is that why the season is called 'fall'?* He realized that identifying individual Netahs in their elk forms would be challenging.

Hesta stopped in front of the two adults with a calf, who was bubbling with joy at seeing Hesta.

Josh followed slowly, noticing several smaller elk watching him with interest from the edge of a nearby pond. He tried the head nod that he and his human friends always used in the school halls, but it didn't seem to register the same with these Netahs. He noticed Hesta stood taller than any of them. Josh dropped his head shyly, as he felt all eyes turn his way. *They must not get many newcomers around here.*

Hesta spoke in a low murmur to one elk, nuzzling her neck. *I'm guessing that's his wife.* The other adult ignored them and stared openly at Josh. The wife peeked around Hesta's bulk and asked with a twinkle in her eye, "Is this our new addition?"

"Yes, my dear," Hesta replied, lifting his chin and looking very proud. "Josh, this is my wife, Ohma. She is the brains of this operation."

She looked at Hesta and beamed. "You don't need to flatter me, my love. I already chose you. You have no competition."

"Others can try."

"Oh, and they do, but you already won my heart."

Josh cringed, expecting a mushy elk kiss to follow. *Competition? Chose you? But they're married!* Josh had to ask, "Are you guys talking about the rutting season?" If he could blush through his fur, he would have. *Why did I just say that?!*

Ohma tried valiantly but unsuccessfully to hide her grin as she turned her attention to Josh. "In a way, yes. We take the rutting season very seriously." She shrugged. "You'll learn all about it in good time."

Hesta grinned and moved away. "Okay, well if you'll excuse us, this young buck and his sponsor are hungry and thirsty." To Josh he said, "Don't worry about the rut, Josh. With the season ended, we are all quite civilized." *But not during rut?*

The calf bounced over and ran circles around Hesta, calling, "Daddy, Daddy, Daddy!" *Okay, so that's his kid.*

The little one then circled around Josh, and peppered him with questions. "Hi Josh! How old are you? Where did you used to live? You fought off a lion? How strong are you? Wanna play?"

The other adult elk broke through the stream of questions and said, "Leave him alone, little bro. He's come a long way and is hungry." Obviously, a girl from her voice, she nodded over her shoulder and quietly said to Josh, "Follow me." Hesta shrugged as he corralled his son back towards his wife, while several other adults joined them and were soon deep in conversation. The girl led Josh towards a small pond. The wind picked up, rattling the branches of the willows on its edges. A small dirt devil swirled towards them, and the girl started to run. "Come on, let's get inside and away from that wind!"

Josh nearly ran into her as she stopped abruptly at a large gray boulder. The female elk transformed into a human and leaned against the boulder, revealing it was a door that blended seamlessly into the landscape and opened easily.

"You need some breakfast?" she asked over her shoulder as she led him down a hallway. Josh guessed she was a little older than he was because of her self-assurance. The thought of food raised his spirits.

"Now that you mention it, yes." Josh attempted to sound nonchalant as he transformed and followed her, marveling at how easily he could pull the boulder slab closed. "Hesta led me to a barn full of hay yesterday, or was that two days ago? That and a nut bar were the last good things I've eaten in a while. What's your name?"

"You can call me Noomi. You're called Josh, right?"

"Yeah. Are you related to Hesta?"

"That's right, he's my dad." The hallway opened into a sunny room.

Josh's jaw dropped as he took in their surroundings. He expected a dark, damp cave or tunnel, but instead he entered a modern, light-filled room with high ceilings. As he removed his jacket and boots and placed them next to Noomi's, his eyes took in the ceiling of the entryway, which looked like glass, but the light coming through moved like waves. Josh decided there must be water on top of the glass. The walls looked like compacted clay, dyed green. A smooth floor of red rock slabs felt nicely warm underfoot. He approached a wall of windows framing a stunning view across rolling plains. A stone overhang shaded the windows.

"Whoa, this is so cool! It's an earth home, right?"

"I guess you could call it that," Noomi laughed. She led him to an open-plan kitchen. "Want some eggs and toast? I can fry some up in minutes. I'll bet some human food would taste good right about now."

"You read my mind, Noomi. Thanks. Um, can I help?"

"Sure. Here's the bread, there's the toaster, have at it." Noomi reached for a basket of colorful eggs sitting on a shelf and cracked one into a bowl with cool efficiency. "How about some scrambled eggs with herbs and mushrooms? It's my specialty."

"Sounds awesome. Want a piece of toast, too?"

"Sure."

Josh dropped two slices of bread into the slots and pushed the button. He watched Noomi for a few seconds, admiring her thick dark braid and big amber eyes. His heart might have skipped a beat. *Get a grip!* His eyes roamed the room. The open-plan living space, complete with couches, tables, and lamps looked like any modern human home, except the roof was the bottom of a pond. Then it dawned on him.

"How does this happen?" He waved his hand to encompass the living room and kitchen. "Where's your power?"

"The roof is solar panels," Noomi answered.

"How? All I see is what looks like water on a huge skylight."

"The panels are just below the surface of the water for camouflage."

"Genius!"

"Yes, and all the cables are underground."

"Do you have computers?" Josh's heart raced. He thought he'd never see another phone or computer ever again. This changed everything. He searched what he could see of the house for computers, monitors, or phone chargers. He didn't see any.

Noomi kept her eyes on the pan of mushrooms, stirring slowly. A light brown curl fell into her eye and she absentmindedly tucked it back into her braid. The earthy smell of mushrooms filled the room and made Josh's stomach growl in appreciation. He noticed she had not answered. "What? What did I say?"

"Oh, nothing," she said a little wistfully. "Yes, we have computers, but it's kind of an issue around here. The elders are basically Luddites. The old story about how they never needed them, why do we?" She wagged her head mockingly. "My generation embraces high tech!"

"So, you do have computers?" Josh wanted to clarify.

"Yes, but only a few of us have access. They are highly restricted, you know, like classified." Noomi poured the eggs into the pan with the mushrooms and sprinkled a pinch of herbs over the top. Josh's elation plummeted. *So much for getting back to gaming.* He snatched the toast from the slots and dropped the slices on a plate before asking, "Butter?"

"First cupboard on the right, knives for spreading in the drawer in front of you. Good timing, these are ready." She slid the eggs onto the toast plates. They sat down next to each other at the counter and dug in.

Josh took several ravenous bites before he looked around again, searching for computers. "So, who gets to use the few computers?" He picked up his toast and tasted it.

Noomi said, "I bet you have a million questions. What else do you want to know? Fire away."

Josh finished his bite, noticing she didn't answer his question. "Just one more about computers. Are you connected to the internet?"

"Yes, of course. It is a different kind of network, though; we are not on the same one as the humans. It would be too easy for them to find us."

Right, Josh thought, taking another bite. "Your own network? Who designed that? Do you have your own colleges then?"

"Yes. Are you interested in college?" Noomi asked, resting her chin on her hand and watching Josh sop up the last of the eggs with his toast. Josh waited, noticing how easily she deflected questions she didn't want to answer. *How the heck am I going to learn how these people live if they won't answer my questions?*

To hide his frustration, he stood up and said, "Mmm, great eggs!" He picked up their empty plates and took them to the sink. "Yes, I am interested in college, especially computer science."

"Huh." Noomi followed him to the sink and began washing the dishes.

Josh picked up a towel and dried for her. *She's inscrutable! I wonder what she's hiding.*

She said, "You might want to keep your interest in computers under your hat for a bit until the elders get to know you. It might alarm them."

"Because they're Luddites?" Josh asked.

"Precisely. Come on, I'll give you a tour of the house. It is filled with science that you won't find in human homes. I think we'll skip my brother's room. He's a slob." The rooms were bright and modern, with no clutter. The pale walls had a rough texture and red stone floors gleamed throughout the house. He saw no innovative science; it must have been well hidden.

"You don't have a car?" Josh asked, noticing no garage.

"No, not as a family, but there is one available for the community. Did you see any roads down here in the valley on your way in?"

"Only one that runs along the edge of your land, Hesta said. Is that another way to stay off the radar?"

"It's not the only way," Noomi answered. She led him outside again and they both transformed back into elk. They stepped around the boulders next to the pond, its edges filled with cattails and reeds. "Look around. What do you see?"

Josh searched for a telltale sign of high technology. He looked for reflective surfaces, but found only the frozen ponds. He searched for wires, poles, anything artificial and man-made, but could find nothing. "It's amazing. How?"

"Shielding devices. Just like James Bond!" Noomi laughed.

"Where are they?"

"If you could see them, it would defeat the purpose. They are shielded, as well. Just like our wind power is driven by structures that look like evergreen trees. As they move in the wind, it translates to power that we store. Our batteries are underground, our solar panels under water, and we use geothermal power to heat the floors of our homes."

"Huh, it all sounds so . . . very . . . sustainable, and what's the word? Renewable!" Josh's mind was blown. The Netahs were very advanced. He stared into the pond, surprised by the big elk face reflecting back. *Idiot, you just transformed, remember?* He caught the movement of a couple of fish just below the surface. Noomi came over and stood next to him. Josh noticed the coloring differences between their male and female elk bodies in their reflections in the pond.

"Wait, you said there are solar panels in there, I don't see them. All I see are the . . . are those trout?" he said.

"Yeah, I'm pleased at how the panels disappear under the water. The fish were my idea. Dad was furious the first time it leaked into the kitchen. He'd said it would leak and it did. It took a little extra engineering, but we fixed it."

"Cool."

Noomi said, "It's a lot to take in at once, I know. Don't worry, take your time." Warmth radiated from her furry side.

Josh felt his knees go a little weak and heat traveled up his neck to his cheeks. Noomi stood very close and he noticed her long lashes. He lowered his eyes and watched the fish move slowly through the pond at his feet. He asked, "Do all Netahs live like this? I mean, your homes are very green. Why don't you share it with humans?" He thought he knew why they didn't share but wanted to hear how she felt about it.

"Oh, you know, the usual, secrecy, camouflage, it's all for your own good, protection from the big bad outside world." She tossed her head, scoffing.

Josh laughed. "I'm from the big bad outside world. What's protecting you from me?"

Noomi tilted her head and raised her eyebrows. "You've been vetted by a crack team of experts. You thought they were just high school students? No way! Spies! Oops, I shouldn't have said that!" She giggled in a very girlie way and suddenly seemed much younger. Josh couldn't guess her age. She could be his age or maybe a little older.

Just then, Josh sensed the presence of someone else. He hadn't heard any footsteps. He took a few steps back from the pond and looked around, as a large elk stepped through some twiggy bushes and transformed into a slim, bearded young man with massive shoulders who scowled at Josh.

"Who said you could talk to my girl?" the man asked in a deep voice. "And what shouldn't you have said, Noomi?"

Noomi looked annoyed, so Josh relaxed and asked, "Your girl? That right, Noomi?"

She shrugged and said, "That's what he wants me to believe." She turned to confront the man, defiant.

"Aw, come on, Noomi," the guy's voice took on a teasing tone. "Quit fighting it. You know you like me." He crossed his arms over his broad chest and looked at her with a twinkle in his eyes and obvious affection. Josh read their interaction as a friendly tease rather than perhaps a stalker and his prey. The man shifted his gaze to Josh and turned serious. "Say, you're the new guy, the clueless halfling, right?"

"Oh, Rodan, why do you always have to be so confrontational?" Noomi asked. "Give him a break." She did not sound like someone talking to her boyfriend.

Several male voices guffawed, but Josh couldn't see the guys. *How do they do that?*

"Try to be civil for once, Rodan," a disembodied older male voice advised.

Rodan shrugged. "There is a time for civil and a time for challenging! Civil will come later. If he wants to hang out with my girl, I get to challenge him." Rodan transformed into an elk. He towered over Josh as he slowly inspected him. "You feel the heat yet?"

"Uh, I don't know. Maybe?" *What, like summer, a fever, am I blushing?*

"Well, what are you going to do about it?" He gave Josh the slightest nudge with his shoulder as he circled around him.

Josh got annoyed but stood his ground. "What are you talking about?" he demanded.

Noomi moved between them and said, "Stand down, Rodan. He is no threat to you or any of us. Leave the poor kid alone. I mean it."

"Or what?" Rodan sneered.

Rodan couldn't see the elk approaching through the willows behind him. He might have noticed both Noomi and Josh looking over his shoulder, though. Rodan went still. The new elk calmly waited, his head held high, glaring. "Do you really want to challenge this kid, Rodan?" Josh recognized Hesta's voice and grinned at the twinkle in Hesta's eyes.

"Isn't that what you want?" Rodan asked, turning towards Hesta.

"I don't expect you to accept him without question, but I do expect you to be fair. Since he just arrived, rather than challenging him, teach him. He is your tribe now."

It's good to have friends in high places! Josh relaxed.

"Okay, sure. I can do that." Rodan turned back to Josh. "Ready for your first lesson?"

"Um, I guess?" Josh answered with no confidence at all.

"Lesson number one, don't mess with another guy's girl."

Hesta said, "That will be all for today, Rodan. I know you and your crew have more important things to do."

"Sure, sure," Rodan said, rolling his neck as if to relieve tension. "Sorry, sir. I just wanted to meet the new guy." To Josh he said, "Welcome to the village, Josh. See you around, Noomi." At that he bugled, and galloped off over a rise to disappear from sight.

Meanwhile, Josh watched a couple more elk break their cover and thunder after him. Noomi stayed by Josh but addressed her father. "He is getting very annoying, Dad. I wish he'd knock off this 'my girl' business. I don't know what all the other girls see in him. Yeah, he's big, but so what?"

Hesta nodded. "None of us is perfect, and yes, he can be annoying. Do you want me to say something to him?"

"Nah, that's all right. I can look after myself."

"I know that." Hesta studied Josh. "Did she feed you already?"

"Yes, we had eggs and toast." Josh nodded with enthusiasm. "And then I got a tour of your house. It's amazing. The style is really cool, especially all the shielding and stuff."

"She told you about that, huh?" Hesta raised one eyebrow, as if deciding whether this was a transgression or not.

Elk have eyebrows? "Yes, why? Is that a problem?" Josh asked innocently, realizing he'd been testing their conviction about secrecy all morning.

"No," Hesta said with a sigh of resignation. "You'll have to hear our secrets eventually if you're to live with us. I guess I thought we'd introduce you to it more slowly."

"Daddy," Noomi said, with the tone of a daughter scolding her father for being unreasonable. "He's old enough to understand. He's been treated with suspicion for so long, isn't it time we trust him?"

"You trust him already?" Hesta almost sneered, but corrected himself, softening his tone. "You've only known him for what, an hour?"

"I'm a good judge of character, and so are you. That's all I'm saying."

"I hear you." Hesta looked amused. "Now, don't you have a job to do or something? I need to borrow this young buck."

"By all means, he's all yours. Bye, Josh," Noomi said with a smile and then galloped away.

Hesta moved next to Josh as they watched her go. "It didn't take long for my daughter to take to you."

"In my defense, sir, she approached me and offered me some breakfast."

"Of course she did." Hesta nodded. "What'd I tell you, Josh? Our girls are not shy, especially not my daughter."

"No, sir, she's very nice." Josh paused, waiting to find out why Hesta needed to borrow him. Then, before he forgot, he asked, "How does the shielding work?"

"Ah, well, all in good time. First, we have a job to do. Follow me." Hesta walked away, still in his elk form towards a clump of tall spruces.

CHAPTER 4

Playing Cowboy

Hesta walked through the trees and disappeared. Josh followed him and saw that Hesta had transformed into his human self, built like a tank, wearing a black felt cowboy hat, and a green plaid shirt jacket with a logo on the chest. Josh transformed, as well. Hidden by the spruces sat a Quonset hut covered in a silvery film that reflected its surroundings, making it nearly disappear. *Is it shielded? Is there a switch somewhere? Hesta must have just turned it off.*

Through a door in the side of the building, Hesta flicked a switch. Bright lights revealed an ancient pickup truck, a fire engine, and tall shelves piled high with crates marked "clothing," "scrap metal," "pipes," "cables," "lumber," and "tools." Josh realized this was where they kept the community vehicles that Noomi mentioned.

Josh decided the prospects for that day's adventures had just improved. Josh's human dad, Danny, used to joke about not knowing which end of a hammer to hold. Distracted by the surprise at what surrounded him and the sadness of thinking about his dad, Josh lost track of Hesta, but soon found the guy sorting through a pile of folded green plaid jackets on a shelf. He tossed one to Josh. *A man of many words.* It had a logo, too. Josh read it. "Rocky Mountain Land

Conservancy" circled a badge shaped like a forest ranger's shield. *Okay, so this is their disguise. They made up a nonprofit to hide behind.* Josh shrugged on the jacket as he followed Hesta.

Hesta waved towards the end of a table, where a stack of black cowboy hats waited. "Find one that fits and follow me," he ordered.

Awesome! Josh had always liked cowboy hats; he just didn't have any excuse to wear one in the suburbs. Things were definitely looking up.

Josh heard the quiet whine of an electric motor and the crunch of gravel as Hesta pulled the battered, old rusty pickup towards a garage door. He motioned for Josh to climb aboard. Outside a light snow had begun. Josh took in the modern dashboard. "An e-truck disguised as a beater, amazing!" He peered into the rearview mirror beside him and watched the plume of dust and snow billowing in their wake. "This isn't very subtle," he said. "I thought you guys were trying to hide out here."

"Sure, but what's more natural than a nature reserve?"

"The cowboy hats are a nice touch." Josh laughed, as he adjusted his hat to sit more comfortably. *How great is this? Who'd have guessed I'd be wearing a cowboy hat, riding in an electric pickup truck, driving cross-country like a local ranger on my first day in the valley?* Josh studied the flat screen and several unmarked buttons that made up the dashboard.

"That hat suits you," Hesta said. Then he reached over and pulled it a little lower over Josh's eyes. "That's even better."

"Thanks." Josh's grin grew as another thought occurred to him. He wondered out loud, "Is sixteen the legal driving age for Netahs?"

"Certainly."

"Do you have driver's ed?"

"Nope, but I'll teach you when you're fifteen and a half."

"Huh, um, what month is it?"

"November."

"So in seven months. Promise?"

"Promise."

They passed a small stand of cedars and made a turn. Josh looked over his shoulder and tried to see any signs of human presence, other than the tire tracks they'd just made. There were no flashes of light on windows or pieces of metal, no telltale smoke or steam escaping a chimney, not even any other plumes behind a vehicle. *How could there be over a hundred Netahs hiding somewhere back there?*

"Is your whole town shielded? That would be, like, crazy technology!" Josh said.

"Good question," Hesta laughed. "First, this is now your world, too, and don't forget it. To your question, we've been at it for a long time. We decided some 8,000 years ago that our only chance at survival was to remain hidden. We had some bad encounters with the natives. Some good ones, too, but generally, they wanted our hides and antlers for talismans. Some thought we were gods. It got messy."

"I can see how that might be," Josh said.

"Yeah, we had low-tech solutions for a long time, like plantings to hide our farms, and homes in cliffsides or under hills. Then we resorted to things like barbed wire when that became the norm around here, which frankly only encourages some types to explore further. Nowadays we have more sophisticated systems and simple camouflage."

"Do you keep cattle or horses?"

"No, no need or use for them. I mean, think about it. As elk, we can forage anywhere we want, like a buffalo, and we have strong legs to carry us cross-country like a horse."

"Yet, you have trucks like this one," Josh pointed out.

"When there is equipment to be carried, yes. Best of both worlds, right?" Hesta shrugged.

Josh ran his hand over the door panel. It felt like wool. He said, "Where did this truck come from? I've never seen anything like it."

Hesta chuckled quietly. "Wondered when you'd notice. We may have made a few little modifications of our own. I'm no mechanic, so I can't elaborate."

Josh sighed and gazed out his window at snow squalls across the valley, while scrolling through the growing list of questions in his mind.

He asked, "So how do you keep humans out? What if someone gets too close?"

"There's a boundary alarm. It registers outside the hearing of humans, but we elk can hear it loud and clear. If you hear it, become an elk, immediately."

"Kind of like a tornado warning?"

"Yep, but a human warning that they cannot hear," Hesta chuckled.

"And you farm? Are you able to grow enough food to be self-sustaining or do you have to make runs to towns for groceries and stuff?"

"We don't need the outside world at all, although if you ask our young people, that's," he switched his voice to a high girly squeak, "like totally not true!" Hesta bobbed his head for this imitation and then chuckled. He pushed his sunglasses back up his nose.

"That's what your daughter says?" Josh grinned.

"Certainly. She hears about things and decides she *needs* them. Ridiculous. We have what we need, the rest is fluff!"

"Trucks and Quonset huts don't just grow from the land," Josh observed, and then realized he might have stepped over the line into snarky.

Hesta peered at Josh over the top of his sunglasses with a frown. "Careful, I know you have questions, but watch your tone."

"Sorry, sir. I meant no disrespect."

Hesta nodded. "Of course not. And, yes, okay, you're right. We will, on occasion, and very infrequently, buy things we cannot make."

"What do you use for money?"

"We have money, plenty, we just don't need it for much."

"Okay, but . . ." Josh hesitated then decided to drop that line of questions. Hesta sounded defensive, and there were plenty of other things he wanted to know. "Where are your farms?"

With a big sigh Hesta continued. "We have underground hydro farms. Each family unit and lodge have a specialty and we share our crops with each other. When you go to market, notice how no money changes hands. We don't use it. You'll see, wait until dinnertime. Ohma is a gourmet cook."

"I'm looking forward to that. Noomi did a great job with the eggs, and I can handle toast. I think I would like cooking. Will your wife let me help?" *Wait, if I am going to have dinner with Hesta's family, will I sleep there, too?*

"Sure, Ohma doesn't mind help in the kitchen."

Josh laughed, and then fell silent. He remembered how his mom never allowed him into the kitchen. The kitchen was her zealously guarded domain. He'd always sort of resented that, thinking he could at least help clean up pots and pans. On the other hand, had he really been all that eager to do dishes with his mom? Not really, and at this point he wished he had, a missed opportunity. With a sigh he gazed out the truck window and realized he'd discovered two advantages of being a Netah, in one day. Hesta could fix things and teach him, and Ohma would teach him how to cook. Three things, if he included high-tech electric trucks. For some reason, these thoughts led to memories of his mom's casseroles. He was curious to find out what the Netahs ate. "What's your family's specialty?"

Hesta laughed, "Peppers, the hotter the better."

Josh did not love spicy peppers, so he responded with a noncommittal "Huh."

Hesta asked, "What else would you like to know?"

Josh hesitated. *What can I contribute to a society that is technologically advanced and peaceful, if a little competitive about the females? I like gaming, skiing, trail biking. I'm a fair swimmer, a I love building models. How would that be useful?*

"Come on, don't be shy. What do you like to do?"

"You know I'm only in ninth grade, right? It's not like I've chosen a major in college or anything."

"Sure, I know you're just a kid. What classes do you like?" Hesta kept his eyes ahead, driving straight over the undulating terrain on a route only he could see.

Josh noticed the word 'do.' "Do you have schools here?"

"Not like yours. We learn by doing. What do you like to do?" Hesta was being annoyingly persistent.

"I like computers. I'm great at leading our games." That sounded lame, and he realized video games would probably not get Netah approval. Then he remembered Noomi's suggestion that he keep his interest in computers under his hat for a while. He tried to cover with: "I also like being outside, skiing, biking, that sort of thing."

That got a good laugh out of Hesta. He waved his hand past the windows, a sweeping gesture taking in the whole horizon. "Outside we got!"

Josh nodded then thought of another angle. "I like building things, like models. I like working with my hands."

Hesta rubbed his chin. "Well now, let's see. What jobs require one to build models? Architects build models, so do engineers. Maybe you'd be a good fit there. We can set you up, see how you take to it."

"Wow, really? That sounds amazing!" Josh could hardly contain his excitement. "I didn't think I could try anything like that for years, like not 'til college, anyway."

"Okay, I'll hook you up with the apprentice builders tomorrow. That's a good place to start. Meantime, we're here." Hesta pulled the truck to a stop. Nothing broke the view for miles and miles except dried grasses poking through drifts of dirty snow and a hazy line of mountains on two sides of the valley.

Josh asked, "What's here?"

With a chuckle, Hesta turned off the engine and hopped out. He opened the back gate. As Josh approached, he caught a pair of leather gloves tossed in his general direction. "Grab a spool and those pliers and follow me." Hesta walked away with his own spool of wire and set it down next to a pile of tumbleweeds. "You ever work with electric fencing before?" he asked.

"No, but I'm ready to learn," Josh answered, realizing he had looked right at that line of wire and not even noticed it. Then again, he hadn't noticed the tumbleweeds, either. It looked so normal, not something to notice.

Hesta drawled, "Well, okay then, cowboy. Do as I tell you and you'll be a good ranch hand in no time." Josh watched as Hesta checked a small device he pulled out of his pocket. Then he reached into the tumbleweed and removed a length of wire.

Josh suddenly realized what was happening. "You hide the wire stakes in tumbleweeds?"

"Yes." Hesta handed Josh the device. "Why don't you see if you can figure out where the next break is with that?"

Josh looked at the small screen. It showed a terrain map and several blinking lights. "The lights show breaks?"

"Uh-huh."

"Which one is us?"

"Do you see a yellow spot? That's this break, because I'm replacing it. Look for the next red one."

"Got it."

"Great. Almost done. There. Let me see." He glanced at the device. "We'll need the truck to get there. Come on."

They worked through a light snow, until the sun disappeared behind the far mountains and tinted the tops of the clouds with its last glow of gold, and then they packed up. Josh tucked his hands under his armpits for warmth as Hesta reached into another tumble-weed. "Are you resetting the alarm?" Josh asked.

"Good guess. Yeah. See that little nail? That's it. Doesn't light up or anything, just a sensor that triggers a sound only we can hear." Hesta stepped back so Josh could inspect it up close. "Pretty slick, eh?"

"I'll say."

"We're goin' for unobtrusive." Hesta waved him back towards the truck.

Josh asked, "What do you think broke that fence?"

"A couple of ornery buffalo live in these parts." Hesta waved a hand to include the entire valley. "They broke out from a ranch, is my guess. Sometimes they run from the coyotes right into our lines, barreling through them like they were string. Don't ever mess with a buffalo, son. They're mean, worse than that mountain lion you ran into."

"Are there a lot of coyotes?" Josh asked.

"Sure, and the buffalo are mighty big. Wires don't stop 'em. We transmit sounds they don't like. It helps a little, but if there's a big enough pack of coyotes that get them riled up, they run right through like bulldozers."

Josh gaped as the first stars winking on overhead lit the snow enough that Hesta could navigate with no lights on. Back inside the barn, they hung their hats on hooks to dry from the snow and then walked outside. Hesta passed through the spruces, flicking a branch on his way by, then turned into an elk and began galloping across the rolling landscape. Josh transformed and ran after Hesta, wondering if a home hid underneath each pond.

Hesta stopped at one for a drink. Once sated, he sighed and turned back into a human. "You did a good job. How are you feeling?" he said as he stretched his neck and rolled his shoulders.

"Great," Josh said, before tasting the water for himself. "This is fantastic! Is it filtered? I didn't realize how thirsty I was."

"Yes, it's filtered. You like workin' with your hands, eh?" Hesta probed.

"I do, although I haven't had much chance before," Josh admitted.

"Why not?"

"My dad wasn't handy." Josh's voice trailed off sadly as he transformed too.

"No grandpa or uncles to show you stuff?" Hesta pressed.

"Nope."

"Huh, well . . ." Hesta let his gaze drift to the horizon. "You will have plenty of opportunity to learn new things here. Like for instance, yeah, the water is filtered by the plants we put in and the system that connects all our ponds through channels and rocks. Tested often, too, so don't worry."

"Are you saying it's naturally filtered, no chemicals or anything?" Josh only knew about water filters in a pitcher, like the one his mom kept in the fridge.

"No chemicals, just nature." Hesta nodded. He waited by the pond, in case Josh had further questions. When no more came, he continued, "Right, well, we'd better be getting inside. Ohma will have supper ready and we don't want to keep everyone waiting."

"Are we close?"

"We're here. Come on." Hesta pushed on the rock behind him, then walked inside.

"Wait, what?" Josh hadn't seen any signs of the home in the dark. He hadn't smelled dinner or noticed light peaking under doors or out windows or rooftop ponds. *Do they live in the dark?* Nope, inside, the house was bright, warm, and cheerful.

Ohma served a hot vegetable soup that reminded Josh of his mom's minestrone. Ohma's had small cornbread mounds across the top. Josh took tentative first bites, expecting it to be spicy with the house peppers, but it wasn't. After dinner he helped clear the dishes. No one objected. He and Noomi made a good team as he dried plates and she pointed out where to put them away.

They joined the rest of the family in the living room. Noomi's younger brother lounged on pillows on the floor, looking at picture books. Hesta and Ohma snuggled together on a couch with books in their hands. They appeared happy and content, in spite of the complete absence of electronic devices.

Ohma looked up and put her book down when they walked over. "You're probably wondering where you'll sleep tonight, Josh."

He snorted. "Funny, I hadn't even thought about it." Well, okay, he had, but he'd been quickly distracted learning how to mend boundary wires.

"We've made you a room downstairs. Noomi will show you. Anything you need, just ask."

"Thank you. I guess I could use a shower. Otherwise, may I borrow a book from your shelves? Reading helps me fall asleep," he said, fighting back a yawn.

Ohma dipped her head in agreement and waved him towards the bookshelves. Josh noticed the little boy make a face at him, so he made one back. The boy giggled and held his nose. "Sorry about that, kid," Josh said, getting a whiff of his own odor. *So halflings don't have the gift of no smell!*

Noomi led him to the lower level. "The shower room is at the end of the hall. Mom laid out some clean clothes, including pajamas, on your bed." She opened a door and he saw the clothes and a towel.

He sat on the bed and bounced a little, testing. Nodding his approval at Noomi, he kicked off his shoes. "Thanks! If you don't mind, I think I'll turn in soon. I've been awake for days, it feels like, and I'm looking forward to sleeping in a human bed for the first time in months."

"Sounds good." Noomi left.

Josh grabbed the towel and followed her out. She entered another room and closed her door. Josh continued down the hall to the bathroom. The walls were natural gray stones stacked tightly together and the floor looked like pebbles in sand, but the sand was solid like grout. A showerhead poked out of one wall in a corner with a drain below it. A stone ledge held a bar of soap, and a curtain hung from a rod to close off the corner. A typical toilet, small mirror, and stone sink completed the room.

Josh glanced in the mirror while he waited for the water to turn hot. He gasped, horrified. In the months since he'd disappeared into the wilderness, his dirty-blond hair had grown several inches and it stuck out in all directions. His skin was reddened from sun and grimy with layers of dirt. He ran a hand over his cheek and felt a light stubble. He sniffed his armpits. *Guh! Definitely ripe!* It took only moments for the shower to heat up and the room filled with steam as he stood under the water. He soaped up, rinsed off, sniffed, and started over. There being no shampoo in sight, he used the soap, loving the pine scent. His mind wandered back to his human house and family. He pressed his palms into his eyes and stood under the water for a few extra moments before he switched off the hot water. *Now is not the time to wallow in self-pity. I should be grateful! I am alive and safe. Suck it up, man!*

Slipping on the soft flannel pajamas nearly sent him over the edge again, but he took a deep breath and let it out slowly. Studying his face in the mirror, his grin spread from ear to ear. He stroked the thickening blond mustache. A small jar sat on a shelf at eye level. He opened it, sniffed. *Mint?* He dabbed a bit on his finger and tasted it. *Toothpaste!* With no brushes in sight, he settled for using his finger. That made him feel almost human again.

No natural light entered his bedroom, but a switch by the door lit the small reading light by the bed. The bed invited him to climb under the covers and he couldn't resist. Relaxing into the pillow, he studied the ceiling in the dim light. Its unblemished solidity held no distractions, and he didn't have the energy to pick up the book. He turned off the light, expecting to be asleep in seconds. Instead, he lay there listening to the sounds of the house. Floors creaked, a door closed too hard, chairs slid into place in the room above him, water ran.

Josh remembered Rose, the undercover Netah skunk who liked to curl up under his bed. Images of toddler Rose, his parents, his old life, and his new Netah friends flashed behind his closed eyes. He'd had no time to feel sorry for himself until that moment. He rode the roller coaster of emotions evoked by Rose (gratitude), his parents (sadness), his new friends (joy). Josh tossed onto his side, squeezing his eyes shut to erase the images and emotions.

It didn't work. His throat ached as he worried whether his parents had grown closer or started fighting. Would they consider fostering another child since Rose had been adopted? Josh tossed onto his other side, his breath catching in short gasps as he realized that if they did, he wouldn't be there to see it. On his back, a warm glow washed over him as he imagined them with another child, laughing, playing, happy. *Can I ever reach out to them and tell them my story?* Not according to the Netahs, he couldn't.

Tossing again, the warm glow turned to red-hot heat. *When did I become needy? When was the last time I felt a hug like Dad's?* The calmer voice in his head said, What about Fern's hug? And as for your mom's minestrone, you have to admit that Ohma's was delicious. Josh rolled onto his stomach. *The Netahs aren't saints. They'd torn him away from his family, banished, one of their most terrible punishments. They'd taught him their ways in exchange for his promise to keep their secret.* The price was getting shot, but he'd been deemed a hero and now he lay in bed, exhausted, unable to sleep.

Cut it out! Think of something positive! There has to be something. *Okay, well, the Netahs have watched out for me while I learned how to transform. I like being outside in the wilderness.* Even in the winter? *Elk fur is warm. We turn into humans at night. Noomi is nice.* All good things.

What might have happened if the Netahs had never found out about you and taken you away? *I might have turned into an elk right in the middle of school! I wouldn't have known what to do. I would probably have been taken away from my family by some agency that wanted to lock me up in some lab.* Maybe you watch too much TV about government cover-ups and mad scientists. Maybe it would have been okay. *Probably not.* Deep down Josh knew that the Netahs had protected him, and he should be grateful. At any rate, staying home was not an option.

So much for sleep. Josh switched on his light. He chuckled as he read the title of the book he had grabbed, *My Antonia* by Willa Cather. He recognized the author's name from his school reading list. He had never had time to read it before. *What the heck. Maybe it will be a good distraction.* He read the back cover synopsis first. A story about Nebraska homesteaders? An ode to pioneering souls? *Oh, the irony!*

CHAPTER 5

Making New Friends

The smell of waffles and coffee made it into Josh's dream about badgers and starlit nights. Sitting on the edge of the bed, he tried to recall the dream. He could only remember a very strong wind that he couldn't escape. Perhaps his bedtime reading had slipped into his dreams.

Muted light suffused the room, making it feel like the sun just came up. The light seemed to come through the ceiling and walls. The red, black, and cream Navajo blanket had been tossed to the floor, so he shook it out and straightened it across his bed, fluffing the pillow. He pulled open the drawers of the dresser and found jeans and a flannel shirt. He checked the sizes. *Lucky guess. Or was it?* They did have spies. He supposed Rose could have noticed that detail and passed it on.

As he dressed, his mouth dropped open. *Lightbulb!* Whatever the Netahs wore as humans was what they'd be wearing after they transformed back from their animal! Why hadn't he figured that out? His Netah friends had all been wearing the same clothes all the time they were together in the wilderness. When Crawley appeared in her ski outfit, she had been away. *So that's how it works!*

He grinned widely as he pulled on socks. He'd been famous for mismatched socks in school, a studied nonchalance about clothes and colors. His friends at school used to say things like, "Orange shirt and red pants? What team wears that?" A girl he hardly knew said, "I can go shopping with you, if that would help." *As if that would ever happen. Shop? No way!* He carried his dirty clothes upstairs with him to take to the laundry room, if he could find it.

At the top of the stairs, he saw Noomi pry a waffle off a machine on the counter and stack it on a dish. "Just in time," she said, waving the fork at him. "Oh, take those down the hall. The laundry room is the last door on the left."

Josh returned and slid onto a stool next to Noomi. They tucked into their waffles with gusto. Fresh blueberries stained the waffles and syrup dripped off each morsel. It tasted like home. He'd missed eating like a human.

After breakfast he asked Noomi's mom, Ohma, if he could run his laundry.

"Sure. Come on, I'll show you."

Josh followed her. "Where's your dryer?"

Ohma rolled out a floor-to-ceiling rack hidden inside a cabinet. "It saves energy."

"Okay, cool, efficient, too. Thanks."

Ohma crossed her arms and leaned in the doorframe as he started the washer. She asked, "What would you like to do today? It's our day off, no working, no school."

"But you're not absolutely strict about that, because we can run laundry?"

"Oh, sure," she looked puzzled, then waved towards the machine, with a grin. "Especially if it's really stinky laundry."

Josh laughed. "I had a Jewish friend whose mom couldn't even cook dinner on Sabbath, it all had to be made the day before. You're not that strict?"

"Nope. So, you want a tour of our valley? We could go for a nice long walk. It's supposed to be warmer today."

"That sounds great."

When they returned to the family room, Ohma announced their plans. The little brother wanted to come, too. Hesta said he preferred to relax in a nice quiet house with a good book. Josh, Ohma, and Noomi waited while her brother went to the bathroom, finished his waffles, and generally dawdled. Once outside, everyone transformed into elk and rambled around the ponds whose edges had frozen overnight.

"This is what my parents would call a bluebird day," Josh admitted wistfully, as he noticed yesterday's snow had all melted.

Ohma paused and said, "Do you miss them terribly?"

"All the time," Josh admitted. "But I know it's necessary."

Noomi had stopped, as well. She said, "It doesn't make it any easier for you, I'm sure."

Ohma moved next to Josh. He wasn't sure what to do, but then she rested her head on his shoulder. He felt strangely comforted. She said, "We're your family now." Having spent a nearly sleepless night missing his mom and dad, Josh's feelings about the word "family" were still raw. *Can I really become part of this family? I'll have a brother and sister! I won't have to hide who I really am. Change is life, and it beats the alternative!* With a twinge of guilt at leaving his mom and dad behind and in the dark about what was happening to him, Josh struggled to be happy with the family Ohma was offering. Even so, he said, "Thanks. You're very kind."

Ohma led them to the top of a mesa. Josh studied the snow-capped mountains in the distance but didn't recognize them. He was always lost. Rocks on the side of a nearby mesa revealed a rusty red, sandy yellow, and one band of deep black.

"Is that a coal seam?" he asked Ohma, pointing with his black nose and eyes.

"Yes, I believe you are right," she answered.

Noomi spoke up. "We don't use coal here. That's why it's still in the ground, undisturbed."

"Hmm. Do you only use renewables?" he asked.

"Yep," Noomi answered, maybe a bit too proudly.

"Noomi is one of our energy scientists," Ohma explained with pride. "She is rather outspoken about renewables."

"When did you start to use them?" Josh asked.

Noomi said, "We stopped burning wood only a few years ago. I finally convinced everyone that not only did it destroy the landscape and pollute the air, but smoke trails coming from our homes could not be disguised. We made it look as natural as possible, like steam from an underground geothermal vent, but you could still smell the burning wood."

Had Josh heard that correctly? She had convinced them? He thought Noomi was his age, but she was a scientist already? "Noomi, if it's not impolite, how old are you, anyway?"

She laughed. "It's okay, I don't mind. I'm twenty-nine. Why?"

Whoa! "I thought you were only my age. I'm terrible at guessing people's ages, let alone Netahs. I mean, you and your mom look like sisters, and I'm not just saying that to flatter you both. It's true!"

Ohma nodded. "Well, thanks. It's one of the benefits of being a Netah."

Noomi explained. "When we return to our animal forms, we recharge. It's kind of like a fountain of youth."

Ohma searched for something. "Now where did your brother go? Do you see him, Noomi?"

"He's probably playing hide-and-seek," Noomi laughed. "Come on, Josh. Let's find him." She called out in a louder voice, "Ready or not, here we come!" They both heard a distant giggle.

Ohma huffed. "I don't have time for this. Will you find him? I'll see you back home." She disappeared down the steep slope towards the house.

Josh studied the ground carefully, trying to find any evidence of where the little elk might have gone. He walked back the way they had come and found a set of small hoof prints. "Check this out, Noomi."

"Good job, Josh." They followed the prints until they disappeared. "This is when it gets challenging," she said. "My advice is we stick together."

"Is he using a shielding device?" Josh asked.

"Who told you about shielding devices?"

"You did."

"Oh, yeah, right—no, they're for structures, not for us, silly." She shook her head in disbelief.

Josh thought about Rodan the day before. "I thought Rodan was invisible when he appeared yesterday. I couldn't see him through the dry branches of a bush that shouldn't have been able to hide him."

"Oh." She paused, which Josh figured meant she had to decide whether or not to tell him yet another secret. "You think we can disappear? That's a laugh. No, we cannot magically disappear. However, we can learn to read our surroundings enough to know where to stand or lie down to blend in. It's not a device. It's something we learn. My little brother is practicing right now."

"So, it's like the instinct that makes a baby fawn lie still in the grasses, so predators don't see it?" Josh asked. "I'm not yet worthy to learn this? Or maybe as a halfling, I can't learn it, because it's an instinct?" His voice betrayed his growing anger. He didn't like to accuse, but she'd touched a nerve.

"Josh, I'm sorry. Please, I'm trying to help, but don't know what is allowed, and I certainly don't know anything about halflings. Of course, you can learn, it's not rocket science!"

Josh sighed. "Who decides what is allowed? I feel like I could use a rule book."

Noomi snorted, "You and me both!"

"Yeah," Josh sighed as he looked downhill in the direction Ohma had gone. He wanted to argue that Noomi had grown up in this society and probably knew the rules by osmosis, where he had to learn them slowly, by trial and error, since the rules seemed to all be unwritten. "I'm just tired," he admitted. "Could you show me where the house is? I could use some time alone." He studied the landscape, fighting to maintain his composure.

Noomi pretended she didn't hear the catch in his voice. She called out to her brother. "Game's over. You win!"

Giggles erupted from three feet away, and then the young calf got up from his hiding spot, his legs all spindly, and a line of spots along his sides. He bounded down the hill and disappeared.

"Did he just go into your house?"

"Yep. Come on. I'll show you."

"Does your brother have a name?"

"Not yet. He hasn't had his naming ceremony."

Josh made mental notes as they walked: a low juniper by a large gray rock, a clump of yellow grass seed heads, and a small spindly pine. *That looks like a Charlie Brown Christmas tree. I wonder if these people celebrate Christmas?* When Noomi stopped, he recognized the large gray rock of their front door. "Know what? I think I'll just explore a little around the house and see if I can spot it from other directions, okay?"

"Sounds good." Noomi went inside and Josh stood there alone. Except he had the sinking sensation that there was someone watching him again, someone hidden and if he guessed it right, maybe even a little angry.

He lifted his head and sniffed hard, trying to pick up a scent. Then he remembered that the Netahs didn't smell. He looked carefully at all the nearby bushes and grasses to see if he could spot someone hiding, a shadow, footprints. "That you, Hesta?" he called out.

"Guess again," a low voice said from behind him.

"Rodan?" Josh spun around to face the voice.

Rodan poked his large head around a tall cedar at the side of the pond. "Yeah, lucky guess. How many of our names do you know, anyway?" His voice dripped with sarcasm and hostility. He paused, then said, "So, I see you've been hanging out with my girl. That's a dangerous choice."

Josh stepped back, then gathered his sense of injustice and faced Rodan man-to-man, or rather, elk-to-elk, no, Netah-to-Netah. He forced his voice into a patient tone. "Hey, look, I didn't choose to live here. It's where Hesta put me. Besides, I only just met Noomi. Also, she's way older than me." He snorted. "You think I'm competition? I'm just a skinny kid. Look at you. I mean, I'm flattered, but I think you have nothing to worry about." He paused and realized Rodan had called it a choice. "Are you saying I have a choice where I live?"

"Of course, you do." Rodan's tone softened, and Josh noticed a slight upwards curl on one side of his mouth. *Elk do have facial expressions!* "You could come live with the bachelors. Didn't anyone tell you?"

"Nope."

"Maybe Hesta just hasn't gotten around to it yet," Rodan suggested. "I mean you've only been here, what, one night?"

"That's true."

"Also, it could be that Hesta feels responsible for you and wants to ease you into things more slowly."

Furrows deepened across Josh's furry brow. "I bet I have to pass another test or something first."

"Huh." Rodan nodded. "Yeah, I heard about how the council made you pass three tests before they'd accept you. What was it: keep our secrets, learn how to transform, prove your loyalty? But, hey, you passed and came out a hero when you saved that littles community. Still, I can see how you'd be tired of tests." The anger had drained out of Rodan's voice. He almost sounded sympathetic.

"You can say that again."

"Say, how old are you, anyway?"

"Um, approaching fifteen."

"Aw, geez! You're just getting started, as a human." Rodan paused, considering the implications, perhaps doing a little mental math. "However," he continued, "in Netah years, you are approaching manhood. Did you grow antlers yet?"

"I sure did. Even gave Crawley a ride on them a little while ago." That might have been a little brag.

"Well then, I'm gonna have to have a talk with Hesta. It's time you joined your brothers in the bachelor's camp. You've got a lot to learn and no time to lose."

Josh heard the words brothers and bachelors. This had taken a nice turn. The new friendly vibe encouraged him to ask, "Hey, could you help me out with something else?"

"Sure, what is it?"

"I can't find my way around here. It all looks the same. Can you give me a clue, a landmark, anything to differentiate Hesta's place from everywhere else?"

"Wow, that would be disconcerting. You feel lost?"

"Yeah, I guess." Josh hated to admit that, it sounded so lame. "I mean, this may be the first time I've been outside by myself since I got here, except that you're here, too," Josh snorted.

"Okay, here's the deal." Rodan nodded. "We try very hard to blend our homes into the landscape so they are invisible. Each home has a unique rock face for the front door. Hesta's is that dark gray granite. Some are yellow sandstone, red, tan, or speckled. For instance, look over here." Rodan motioned with his head towards another large boulder. "See the red veins in this tan rock? This door belongs to my parents."

"But you don't live there anymore? Are you not allowed to?"

"That's right. Once we reach adulthood, we guys move away and live in our own place together. Right now, there's not many of us in the lodge. There's plenty of room for you. The only question is will Hesta think you are ready and old enough."

"Wow, that sounds sick. I think I'd like that. How old do you have to be?"

Rodan looked confused. "Sick? No one's sick, don't worry."

Josh laughed, "No, not literally, it's just an expression, it means that's awesome, great, you know?"

"Ah, okay. So, your question . . . let me see, do you need a certain number of elk or human years? Um, in human years, you're just a kid, but as an elk, you're full-grown. I have an idea. Do you trust me?"

"Dude, I guess?"

"Dude, huh?" Rodan lifted his chin and grinned. "I understand your hesitation. You just met me, right, dude?" He laughed. "Come on, we're gonna get some exercise. We'll check out the lodge, and you can decide if it's for you."

"Yeah, okay. Lead on." Josh barely contained his excitement.

"Right." Rodan took off, splashing through puddles of snowmelt. They galloped across the valley through low bushes and slowed near a stand of aspens. The trees were mostly bare except for a few brown leaf stragglers wiggling in the wind. Passing through the white, spotty trunks of the aspens, they approached a large speckled boulder that nearly disappeared in the dappled shade of the trees. Dried grasses hung over a large boulder next to it, and a trickle of water splashed into a tiny pool at its base. "This is it. Come on in."

Rodan became a human and waited for Josh to do the same before he pushed the rock and it swung aside, revealing a large hall.

"Rode!" A chorus of male voices greeted Rodan as they entered. The men were spread out around the large room.

"Hi, guys," Rodan laughed. "I brought a guest. Try to behave yourselves."

"We always do!" one said.

"Define behave," another laughed.

"Did you bring the mead?" came another voice.

"Um, no. You'll have to make do."

"Jeez, Rodan," one complained. "We ask you to do one thing and you forget it completely. Reliable as usual! And who's the stray?"

Josh stood next to Rodan, taking in the room. He had expected to see timbered ceilings and stone walls, when Rodan called it a lodge. In fact, the place had tall, modern windows, high ceilings, reddish walls, and a warm stone floor like Hesta's home. Sets of leather chairs lined up facing a wide picture window, and a long half-sawn log table lined with benches sat in front of a stone fireplace. Where Hesta's house had colorful children's art and a modern vibe, this mix of earth tones and textures felt very western. Josh loved it. It felt like a fancy mountain cabin.

Rather than introducing Josh, Rodan made a sweeping gesture with his hand, taking in the whole room and asked, "What do you think? Want to see the bedrooms?"

"It's fantastic. Yes." As they walked through the room, Josh counted five guys. They had various stages of beard. Josh rubbed his peach-fuzzed chin and felt a little out of place. "You really think I might be old enough to come live here?"

"I honestly don't know, but I think you could adjust faster if you do live with us. We can teach you what our responsibilities are, show you the valley, get you up to speed faster than Hesta can. He's got other things to deal with." Rodan walked down a hall and gestured to several doors, then opened one. "We all get our own rooms these days. I'll show you mine, because I know it's neat. Some aren't." The room had a single bed, table, lamp, and small bookshelf. It looked like the bedroom at Hesta's house except for a window wall at the end that looked like the opening of a cave. A small empty fireplace looked like it hadn't been used for a while. It all smelled like stone and wood and dirt, like actually being in a cave.

"Wow," Josh said. "Hey, how is this place heated? Geothermal like Hesta's?"

"Yes, but this lodge has been here a while. We just haven't gotten around to removing the fireplaces. I kind of like them. I figure they're our emergency heat. Or maybe we'll figure out something to burn that doesn't have a smell."

"Is someone working on that?" Josh asked, now very curious.

"Your pal Noomi is trying, but so far no luck. The trick, she says, is to have a substance to burn that won't pollute, would be waste anyway, and has no odor. She's currently working on switchgrass. Burning produces carbon dioxide, no matter what you do, so who knows? Maybe I'm just nostalgic for the old days of sitting around a roaring fire telling stories."

"Yeah, me, too. My parents lit their fireplace all the time. Except, it used natural gas, not wood. It's not the same, but it still got warm. It also doesn't smell, so you guys could use that."

"Sounds nice, maybe we should try it here," Rodan said.

"I wonder. It wouldn't smell, but it still releases carbon dioxide. Is that Noomi's concern?"

"Yes. Ever since she heard this term 'net zero' in college, she's been pushing for it."

"Yeah, I've heard of that," Josh said. "I think we're a long way away from it as long as we're using fossil fuels like natural gas. If the Netahs figure it out, that would be awesome!"

Rodan raised his eyebrows. "That interests you?"

"Sure."

"Sounds like you have the makings of a scientist." Rodan rubbed his chin thoughtfully.

Just then a commotion broke out in the main hall. Josh and Rodan rushed back. They found Hesta at the door, angry, demanding to see Josh. The others had all gathered by the front door and appeared just as angry. One guy said Hesta had no right to come barging in on them and making demands on their day off.

"I'm here, Hesta. What's the problem?" Rodan said with authority and self-assurance, standing tall as he approached Hesta. Josh copied his posture, hoping it would make him look just as confident. After all, he hadn't done anything wrong, why was Hesta all worked up?

"Ah, good. The problem is," Hesta stopped, glaring at Rodan and turning kind eyes on Josh, "Rodan had no authorization to bring you here."

"Yeah, Rodan," one of the angrier and bigger guys said. "What do you think you're doing bringing that halfling here without approval?"

Rodan waved his hands in a placating way and shook his head. "Calm down." His voice took on a jovial tone. "There's nothing wrong with showing a young sprout like Josh what he has to look forward to. That's all I did. He didn't even know we had our own lodge. I thought it would do no harm to let him know. It's part of our society, our culture. Hesta, I was only trying to help."

"I'm not about to start babysittin' that smelly kid!" the angry guy said. Josh moved to stand a little behind Rodan, out of the guy's line of sight. The guy continued, "Do we have to take him in? He could go anywhere. I don't trust him!"

Maybe the lodge isn't a good idea. On the other hand, why am I cowering from angry guy? I bet he's all bluster. Josh stood taller.

"Okay, fine." Hesta crossed his arms and spoke to Rodan. "How would you feel about sponsoring Josh into the lodge?" Josh couldn't believe it. Did Hesta not hear angry guy? Josh expected Rodan to instantly turn Hesta down. Hesta continued in a more conversational tone. "He's interested in building. Maybe he can apprentice on Haiman's project."

A silence fell on the men. Josh felt scrutiny from all sides. He understood that they'd be cautious, maybe even suspicious, but didn't love being talked about in the third person.

Finally, Rodan answered, "I'd be honored to sponsor him. When shall we schedule the ceremony?" Voices erupted around him as events, jobs, other commitments were listed. Rodan interrupted. "We could use an extra hand with all those jobs." Murmur, murmur, grumble, grumble, the voices died down.

Josh kept his eyes on Hesta, watching his reactions. First, he looked surprised when Rodan said yes, now he looked impatient. Josh wondered what the ceremony would entail. Would he get a funny hat to wear to lodge meetings? Would he have to pass more challenges? *You know what? To heck with it. I'm tired of being told what to do.*

Josh spoke loudly, "I'd be honored to join the men's lodge, if they'll have me. I am willing to work and learn whatever I need to and contribute to the group. Perhaps I could be admitted on a provisional basis." Netahs seemed to like that word.

The men remained silent. Josh studied the faces around him. Some looked surprised, some unhappy, several nodded their approval. A mixed bag.

Rodan took charge with a nod. "I say we take him on immediately as a junior associate. Let's get to know him and see how he handles our living situation. I mean, he's only a kid as a human, but he's part Netah and has had to do some pretty hard growing up recently. If the council says he's trustworthy, who are we to question it?"

Josh took a breath, realizing he'd been holding it. Now all eyes turned to Hesta. Apparently, he had the last say. "Fair enough," Hesta began. "You will all take responsibility for teaching and helping our newest member. Help him become one of us. Keep him out of trouble. Just remember, he is not your errand boy, he is one of you. I leave him in your capable hands."

"Yes, sir!" all the guys answered like a military chorus, although some of them were obviously being sarcastic, in Josh's opinion.

Hesta looked Josh square in the eye, obviously making a decision. "Josh, if I may have a word."

Josh's eyes were wide with worry as he moved through the guys to stand next to the chief. Hesta put his arm over his shoulder and said quietly, "Walk with me a moment, would you?"

Josh nodded and followed him outside, glancing over his shoulder at the faces in the doorway before it closed behind him.

Hesta only went as far as the edge of the pond by the door. He stayed in his human form, tucking his hands into his jacket pockets. "Listen, I'm pleased that Rodan has taken a shine to you and made this offer. I wasn't sure if he would, mostly because you're young and new around here." He paused, choosing his words carefully. "That said, you're always welcome back in our house if you need a break." He watched Josh nod. "Also, you let me know if they give you any trouble, or if you have any questions. Agreed?"

"Yes, and thank you, sir," Josh answered, picking up on the title the others had used.

Hesta nodded his approval, patting Josh on the shoulder before he transformed and left. When the door closed behind Josh, the room full of men stayed hushed.

Josh broke the silence. "Hey, guys, thanks. I appreciate it. Also, I'm starving. You got anything to eat?" That broke the tension.

"You're in luck," Rodan said. "It's Sunday night, soup night, and it's already simmering on the cooktop." He looked around at the rest of the guys. "What do you say, shall we eat early today?"

"Sure, I'm always hungry," one said.

"That soup's been calling me all afternoon."

"I'll slice up the bread."

As a group they walked towards the kitchen area. One got out spoons and handed plates and knives to Josh. "Come on, help me set the table." They each filled their own bowl from the pot. As Josh filled his, the grouchy guy said, "Hey, leave some for the rest of us! Damn it, what a greedy little bugger!"

Josh handed him the ladle. "Here you go, grumpy."

The next guy in line snorted and said, "Yeah, grumpy." He grinned at Josh, nodding agreement with Josh's new name for the guy. Grumpy mumbled something under his breath but kept his eyes down.

Josh walked slowly towards the table, unsure where to sit. The one who'd been behind him walked past and said, "Come sit by me. I won't bite your head off like some people." Josh followed and watched everyone start to eat, not knowing their dining etiquette.

The short, stocky one with a graying beard said, "Hey, dig in, kid. We're not formal around here. And don't let Arman shake you up. If you're still hungry, go back for more. He's not the food police."

Josh grinned. "Thanks, mister."

The older guy grimaced. "Not mister, I'm Mako. Guys, introduce yourselves." He waved his hand to include everyone sitting at the table.

Josh studied every one of their faces as he heard their names. Esok had a very round face and a neat, dark beard; Haiman's long beard and hair were a dark red, and he was at least a half head taller than most of the others, even sitting down.

When they'd come around the table to angry guy, he looked up and said, "I'm Grumpy. Not pleased to meet you."

The guy next to him laughed and said, "Grumpy or Arman, you can call him whatever you want. Me, I'm going with Grumpy!" That got a growl out of Arman, but the guy looked pleased with himself.

To Josh he said, "I'm Tomo, and I'm grateful that I'm no longer the youngest guy in the lodge!" He stroked his bare cheek and looked around the table for their responses, which ranged from scowls (Grumpy) to surprise (Haiman) to approval (Mako). Josh just got a nod and small salute from Rodan because Josh already knew him.

"Hi, um, nice to meet you," Josh said, trying desperately to remember identifying features. In their human forms he could recognize them. The tricky part would be when they were elk.

Conversation turned to upcoming projects. Josh listened while they discussed building Haiman's house, fence mending, cleaning out the barn, truck maintenance. Guy stuff. Josh took Mako's advice and got seconds. He also helped with the dishes afterwards. As everyone drifted away, Josh found Rodan and asked, "Which room is mine?"

Nodding, Rodan said, "This way." He led Josh to the hallway lined with doors, kind of like in a hotel, and pushed open the third door on the right. "How about this one?"

Josh looked inside and saw an exact copy of Rodan's room, minus books and clothes on the shelf. The walls were whitewashed, but they were odd planes, like rock faces. The dark red floor felt nice and warm underfoot. A small table and lamp cozied up to the wooden headboard and a blanket lay folded at the foot of the bed. "Looks great. Guess I'll have to go get the clothes and pj's I left at Hesta's house."

"We'll do that in the morning. Hang on." Rodan ducked back out the door and reappeared in a minute. He handed a pair of pajamas and a towel to Josh. "You can keep those. I have more." Josh tossed them on the bed and said, "Thanks!" He stood there, unsure what to do next.

"Come on," Rodan said. "Let me show you the rest of the place."

Through a warren of hallways that were all lit mysteriously through what looked like natural cracks in the walls and ceilings, Rodan led Josh past the bedrooms and downstairs, through a workout room filled with equipment, to the sauna, a hot springs pool lined with river rocks, then into a much larger room that held a boxing ring and a pool table. It was an extensive building, or maybe a cave? Josh noticed there were no stalactites nor water seeping down walls; it felt warm and cozy.

The men had spread themselves out, two sparring in the ring, one lifting weights, and one soaking in the hot springs, buck naked, Josh noticed with a wince. *Ha, buck naked! Buck, get it?* When they got to the library, its walls lined with books, overstuffed chairs, and tables, Josh asked, "Can I look around in here?"

"Sure, knock yourself out. I'm going to hit the sauna. Don't let the guys scare you. They're all much friendlier than they look. Well, most of them are." He shrugged and turned to go. "Ask 'em anything. Don't be shy."

Josh nodded. "Okay, yeah, thanks." After Rodan left, Josh stood in the middle of the library and took a deep breath. He knew he could really get to like this place. He just had to get the guys to accept him. No biggie. *Hah, yes, it is!* With a shrug, Josh walked over to read the titles on the book spines. He tried to figure out how they were organized. Then he spotted an interesting title: The First Netahs. *That could be useful.* He pulled it out and sat in a generously proportioned chair that made him feel like Goldilocks in Pappa's chair. Flipping through the pages, he found a short story that sounded like the one Hesta had told him. He reread it and continued on, losing track of time.

Josh stifled a fifth yawn and realized his eyelids had grown heavy. He closed the book and tucked it under his arm. Walking back through the hallways was eerie, because they were now empty, although still lit with a soft warm glow whose source he couldn't determine. No one remained in the sauna, or the weight room. He found the long hallway with bedrooms and counted to find his. Yep, there were the pajamas on the bed where he'd left them.

LISA KANIUT COBB

He returned to the hallway and looked for an open door. Haiman had his back to the door as he pulled off his shirt, revealing a hairy back and shoulders. Josh said, "Um, excuse me, where's the bathroom?"

"End of the hall, big red door." The guy didn't pause as he slid his jeans to the floor. Josh spun away and rushed to the red door. The room reminded Josh of his high school gym bathrooms only nicer, like in a ski lodge. The stone walls and floor were different shades of warm earth, but the white ceiling and soft evening light coming in through high windows over the sinks kept the room cozy. Josh picked up a soap bar and sniffed. It was the same pine soap he'd used at Hesta's house. He also found a small jar of toothpaste and used his finger again. He'd have to ask about toothbrushes. He'd never been comfortable in the boys' locker rooms at high school. Now he'd have to share one with a bunch of strange grown men. That was an uncomfortable thought. Shrugging it off, he retrieved his towel and returned to shower. He wouldn't be called the smelly one tomorrow!

By the time he fell onto the bed, he couldn't keep his eyes open. His first day in a Netah lodge had been quiet and relaxing and filling.

CHAPTER 6

New Foods

D awn broke through the window in Josh's room and filled it with a rosy light. Josh liked waking up with the sun like this; it sure beat waking up in the dark to an alarm. He rolled off his bed and pulled on his jeans and shirt. Heading towards the kitchen, he found himself alone. He looked around for a coffee machine and found a canister of what looked and smelled to Josh like dried weeds. Josh knew better than to help himself to other people's stash. It could be tea, but he wouldn't risk it. Josh peered into a cabinet and found jars of what looked like green smoothies or maybe green tea, and a grayish milk. Nothing had a label and nothing smelled even vaguely recognizable. Not feeling adventurous, he settled for a glass of cold water and walked over to the windows to see what the world looked like that morning.

It was breathtakingly clear and oddly distorted. When he saw a leaf float past, he realized the window was hidden behind a waterfall. The water sparkled, as the sun rose above a range of mountains in the distance. As he sat in a chair and sipped his water, the light blinded him, so he returned to his room to retrieve his book. A different chair avoided the sun. As he read, he sensed motion and searched the view for movement. A herd of elk approached, and he wondered if they were just elk or Netahs.

Moments later the lodge door opened, and the sound of alarmed voices reverberated around the room. He wandered over to see what the fuss was about. Rodan spoke to Haiman. "We've seen this before. The humans call it chronic wasting disease. Is it contagious? That's all I want to know."

"We really don't know," Haiman insisted. "So far, no Netah has caught it, but we don't know for sure that we are immune. Maybe we are lucky or it's because we keep our distance from the feral elk herds and have not been exposed."

Esok said, "That elk died on our land."

Josh wondered if the wired perimeter was meant to keep others out or merely warn of intruders.

Rodan looked at Josh. "Did you and Hesta find any breaks yesterday?"

"Yes, but we repaired everything on the screen." Josh felt heat rise in his face. Were they going to blame him for a dead elk? They were calling it an elk, not a Netah. "We definitely reset the alarm," he added.

"Sure, you did," Arman sneered. "You believe this?" He'd turned to Rodan. "I knew this would happen. He's going to get us all killed! You can't trust him, just like his da—"

"Enough! Arman," Rodan interrupted him, "if Josh says they fixed it, then they fixed it. You don't trust Hesta to do it right?" Arman lowered his eyes and studied his shoes but didn't apologize or answer. Rodan continued, "Sounds like this animal got through before that. Josh, you stay here. Arman, you're with me. We have to report." They left.

Josh closed his mouth, which had dropped at Arman's reaction. He knew perfectly well what the man meant to say. He didn't trust Josh's father, and wouldn't trust Josh. It almost felt like the guy had been betrayed by his father, like maybe they'd been close. Josh decided to keep his distance from Arman. He had enough things to deal with without having to also make amends for something his father had done.

Josh turned to the others. "Uh, guys, I have a dumb question for you."

"Shoot! We've got plenty of dumb answers for you!" The guys chuckled and the tension they'd carried in with them broke. Haiman said, "What is it, kid?"

"Well, where is the coffee?"

After a few awkward moments when no one seemed to know what to do or say, Mako finally said, "Coffee first or food, eh? I say food. Come on, there's still plenty to eat outside. We can wash it all down with coffee when we get back."

Josh thought that meant going outside to a freezer in a garage, but, no, it meant going outside and turning back into elk, then sniffing around. Josh got his second real lesson in finding elk food in the aspen grove.

Tomo was the smallest elk in the group, even smaller than Josh. He found something good and said, "Here you go, check this out." He yanked up a mouthful of a tall, dry grass with a yellow tassel.

Josh tried it. "Hmm," he mused. "Tastes a little nutty, maybe a little like onion. What is it?"

Esok said, "Ha, we got a food critic here guys!" He gave Josh a friendly smile on his way past. Smiles were still smiles, even if they were on an elk face and included grass stuck in the teeth. Josh compared Tomo to Esok and decided that other than Tomo being smaller, they were different colors. While Tomo's fur looked light brown, Esok's shoulders and head were much darker. Would he notice the difference if they weren't standing next to each other? Sure. Esok continued, "I don't know the name of everything. I just know what I like. This is my favorite. I just look for those flat seed heads. They're all over this valley."

Haiman stood a few yards away, casting a long shadow with his big body and long legs. Josh would know Haiman by the red in his fur. Haiman said, "Try this."

Josh tasted something like a sunflower seed. He noticed that Haiman ate the seeds and stems. "This is delicious," he said. He and Haiman ate half of the patch.

"Leave the rest for another time," Haiman instructed. They all wandered a little further, sniffing and poking their noses through the dried stems and patches of snow on the ground.

Josh noticed the dried remains of what looked like a mushroom. He sniffed it. It smelled earthy, maybe a little tangy. "What about this, is it edible?" he asked no one in particular, because the others had all wandered out of earshot.

Josh figured he had the hang of this and decided to be brave. He took a small, ever so tiny bite.

"Stop!" Tomo appeared out of nowhere and shoved him aside. "Did you eat any of that mushroom?"

"No, I, uh, yeah, I kinda did," Josh admitted, spitting out the piece, not liking the tart, stinging taste on his tongue.

Tomo went into high-alert mode. "Mako, we have a problem."

Mako came thundering over just as Josh started to feel his world go upside down. "What?" Mako's voice sounded old and tired, and very annoyed.

Josh groaned, "Oh crap," as the world tilted and he slowly seemed to melt down to the ground, his eyes wide, his tongue lolling.

Josh felt the other guys approach through the ground his ear rested on. He smelled damp earth and a silly grin spread across his face. He heard a small creature skittering under a nearby bush and studied the light through a pale leaf in the same bush. He didn't have a care in the world. He didn't care about tests or food or even coffee. He felt weird, like his face was growing shorter while his legs were what, oh, sure, becoming arms. It all made perfect sense and he laughed.

He heard the guys talking, but their words were jumbled, like they came into his ears in the wrong order. That was weird. He picked up on the tone of their voices. Josh heard concern, annoyance, anger, fear. Josh realized he couldn't move his legs, his head, or his mouth, which had way too many teeth in it. He didn't care, not as long as the sun kept shining so nice and warm on his face. He decided it was the perfect time of day for a nap, so he let his eyes close. He did not sleep.

The ground rumbled like a train approached and suddenly Josh cared. He did not want to be crushed by a train! That would be bad. A nice soothing voice made demands. Josh tried, but couldn't answer the nonsense questions. Other voices sounded annoyed and one sounded amused. Oops, now Josh picked up dismay. *Oh, that's me, but why am I upset? Oh, is it because I'm nauseous?* Josh wished he hadn't laid down for his nap on top of an anthill. The little things crawled all over him. Josh struggled to his feet, noticing he only had two of them at the moment, and the voices grew louder. He felt warm bodies pressing against him and he let them push him, he didn't care. He didn't feel like fighting.

When the icy water sloshed around his ankles, he gasped. He definitely wanted to fight now, but the warm bodies were relentless and next thing he knew, Josh felt the ground slip away and he had to swim. He swam for his life, his breath coming in gasps. He was a competent breaststroker, and he made it to the far side of the pond quickly. He lowered his feet to find the bottom and realized he now had four feet with which to climb out. Shaking the water out of his fur, he spun around to face his friends, suddenly livid at their prank. The nausea returned. He dry-heaved for a minute until he heard the first words that made sense in a while.

"Take a drink!" a woman's voice commanded.

Hmm, bossy much? Oh well, it's probably a good idea. He drank. His tongue cooled off, the ants jumped off, his stomach settled down a little. He drank some more and thought he could drink the pond dry, he didn't. When the fuzz finally cleared from his brain, he looked up sheepishly. "Huh, interesting."

His new lodge mates laughed. Josh noticed a new elk standing among them. He realized she was the female voice he'd just heard. She said, "Follow me. I'll mix you up something to settle your stomach and counteract the toxins." Where had he heard that voice before? Noomi? Horrified, he realized he had no clothes on, but wait, he had elk fur. He relaxed. *Toxins? From a little bite? What kind of place had mushrooms that could nearly kill a guy? Okay, maybe not kill. Just tickle, numb, make dizzy and nauseous.* He followed her to the large black rock. She became a woman and Josh recognized Ohma.

Josh transformed, as well, which went smoothly, surprising Josh. He half expected to transform partly. He'd seen what industrial fertilizers at an illegal marijuana grow had done to the littles a few months ago. The squirrel baby with a human head and hands was unable to climb trees or eat nuts. Even Josh was affected as he became part human and part elk, kind of like a centaur. *Maybe I didn't eat enough of the mushroom to have that effect, and my size might have made a difference?*

Ohma put her hand on Josh's chest, studying his eyes, and said, "Come on, let's get you inside."

He nodded, moving a little unsteadily. Tomo approached from inside and wrapped a blanket around Josh while Ohma steered him to a barstool. Next, she mixed up a concoction that looked and tasted like green mud. "Drink up," Ohma insisted.

Rodan walked in and sat down next to Josh. "How you feeling now, little buddy?"

Josh took stock for a moment then answered, "Okay, I guess." He registered the fact that Rodan had called him the same nickname George used to use.

Arman grumbled, "Jeez, can't leave the kid for a minute before he gets into trouble. What a pain! He doesn't belong here!"

"Perhaps," Rodan agreed with a frown. "But I'm willing to give him another chance. From now on," he spoke to Josh, "you don't eat anything outside without checking with one of us first. At least not until you learn what's what out there. Deal?"

"Deal, except . . ."

"Here it comes, it's always something with this kid," Arman groused.

"No," Josh scowled. "I mean, will someone please tell me what that was so I know for next time?"

"Don't sign me up for babysitting," Arman insisted. "I got better things to do," and Josh was relieved to see him walk away.

Rodan raised his eyebrows at Ohma and she nodded and said, "Right, so that was an Autumn skullcap, a gilled mushroom that grows in rotting wood. If you'd eaten more, we might not be sitting here talking about it." She looked up at Rodan. "You really shouldn't leave those things lying around."

"On it," Rodan said, heading for the door, presumably to remove the offending and deadly mushrooms.

"Come on," Ohma said. "Time to get some rest. You'll feel better after that, I promise."

Josh had no will to resist. He meekly let her slip an arm around him and steer him to his bedroom. At the door, she stood aside and waved him in. Quietly, Josh said, "Sorry."

"Yeah, me, too." Ohma smiled reassuringly.

Josh sank onto the bed and rolled over to face the wall. He heard the door click shut. Tears welled and Josh wiped them away angrily. Rolling his face into the pillow he yelled into it. Coming up for air, he pounded the pillow to a pulp. He felt slightly better, even though he'd never been so mortified and embarrassed in his life. With a final sob, he took a deep breath and let it out slowly, continuing until he slipped off to sleep.

When he woke up, the intensity of the light in his bedroom had dimmed. Josh wandered out into the great room. He noticed that Haiman and Esok were talking quietly. He walked towards them. Esok turned his back, so Josh walked on. Arman looked up from his book and said, "It lives. Look, guys, our little drug addict has risen from his widdle nappypoo!"

Josh avoided Grumpy. *The guy has the maturity of a high school bully!* Tomo sat alone at a long table. When Josh caught his eye, Tomo shrugged. That being the warmest reception he got from anyone; Josh settled down across from Tomo.

What had happened? They were all friendly that morning, what had he missed? He asked, "Tomo, what's gotten into everyone? Was it the stupid mushroom?"

"What? No," Tomo laughed. "Don't be so sensitive. We're just worried, I guess."

"What are you worried about?"

"The elk? Remember? Jeez, either you have a very short memory, or really don't have a clue what's going on around you." Tomo returned his eyes to his book as if he really didn't want to talk.

"Oh, you mean the elk with chronic wasting disease. Yeah, I heard you guys talking about that. I thought it wasn't contagious," Josh persisted.

"We don't know if it is. That's different." Tomo didn't look up.

"I get that, but I don't get why everyone is suddenly grouchy." Josh sensed a change in the room.

"Maybe it's because we had to spend the morning babysitting you," Tomo said, his eyes closed, acting like he'd never been so bored, and it should have been obvious.

Josh was flabbergasted. He hadn't had a babysitter for years, at least four or five years ago, and hadn't he been on his own for the last several months? He didn't have his family looking after him, but he always seemed to have minders, he realized. His empty belly rumbled and churned. *I'll never fit in if I'm always treated like a kid or an outlaw like my dad. My connection to him is inescapable. I have to always prove myself! It's so unfair!*

Rodan disturbed his fuming when he entered the lodge and announced in a voice meant to be heard by everyone, "All right, Netahs. You know the drill. Ohma has declared a lockdown for three weeks."

"Three whole weeks?" Tomo whined.

"That's right. Everyone stays in the lodge."

Josh leaned over and whispered to Tomo, "What's he talking about? What's the drill?"

Tomo spoke slowly, like he was talking to a toddler who didn't understand words, not bothering to whisper. "Uh, okay, so a lockdown is because there's a threat to the community."

"Yeah? What threat?" Josh asked.

"We can get sick, duh." Tomo turned away to listen as Rodan continued, looking directly at Josh.

"We stay human for three weeks and we will be examined regularly by Ohma. She will give us the all-clear when it's safe."

The others grumbled their agreement to the order. That settled, the men got up and wandered away, most heading downstairs to the gym. Josh' stomach growled noisily. He saw a grin form on Tomo's face, even though Tomo kept his eyes on his book. Josh kept his voice even like Tomo had just done. "I'm starving. What do we eat if we have to stay human?"

Tomo looked up and his expression softened. "I bet you are. Come on. I know just the thing." He led the way to the cold cupboard, which Josh learned was a big metal box that stayed cold because of the trickling spring water that seeped through stones surrounding it. Tomo pulled out a jar filled with a thick green liquid. He poured some into a glass, cut it with some water at the sink, stirred and handed it over. Josh sniffed it, then watching Tomo's eyes for signs that he might be kidding or something, he sipped. It tasted like cucumbers and mint. Josh's eyebrows shot up with surprise. Tomo poured some for himself and lifted it. "Cheers."

Turns out, there were worse places to have to spend a few weeks with strangers. After all, the lodge had a workout room, a pool room, the kind with cues and balls, not water, even a hot springs and sauna. Josh even had his own room and he loved the library. It was pretty darned good.

Josh guessed he'd made it through at least one week, when he rounded the corner by the kitchen area and saw Rodan peering at something on the wall. He went to investigate and found a chore chart that rotated responsibilities within the lodge. Josh had just decided to go check out the library again when Rodan said, "So, Josh. I think we'll add your name to the list in a few days. Meantime, you're with me. I'll show you the ropes."

Josh peered at the chart, found Rodan's name and job. "Says here you're the cook."

"Oh good, you can read," Rodan snorted.

Josh fought the urge to return the sarcasm, he saluted and said, "Captain Obvious, at your service!" That got a smile from Rodan. Josh continued, "Do you plan the meals?"

"Nope. Basically, we improvise with what we have, so we don't waste food. It's efficient."

"You have a storeroom somewhere? Where do you shop?"

"We don't shop," Rodan answered while reading a list tacked on a board in the corner of the kitchen. "We have a swap meet every week and exchange surplus."

"Oh, yeah, Noomi told me about that. She said her family specialized in peppers. What's our specialty?"

"Uh, I guess you could say we grow the best potatoes. Hope you like them." Rodan shook his head. "Truthfully? I'm getting a little tired of potatoes." He chuckled.

Josh read the piece of paper. It said vegetable soup, period. "Is this a joke? That's all you ever eat? Vegetable soup?"

"Why? You got a problem with that?" Rodan laughed and crossed his arms.

When Josh didn't respond, Rodan continued, "Mostly we eat outside, but soups and casseroles fill us up when we can't, like now, in lockdown. This time of year, we usually cook one night a week. This lodge does it Sunday nights. Eventually, later in the winter, we might be eating soup three or four times a week. It depends on snowpack mostly. Don't worry, you won't starve. Sometimes we get surprises. Tomo is the most adventurous. He'll throw in things he forages to spice things up."

Josh nodded. "Okay, simple is good. You know, my mom never let me in her kitchen back at home, but I'm ready to learn."

"Why not? Were you dangerous with knives?"

"Don't know, I never got the chance to try."

"It's not hard, as long as you know a few tricks. I'll show you. Don't worry."

"Worry? No way, when do we start?"

"Hmm." Rodan looked out the window to gauge the time. "We can start now." He picked up a couple of baskets and said, "Follow me. Time to scrounge up some grub."

"All right!" Josh followed Rodan downstairs to a door he had not noticed before. Beyond that door they found a cold cellar. A single lightbulb hung from a cord in the ceiling, dimly lighting wooden shelves along three walls carved right into the bedrock. The space was dry and cool. They spent a few minutes filling their baskets with potatoes, assorted vegetables, nuts and greens. Back in the kitchen, Rodan carefully demonstrated how to curl the fingers out of the way of the knife blade. As they worked together, washing, chopping, and peeling, Rodan lined the vegetables up in the order they'd be added. Rodan sighed contentedly and Josh's shoulders loosened. Josh chopped what he thought looked like white carrots very slowly.

"Nice work on those parsnips, Josh." Rodan grinned as he rinsed his hands in the sink. "You'll make a fine chef someday."

"Chef?" Josh kept his eyes on the movement of the knife.

"Yeah, sure, lots of guys are chefs." Rodan pulled a big soup pot out of a cupboard.

"Are you going to marry Noomi?" Josh didn't know where that came from, but there the question hung, waiting, the subject changed.

"If she chooses me, but who knows? Maybe she'll choose you!"

"Nah, she hardly knows me." Josh waved away the notion. "That's ridiculous. Besides, I'm too young for her." He scooped the turnips into a bowl.

"You may be right. Maybe I do have a chance." Rodan grinned and gave Josh a playful nudge. Luckily Josh had already put down the knife. Josh marveled at how quickly Rodan had gone from rival to mentor. It gave him hope for the others, except maybe for Grumpy.

When it was time to start cooking, Rodan turned the heat on under the pot. It appeared to be natural gas but didn't smell like it.

"What kind of gas do you use?" Josh asked.

"Vegetable oil," Rodan answered.

After pouring a clear oil into the pot, Rodan handed Josh a wooden spoon and said, "Time to dump that first bowl of veggies into the pan. Keep stirring so nothing sticks."

Josh stepped back a little to avoid the spattering oil, and his mouth watered at the scents coming out of the pot.

Rodan peered over his shoulder. "Next bowl," he commanded.

As Josh stirred the ingredients, steam wafted up, and he squinted into it. Rodan turned on an overhead fan. Josh continued to stir while Rodan poured a mystery liquid from the cold cupboard and water into the pot and said, "Put the lid on. We let it come to a boil, then let it simmer for a while." A peppery fragrance almost made Josh sneeze. Rodan continued, "Later we'll add the last greens and serve. Have you really never cooked before?"

"Does putting a hot dog on a stick and holding it over a campfire in Cub Scouts count?" Josh grinned crookedly, knowing the answer.

"Hot dogs? That's not food. It doesn't count." Rodan snorted, as Josh rolled his eyes and nodded in agreement.

Rodan filled a tea kettle, while Josh finished putting away their knives and board. He scooped up peels and ends and stood still, looking for a bin. "Here, dump those in here," Rodan said, holding out a small saucepan. "Now fill that to the top with water and put it on the other burner to boil." Rodan reached for a jar of what looked like dried herbs. He sprinkled it into the water and covered that pan, as well.

"What's that for?" Josh asked.

"Broth. Lots of vitamins in those parts."

"Huh." Josh liked the efficiency of it. He asked, "So, are you worried about this disease? I mean, I've heard of it. I read reports in the *Denver Post* last year. It's nasty."

"Yes, it is, and no, I'm not worried. Ohma is a good healer."

"Is it like what happened to the littles?" Josh asked. "The way they couldn't change as usual because of the chemicals in the water?"

"Who knows? No Netahs have been infected." Rodan shrugged as he thought a minute. Josh wiped the counter. Rodan continued, "I forgot you were involved in that littles incident. Nice work, by the way. Because we are Netahs, we cannot go to human doctors. Obviously, but we have our own healers, our own medicines and treatments. Anyway, don't worry so much, kid. We can handle this."

Josh chewed on his lower lip. *Kid? Maybe I am the youngest person in the lodge, but I'm not a kid.* A calmer voice in his head said, Take it easy, it's a term of endearment! That voice was oddly similar to his mom's voice. Josh sat on a stool and stewed as Rodan moved around the kitchen.

Rodan arranged two cups on the counter, two spoons, a couple of wafers, and the canister Josh had found in the morning. Rodan scooped a spoonful into each cup, poured the water, and stirred before handing one mug to Josh. Josh continued to stir it, because that's what Rodan did. The liquid smelled like fresh spring grass. Rodan watched the herbs sink to the bottom, then took his wafer and dipped it. Josh copied him. The wafer tasted nutty with a hint of cinnamon. Rodan asked, "What do you think?"

Josh said, "I could get used to this. Do you guys not drink coffee?"

"Ha, a coffee man already, huh?"

Josh grinned. *Ah ha! Now I'm a man!* That other voice in his head said, *It's just an expression.* On the other hand, he'd been invited into the bachelor's lodge, and they were all presumably considered men. *I can't be so sensitive. In time, I'll fit in, I have to.*

Rodan continued, "Well, we have something similar. It's herbal but has plenty of caffeine kick. If you want to make yourself some in the morning, it's in that second canister. Prepare it just like this, one spoonful, water, stir. Only have one cup, though, it's pretty powerful." Rodan sipped his tea. "This will help keep you healthy. Lots of good stuff in this. I have some every day."

They sat in silence for another few seconds, then Josh thought out loud, "I'm looking forward to being an apprentice builder."

"Oh, right, Hesta mentioned your interest," Rodan hemmed, squirming on his seat. "Let me first say I thought you were older when we met."

"You said that."

"Yeah, because you're tall, but when you're older, you have some basics from school to build on."

"Like algebra and geometry?"

"Right. How much of that have you studied?" Rodan asked.

"All I know is I liked math before all this started."

"That's great. You'll be fine." Rodan encouraged him. "Hey, I think we have some text books around here somewhere. Let me dig them out. Just ask me if you have any questions." He stood up and left, taking his tea with him.

The main hall was empty. Josh watched the light change the landscape out the big windows as clouds raced across the sky. Small piles of snow pooled in the shadows. As he waited for Rodan to return, he decided to take the books to the library downstairs and take the opportunity to see if he could find out any more about the Netah's technology or about his birth dad.

Rodan returned with a couple of thick books. "Now's as good a time as any to get started," he said. "Let me know if you have any questions when we sit down to dinner. I have some work to do now, so see ya later."

Josh went to the library and set the books on a table as he roamed the room, getting a feel for how the shelves were organized. He found a history section, some textbooks, and a large collection of beat-up paperback westerns. There was nothing recent, like a newspaper or magazine that might talk about his dad. He returned to the math books and worked his way through several chapters before he looked up as a couple of the guys came in. Josh thought he recognized Tomo and Arman.

Tomo spoke as they approached. "You need a break? How'd you like to come blow off some steam?"

"Absolutely!"

"Follow us." They led Josh to the workout room and over to a punching bag.

"Ever box?" Arman asked.

"Nope, but I've always wanted to try it," Josh admitted.

"Okay, let's see what you've got." Tomo laced gloves onto Josh's hands, then cinched up Arman's gloves. Josh figured they'd start on the punching bag, but no.

Tomo showed him how to stand, and then Arman began throwing punches at Josh! The first swing connected with his mouth, and he could taste blood on his lip. Arman watched him for a reaction. "You wanna quit like a baby, halfling?" he taunted. Josh scowled. *It is a test.* He held his hands higher and set his feet. He took a punch to the stomach and bent double, gasping for breath.

"Hey! That's not what we agreed on!" Tomo yelled, pulling Arman back.

Arman shrugged off Tomo and danced from side to side in front of Josh, laughing. "Come on, don't just stand there. Do something, you worthless halfling!" he commanded.

Josh tried to move around Tomo and take a couple of swings, but Tomo stayed between them. "Okay," Josh said, nodding and backing away. "Very funny." His eyes went from Tomo to Arman. "You got a problem with me or something?"

"What's the matter, you scared?" Arman jeered.

"Stop it, Arman. You know Rodan would be furious!" Tomo insisted.

"Screw Rodan," Arman spit out. "Come on, baby face. You want to live with the men, act like one!"

"What do you want from me?" Josh yelled back, his anger boiling to the surface. "I'm tired of guessing. You start out all," Josh used his stupid human voice, "welcome to the club, Josh. Come on in." He reverted to his own angry voice, "You, on the other hand, Arman, have always made your feelings about me clear. What's your beef? It's something to do with my dad, isn't it?" His scowl bored into Arman as he stood his ground, arms up in case Arman took another swing at him.

Arman froze, alarmed at the confrontation. He sputtered, "Your dad is a . . ." Arman stopped himself and shook his head. "No, I'm not going to debate the merits of your father with you. You don't know him. It's a waste of time." He rolled his eyes and bit at the laces on his glove, looking self-satisfied. "All I know is, you don't belong here."

"That's your opinion, and in case you haven't noticed, you're not in charge around here. You're just a bully!" Josh spat out as he turned and landed a punch on the bag. Dust flew off it. He swung again, ignoring Arman, although still half expecting to feel another punch.

Tomo moved to stand face-to-face with Arman, and Josh watched out of the corner of his eye. He noticed the size difference between them, like a skinny yearling standing up to a looming draft horse. In a low, threatening voice, Tomo said, "Maybe you should pick on someone your own size."

Arman scoffed, "Like you? Wanna make me?" Arman bounced back and raised his gloves in front of his face. "Come on, or are you all talk, too?"

Tomo turned his back on Arman. Josh thought that was a mistake. Arman yelled, "How am I supposed to make a man out of you if you won't engage? Come on, man up!" He danced around Tomo, challenging him with a couple of air punches. It surprised Josh how nimbly the old guy moved.

"Enough!" Tomo yelled as he spun back around, then said in a menacingly quiet voice, "Walk away, Arman, before you do something you'll regret."

Arman yanked off his gloves and threw them at a wall. Plaster bits sifted out of the dent. "Man, lighten up. You can't talk your way out of everything. How you going to handle rut?"

"You let me worry about that." Tomo's voice stayed quiet and controlled.

Josh admired Tomo's self-control, as he tasted bile rising in his own throat. He tried for a light tone as he said, "I did mention I've never boxed before, right? I was raised by a nonviolent man. We take pride in using our words, not fists."

Arman laughed and said, "Sounds like a coward to me."

Josh didn't hesitate. He took a swipe at Arman's face and surprised himself when he connected with a cheekbone. Backing away, he said, "I guess words are wasted on you." He watched Arman's slow reaction as he touched his cheek and checked his fingers for blood. Arman snorted, "Not bad, for a sissy."

"You got something to say about my dad?" Josh demanded. "Sounds like you know him a lot better than I do. What exactly happened between the two of you?"

"Shut up! Nothing happened!" Arman's face turned purple.

Tomo grabbed him and pushed him back from Josh, struggling to hold him, he said, "That's enough! Get out!"

Arman took a ragged breath and then pushed Tomo away. Looking Tomo in the eye, Arman said, "You say one word to him and I'll make you pay." He stormed up the stairs.

Tomo picked up Arman's gloves and tugged them on, tightening the laces with his teeth. He said, "Come on, hold the bag. I'll teach you some moves."

Josh leaned his shoulder into the bag as he'd seen on TV. Soon he was laughing and insisting, "Hey, let me try." His first punch nearly knocked Tomo over. Tomo leaned in, steadying the bag. Josh punched that bag over and over, harder and harder, faster and faster, until finally Tomo yelled, "Okay! Dude, stop!"

Josh stepped back. He could barely see through the sweat in his eyes, but he liked what he saw on Tomo's face. Could that be respect? *Maybe the punches I took earlier were worth it.* On the way to the showers, Josh asked, "So, you gonna tell me about Arman and my dad?"

Tomo paused, took a breath, and studied the ceiling before saying, "That's a story for another day. Word of advice? Don't poke that bear, steer clear."

Josh wanted to poke that bear, but he said, "He threatened you and you walked away. Is it just us, or does he treat everyone that way?"

Tomo frowned and shook his head. "Not everyone. Look, all you need to know is that he has a short fuse, a rough background, and he's got anger management issues. Knowing that, you decide whether you want to try to be besties with him. It's your call."

The two hit the showers in silence. A bell clanged and Tomo said, "Dinnertime!" Josh dragged his sore muscles upstairs where Rodan served the soup and the guys passed a large bowl of crusty bread. Grunts of approval and a hushed table meant the soup passed muster. No one said a word about Josh's puffy lip. Josh noticed Arman had a bruised cheek. Josh ate with gusto and pride. He'd shown what he was made of, not by choice, but because he had to.

After dinner, Josh sank onto a chair in the great room and found a stack of westerns someone left behind. Arman strolled past and grumbled, "Typical! Leaving your stuff lying around. Don't expect your mommy to come and pick up after you around here, halfling."

Josh flipped a book open and came up with a retort by the time Arman was a safe ten feet away. "You get your sunny disposition from your mommy?" Josh muttered.

"What'd you say?" Arman growled, stopping in his tracks.

Josh did his best impression of Clint Eastwood's squint as he sneered, "Leave my mom out of it, if you don't mind."

Arman shook his head and scowled his way out of the room.

The week went downhill from there. A blizzard overnight made them feel even more claustrophobic because it blocked the natural light coming into the lodge. Having to stay human took its toll on everyone. They'd started out irritable and became hostile and argumentative. Josh laid low in his room or the library and absorbed the math.

Occasionally he missed video games and his high school buddies. One night, he lay awake on his bed and listened to the others snoring down the hall, remembering the last night he'd spent with his human friends. His mom brought popcorn down to the basement game room. His dad proudly played with the foster child, Rose, unaware she was a Netah. Josh wondered where Fern and Crawley and George were now.

Giving up on sleep, he pulled his towel off the hook and went downstairs. Lowering himself into the hot spring pool and resting his head against the side, Josh peered into the shadowy spaces, lit only by starlight through the ceiling and wall openings. In a game of positive/negative, he reviewed his situation. You miss your school friends. *These guys aren't all bad.* You miss school. *I like the math books.* You only had to ask Rodan for help on one part so far. *Yeah, I'm proud of that.* The food is good and hearty. You've learned your way around the lodge and the chores. *What am I missing? I need to buck up.* If missing game nights is the worst thing, you'll survive. With a sigh, Josh returned to his room.

At the end of the second week, Rodan invited Josh to go with him on patrol. "Put on all your warmest clothes. We have a hike ahead of us."

They strapped on snowshoes, because the snow still stood two feet deep. The snow sparkled in the blinding sun and squeaked underfoot. The quiet landscape seemed muffled, like it had been buried under a fluffy blanket.

Josh asked, "Why are we going as humans? Wouldn't it be easier to walk and keep warm as elk?"

"We haven't been cleared by Ohma yet. Probably soon, though. You getting tired of being a human already?" Rodan lowered his head into the wind.

"Well, it's inconvenient, if nothing else." Josh tried to sound cavalier about it, even though he felt as irritable as everyone else.

"You sound like a Netah," Rodan laughed. "Come on, we're almost there. Let's jog a bit to warm up." They couldn't talk and jog at the same time. Josh worried he'd trip himself with the snowshoes, which required an awkward, bowlegged stride.

Rodan stopped suddenly and put his hand out to stop Josh. They stood near the snow-covered road. Snow mounded above tumbleweeds and patches of dried grass.

"What? What is it?" Josh asked.

"This is not right," Rodan said, slowly walking around a big disturbance in the snow. "There are tire tracks, boot prints, piles of snow like it's been shoveled. What do you think we're looking at?"

"It looks like something got dug up. You know what it was?" Josh asked.

"We buried the dead elk here."

"Oh." Josh frowned. "Someone came by afterwards? Are these tracks from the truck in our barn?"

"Yep, and nope, not our truck." Rodan squinted into the cold wind as he pulled a small metal pencil out of a pocket and started clicking it, moving it like a camera. It was the third high-tech item Josh had seen since he became a Netah, but who was counting?

"Is that a camera?" Josh asked.

"Yes, why?" Rodan didn't even look up.

"I guess I'm surprised by how small it is. It's like James Bond or something. It's cool."

"Yeah, I guess it is cool." Rodan looked at the device. "We have lots of tech like this. Give it time and you'll discover all of it." He put it back in his pocket and turned away, pulling his gloves back on. "Come on, we have to report this."

Josh sprinted to catch up, awkward and tired in his snowshoes. With as much respect as he could muster, Josh asked, "Are you part of security or the police or something?"

"I'm head of the security lodge, where you're staying. Didn't you know that? Come on, the sun's going down and it's gonna get a lot colder before we get back."

"I thought it was just the bachelor's lodge," Josh said.

"Well, that's what the bachelor's primary responsibility is, security. I thought someone would have told you by now."

"Nope."

"Huh," Rodan grumbled almost to himself. "Not the first time I've been accused of not being a great communicator."

Josh stifled a laugh. "Who said that, your girlfriend?"

"No, well, uh, yes, at least once. But I say, look, I'm in security. Secrets are my job!"

Josh did laugh at that. "Do I have to stay there if I want to be a builder?" Josh asked. He still hadn't seen a normal routine at the lodge since they were all in quarantine. "When can I start learning that?"

"Tired of us already?" he chuckled. "Hey, ignore Arman. He's mad at the world, not you. As for building, we have to wait for Ohma to clear everyone. How're you doing with the math books?" Rodan asked, keeping a steady pace and clutching his jacket neck against the bitter wind.

"I'm done."

"Good, I'll speak to Haiman when we return. They'll get back to work whenever it warms up a little." He stopped in front of the dark gray boulder that Josh recognized as Hesta's door. He didn't knock but pushed it open. Josh snorted to himself. *Of course, he didn't knock, it's a rock!* They got inside quickly so they wouldn't let out all the heat.

Hesta walked over to greet them as they unlaced their snow-shoes. After Rodan made his report, Hesta looked very worried. He called Ohma over. She'd been listening from the kitchen. "What do you think?"

She put her hand on his arm. "There's nothing you can do about it tonight in the dark. Have the men double-check the feeds to make sure there were no other intrusions."

Hesta and Rodan nodded in agreement. Hesta said, "Let me know what you find." Josh was sure they were hiding something.

Then Ohma checked them for signs of the illness. "Still good," she declared. "Here, drink this before you go back outside." She handed them cups of milky tea that tasted spicy and sweet.

It served to get them back without freezing, but Josh still headed straight for the hot springs pool. He let the water warm him through and thought with satisfaction about Rodan inviting him on the job. It had been bitterly cold, but it had lifted his mood. Maybe it was the exertion, or feeling included.

Josh wondered if he could help lift the mood in the lodge. Arman wasn't the only grump. It was probably because they had to stay humans during the lockdown. Maybe he'd try some jokes on them. Maybe it would break up the stress. He reviewed the jokes he could remember. The only one that came to mind was the banana/orange knock-knock joke. That would probably get him kicked out into the snow. He'd have to think harder.

CHAPTER 7

Mud Fight

With the possibility of only a few more days of lock-down, Josh expected the mood in the lodge to lighten up. It didn't. Mako and Arman got into a shouting match while making dinner. It ended with broken dishes. Rodan and Arman monopolized the boxing ring. Arman had taken to muttering "worthless," or "halfling" under his breath as he passed. Josh always waited until Arman was mostly out of earshot to mutter his response, "You bet, Miss Congeniality!" he'd say with a cheerful smile. Haiman overheard him one afternoon and they both had a good laugh about that, so at least Haiman had a sense of humor. Josh wondered if he belonged in the lodge after all, until the day he worked with Tomo on laundry. First, they stripped the sheets off all the beds and ran them in two loads. They strung up a drying rope in a hidden courtyard. The winter sun tried hard to dry up patches of mud on the ground from the melting snows. The boys tried hard to avoid the icy puddles.

Josh and Tomo worked in sullen silence. Eventually Josh could not take it another minute. "Why haven't we been cleared by Ohma yet?"

"Don't know."

"It's been four weeks. Rodan said it would be three."

"Yep."

"Do we have any options?"

"Nope."

"Hey, what gives? Did I do something wrong?"

Tomo shrugged, finished pinning up the last sheet and picked up the basket, heading back inside.

Josh ran up and grabbed the basket, seething inside. Tomo held tight and they struggled for the basket until they both slipped and fell on muddy ice. Neither one let go of the basket, and they ended up rolling and struggling to get solid ground under them, until they were both covered in mud. Josh finally let go and watched with satisfaction as Tomo fell backwards.

Tomo looked like a mud monster when he sat up. As brown sludge dripped down his neck, Tomo grinned and wiped mud from his hair. He slung it at Josh, who scooped some from the ground next to him and flung it in response. Giggling quietly, they both tried to stand, fell, got on all fours for stability, slipped face-first, and finally rolled onto their backs, laughing so hard they couldn't breathe.

"Man," Tomo laughed.

"Yeah," Josh agreed.

"Yeah, what?"

"What do you mean?"

"I mean," and Tomo rolled onto his elbow to smile at Josh. "It feels good to laugh."

"Yeah, that's what I meant, too. I mean everyone is so friggin' grumpy!"

"It's the lockdown." Tomo shook his head. "Don't kid yourself, you are grumpy, too. I mean you sulk when no one laughs at your stupid knock-knock jokes. It's like, come on, banana? Move on!"

"Yeah, I know, it's a lame joke, but it's not like I can google a new set of jokes. That's all I can remember. I'm just trying to lighten things up," Josh said, trying to get to his feet.

"What's google?" Tomo asked.

"It's a search engine on the internet that humans use to look up everything."

"Everything? Like how to stand up in a mud puddle?"

"Yeah, like that," Josh laughed as he got his hands and knees under him, feeling relatively stable until he tried to shift from a knee to a foot. He got a mouthful of mud. He pushed back up to his elbows and knees, frowning with frustration. While their situation was funny, Josh remembered that warm days in winter quickly turned cold. They had to figure out how to get up and get inside.

Tomo watched Josh's efforts and decided to try a variation. He got on his hands and knees and skated them to the wall of the lodge. He reached up for the door handle. It released the latch and swung open, swinging him back to the ground.

With a sigh, Tomo closed his eyes and tipped his face to the sun. He said, "You should be glad they're just grumpy. They've been taking it easy on you. You should have seen what I had to go through." He seemed to have given up on getting up.

"Really? Like what?" Josh asked, scrabbling to stay out of the mud but failing once again. "Shit!"

"Shit," Tomo snorted as he reached his hands up along the wall, searching for something to hold on to. Sighing, he continued. "Rodan took you under his wing and wouldn't let anyone haze you. When I arrived, they told me it was tradition," he said petulantly.

Josh made it to the wall and sat back against it, feeling the warmth it had soaked up from the sun radiate through his wet shirt.

Josh said, "I hate traditions," as Tomo moved next to him.

"Yeah, me, too," Tomo agreed.

"Shit, shit, shit!" Josh scraped mud off his hands.

Tomo laughed. "You look like shit."

Josh sniffed. "You smell like shit."

"You eat shit!"

"You . . ." Josh ran out of stupid insults. He clenched the mud into a ball and threw it, managing to miss the clean sheets and hit a nearby pine. Under his breath he said, "are a shithead."

Tomo giggled. "Shit shoveler," he muttered.

"Chicken shit!" Josh laughed.

Josh wondered how old Tomo actually was, but figured it wouldn't matter, because Netahs aged differently from humans. They army crawled into the building and finally stood on the mat inside the door, wrapping their arms around their shivering torsos.

Tomo kicked off his shoes. "I'm taking my clothes off here. I mean, look at us. If we don't, we'll just have more to clean up, like floors."

"Are you kidding? You're not freezing enough already?"

Tomo shrugged and pulled off his sweatshirt, revealing a very thin, nearly frail frame.

They ran for the showers, dumping their clothes in a sink. Keeping his eyes on the walls and ceilings, Josh asked, "Want to talk about the hazing?"

Tomo didn't answer right away. Eventually, with a sigh, he squinted through the steam. "They made me do all the jobs for one week while they sat around drinking mead. I wasn't allowed to wear clothes inside as a human. I had only bread and water to eat. In the end, they shaved my head. Then they finally gave me full membership."

"That doesn't sound too bad," Josh said. "Except for maybe the food and shaved head. But your hair grew back."

"That's true, but they humiliated me." Tomo tilted his head back to let the water rinse his short black hair. "I don't like being a naked human." He crossed his skinny arms across his chest.

"That's funny, 'cuz we don't wear clothes as elk."

"Right, but we have fur coats."

Josh snorted and nodded, "True."

"They said they all got hazed when they arrived, so I figured I had no choice."

"Is that why you're mad at me, because I didn't have to?"

"Maybe." Tomo shrugged, not raising his eyes to Josh. "I guess it's stupid."

Josh saw that the hot water at his feet no longer ran brown down the drain, so he turned off the water and grabbed a towel. "Nah, I get it."

"You're all right, Josh, no matter what the other guys say," Tomo said as he toweled himself off.

"Wait, what?" *Can I not ever get a break? One second, I'm all right, then boom, knocked right back down.* With a sigh of resignation he said, "What do they say?"

"That you're a spoiled kid who can't be trusted," Tomo blurted, then gasped and covered his mouth with his hands. His face was scrunched up as if in pain as he turned to look at Josh, clutching his towel at his waist.

"Spoiled?" Josh's voice screeched. "By whom?" he demanded, his arms akimbo. "Trusted? What the hell do I have to do to prove myself around here?" He spun around and marched towards the door, tucking his towel securely around his hips.

"Well, it doesn't help that you're working with Rodan on math," Tomo called after him.

"Why?" Josh stopped, keeping his back to Tomo.

"You know."

"Uh, know what?" Josh leaned his back against the doorframe, his arms crossed, waiting for an explanation as he studied his wet toes. Tomo hesitated, clutching his towel to keep it from falling off his skinny hips. Josh's voice went singsong and sarcastic and he wagged his head from side to side, saying, "Let me guess, it's a deep dark secret and you're not allowed to tell me. It's something everyone else in the lodge knows except me." Anger crept into his voice. "You want to talk to me about what's fair? How about you be my friend and let me in on what's going on around here? Oh, and by the way, I didn't miss that bit about membership. What's that all about?"

Tomo finally looked Josh in the eye. He looked around cautiously before he motioned for Josh to come closer and spoke quietly. "You're right. I want to be your friend, I mean, you're probably the only guy here close to my age. We should stick together. But, if I do tell you things, you have to act like you don't know. You have to act surprised when one of the other guys decides it's time to tell you our secrets."

"I can act," Josh said, walking over to the sink that held their muddy clothes. He turned on the faucet and watched the mud detach from his pants.

"Good. Listen, I'm sorry." Tomo joined him, grabbing a brush to help loosen the mud. "I shouldn't have taken it out on you. Maybe it's being cooped up as a human, you know?" They worked silently for a few minutes. "But, I mean, you were taken from your family to a strange place. You get bossed around with no one to stand up for you, right? At least I knew what I signed up for when I moved in here." Tomo had a faraway look on his face, then he continued with a sigh, "I'm sorry."

"Yeah, don't sweat it. Oh, and I know a few things. Like my dad's an outlaw." Josh suspected this fact colored everything. Out of the corner of his eyes, he watched as Tomo's jaw dropped and his eyes widened.

Tomo recovered before saying, "Right, which is why you are under so much suspicion. No one really knows if you and your dad are working together."

This made Josh's blood boil. He sucked air in through clenched teeth. "My dad?" he growled, shaking his head vigorously, holding his hand up to stop Tomo from saying anything else. With a very even voice he continued. "You mean my human dad who always treated me like an equal, a teammate, a smart and likeable kid? That dad? The one who probably thinks I'm dead now? No, of course not. You're talking about the dad who abandoned me and my mom, who I never knew existed until a few months ago, when I also discovered I could turn into an elk, like all of you guys, but not like you guys, because I'm only a halfling." Josh took a breath. "Two strikes against me, my blood and my ignorance. Neither of which are under my control!" He stepped back from the sink and noticed they had gathered an audience of faces peering in at the bathroom door. Tomo kept his eyes on the sink, his shoulders hunched under the barrage of angry words.

Josh spun on the others. "What part of that is wrong?"

The guys sheepishly avoided his eyes. Haiman's face turned deep red, Esok studied a crack in the ceiling, but Mako stepped into the shower room. "You nailed it, kid, and you're right, it's not fair. Life is rarely fair. I do, however, have a bit of good news that might help you feel better."

"Yeah, what?" Josh snapped.

"Well." Mako stroked his gray, scraggly beard, thinking. "Two things, actually. First, we've been given the all-clear by Ohma. No one got sick, so we are now free to leave the lodge and transform. Noomi came over to tell us. Also, she wants to see you, so we came back to find you."

Now Josh's mouth dropped open. He would be very happy to see Noomi. He'd missed her ever since he'd moved into the lodge. Josh composed himself and moved towards the door. The guys moved apart to let him pass and avoid his elbows. He dressed quickly and went to the great room, combing his hair with his fingers.

Noomi's slender figure turned from the big wall of windows as he approached. Her face broke into a beautiful smile and Josh's mood lifted instantly. She opened her arms to give him a hug. The other guys in the lodge wandered back into the room, their curiosity getting the best of them. "Hi, guys," she said. "Mind if I borrow Josh for a few minutes?"

Tomo started to object but seemed to think better of it. The rest of them shrugged or shook their heads, and the two walked outside. They turned into elk and galloped away across the valley. Skirting willows along a stream, they leapt across the frozen water and continued on for several minutes. When Noomi slowed, Josh caught up with her. They were both a little winded.

"Wow," Josh admitted. "That felt great but am I out of shape! How often do we have to go into lockdown like that?"

"It's pretty rare," Noomi admitted, turning back into a young woman and sitting down on a sunny rock. Josh transformed, too, and sat next to her. "It always takes a little time to get your elk legs and lungs back, so don't feel bad. It's normal."

"Okay, that's good. So, what's up? Man, it's great to see you!"

"It's good to see you, too," she said. She studied his face and reached over to brush a lock of hair out of his eyes. "Is everything all right?"

"I guess it's just being cooped up, you know?" Josh said, not really wanting to complain. He picked up a stick and began pulling the bark off. "The lodge is okay, but no one tells me anything. Of course, how could I learn how Netah elk normally live when we're in lockdown as humans?" *Stop complaining.* "Rodan gave me a couple of textbooks to study and said to ask him questions if I got stuck, even though he's rarely around. The other guys leave me alone, mostly." He shrugged and glanced up at Noomi. "I got in a mud fight with Tomo just before you got here."

Noomi snorted, then tried to hide her smile. In a very sisterly voice, she said, "That sounds like fun and also explains why you have mud in your ear. What started it?"

"Oh, he acted like a shit, you know, like one syllable answers to my questions. I guess I kind of lost it. I mean what did I ever do to him?"

"Did you figure it out?"

"Yeah, turns out he got hazed when he got here and I didn't. He resented that, I guess." Josh started to dig his finger into his ear to remove the mud.

Noomi grabbed his hand and said, "Stop, you'll just shove it in further. Rinse with warm water when you get back inside. It'll be fine."

"Also," Josh continued, anger seeping into his voice. "He said something about everyone thinking I worked for my dad. I mean, I've never even met the guy! Why is everyone so suspicious? What did he do besides knock up my mom and leave her? I mean, that's horrible, but why would it have anything to do with me? It all happened before I was even born! I don't even know what he did before you guys outlawed him, I mean for a living. Do you know?"

"Yep, he developed our undernet."

Josh squinted, unsure he had heard her correctly. "Undernet?"

"Sure, it's kind of like the human internet."

"I see, but it's under?"

"Mm, hmm."

Josh wanted to laugh, but saw she was completely serious. "Okay, is that why computers and the internet are restricted, because he developed it? Did my father invent other technology, too? Is that why everyone is suspicious?"

Noomi gazed at the horizon as she decided how to answer. She said, "I'm not sure how much I'm allowed to tell you. You know how it is."

"Yeah, I guess—trial period or something, prove myself to the community and all that." He shrugged, letting it go for now. "Are the math textbooks a stall tactic because they think I want to help my outlaw dad?"

"Maybe." She moved uncomfortably on the rock seat.

"Yeah, but I never knew what he did for a living."

"How would we know?"

"Oh, so now I'm getting in trouble for things I didn't tell anyone I didn't know?" he asked in exasperation.

Noomi took a slow breath before she took his hand between both of hers. Josh struggled to keep staring into her beautiful brown eyes rather than look away. *Listen, don't squirm.*

"It sounds impossible." She dropped her gaze to their hands. "I'm sorry. Listen, I'll give you a little information about your father. Maybe it will help. You know he wanted to share some of our technology with the humans? He said he wanted to help them. He developed our connection to the undernet, which is how we communicate through plant roots, and its security. He made sure of that, had to, or the elders wouldn't approve it. It's been a game changer, connecting us to our kind around the world. It's also been a headache. The elders still don't trust it, they're afraid. They want us to go back to living simply off the land. Instead, we learn how the rest of the world does things and want those changes. Old folks hate change. They think we'll be discovered."

"What would happen if someone let it slip?"

"They'd be banished or worse, probably erased."

"What's erased?" Josh watched her face. She didn't flinch.

With a sigh, she answered, "It takes away the ability to transform and locks a person into their animal body, but with no memory of Netahs or how to transform."

Josh considered the ramifications of this. "Where do they live? I mean, they can't live among the Netahs anymore, right?"

"No, they can't," Noomi agreed. "They are taken to a remote reserve in Alaska to live out their lives as animals."

"Do they survive the winters?"

"As well as other animals do."

"Huh, sounds pretty humane," Josh mused. "So, you have brain surgeons?"

Noomi looked frustrated. "It doesn't require that, but you have to understand. We know it's cruel, so it is rarely done."

"You don't have the death penalty?" Josh asked.

"No."

"It would be kinder."

"Maybe that's the point. It is reserved as punishment for only the most heinous crimes."

"Like what?"

"Murder."

Josh rubbed his face with both hands, squinting his eyes, trying desperately to remain calm and not blow up again. "Okay, so, my dad didn't commit murder, but he was banished to an ag facility and is growing vegetables. So what? He doesn't sound like a hardened criminal, although if he figured out the undernet and other stuff, he must be very smart. Is that why everyone is so scared of him?" Josh stood and paced. He struggled between feeling sorry for the man and being angry. His head swam. It helped a little to know this much about his dad. He turned to Noomi.

"Listen . . ." she started.

Josh put his hand up and quietly interrupted. "No, you listen. I just want you to know how much it means that you trusted me with this information. It sounds like people think he's a traitor." He pulled up his hood to ward off the late afternoon chill. He kicked at stones as he asked, "Is he evil? I mean, if he just wanted to share and help humans? Why is that so bad? Couldn't he help humans without giving up Netah secrets or is he a sociopath with no moral compass?"

Noomi considered. "He said he wanted to share, but we have channels to do that, and he acted outside of those channels. Is he a sociopath? That's for our healers to determine and it's still up for debate. At any rate, he lost the trust of the elders. That's very hard to get back."

Josh paced while he gathered his thoughts. "Okay," he stopped in front of her. "So, how could I possibly be working with him? I mean, if he's banished to an ag complex, how is that enforced? Does he have a tracker on him or something?"

Noomi took a big breath. "Right, well, here's where it gets complicated. Yes, he has a tracker, but it is no longer working. It should have been permanent, unless . . ." She paused.

"I'm not supposed to know this, right?" Josh sounded disgusted.

She sighed. "Unless he could figure out how to turn it off."

"Huh." Josh ran his fingers through his hair. *Interesting.*

"It's never happened before, that it wasn't permanent, but he is very good with technology."

"Is he still in the facility?"

With her eyes on her hands and a quiet voice, Noomi said, "No."

"Shit!"

"Yep."

"It's not fair." Josh stopped pacing, his eyes glazing over. There was that word again—Mako had talked about what's fair earlier. "I wish I could have met my father. Then I could maybe judge for myself. I don't know him, though, so I have to trust the judgment of the council." Josh studied Noomi's profile. "And now he escaped?"

"It appears so."

"Alone?"

"No."

Josh sat down hard and dropped his head into his hands. When he finally looked up, he said quietly, "That's why they wonder if I'm working with him?"

Noomi made a pained face.

"Any advice?"

She sighed and put her hand on his shoulder. "Just continue to be your honest, hardworking self. The others will learn to trust you like I do. Be patient with us. Oh, and be careful. No one knows where he is. He may be trying to find you."

Josh grinned. "Be yourself, you say? I don't know who else to be, so that's easy! As for careful, what are you saying? Do I need a bodyguard?"

"I don't know. Just be smart. I'm sure security will be tightened. Rodan knows what's going on. Let him worry about it." She turned as if to go, then hesitated. "Oh, and by the way, Dad wanted me to invite you to dinner tomorrow night."

"Cool," he said. "What time should I come by?"

"When did you last see a clock?" she asked, her grin widening.

Josh tried to picture the insides of the lodge. He couldn't remember seeing a clock anywhere. How did they know when it was time for dinner, breakfast, whatever? Everyone seemed to get hungry at the same time. It just happened. How had he never noticed the lack of clocks before? "Back in my school," he admitted.

"Right. So how about you come over when the sun reaches the tops of the trees?"

"I can do that," he said. "Should I bring something?"

"Sure." Noomi thought a minute. "Some of Rodan's tea would be good."

"I can do that." He wondered what he could carry it in. Maybe Tomo would have an idea.

"See you later, then," Noomi said as she walked away, flicking her braid over her shoulder so that it hung down her spine between her shoulder blades. Moments later she transformed into an elk and the braid blended in to the brown of her back as she trotted across the snow-dusted hills.

Josh transformed and then quickly retraced their route from the lodge. He thought about his dad out there somewhere, possibly looking for Josh, and the fur on his shoulders bristled. His ears twitched as they picked up the sounds of small animals on the plains. If the tracker was off, he could be anywhere. He could be spilling their secrets to the humans already. How would humans take it, though? Would they lock him up as a crazy guy?

Josh reached the lodge door and he remembered Tomo and the laundry. He headed to the laundry room. As they folded shirts and pants, Josh had an idea. "Hey, Tomo, is there any red pepper around here?"

"Sure, why?"

"I thought of a way to pay the guys back for hazing you."

"Really? Cool. I'll be right back."

Minutes later, they were sprinkling red pepper inside a shirt cuff here, a pant leg there, a pair of socks another time. They kept up a loud running banter about how happy they were to all pass the health test, to hide their activity. Everybody had names inside their clothes. The two conspirators neatly stacked the clothes on the counter. The guys would pick them up when they had time. Tomo and Josh made sure there were no signs of their activity before they went to dinner. Sitting together, they nudged each other under the table to contain their glee.

Eventually Arman sat back from his bowl and looked around the table. Josh knew that Arman was second-in-command here. He had noticed a definite pecking order, not based on age, but obvious when you watched who deferred to whom. Arman watched Josh and Tomo for a few minutes, then sneering, he scratched his curly black hair and said with false enthusiasm, "I never knew how much fun doing laundry was." All eyes turned to him, puzzled. "It seems to have raised their spirits a great deal," he said, nodding towards Tomo and Josh. His voice rose into a girly falsetto. "You guys looking forward to it as much as I am?" The others laughed, pushing back their chairs, and patting the boys on the shoulder as they walked away.

Josh and Tomo laughed with them and shrugged their shoulders, while thinking . . . if only they knew!

The chores in Josh's lodge rotated daily, so the perpetrators of the pepper caper were never revealed. Guys would pull on a shirt one day, or a pair of pants three days later, and they would get itchy. They suspected a bed bug infestation and fumigated the lodge and all the bedding. No one had any idea who did it. Tomo and Josh, however, were now fast friends.

That night, Josh's thoughts returned to his father. He assumed there were things he had not been told, things that made his dad worse than a Netah who liked humans and abandoned his wife and son, and worse than a tech genius. He sensed fear from the others. Was the man some kind of sociopath? Did Josh need protection? He fell asleep thinking about pepper spray, how to make it, how to carry and conceal it. His dreams included lots of running away from something shadowy that he couldn't quite see.

CHAPTER 8

Family Dinner

The next morning, Josh asked Tomo to help him find his way to Hesta's house.

"Sure, you can walk over with me this morning. I will be doing home visits with Ohma."

As they walked, Tomo helped him find markers such as a willow stand, a small stream, and the pond that made up Hesta's roof. Josh made the reverse trip on his own and finding all the landmarks, he felt confident he'd be able to find his way that evening. What he didn't like was the tingling sensation that he was being watched.

Dinner at Hesta's house would provide Josh with a welcome change from the lodge. He showered and brushed his teeth. He grabbed a jacket for the walk and tucked a bandana filled with tea in his pocket. Snow pasted inself to the north sides of trees and the ground remained frozen hard with icy spots. Josh couldn't tell if his neck prickled because of the cold wind blowing at his back or because there were eyes on him. He wondered if the local lioness he'd heard about from Hesta was in the neighborhood. He told himself the security guys were out there. Also, luckily, Hesta's house was not that far away.

The granite door did not invite knocking, but Josh noticed a small red rock set in a niche on the wall. He pressed it and a bell sounded inside the house. When Noomi opened the door, Josh asked, "Is there a special occasion?"

"You bet." She stepped aside. "It's my brother's naming ceremony. Come on, we're ready to get started. You can put your jacket on the bench."

Josh obeyed and followed Noomi into the house.

Ohma pulled Josh aside on his way past the kitchen. The top of her head came no higher than his chin, and he noticed the sparkle of occasional gray in her glossy black hair. A curtain of it covered one eye, which she tucked behind her ear before whispering, "Just so you know, he will ask lots of questions. Answer as honestly and simply as possible. It's kind of a game, kind of a way to narrow down our name choices."

"Okay, thanks for the heads-up." Josh remembered the tea and handed it over. "This is for you."

Ohma accepted the package and held it to her nose. "Is this Rodan's secret mix?"

"That's right, I hope you like it," Josh said.

"Oh, it's our favorite. Thank you." Ohma's smile filled the room, and while Josh basked in the warmth of that, she wrapped her arms around him in a hug, and rested her head in the hollow of his shoulder, just like Josh's mom used to do. Ohma stepped back, keeping her hands on Josh's arms and looking into his eyes. "I'm so glad you could come tonight. It's a very special family ceremony."

The mere mention of family set Josh's heart thumping harder. *Did she just imply I am family? Oh, what I wouldn't give for that!*

Ohma turned away and placed the tea on her counter, returning to her pot of soup. "Go ahead. Start without me." She waved him away with one hand, and a knowing grin.

"Okay, thanks. That is unless you need any help?"

"Very polite, but I've got this. Go on." She shooed him out of the kitchen area.

A blue tablecloth covered the dining table and green napkins sat under the silverware. A large brown cake sprinkled with powdered sugar waited on the counter and smelled like gingerbread.

Josh wondered why the kid wanted him there; he'd never said a word to the kid when he'd been in the house before. Josh walked over while Hesta continued to read the little boy a book. Noomi sat nearby and listened with her eyes closed and a serene smile lighting up her face. She roused as Josh approached and motioned for him to join her on the couch. Josh recognized the origin story Hesta had told him when they walked to the valley.

When the story finished, the little boy looked up from the picture book and noticed their visitor. "Hi, Josh!" He leapt to his feet and came over to stand by Josh. Josh thought maybe he wanted to climb into his lap, so he held out his arms, and the boy did climb up, pointy elbows and knees and all.

"Oof!" Josh said, and then decided to tickle the boy in defense. The kid was very ticklish.

Hesta laughed and said with his deep, kind voice, "Hey, you two, settle down. You won't be able to eat if you get all riled up." Josh stopped tickling, and the boy relaxed into his lap. The snuggle reminded Josh of when he held Rose this way, what was that . . . centuries ago? He choked up a little.

Hesta asked, "How're things going at the lodge? You settling in okay?"

"Oh, yeah, great. Of course, it'll be even better now that we can transform again."

Hesta rubbed his chin. "I bet things got a little tense."

Josh shrugged. Ohma carried a steaming pot of soup to the table, saying, "Okay, gang. We don't want it to get cold."

Noomi showed Josh his place at the table. They passed their bowls to Ohma and once Ohma sat down, she said, "Okay, dig in!"

"Thanks for inviting me," Josh said.

"It was his idea," Ohma said with a twinkle in her eye, nodding at her son.

As they enjoyed the delicious vegetable stew, the boy asked Josh questions before every bite.

"What was your daddy's name?"

"Danny. What's yours?" Josh had not been instructed to respond with questions, but it seemed like a fun game.

"Hesta, silly, you know that. Where did you used to live?" His lisp reminded Josh of Lorna.

"In a house on a hill in the suburbs of Denver. Where do you live?"

"In a house under a pond in a valley." The boy sat up straighter, warming to this game. "What's your favorite thing to eat?"

"Carrots and cashews. What's yours?"

"What's cashews?"

Josh paused. *How to describe them?* "They're sweet nuts, best salted, nice and crunchy."

The boy clapped his hands. "I love salty and crunchy, too. What does your name mean?"

Josh pursed his lips, considering his answer. "Hmm, I'm not sure. I wonder if we could look it up."

Hesta raised his bushy eyebrows. "No need, I know the meaning. It has Hebrew roots, and means salvation. Josh led the Israelites after Moses."

Noomi spoke up. "I looked it up in the urban dictionary. It said a funny, cute, adorable guy with a naughty side." She tried unsuccessfully to keep a straight face.

Everyone snickered and Josh was slightly insulted.

The little boy squinted hard, wrinkling up his freckly nose. "What's salbayshun?"

Hesta fielded this one again. "It means being saved."

"From what?"

Josh and Hesta exchanged a smile, then Josh shrugged. "From something bad, I guess."

"Like a superhero?" The boy's eyes grew wide.

"Definitely."

More laughter and Josh blushed.

Hesta looked around the table before standing. "Okay, looks like we're all done. It's time to begin. Follow me, everyone." He led the way to the two sofas facing each other in front of the fireplace and motioned for everyone to have a seat. He stood next to the little boy, his hand on his shoulder and said to the rest of them, "It's now our turn to ask the questions."

Ohma asked, "What do you want to be when you are grown?"

The boy thought hard, a frown creasing his forehead. "I want to be a saver."

Noomi asked, "Savior? Who will you save?"

"Netahs!"

Josh asked, "How will you save them?" He thought he noticed a pattern here and that this should be the logical next question.

The boy rolled his eyes then shrugged. "I don't know."

His dad said, "Then how will you find out?"

"Ask questions."

"Very well." Hesta nodded. He looked to Ohma for approval. She nodded as if they had already decided previously. "You will be Mesenova, a boy who discovers and finds out about things." Hesta looked at the others and said, "It is time for cake."

"Yes!" the boy giggled and did a fist pump before rushing to his seat at the table.

As they walked back to the table, Josh asked Noomi, "Mesenova? What language is that?"

"It's Netah," she answered shyly. "No one speaks it anymore, but we base our names on it, and children learn to read it."

This surprised Josh. No one had mentioned anything about their own language. That explained their interesting names, though. "Is it related to any human languages?"

"The Cheyenne language has some similar sounds and words, I think," Ohma answered, shrugging as she placed a piece of cake in front of Josh. "Are you a student of languages?"

"I took a couple of years of Spanish, but I don't remember much," he admitted.

Mesenova cut a forkful of cake and held it towards Josh. "Cheers, Josh."

"Cheers, Mesenova." Although he suddenly felt less than cheerful. The cake reminded him of his own birthday, the cakes his mom had always made for him, his home, his previous life. He sat and listened to the others talk about nothing. At least he assumed they talked about nothing because he stopped listening. When everyone finished, he tried to help clean up, but Noomi and Ohma chased him out of the kitchen. Josh was struck by how similar they looked, with the same high cheek bones, nose and chin structure, and long braids, except Ohma had several long strands of silver glinting in hers.

Hesta said, "Come with us, Josh. I'm going to tell Mesenova a bedtime story. You might like to hear it. Come sit with my son and get comfortable."

"Okay, sure."

Hesta sat in one couch while Mesenova curled up in a corner of the opposite couch, pulling his feet under him. When Josh sat next to the boy, he moved over to lean against Josh. Josh soaked up the affection as he put his arm around the boy, who beamed up at him and snuggled closer. Josh's sadness fell away and was replaced by a warm sense of belonging. Hesta sat up straight and cast his gaze over their heads.

"In the early times, there lived a young man. He lived in a big house with his mom and dad. He had good friends and a good life, until one day he had to leave it all behind and live in the wilderness. Everything about his life changed, except it didn't.

"He still lived in a beautiful place, filled with amazing things that he had never known existed. He made new friends and they became very loyal to him and kept him safe in his new place.

"The young man missed his parents. He carried a constant sadness that made it difficult for him to see all the good people around him. This made it hard to be a new person in his new place. He didn't know who he wanted to be and couldn't find happiness.

"One day he was given a mission. He must capture an evil sorcerer and bring him to justice. While he climbed mountains, pushed through forests, swam across wide rivers, and found the sorcerer, the young man learned who he was: a brave, strong, wise, and good man, and his happiness returned.

"That is the way of the Netahs."

Mesenova pulled away from Josh. "Daddy," he said, his hand on Josh's knee. "Did the young man have a name? Was it Josh?"
Hesta looked at his lap for a moment.

"Sir? May I answer?" Josh asked. Mesenova's brows rose. Hesta nodded consent, so Josh said, "I think it is the story of every young man as he grows up."

Hesta confirmed that with a nod. "Very good, Josh. Yes, it is a parable."

"What's a pabula?" Mesenova bit his tongue.

"A parable is a story with an important message about how to live your life," Hesta explained.

"Hmm." The boy waited a beat before asking, "What's a sorcermer?"

"A magician."

"Oh! I like magic." Mesenova hopped off the couch, his mood brightened. "Daddy?"

"Yes?"

"Next time can the sorcerer be a dragon or maybe a dinosaur?"

"I'll consider that," Hesta said with a very straight face. Mesenova skipped over to his big sister while Hesta and Josh laughed quietly. Moments later the little guy returned for a good-night hug before skipping off to bed.

Mesenova stopped suddenly and asked his father, "Will you come tuck me in?"

"Yes, in a moment."

Mesenova turned and hummed his way into his bedroom.

"Um, Hesta?" Josh asked. "Did you tell that story for my benefit?"

"Hmm? Oh, no, it's just a story fathers tell their sons so that they will try to be strong and brave as they grow up. Why?"

"I would have added a dragon," Josh joked as he got up. "I should be going. Thank you for including me tonight."

"You're welcome." Hesta stood and followed him towards the entrance. "Oh, I wanted to ask, have you noticed anything strange happening in the lodge?"

"It's all strange to me, so I couldn't say. You worry too much." Josh shook his head.

"As a wise young man once said to me, I think I worry just about the right amount," Hesta answered as he patted Josh on the shoulder, steering him towards the front door.

"Thank you for dinner, Ohma," Josh said as they walked past the women. "See you later, Noomi."

They both looked up and said, "Bye!"

The night was bitterly cold, so Josh transformed and moved quickly. The dark, moonless night made the few landmarks difficult to find, especially since he was distracted by thoughts of his father possibly lurking in the shadows, and about what Noomi meant when she said security would be tightened.

As Josh galloped, he admired Mesenova's curiosity. The ceremony had been simple, but odd. How strange that a child could help determine his own name. Mesenova seemed much wiser than a three-year-old. Josh turned the parable over in his head as he walked. It occurred to him that it was a story from a father to a son, and that Hesta had chosen it for him as much as for Mesenova, since his own father wasn't around to tell it.

Would it have been better if the young man had to battle a dragon? *Maybe, but sorcerers were also fun.*

He nearly leapt out of his skin when a large figure materialized suddenly in his path.

The friendly voice of Haiman said, "Lovely night for a stroll, eh, Josh?"

Josh snorted. "Nights like this make me grateful for fur!"

"Me, too." As he walked along with Josh, Haiman asked, "How was the ceremony?"

"Interesting."

"What did they name the kid?"

"Mesenova, which I think means listen."

"Huh, interesting indeed." He paused, and said, "See ya later," before disappearing into the night.

Josh realized they were standing in the aspen grove at the front door to the lodge. He pushed the door open and went inside.

As he lay in bed, he thought about Haiman on night patrol and felt grateful. He analyzed Hesta's story, which hit awfully close to home. Was he trying to warn Josh? If so, would Josh live up to his name as a savior, or cower and fail? Did Josh's parents know the significance of his name or just like the sound of it? They had not been religious, but he wouldn't put it past them.

Josh had a sense that things had shifted slightly in the last few hours. Maybe it was the freedom to transform again, or the delicious soup, or the warmth of family he'd experienced that night. Or maybe it was the sense of foreboding building around him. His dreams were filled with dragons and dinosaurs, sorcerers and spies.

CHAPTER 9

Apprentice Builders

The next day life in the lodge returned to normal. His lodge mates all talked at once, their spirits high as they sipped their tea. Everyone seemed excited to get back to work. Josh heard Haiman talk about his new house under construction, and was delighted to be invited to come help.

"Thanks," Josh said. "Do I need to bring anything?"

"Nope, everything we need is there. You almost done with your tea?" Haiman asked.

"Give me five minutes, okay?"

"You got it. I'm going outside for breakfast. See you out there." Haiman left.

Tomo sat at the end of the counter. Josh drank another gulp of tea and asked him, "Where are you going this morning?"

"Back to the infirmary. I'm trying to decide if I want to pursue healing."

"Will you go to a human university?"

Tomo shook his head. "Not for a while. I have loads to learn still from Ohma."

"When do you have to decide? Do you have to be a certain age?" Josh asked.

"Nah, we have to pass a certain level of knowledge in the field, usually decided by the head of that team. When they think you're ready, you get permission to go."

"Is that why there aren't very many guys our age in the lodge right now? Are the rest of them all off at school?" *This could explain a lot.*

"Sort of, yes, some are at uni, but others have moved on."

"To other Netah elk villages? Are there a lot?"

"I guess. We're spread out all over the west and into Canada. But also, when you pick your mate, you build your own home like Haiman's doing. This lodge is only for bachelors."

"Huh." Josh finished his tea. "I guess I shouldn't make Haiman wait, then. See you later!" As he walked out the door and transformed into an elk, he realized he had learned more about Netah life in five minutes than he had in the previous several weeks.

Outside, he saw Haiman nibbling brown leaves off nearby aspens. He noticed dozens of small groups of elk moving around the valley. Now he knew they were all going to work, just like in human communities. Josh wondered what other jobs there were in the valley. He walked over to Haiman. "How far away is your new house?"

"Not far. Come on, follow me." They galloped to the top of the mesa. Their hooves thundered across the frozen ground. As the sun warmed his fur, Josh decided that becoming a Netah might just be the best thing that had ever happened to him.

Several other Netahs were heading in the same direction. Haiman slowed to a walk and pulled up beside three others. Josh struggled to decide whether they were boys or girls, old or young. He noticed that Haiman had antler nubs beginning to appear again, and the elk he talked to had no signs of antlers. *Clue number one: the ladies don't grow antlers!* Josh held back so Haiman could move ahead, and the two other elk slowed down to walk with Josh.

"Hi, I'm Josh," he said. "What are your names?"

The smaller one said, "I'm Ano, this is Eve. You working with us today?"

"Seems so. Nice to meet you. Hi, Eve." He peered past Ano to see her friend.

Eve grunted. "Hi."

Josh raised his eyebrows. "It sure is great getting out of the lodge."

Eve coughed. "I hate being cooped up."

"We got on each other's nerves a little," Ano admitted.

"You two live together? Are you sisters?" Josh asked. "That is if you don't mind me asking. I'm not trying to be nosy, just trying to figure out how things work around here."

Ano almost whispered, "I get it. You're the new guy, right?"

Eve said, "Of course he is. Duh! We know everybody else in the whole valley." She said to Josh, "It's a small community. Oh, and yes, we share our home, but no, we're not sisters." She moved off to catch up with Haiman and the lady elk.

Josh watched her move away and wondered if he had insulted her. *Maybe she's just not into me.*

Ano walked beside him for a bit before she said, "You must be overwhelmed with questions." *Did she just read my mind?* "I know I would be. What do you want to know? Don't worry about Eve, she got up on the wrong side of the bed this morning."

"I heard that," Eve called out over her shoulder.

Josh laughed. Turning to Ano, he said, "I know families live together and the bachelors live in a lodge, but I don't know how or where all the girls live."

"Right, well, I can explain." Ano had a soft, purring voice. "We live with our families while we're young, learning basics at home, you know, reading, writing, and arithmetic, then we start our apprenticeships. That's when we can move into the lodges with fellow apprentices. It's pretty great, because we learn on the job and from each other. Sometimes there are lots of apprentices and they get a bigger house. Not many girls go for construction, so for now it's just Eve, Nohka, and me. That's Nohka with Haiman."

"Interesting."

Ano asked, "How do you like the bachelor lodge?"

"It's kind of great. Kind of like a big dormitory where we share chores, but there's lots to do in our downtime, too."

"Have you made friends?" she asked.

"Yes, Tomo, the only one who is close to my age. The others all seem much older."

"I know Tomo, he's cute." Ano pursed her lips, too late to take back her words.

"You like him? Does he know?"

"I think so, but he's kind of shy, so he doesn't show it." She giggled.

"Shy? Huh, I thought he was just quiet." They caught up with the others, who had gathered with twenty other elk. Moments later they became a group of humans. They lined up at a shed and took turns pulling out work gloves and yellow safety helmets. Haiman found spares for Josh. Then he called out, "Okay, people, listen up. I want to introduce a new apprentice. This is Josh." Some waved, others smiled, a couple nodded. "Let's introduce ourselves as we work with Josh today, rather than loading him down with all our names at once." They nodded agreement. Josh wondered if Haiman was the team leader.

But then an older man spoke. "Thanks, Haiman. I know all of you will make Josh feel welcome. Now let's get to work." The man walked over and put his arm over Josh's shoulder as they followed the others. "Josh, I'm Kim. Let me explain how we do things around here. First, we check out the progress of one team. We get a report, ask questions. That's how we learn. After that, I want you to explore the building site and see what the others are doing. I'm going to let you decide which team to work with today. Each day, I want you to choose a different group until you've worked with each one. I may assign you a task if we need extra hands. Otherwise, you decide what to try, with the team's consent, of course. Questions?"

"No, sir, thanks." Josh loved everything he'd heard, like about teams, getting a choice who he would work with, and on what.

"All right, can everybody see?" Kim asked as they approached a corner of the house where the others had gathered. "Ano, why don't you start us out with your report," he instructed.

Ano faced the group, her brown curly hair poking wildly out from under her helmet. Three guys with long hair in man buns stood beside her. "Okay, well, last time we were here," Ano started and then paused as quiet laughter erupted. She nodded. "Right, before lockdown, we managed to coat the foundation with our waterproofing material."

Kim asked, "What did you use for the waterproofing?"

Ano hesitated and looked at a tall, skinny teammate who nodded and spoke, "We decided to make pitch from pine resins. I found a formula on the undernet."

Kim asked, "Problems? Successes?"

Ano took over again, "Yes, sir. We had problems finding the resin because all the trees are dormant, until we found a cedar by the hot springs. It had a broken branch and fresh resins pooling up where it broke. We gathered a bit to test, heated it, strained it, and added . . ."

A teammate broke in enthusiastically, "Dried elk duds and fat rendered from a fish."

Laughter broke out. Haiman spoke. "Good. Innovative recycling. How did it smell?"

Ano's team covered their noses and shook their heads. "Not good, sir."

"What did you do to remedy that?"

Ano nodded. "We tossed that batch and made a second batch with beeswax, sir."

"Problem solved?"

"Yes, sir. It smelled great, held together, and spread well over our wall."

"Your wall, for Josh's benefit, was made out of what?" Kim prompted.

"Compacted bricks of mud and hay."

"Did you finish sealing the wall and did you have enough materials?" Eve asked.

"Yes, all done," Ano responded. Several apprentices went over to inspect it. One smelled the pitch and nodded approvingly, one dabbed at it to test its texture, another picked up a small pail of water and asked, "May I?"

Ano nodded and he slowly poured the water down the wall to check its effectiveness. The water beaded up and drained away down the hill.

"Good, what's next?" Haiman asked.

"We're going to double-check the drainage before we begin the final landscaping."

"Great." Kim nodded. He looked around the sea of faces standing there in the cold. "Does anyone have any questions before we get to work?"

No one did. Some stamped their feet; others blew on their hands to warm them.

Kim said, "Okay, let's get to it. This house won't build itself!"

Josh walked around and noticed how the house blended into the natural contours of a low hill. Trees and bushes that looked original to the site hid its existence. The hill had one side dug out like a cave. A curving roofline created with bent saplings and turf above it, reached beyond the cave opening, creating a covered entrance. Large boulders lined one rear wall. As at the lodge, a long line of windows was tucked under an overhang, and a pond over a skylight hid solar panels. Josh stepped up to the pond to see if he could see the solar panels. He couldn't find them, but he did notice the pond had steam rising from it. He reached down and dipped a finger in. It was hot, not just warm!

Josh found Haiman and asked about the hot pond.

"You noticed, huh? That's why we chose this spot, Nohka and I. The hot spring runs down behind a false wall, radiating heat into the house."

"So no furnace or fireplace needed?"

"You catch on fast." Haiman looked impressed. "What else have you noticed?"

"Well, I couldn't see any solar panels in the pond, like at Hesta's house."

"Oh, they're there, just colored to blend in with the rock pool."

"How hot is the pool?"

"A perfect 102 degrees! We have our own natural hot tub!" Haiman grinned. "It'll be great at the end of the day."

"Awesome!" Josh nodded, then looked puzzled. "But what about in the summer? How will you cool off the house?"

Haiman laughed. "We simply reroute the spring into the lower pool!"

Josh shook his head in wonder as he investigated what each of the teams worked on. One group mixed cement, another made clay bricks and tiles, one spread plaster, while Kim and Haiman checked drawings. Josh offered to help the tile team, pressing the clay into molds and stacking them to dry for the rest of the morning.

At lunchtime, they all turned into elk and went foraging. Eventually, several Netah elk gathered in a clearing. Josh walked over to see what was going on. A line of small stones marked a starting line and the Netah elk jostled for positions. Josh recognized the older guy who was in charge of the tiles, as he held a large branch in the air. All eyes turned. He lowered the branch and cracked it against a boulder. The elk shot off, pounding the ground, churning up dust and mud. They made a wide curve to the left and then circled back to the line of stones like horses on a racetrack.

Josh picked out the smaller, but agile, Ano and Eve in the front of the race, but they were soon passed by a taller male. Josh thought it looked like Haiman was the winner, and that maybe the others had eased up a little to let him win. Nohka walked up to him at the finish line and they nuzzled each other's necks while everyone else turned back into humans and returned to work.

Josh returned to the tile group. "Hey, Manny. I had an idea. Do you use these tiles on inside walls? If so, can we make them more decorative?"

"Sure. We use them in the bathrooms, kitchens, and floors. What did you have in mind?"

"Well, I thought it would be cool to have some different textures. I could etch a design into them, or I could use something as a stamp."

"Interesting. Why don't you experiment with that stack of fresh tiles over there." He pointed to the pile they'd made that morning.

"Are you sure? We just finished making those," Josh asked.

"Sure I'm sure. You need them to still be pliable, right? It's perfect timing. Let me know if you have any questions or problems." Manny walked over and helped stir water into a big vat for a new batch of clay. Josh could see why his arms were so muscular.

Josh couldn't believe his luck. He began by once again walking the perimeter of the site and searching for items he could use for etching or stamping. He picked up a sturdy stick, a branch of cedar, a pinecone, and several twigs with interesting shapes. Back at the cave he found a rock in the sun he could use for a stool and went to work. He rolled the pinecone across one tile. It made very satisfying ridges, but left bits of pinecone behind, looking messy. He pulled the bark off a twig, then pressed it into another tile, moving it and pressing until he had a good pattern. He picked up the sturdy stick and decided it needed to be sharpened.

He walked over to Manny. "Hey, Manny. Do you have a pocket-knife? I want to whittle a point into this stick."

Manny looked up from smoothing the clay into its brick form. "Let's see," he said as he reached into his back pocket. "Will this do?"

"Perfect. Thanks. I'll return it at the end of the day."

"No problem, leave it in the shed when you're done."

One of the team members looked up. "Uh, Manny? Mind if I go work with Josh?"

"Go ahead." He waved them off.

The tall, stringy guy wiped his hands on his jeans and held one out to Josh. "Hi, I'm Pehpe. I like what you're trying over there and had some ideas. You mind?"

"Not at all. Nice to meet you, Pehpe." Josh showed him what he'd done so far.

"I like it. Okay, I'm going to go look for some other objects. Be right back." He tucked a dark curl that had escaped from his man bun behind his ear and he walked along, eyes on the ground.

Josh settled to his task and soon had a workable point with which he could make crosshatch marks, stripes, circles, which were harder, swirls were very challenging, simple shapes like a series of triangles, dashes, and dots that could be grouped together to make patterns. He'd gone through a quarter of the tiles before Pehpe returned with bulging pockets.

He sat on the other side of the tile stack and pulled a tile onto his lap. From his pocket he retrieved a handful of pebbles. He dropped them on the tile and pressed them gently in, moved some, repeated the process. Pehpe dumped them off and studied the effect. On the next tile, he pressed a sharply edged rock, studying the effect of each impression, deepening some, smoothing out others. The two worked silently for a while. Eventually Josh rubbed the back of his neck and watched Pehpe work.

"Pehpe, you mind if I ask you something?" Pehpe moved his sharp rock to create a mountain scene.

"Nope, what's up?"

"Is there a construction lodge?"

"Yep."

"But only for the guys?"

"Yeah, I don't know why. I mean, most of the other lodges are co-ed, but the building guys are old-fashioned." Pehpe rolled his eyes. "Maybe it's a space issue. Our house is small."

Josh snorted, "Huh, I thought Netahs were more advanced than that." He'd meant it sarcastically, but then realized he might have believed it.

Pehpe straightened and looked at Josh. "You ready to get out of the security lodge?"

"No, no, I'm fine there."

"Arman?" Pehpe asked, one eyebrow raised.

"Ha, you mean Miss Congeniality?"

Pehpe laughed. Josh shrugged. "Takes all kinds. Do you like your lodge though?"

"Yep, I guess. I've only been there a year or so. You have to decide your trade, before you move in."

"How many lodges are there?" Josh had thought there was only the one.

"Well, let's see." Pehpe looked up and appeared to be counting things in the sky above him. "Maybe twelve?"

"Huh," Josh mused. "So is my lodge for guys who haven't chosen their trade yet?"

"Well, not exactly, it's the security lodge. No one told you?"

"Oh, right, I did hear that. In that case, why is Haiman here if he's security?" Josh asked.

Pehpe laughed, "Oh, well he's dating Nohka. They're engaged. This will be their house. Bringing you here gave him an excuse to see her today, that's my guess."

"Huh. I wonder why no one said anything about that at the lodge. It's strange, I've been there about a month, and I know so little about how things work around here."

"That must be annoying," Pehpe sighed and smoothed his hair back, leaving a smudge of dirt on his forehead. "The lockdown didn't help. You want my advice?"

Josh nodded. "Sure."

"Give it time, relax. There's a lot to learn, but you're in no hurry. You're not planning on going anywhere, right?"

Josh snorted, "Yeah, right. Where would I go?"

Pehpe shrugged and returned to his work. "You're pretty creative. This could be a good fit for you. It's not all art, though. What will you try tomorrow?"

Josh looked around at the different groups. "Maybe I'll help with the concrete. Something more physical will keep me warmer, right?"

"Good idea. Start with us tomorrow, though, so we can show off what we've done and get some feedback, okay?"

"Sure, sounds good." Josh wondered if Haiman would walk him back, or if he'd be able to find his way by himself. "Where is the construction lodge?" he asked.

"Not far from your lodge. Why?"

"I'm still trying to find my way around here. Maybe we could walk together in the morning?"

"That's a great idea. I'll swing by for you." Pehpe put down the last tile and looked around the work site. "Looks like folks are finishing up. Want me to walk you back today, as well?"

"Yes, thanks," Josh happily agreed. "What should we do with these?"

"Let's show Manny and let him decide."

Manny came and inspected their work. "This is great, gentle-men. Let's share it in the morning. Which one of you wants to talk about it?"

Josh and Pehpe looked at each other and both shrugged. Josh realized he'd started the project, so he should do the talking. "I'll do it," he said.

Manny nodded. "Good. You don't have to go into much detail. Maybe say what inspired you, what you liked and didn't like. Then we'll get Nohka's opinion. Okay?"

"Yeah, absolutely."

"You can leave them here to dry overnight and we'll gather here in the morning. I'll let Kim know we want to present." Manny turned to go.

"We free to go home now, Manny?" Pehpe asked.

"Sure thing."

"Good, I'm going to walk Josh home. See you back at the lodge."

Josh asked Pehpe, "Have you seen Haiman? I should probably let him know we're going."

"Oh, right. Come on, let's go find him."

They found Haiman working with Nohka, to no one's sur-prise. They were painting a wall and talking in low murmurs. The boys walked up and Pehpe cleared his throat very loudly to get their attention.

"Uh, Haiman, if it's okay with you," Josh said. "Pehpe will walk home with me, so I don't get lost."

"Okay, great." Haiman looked very happy as he wrapped his arm around Nohka and pulled her close to whisper in her ear. She giggled as she resumed painting.

Josh realized they might appreciate a little privacy at the end of the day. "Yep, okay, bye then."

As he and Pehpe walked away, they both transformed into elk. They trotted for a while, which worked the kinks out of sore muscles, then slowed to a walk. Josh noticed his new friend was taller than him in elk form. He asked, "So, if I'm supposed to be trying different fields before I choose one, how long do I work at each one before I move on?"

"Well, I guess until you've tried each thing at the site?" Pehpe thought about it a few moments. "I mean, there are a lot of different parts to this field. You probably shouldn't rush through it, unless maybe if you hated the first five days, that would be a good indication you should move on."

"Well, so far I'm fascinated by all the things I'm seeing here. I guess I'll be back for a long time."

"Great."

"But I have to try other fields before I can choose my new lodge, right?" Josh wanted to be clear on this. "Say, is there a lodge for guys studying healing?"

"No, Tomo is the only one at the moment. That's why he's in your lodge. They had the extra room."

Josh nodded, it made sense. He seemed to be in the overflow lodge. "One more question, if you don't mind."

"Shoot."

"How do you meet girls!?"

After they both had a laugh, Pehpe said, "Well, on our jobs and also during the summer games. Wait till you see that! You know how we all raced at lunchtime? We have one of the best racers in the valley. You a runner?"

"Used to be, as a human," Josh admitted. "Yeah, I like running."

"Perfect. Join us tomorrow," Pehpe insisted. "We need to get in shape, sooner the better!"

Josh realized he had not been paying attention to their route or landmarks, although he recognized the tracks of hoof prints from the morning. *I'm still totally lost.* He was glad for Pehpe's company. The sun sat just above the tops of the trees, like the night he'd gone to dinner at Hesta's. A familiar stand of aspens came into view. "Hey, are we almost there? Is that my lodge?"

"Yep, see? You're not as lost as you thought." Pehpe paused. "So I mentioned the summer games, right?"

"Summer games?" Josh repeated. "Yeah."

Pehpe laughed. "Did I tell you that we all go to the high country in the summer, staying elk all the time."

"No, why?" Josh could hear the excitement in Pehpe's voice.

"You and I can train every morning on our commute!"

That sounded exhausting to Josh, but probably worth it. "Hey, thanks for walking me back."

The rest of that week Josh worked his way through the French drain builders, hauling away wheelbarrows full of soil, and lining the bottom of the drain with small river rocks. He helped build an interior brick wall, hauled and lifted where required. He spent one day studying the drawings and pointed out a wall in the wrong place, which he then had to help demolish and rebuild. He got really good at mixing mortar and troweling it on. The physical demands of the work took its toll, and Josh went to bed early every night.

On Friday night, Pehpe invited Josh to the construction lodge for a glass of mead. Josh went, but the mead, even on a full stomach, made Josh so sleepy he excused himself early and headed back to his own lodge while the sky still had some light left in it. The night wind blew cold, and the trees in the aspen grove shone white in the moonlight. Josh followed a faint path through the trees, his hand tightly grasping his pepper spray, and was creeped out by the time he found his lodge. The scars where branches had fallen off the aspens all looked like eyes following him. He nearly squealed at the sight of movement, but seeing it was Esok, he quickly caught up to follow him through their door.

"Where've you been? You're not usually out late like this," Esok observed.

Josh leaned against the entrance hall wall, barely able to keep himself upright as he kicked off his shoes. With a sigh he said, "Went to the construction lodge for an end-of-week celebration. Pehpe invited me. I wanted to see how they live. Their place is a mess!"

Esok laughed, "Huh, I've heard that. I guess we should be grateful Mako expects us to keep this place neat. He hates messes."

"I guess I never noticed him get grumpy about it. How do you know?" Josh asked.

"You've never seen it, because the rest of us learned our lesson and will not let it happen again. Lucky you're not a slob. You seem to be neat naturally." Esok stroked his trim beard as he turned towards the great hall. "Besides, it makes it easier when we host the weekend dinner."

"What's that you said? Host the weekend dinner? We haven't done that since I arrived, right?" Josh asked.

"No, right, guess not, because of the lockdown," Esok agreed. "Well, it will happen tomorrow night, so don't make any messes tonight!"

"No chance," Josh laughed. "I'm ready for bed already. Is there anything I can do to help?"

"Nah, just bring your game face. It's about the only time we get to mingle with the ladies and families. G'nite!" Esok wrinkled his nose before he limped away towards the great room.

Josh pushed himself away from the wall and got a whiff of his own odor. Begrudgingly, he dragged himself to the showers before falling into bed. What a day it had been, a good day, a tiring day, a very informative day.

Better get some sleep. This is not my game face. As he rolled to his side, he wondered when he had become neat. Maybe not having a bunch of stuff helped. He glanced around his room. The only sign he lived there was his stack of math books. *That must be the trick. Don't own anything!*

CHAPTER 10

Unexpected Visitors

With all chores finished, Josh and Tomo checked the weather forecast on the instrument in the great room before heading outside into a crisp winter morning. Gray clouds rushed by in a stiff wind, chasing patches of sunlight across the landscape.

"It's days like this that I'm grateful for my elk coat!" Josh laughed.

"It has its advantages, for sure," Tomo agreed.

At the top of a hill, they surveyed the valley, squinting and leaning into the wind. Elk are particularly good at seeing small movement where there shouldn't be any so the little puff of snow blowing several hills away caught their attention.

"Is that the security detail out there?" Josh asked.

"No way, they're better at concealing their presence. They would never do that!"

"Should we go check it out?" Josh suggested hopefully.

Tomo grinned. "Why not?"

They skirted a patch of snow drifted against the north side of a cedar. Water trickled away and created ice patches that forced them to walk carefully.

Josh asked, "So, how big is this village? I mean there are security wires at its boundaries, right?"

"Right, but not in all directions. From here to those mountains, it's pretty wide-open country. We thought wires would be suspicious, but we still have sensors."

"I wonder if I will hear the alarm, because, you know, I'm only a halfling."

"I wonder, too."

"How often does it go off?" Josh asked.

"Rarely, in fact I can't remember the last time it happened."

They walked along in silence for a while, grazing, sipping at icy creeks, sniffing the air for smells that would indicate the presence of other animals, or something green and fresh pushing through the soil.

Josh said, "I love the way it smells here. It's not like the suburbs where I lived. It used to be a cattle ranch, so as soon as the frozen ground started to warm up, you could smell ancient cow dung."

"I've noticed that sometimes, too," Tomo admitted. "Also, I bet your nose is getting more sensitive, the longer you live as a Netah."

Josh sniffed and wrinkled his nose. "Can you smell the difference between frozen and soggy ground?"

"Certainly. You should start to recognize your favorite foods by their smell if you haven't already." Tomo checked out the position of the sun. "It's still early, and the wind seems to have died down after blowing away the clouds. I think we'll have a better day than we thought," he said. "Do you see signs of anything moving around out there anymore?"

"No, I lost it," Josh admitted.

"Me, too. Maybe it was just a dust or snow devil. How about we rest here for a little while? The sun feels so good, you know?"

"Why not? We just need to be back in time for the weekend meal." As they settled down on the hillside, the sun's warmth reached deep into their coats. Josh couldn't remember the last time he did nothing like this. He usually plugged into some game when he had free time as a human. As a Netah he would read his text books, do chores, or workout. He felt like he'd earned this time. He let his thoughts roam. He wanted to embrace the peace and quiet. Also, being outside with Tomo made him feel safe.

His faceless father intruded on his thoughts, how he lived among the Netah bachelors, worked on security, invented high-tech devices. What had happened to him? Something happened with Arman, Josh was sure of that. No one would talk about it, though. So that was a secret, his dad's location was a secret, the Netah's very existence was a secret. *I am so sick of secrets!* His insides churned as questions about his Netah dad's character swirled through his mind. *Is he a good guy or bad?* The jury was still out.

A fly buzzed nearby, and Josh flicked his ear. *A fly at this time of year?* He looked at Tomo, whose ears were perked up as well. They got up at the same time.

Tomo asked, "Do you hear that?"

"The fly?"

"Not a fly, it's the alarm. We don't have to worry, we're already elk. It means a human has come onto our land. We should go back but keep our eyes open for anything out of the ordinary."

Josh followed Tomo and rolled his eyes. *What's ordinary?*

Within minutes they saw two young people carrying large camping packs, the metal frames flashed in the sunlight. Tomo and Josh stood very still, watching the couple walk just downhill from them. The girl found a piece of ice and squealed as she nearly went down under her heavy pack. She planted her poles, adjusted her pack, and followed her companion, who had his face glued to his phone.

Tomo whispered, "It's just a couple of back country campers. Hopefully they'll move on. Let's watch them discreetly." He paused, let them gain some distance, and then started after them again.

"Can he get a signal on his phone out here?"

"Probably not," Tomo said. "We're a 'no service' zone."

"What if they don't move on?"

"We have our ways." Tomo grinned a mischievous elk grin.

"So much for a peaceful afternoon," Josh said.

"I always like a little excitement and mystery," Tomo admitted. "Who knows? Will they stop, settle in, start a campfire?"

"We can't let them do that, can we?"

"Look!" Tomo nodded towards a couple of large elk walking casually along the opposite mesa and out of sight of the hikers. They were obviously trailing the hikers. When the couple sat on boulders to rest, the elk stopped and lay down. When the couple walked off, the elk followed.

"Who is that? Do you recognize them?" Josh whispered.

"It's Hesta and Arman," Tomo said through closed teeth.

"What should we do?" Josh hissed.

"We'll follow in a minute. I'm curious." Tomo could barely contain his excitement.

Josh grinned. *It's been a long lockdown. He's starved for entertainment!*

The other two elk leaned towards each other, nodded, then suddenly slipped out of sight. Josh moved to stand and try to find them, but Tomo whispered, "Stay down!"

"Now what?"

"Watch. This could get good."

The hikers started to gather twigs for firewood. That was the signal, apparently. Moments later, before they could start to build their firepit, a wolf howled nearby. The couple froze, then gathered their stuff and quickly moved on. Josh heard stealthy footsteps approach. Hesta and Arman pretended to graze near the boys.

Hesta spoke, quietly, "How'd you boys like an assignment?"

"Sure," Tomo answered eagerly.

"You be our scouts on these two. Stay with them until they leave our lands. If they try to come any closer, Tomo, send us a signal. We can ask our bear friends to wander by. That should scare them off."

"Yes, sir! What if they stay nearby for days? Stay with them?" Tomo asked.

"You bet," Hesta answered. "You two have been working hard. Rodan says you could use the break. Okay?"

Arman interrupted, "Are you sure you can trust this stupid half-ling with such an important assignment, Hesta?"

Hesta shook his head. "Let it go, Arman. I've heard your opinion."

"You can't say I didn't warn you."

Hesta turned back to the boys. "You in?"

"Yes, sir!" both Netahs answered.

"All right, then. When they leave the valley, report back to me. See if you can find out what they're doing here, are they looking for something, hunting, fishing, just sightseeing?" Hesta turned and the two large elk walked away. Josh felt their footsteps vibrating through the ground, growing softer over time.

"Question," Josh said. "If the bears come by, will they hurt the people?"

"Pfff!" Tomo said, keeping his voice quiet. "We wouldn't hurt them. Think about it. There would be search parties, the bears would be found, investigated, and maybe killed, the whole area combed for clues. No, nothing as drastic as that. They'd just scare them off, you know, eat their food, rip their tents, make life uncomfortable."

Josh asked, "Wait, are they Netah bears?"

Tomo nodded. "Not all of the bears around here are Netahs, no," he clarified, "but several are on our patrol team. You don't need more than a few bears to scare off humans. They have a reputation for messing with campsites, so it's perfectly natural, except regular bears are all hibernating. That's even more scary for humans, because they assume the bears are hungry and want their food!"

"The bears have their own lodge of security guys?"

"Of course. I mean, we could live together, but their diet includes meat. It's kinda disgusting." Tomo paused, then nodded. "Yes, they're neighbors, we work together, but we're different. Kind of like Catholics and Protestants, or Democrats and Republicans in the human world."

"Huh." Josh liked that Netahs didn't all walk in lockstep, they had differences. He thought about what it would be like if the bears charged the hikers. "If I were those hikers, I would not stick around once I saw a bear."

"That's just good common sense."

"Agreed." He glanced towards the humans and his eyes grew wide. "Uh, Tomo? Where'd they go?"

The Netahs leapt to their feet and trotted along the top of the ridge, searching. The light had dimmed; the sun dipped behind the far mountains. A campfire gave the humans away. The Netahs drew closer, then settled down to watch and listen from behind a screen of willows, where the cold, humid night air carried the human voices clearly.

The longer he listened, the more Josh thought they sounded familiar. Then the girl said, "Do you really think Josh just ran away and is out here somewhere camping and living off the land like some kind of Huckleberry Finn? If he is, why?"

The guy answered, "Maybe it's wishful thinking. I'd like to think he's out here enjoying himself. I don't want to think he really got killed by a bear."

A tear slid down his cheek as Josh stole a glance at Tomo, who didn't appear to be paying attention. He bit at something on his back leg.

Josh recognized the voices of his friends Anton and Sarah. They'd just confirmed what Crawley had reported about the theory of Josh's disappearance. Josh considered Anton's idea. It was a good story. If he ever found a way to return to his human friends, he needed a reason to leave his comfortable, happy family in the suburbs, which still eluded his imagination. Meanwhile, the day's mystery continued. He had to pay attention and not miss any clues.

Tomo leaned close. "Hey, we should eat something before we go to sleep. In fact, we should also take turns being awake. Come on, follow me. I smell something good."

"Okay, looks like the humans are settled down for the night." Josh didn't think Tomo had heard what his friends said. The sun was fully set as they returned to their hiding spot. Josh took the first watch, while Tomo dozed. It was time to work on his story again, the one he could tell his human friends and family when he was allowed to see them again, the excuse he'd have for having disappeared, the story he'd use after he became a trusted, full Netah. *Okay, so I ran away. Why? A bully at school?* Well, yeah, George pushed you around, but that's not enough! *I joined a gang?* Hardly. *I was kidnapped by a drug cartel and held for ransom?* No ransom note. Nope. *Jilted by a girl and unable to face my friends?* That would work if you had a girlfriend. A puff of breath hung in the air in front of his face.

Maybe I ran away with Fern or Crawley. They would have disappeared at the same time I did. Crawley was a known truant, and Fern said she came from a military family. They moved all the time, so that could work. *If I wasn't unhappy or depressed, why run away? I had friends, gaming buddies. Maybe I was kidnapped, hit on the head, and had amnesia.* You'd have surfaced by now.

The corner of Josh's lip curled up as it occurred to him that the Netahs had basically kidnapped him.

Josh dropped his chin and rested it on the ground, his eyelids suddenly heavy. *This isn't helping.* It also didn't help that Anton decided the willows would make a good urinal. Josh froze as he heard Anton's zipper, and a splashing of urine uncomfortably close to his head. He held his breath. *What has he been eating? If only Anton knew I was here. What would he do?* He'd probably jump right out of his skin. *Maybe someday I'll be able to tell my friends about my adventures.* Um, no, you'll never be able to tell anyone. *Not even my mother?* Maybe her. Probably not.

Josh wished his friends would discuss why they were out here by themselves. He didn't see signs of a romance. Were they really looking for him, or was that just an excuse? Josh knew Anton had trouble with women, usually jumping from first eye contact to puppy love in seconds. It scared the girls off. Anton and Sarah had known each other since kindergarten, so he didn't scare her.

Sarah spoke into the damp night air, her voice carrying easily to Josh. "This really is fantastic, Anton. The sky is filled with stars. It's beautiful. No wonder you love it out here."

Josh glanced up at the night sky and was astonished at the number of stars visible.

"I told you we wouldn't need flashlights," Anton laughed. "I'm glad you like it. Josh's family and mine used to do this all the time. Our folks would set up a big camp, and they'd let us go off on our own for a night, just over a ridge, not too far away, but it felt like we were on our own. Our parents knew exactly where we were. I mean, you never know what wild animal is lurking around in the dark."

Tomo gasped. Apparently, he had woken up.

"Shhh," Josh insisted. "Just listen."

Sarah pulled on a beanie and pulled her hood over it before she snuggled down into her sleeping bag on the opposite side of the fire. "You're not trying to worry me, so I move closer, are you?"

Anton snorted, "Too obvious?"

Giggling, she said, "Maybe?" She shook her head, "Actually, I'm sure your Boy Scout skills will get us through. If we weren't like brother and sister, my parents would probably never have agreed. You have a good heart, Anton. It's one of my favorite things about you." *Aha! He's playing it cool and letting her make the moves. What a sly fox you are, Anton.* She said one of my favorite things, so there are other things. Josh sniffed, detecting a hint of romance in the air and no puppy love. Had Anton finally learned from years of Josh's coaching advice? Josh felt Tomo's eyes boring a hole into his head. He turned to his friend and whispered, "I'll explain in a minute. Let me listen."

Tomo nodded and shifted to get more comfortable while he waited.

Sarah said, "We only have food for today, so we have to go back tomorrow morning, right?"

"Uh-huh," Anton agreed. He unrolled his sleeping bag onto a mat and unzipped it. "Let's get some sleep."

"I'm glad your parents set this up." Sarah sighed as she pulled off her shoes and slid into her bag. "I can't imagine what Josh's parents are going through. Maybe the fresh air and change of scene will help them." She rolled onto her side. "Hey, Anton, is it okay to leave my shoes like this?"

"Um." Anton hesitated. "Might be better to stuff them into your pack."

"Okay." Meanwhile, Anton smoothed his bag and slid inside. Still sitting up, he said, "Thanks for coming. I really miss that little booger."

Josh frowned. He heard their bags rustle as they got comfortable.

Once they both were quiet for several minutes, Josh took a deep breath to calm himself. His friends lay only a few feet away, and he couldn't talk to them. *Well, I don't have a good story to tell them yet, anyway.* He snorted in frustration.

Tomo nudged Josh's shoulder and whispered, "Come on, we need to talk." They quietly walked away from the campers. "Josh's parents?" Tomo whispered.

"I heard that."

"You?"

"What? No! I'm not the only Josh in Colorado, you know." Josh shook his head and frowned at the absurdity.

"They're out here looking for you. They're friends of yours." Tomo didn't miss a thing.

Josh didn't love secrets, especially one that could drive a wedge between him and Tomo. "Yeah, you're right."

"Okay," Tomo said. "We got this. Thanks for being straight with me. It's our little secret. We just have to make sure your friends leave safely."

"Yeah? No harm, no foul?"

"Ha," Tomo snorted then parsed it out. "They're not going anywhere tonight, so no harm. Let's get some rest. We'll ensure no foul in the morning." Tomo went back to their hiding spot and settled in.

Josh settled and said, "Hey, I'll keep watch. I'm not tired. You go ahead and get some sleep."

"You got it," Tomo answered and closed his eyes. Moments later, his head popped back up and he exclaimed, quietly, "Shit, we missed it!"

"What?" Josh whispered with some urgency.

"The first gathering for like, what, a month? We're stuck out here on intruder duty and we missed the party! Damn!"

"Aw, man! I'd forgotten about it. How often do they happen?" Josh asked.

"Two weeks," Tomo answered with a sigh as he settled back down and began to snore.

Josh couldn't get comfortable. He still had no story to explain his disappearance, but he kept working through ideas, even though they became increasingly ridiculous. First there was him in a corral, under a Talking Elk sign on a family ranch. Then he imagined a circus tent for the amazing elk-boy. Maybe the wintry air led him to pulling Santa's sleigh, like the Grinch's dog, but way more majestic. All impossible, just like his situation. No human could know. It was forbidden.

But, could he see his parents again? If they were camping nearby, couldn't he see them at least? He could stay an elk, they'd never know, but at least he could see how they were doing.

What had Crawley said? Something about trusted humans. How? Josh needed to research that. Maybe Noomi would know. The thought of seeing her again, and getting some answers startled Josh awake. He nudged Tomo, who looked up groggily. "You better take over, I just dozed off," Josh whispered.

"Okay, sure thing." Tomo blinked himself awake.

Josh woke with the sun. The campers rolled over a couple of times before they finally roused themselves. Anton made coffee, which nearly pushed Josh over the edge. Tomo shoved him away, and they pretended to eat. *Just a couple of elk, doing their thing. Nothing to look at here.*

Sarah noticed them even so, and hushed Anton, pointing. Josh and Anton stood looking each other straight in the eye for several beats. Anton pulled out a cell phone and took a couple of photos. Josh pretended to eat, while struggling with the knowledge that his best friend just took his photo and would never know it was him. Eventually the campers were ready to leave.

Josh and Tomo trailed behind the campers for the entire morning. When they stopped for lunch, the Netahs moved closer to listen to their conversation.

"I'm so glad to hear your little sister is feeling better," Sarah said.

"Thanks," Anton said. "She got very sick, in ICU for a week!"

"I hear they traced the illness to some tainted elk meat in the school cafeteria?"

"I heard that, too, but don't know if I believe it," Anton said. "I mean, since when do they serve elk in school cafeterias?"

"Someone donated it."

"Suspicious much?"

"A bunch . . . She's going to be okay, though, right?" Sarah asked, folding up her paper towel and tucking it into her pack, she pulled out a water bottle. "I'm going to fill up and let the filter work for a while. You need a refill?"

Anton handed her his bottle and stood, checking his phone. Josh remembered they had to get to their parents' camp.

The teens came upon a pile of bear scat, which unsettled Sarah. "Are you sure this is from a bear, Anton? Aren't bears supposed to be hibernating now?"

"They wake sometimes," he said, shrugging it off.

"We're almost back, right?"

Anton nodded. "Yep, It's just over that ridge. Are you okay?"

"I can make it." She shifted her pack and lifted her chin. "Lead the way."

The ground leveled out and the two made better time. Eventually Tomo stopped. "We're at the edge of our land here. Should we stay with them or let them go?"

"I want to make sure they get back safely," Josh said.

Tomo sighed. "That's not our assignment or our problem."

"You don't care if a bear gets them?"

"He won't," Tomo laughed. "He's one of us. Big guy. You might know him. Name's George."

"Get out!" Josh looked around, squinting into the sun. "George is here? Why didn't anyone tell me?"

"I guessed; I didn't know you knew him. Was he the guy in school with you when you escaped?"

"That's him, good ol' George." Josh shook his head, remembering. "Hard for that big brown fur ball to hide."

"Nah, he's an expert."

"Like it's his job?" Josh's eyebrows lifted then pinched together. "What's he doing here?"

"Heck if I know. After we report to Hesta, we can ask about George."

"Agreed. Can we follow my friends, anyway? Anton said they were close."

"I guess. No foul." Tomo winked and so they followed the hikers, keeping their distance.

Sarah stopped several times climbing the ridge. Each time she pulled her pack back on it looked harder. Eventually, Anton took it from her and carried it on his front, joking around about being her Sherpa. Once the teens arrived at their campsite, Tomo said, "Okay, time to go."

Josh pleaded, "Give me a minute. I'll be right back." Tomo had no chance to object as Josh moved through the aspens. Six adults sat talking on camp chairs, a pot of chili steamed over their campfire. Josh's parents were quiet. His mom had deep circles under her puffy eyes. She looked in Josh's direction and seemed to stare at him for a beat, then looked away. She didn't say anything to the others. Danny sat as close to her as he could get and held her hand. They had each other.

Josh tore himself away. There was nothing he could do. Everything he'd done since transforming into an elk had been to protect her, and yet she'd been hurt. It wasn't his fault and it wasn't his to fix. At least not now.

He turned to see Tomo watching him from just a few feet away. With a nod, Tomo led Josh across the mesa where he had first seen the valley. There were only a few elk visible from where they were, and the sun had just set, but the sky still glowed dark blue over the western side of the valley. "Where's Hesta's place?" They had not spoken a word since leaving the campers.

Tomo said, "Hey, I'm sorry about your parents. I'm glad you got to see them. Don't worry, no one here needs to know. Follow me."

Their report failed to mention the fact that Josh knew the hikers. They were just a couple of random people, as far as anyone knew. Josh did mention what he'd heard about the tainted meat in the school, however.

"We never did find out what had happened to the carcass from our fence line, did we?" Josh asked.

"That's true," Hesta said, shifting on his sofa. "Are you suggesting those two things are related? Why? What are you basing that on?"

"You're right, I have nothing, no evidence, except that the timing seems a big coincidence," Josh admitted.

"We don't even know what school the kids were talking about, do we?" Hesta said.

Josh and Tomo stood shoulder to shoulder, making their report. Josh asked Tomo, "Did you hear them mention which school?"

"Nope, nor their city or state." Tomo shrugged.

"They had Colorado license plates," Josh offered.

"Huh, well, that's not much help," Hesta said. "Colorado is a big state. I'll see if George heard anything."

"You're talking about George, the bear?" Josh asked, wondering if they had not been trusted with their simple assignment after all, since George was working security, as well. No surprise there. However, if George recognized the hikers, he'd know Josh was hiding something. That could be a big problem.

"Yep, that George," Hesta said, his eyes unfocused, peering out the window. He blinked and returned his gaze to them.

"Um." Josh hesitated, knowing the Netahs saw conspiracies everywhere. He squared his jaw and asked, "Can I see him?"

"Who, George? You know him?" Hesta sounded surprised and gave Josh his full attention. Josh clearly recalled Hesta being in the clearing when Josh said goodbye to George. *Is Hesta losing his memory?* Hesta pushed himself out of the sofa and put his hands on their shoulders, steering them to his front door. "Sure, I'll speak to him," Hesta said, opening the door. "Good work, fellas. Thanks."

It had been a long couple of days, and they'd covered a lot of ground. Josh was pretty sure he could find his way back to the lodge. They walked slowly, taking in the star-filled night sky, whose light sparkled off bits of mica on the ground. Josh looked forward to seeing his old friend George. Plus, he needed to find out what George knew about the hikers.

"Is it too late to stop and eat?" Josh said, as his stomach growled.

"We might be able to find leftovers in the cold box back at the lodge," Tomo said. "If not, there's always good eating near our ponds."

"Is that why there are so many in the valley?"

"One reason, yes. It's kind of like an elk grocery store. Also, the plants filter the water for us, so double benefits." Tomo glanced around quickly, then said, "Come on, race ya!" He took off at a gallop and Josh soon overtook him.

They found leftover bean stew and bread in cold storage and heated them up for supper. Dishes done and put away, Josh laughed, "I can't believe how much I'm looking forward to my own bed tonight. I must be getting soft."

"I know, me, too," Tomo agreed.

CHAPTER 11

A Special Assignment

The next morning, Josh came into the great room to find the guys relaxing and laughing. A bell sounded and they all gasped, not having heard it chime in a long time, and not expecting it. Haiman got up to open the door.

George stood at the lodge door and asked to see Josh. Josh grinned to himself when he noticed his lodge mates looked a little nervous. George's human bulk filled doorways. Josh put down his cup of tea and walked right up to his old friend, holding out his hand. George ignored the hand and pulled Josh into the proverbial bear hug. Once he let go and Josh got his breath back, they both laughed. They inspected each other until Josh finally said, "Man, it's great to see you. You want to come in, meet the guys?"

George looked at the men watching them from the great room. He waved and shrugged. "Now that you ask, sure, let me see how the elk bachelors live."

Josh introduced George to the men as they each walked over. George peered at Arman, not in a "great to see you" way, more like an "I know who you are, and I've got your number" way. Josh rolled his eyes. *It's always something with Arman.* Rodan offered George a cup of tea, and he accepted heartily. Josh led his friend over to the leather chairs by the windows, and the others drifted off, giving the two friends their space, but remaining within earshot, pretending to clean up the kitchen or lingering at the counter stools with low conversations.

Josh studied George, a smile pulling at the corner of his mouth. George asked, "What? What's making you smile?"

"I can't get over your transformation. You lost weight, which is probably normal, right?"

"Yup, sure, I guess," George sighed as he settled himself more comfortably in his chair.

"How many times did I see you as a human?" Josh asked.

"Not many times, that's true. I mean, I usually stayed behind you in the school hallways."

"Ha, yeah, before you'd send me flying, you mean?"

"It was part of my cover, you know, the school bully," George chuckled. "Also, testing whether I could trigger your transformation."

"That's your story, huh?" Josh teased. "I mean, look at those arms!" George made a fist and the muscles bulged. He reached over and gave George's biceps a squeeze.

"Rocks!" George grinned.

Josh rolled his eyes. "Now you're just showing off."

With a sigh, George relaxed and waved towards the rest of the lodge. "Come on, how about a tour." He ran his hand over his neat black stubble, and his dark brown eyes crinkled at the corners.

As they walked past the kitchen, George said, "Gentlemen, at ease." The others chuckled nervously and shifted as if to comply. George followed Josh down the sleeping quarters hall and asked, "They feeding you okay, kid?"

"Sure, plenty," Josh laughed.

"Not making you forage out there on dried winter grasses?" George asked suspiciously.

"Well, yeah, but we eat regular people food every weekend, and for three weeks when we went into lockdown. We eat lots of chili and spaghetti, all vegetarian, of course. Esok bakes breads to die for." He looked content and proud as he said, "This is my room. They're all the same."

George poked his head around the door and nodded. "Not bad. Private, eh?"

"Yeah, and quiet. These walls are solid. Come on, I'll show you the best part." Josh led George to the basement stairs. "So, do you hibernate?"

"Sort of." George paused until they both got down the stairs, awkwardly hunching his broad shoulders to make it through the narrow hallway. "I mean I had a nice long sleep once you left, maybe a few nights. After that, I mostly ate and worked out." His eyes took in the room. "Whoa! This is sweet! You use this stuff?" He waved his hands towards the weights and boxing ring.

"What do you mean, do I use it?" Josh feigned hurt feelings as he made a fist to show off his biceps.

"No, I mean, obviously you do." George nodded his appreciation at Josh's biceps. "Not bad! What else?"

Josh finished the tour of the facility and then led George back up to the great room.

George put his hand on Josh's shoulder to stop him and then asked quietly, "You find any babes in these parts?"

Josh bit his lower lip, lowered his voice, and leaned in to admit, "Yeah, a few. One is kind of a favorite of our lodge leader. Gotta behave."

Of course, Rodan chose that moment to turn the corner with George's tea. He handed it over and said, "Come on in and relax." He led the way to the chairs grouped by the windows. "What's this? You gotta behave, Josh?" Rodan teased. Turning to George he said,

"Don't worry about this kid, he's settling in just fine. Keeps his nose clean, does his chores, no complaints."

"Good, that's good." George nodded as he raised the tea to his nose. "This is your brew? I've had it before, very good, healthy. Thanks."

"Yep. It's mine." Rodan settled back into his chair and crossed an ankle on a knee, trying to look relaxed, but not succeeding. He radiated nervous energy and Josh wondered why. "So, what brings you to these parts?"

"Oh, this and that. Wanted to check on my little buddy here. There's another matter Hesta called me in about, as well. I do some security work, okay? Something about a diseased elk carcass? Hesta said you found it."

"That's right. Why?" Rodan frowned.

Josh studied Rodan's unusual nervous posture. *What's gotten into him? Does he think George was called in for backup? Is Rodan hiding something?*

"Are you trying to figure out where it disappeared to?" Josh asked, because he wanted to know, as well, especially after hearing Sarah and Anton discuss the illnesses at the grade school.

George leaned forward, staring into his cup, elbows on his knees. He weighed his words. Josh had never seen him do that before. Would George hide things from him? George squinted at Rodan. "Among other things," he said. The phrase hung in the air like a warning. Rodan shifted in his seat. George took another sip and then put his mug down, moving as if to stand up. "You mind if I take a walk with my little pal here? Just for old times' sake?" A chill ran up Josh's back.

Rodan sighed, obviously he would get no more information out of George. "Sure, knock yourself out. You got your tour?"

"Yep, nice place you got here," George confirmed. "I mean, that lower level is impressive." He looked at Josh. "You could have done worse, eh, squirt?"

"Yeah, it's not bad," Josh admitted. He kept to himself the fact that while he liked having guy pals around all the time, he still missed his family. He wasn't a kid anymore, and with George standing a full head taller next to him, Josh already struggled to project a manly presence.

"Let's take a walk," George said, heading towards the front door. "Come on."

George led them away from the building for several yards and Josh felt a keen sense of déjà vu. "We need to talk, but not here. Let's transform and put some distance between us and the lodge. You know anywhere private?"

Josh thought about that. Up on the mesa top they could see anyone approaching. Maybe if they didn't want to be heard, they should head to the stream, which ran loud and fast with snowmelt. "No place is truly private around here," he said. "However, I know a place where we won't be heard."

"Good enough." His friend nodded. "Is it far?"

"Maybe a ten-minute run?"

"Perfect." George paused. "I'm going as a bear, get some exercise. You lead."

"Sure thing." Josh transformed and ran at full gallop, testing George's speed. He reached the spot and turned to watch as George thundered through the sagebrush towards him. George didn't do subtle or quiet. His big paws kicked up rocks as he stretched into his own version of a freight train. He slowed in front of Josh, looked around, and nodded his approval. They both turned back into humans and settled down on a log near the rushing stream. Josh waited for George to speak.

"It's about your dad," George started.

"Okay," Josh said, drawing out the last syllable as a question.

"I don't know how much they've told you around here."

"A little."

"Did you know he was in a work facility?"

"Uh huh, but it was more like a prison, right? Wait, was?"

"Right, he broke out." George let that hang in the air as he watched Josh's face. "You knew that, didn't you?"

"Well, I heard his tracker had failed. It was pretty obvious. Are you here to protect me or something?" Josh's eyes widened as it hit him. His voice climbed into a higher register. "You think he's coming here, for me, don't you!"

George raised both hands. "Calm down! Yes, I'm here for you. Your dad left a trail of bodies behind when he broke out. He's not a good guy. In fact, we suspect he had something to do with that carcass disappearing," George explained. "We, I mean the council, thinks he's posing as a hunter with his pals from the ag facility. We suspect they sold the meat at bargain prices to a school that's trying to keep their costs down. We think he's hanging out around here because he wants to talk to you, see you, I don't know, maybe recruit you."

"Recruit? For what?"

George cocked his head, then shrugged. "I don't know, for his evil, nefarious gang of killers! For his princeling, his heir. What do you think? Why else would he hang around here?"

"Man." Josh let that word hang in the air, aware of the irony of it. He shook his head and let out a big sigh. All he needed, just when he had started to win some trust from his fellow Netahs, would be for his dad to come along and mess it all up.

"What, you haven't seen him, have you?" George asked.

Josh groaned. "How would I know? I can't tell one elk from another around here as it is. He could be anyone, but they'd know him, right?"

"Yes, unless someone from here is working with him."

"Aw jeez." Josh dropped his head into his hands. *It's Arman, that's who he's here for. They're in this together, I just know it, but I have no proof, so shut up! Don't be stupid, calm down!* He rubbed his scalp furiously. That explained why George wanted to be somewhere private. "Could this get any more messed up?" Josh stood up and paced. "I don't think so. Nope, no way. I'm trying to act normal. I'm still learning what that means. I do everything I can to gain trust and acceptance. Now this. I . . ." He'd been talking with his hands, which he raised in surrender and then dropped in frustration, unable to continue.

"Listen, we can handle this. I got you," George urged. He reached out and grabbed Josh's arm.

Josh studied the ground, his head hanging, shoulders drooping.

George spoke quietly, "Listen, I trust you. The council trusts you. You want to show everyone else what I see? I got a job for you."

Josh looked into his friend's eyes. Did he see hope, danger, what? He waited.

"We have to catch him. You can help."

Josh gasped and looked wildly around, as if trying to find an escape route. He pulled away from George's grip and paced again. His head said no, but words failed him.

"Look, Josh, I know it sounds crazy, but it could work," George continued, now pacing with Josh. "We think he's here to meet you, to find you, to talk if nothing else."

"Nothing else? You mean, like he won't try to turn me into his evil sidekick? He poisons kids, you suspect, and now you want me to be the bait to catch him?"

"You'll have an army to protect you."

"An army? And he won't notice that at all." Josh let that statement drip with sarcasm.

"We know how to blend in, disappear in our surroundings. You know how to, as well, although you could use more practice."

Josh stopped. What did George mean by that? "Practice? What are you talking about?"

"Nothing. Forget I said that. It doesn't matter." George shook it off, studying his boot toes.

Josh stood his ground. "If you're trying to say something, just say it. Don't beat around the bush. When did I not hide well enough, in your opinion?" *Did George see me watching my parents? How long has he been hanging around here? Will he tell the others?*

George hesitated before he began again with a big sigh. "Look, we, the council, thinks there's a co-conspirator inside the lodge."

"Conspirator working with . . . ?" Josh thought maybe, just once, he'd be let in on a secret.

"Your dad and his pals. A sympathizer, at least. We don't know who it is."

Josh nodded, as it dawned on him that maybe George needed his own inside spy. Wait, George needed him? This could be fun. If the council suspected someone at the lodge worked with his dad, who could it be? *This is my chance to take down Arman! He's involved, I just know it!* George's hint that he could practice blending in might mean he'd seen Josh near his parents, but it appeared George was ready to keep that to himself. "You convinced Hesta to get me on the team?"

George paused then looked Josh in the eye. "Look, I'm not completely going along with their program as it is. The council wanted to keep you in the dark. I didn't think that was fair to you. I'm trying to help, to protect you, and to get this guy caught and . . ." He didn't finish his sentence.

"Killed, erased?" Josh said quietly, controlling his voice. "Is that what they'll do?"

"Yes, Josh. I'm not going to lie to you. I think so, yes. This is even more serious than before. This is murder."

Josh gulped. "Murder?"

George nodded. "Yep, six guards and three ag workers. The security system at the facility was hacked."

Josh breathed, realizing he had held his breath. He said, "I'll do it," before he could change his mind.

George patted Josh on the shoulder, pulling him into a side hug. "Good man. Okay, so here's what's gonna happen. You go back to the lodge, act normal." Josh snorted. "I know, what's that, right? Just act. Tell the guys you and I are going on an overnight camping trip for old times' sake." *So, we are sneaking around behind Hesta and Rodan's back!* "Meet me outside your lodge door after dinner. I have stuff to do. We have a plan; we just need you to do your part." George turned towards the lodge.

We who? "Like dodge a sympathizer and dangle from the hook, looking all innocent?"

"Right." George hesitated. "Speaking of which, no, never mind. I'll eat later. I've got to get things rolling." He took both of Josh's arms and studied his face. Josh studied George's shirt buttons. "You're sure about this? You have any questions?"

Josh shook his head, unwilling to articulate the scary and exciting reasons for his speeding heart rate. He might either cry or laugh out loud. He shook his head slowly and with determination. "I . . ."

"It's a lot to take in, I get it," George spoke with a soothing voice, calm and quiet. "Do you want to sleep on it? Think it over?"

"I don't think I'll sleep until this is all over." Josh shook his head slowly. "I won't be able to. I want . . ."

George pulled him down to sit on the log again. "What? What do you want? Has anyone asked you that recently?"

Josh bit his lower lip. *Stay in control! Be strong!*

"You look like you might be a bit overwhelmed," George said.

Josh frowned, still not looking George in the eye. *Definitely.*

"But I trust you," Josh said. "And yes, the council asked me what I wanted after I helped with the littles. I asked to join a Netah elk herd. They let me. They did admit to a situation in Wyoming, but never elaborated." Josh saw pieces of the puzzle fly into place. *Am I feeling an adrenalin rush at the thought of meeting my dad? Whatever, use it! Embrace it!*

With resolve Josh looked George square in the eyes, where he saw concern. Josh said, "Thanks for asking, George. Look, I'm in. I will do whatever you need me to do. Let's get it over with." He reached over and put his hand on George's shoulder.

George rested his hand on top of Josh's and nodded. "You got it." He stood up and turned into a bear. "Come on, let's get you back to your lodge." Josh transformed, and they walked together in silence until they spotted the lodge's door. "See you out here in a couple of hours. Don't be late." George took off and soon disappeared into the night.

"Yes, sir!" Josh gave him a mock salute. He pushed open the door to the lodge, his thoughts turning to the possibility of a spy working with his dad. That was certainly a complication and a concern.

Josh told Rodan he'd be out with George that night. Rodan asked no questions, which was so weird it made Josh wonder if Rodan might be the spy.

Tomo joined Josh in the great room after they'd all eaten. Food was getting scarce outside, so they supplemented it with some buttered bread and apples most nights.

Rodan made an announcement once everyone settled down inside. "Looks to me like we need to start eating inside more. What do you say we make it Tuesday, Thursday, and Sunday nights? You guys in favor?"

Mako said, "Sure thing. We should stock up from the ag facility, though, our stores are getting low. I can handle that if you want."

"Good idea," Haiman said. "I'll adjust the chore chart."

Arman said, "Give me extra clean-up duties. I don't like cooking."

Esok said, "That's one way to get you to clean your fingernails!" The others laughed as they inspected their own nails. Esok continued, "I'll take Arman's cooking times."

Rodan nodded approval. "That's settled then. Mako, stock us up tomorrow and we can eat inside tomorrow night. It will be good for all of us. Thanks."

While the others drifted off to their various evening activities, Tomo turned to Josh. "So, tell me about you and the bear. How'd you meet? What's he like?"

Josh, trying to keep it light, told Tomo about the cave. "I had just turned into an elk, had no idea how to do it or control it, you know?"

"Sure, okay."

The others turned back, looking through kitchen cupboards and drawers, milling around nearby, pretending not to listen, but they were quieter than usual. They didn't fool Josh. He could act cool. *Boy wonder, that's me, a hero who helped bring down his evil father. Just you watch.* He continued, "So George scrambled to get me away from school, and we climbed above the tree line to a cave he knew. By then, I was an elk. It just happened. I also couldn't talk very well, never having talked with an elk mouth! Anyway, it was stupidly cold, and I couldn't go into the cave."

"Why?" Tomo asked.

Josh pointed to his head and said, "Antlers." Josh heard snorts from the others.

"That time of year?" Tomo sounded doubtful. "You should have lost them in the fall. Maybe your Netah side got confused because it had just begun to manifest itself? Anyway, what'd you do?" Tomo had gotten caught up in the story.

"I went to sleep outside on the hard, rocky ground. I found a spot behind the rocks, which cut the wind. I realized I'd be fine, because of my nice warm fur. But then I fell asleep and when I woke up in the middle of the night, I had transformed into a naked human."

"Shit." Tomo sat forward, his usually wild hair spiking in all directions as he ran his fingers through it, a nervous tic Josh had noticed before.

"Right. Well, of course, I could then crawl into the cave, which I did, and got as close to the bear, George, I mean, as possible. I eventually stopped shivering and fell back to sleep."

"Smart." Tomo sounded impressed, he pushed on the arms of his chair to tuck his feet under him.

"I guess, but I had no idea how to change. In the morning I woke up cold again. George had disappeared and there I was—still human and naked."

By then, all the guys had moved closer to listen, pulling up chairs. Josh glanced at them, enjoying the attention. He liked the role of a storyteller. "Well, I can't stay inside and freeze to death, so out I go. No sign of George. I'm all alone on the top of a mountain in a bitter wind, standing there completely naked. First, I crouch down and make myself as small as I can, hugging my knees into my chest, my back to the rocks of the cave. There's a little warmth coming off the rocks, probably from the sun, and I'm out of the wind mostly. My teeth are chattering, by toes numb. Next thing I know a big black raven flies in out of nowhere. She transforms into this beautiful goth chick I know from school and drops a package at my feet. It's, like, ski gear. I'm saved."

"Who was the girl?" Esok asked, his round face looking rounder because his eyes were nearly popping out of his head.

Josh shrugged, trying to look nonchalant as he dropped a big name. "None other than Crawley. You know her?"

"The one on the council?" Haiman asked, one eyebrow rising towards his hairline.

"The same."

"Wow, they pulled out all the stops to help you, didn't they?" Rodan shifted in his chair.

"I guess. What did I know? The day before I had just been a high school kid with a couple itchy patches on his head." Josh scratched his head for effect. The others laughed.

Tomo asked, "Did the bear come back?"

"Yeah, and he stayed. George didn't leave until I knew how to transform."

Haiman frowned as he tried to picture that. "How long did that take?"

"Most of the fall. First, we figured out that if they scared me, I'd transform. So, George and the others spent a lot of time jumping out of bushes, pushing rocks down mountains at me, that sort of thing."

"What others?" Esok asked, stroking his trim mustache.

"Oh, we were joined by my friend Fern, she's a fox." The guys erupted in catcalls. "No, I mean, really, the animal, a Netah, of course. And Rose came along." More whoops and comments circled the room.

"You're in the woods with two dames?" Mako's eyes crinkled and he stroked his peppery beard. "And you're trying to tell us nothing happened?"

"This kid? He wouldn't know where to start!" Arman sneered, his back to the gang, his arms crossed, as if he wasn't listening as hard as the others.

"Right?" Rodan gave Arman a playful shove.

"Yeah, but they're a fox and a skunk!" Josh rolled with it. "It's not like we could make out or anything." More whoops. Josh laughed sheepishly. "Crawley showed up now and then, too."

"Three girls!" Haiman howled, throwing back his head. Josh had never seen the guys having so much fun. He didn't mind that it was at his expense.

"Why didn't they get one of us to help? We could have shown you how to change," Haiman asked.

"Like we'd know anything about training a halfling," Arman muttered.

"Exactly." Josh pointed at Arman and at his own nose. "They said that since I was a halfling, I had to figure it out on my own."

"How did you figure it out, then?" Tomo tried to keep him on track.

"I thought about something I really liked as a human. I had to be quiet and concentrate, and then, pop, I'd be human."

"What was it?" Esok asked.

"Hamburgers."

"Figures," said Rodan.

"Maybe, except as a human I didn't eat meat. It worked, anyway."

"What did you think about to become an elk?" Esok asked.

"Oh, you'll love this," Josh said, pausing just long enough to get everyone's attention for the punch line. "Lichen."

"What?!" The guys roared.

Rodan shook his head as he left. "He's likin' the lichen."

The others groaned at Rodan's pun, which ended story time. Esok chuckled to himself as he passed. Mako said, "Good story, kid," and patted his shoulder on his way past. Arman muttered something under his breath and rolled his eyes. Josh soon had the room to himself. He lingered a few minutes and then went outside and waited for George.

Josh blew a series of misty breath clouds, trying for rings. He took in the fresh scents of cedars and listened to the trickle of water from the lodge overhang. His head cleared as he considered the job ahead, proud that he'd been asked to help, but anxious at the obvious danger.

CHAPTER 12

Camping Trip

As George and Josh left the Netah village, their warm coats easily fought off the bitter cold air pouring down off the snowcapped mountains. George led the way and Josh kept his chin down and followed. They couldn't talk over the howl of the wind. Josh lost track of time and distance.

Eventually they arrived at a campground hidden in a deep ravine surrounded by rock walls that cut the wind at ground level. The clouds gave way to a nearly full moon and a riot of stars. Shadows danced on the canyon's forty-foot rock walls, lit by the flames of several campfires. A fast steel-gray river roared behind a line of gnarled cottonwoods. Several tents surrounded a clearing, and people gathered in small friendly groups, talking and laughing.

George transformed into a human and walked towards the largest campfire, with Josh close behind. Several people rose to their feet as they approached the group. "George, you made it," one of them called out. "And this is Josh?"

"Howie, great to see you." George shook his hand. "Hi, Stella. How're the kids?"

Stella nodded and gave Josh a friendly smile. Josh shook hands with each of them. Howie said, "Josh, welcome to our little gathering. You ready to party?"

"Party? Looks like you guys started without us." Josh snorted, looking to George for an explanation.

George waved Josh to an empty chair and sat down next to him. "Sorry we couldn't talk on the way over with that wind in our ears. Let me bring you up to speed. First, Stella is my sister. Howie is Stella's husband."

Josh raised his eyebrows and then nodded at them.

"Hi, Josh," Stella said. "I'm his big sister."

"Except you're smaller," George corrected her. They both chuckled.

George nodded. "Yes, my older sister." He paused, knowing she'd be tempted to swat at his shoulder, which he dodged and said, "Anyway, we are going to make this little campground our home for a bit. We plan to be loud, with music blasting and the occasional mock fight breaking out so it looks like we're drunk, so don't be alarmed. We're having a family reunion. Speaking of which," he raised his voice and called loudly over his shoulder, "Where's the beer?" He winked at Josh.

Howie reached into a cooler at his side and tossed a can to George, who opened it to much fanfare as it erupted with foam. Howie waved one at Josh who nodded that he'd take one, too, and another came sailing through the air to him. That performance earned more loud cheers and pretend drunken laughter. Josh's can erupted with foam when opened, which caused more cheering.

After a few long pulls on their drinks, George leaned over and said quietly, "Careful, little buddy. I know you're underage. Have you had beer before?"

"Sure, my dad would give me one when we went camping," Josh said. "But this is only ginger beer, so don't worry about me."

"That's from a Netah brewer I know personally," George laughed. "You'll never taste anything else like it." He looked around the circle. "Hear that, Howie? Josh likes your beer." Howie raised his can and they all cheered again. It appeared they had agreed to cheer loudly no matter what was said. George continued more quietly to Howie, "Anything happening yet?"

Stella laughed ecstatically, playing her drunken part. If Josh hadn't been warned, he'd think she was crazy. Howie leaned in and spoke quietly. "A small herd of elk has been hanging around on the rim of this canyon for the last couple of days. Our scouts reported that they started to move down into the valley this evening. They should be wandering in any minute. Glad you got here in time. The real party is about to begin."

"Right, and if they were mere elk," George said quietly to Josh, "they'd be going away from our noise. Looks like he's taking the bait." George winked at Josh before he said to Howie, "Okay, time to turn up the volume."

Howie nodded and went into a nearby tent, returning with a boom box. He fiddled with the controls a moment and then a guitar riff screamed out into the valley, bouncing back off the rock walls. Whoops and yells rose from the other campsites, as if that had been a signal. More people joined the big campfire, carrying chairs and beers, some wrapped in blankets, some tripping and laughing. Snacks were dumped on the nearby picnic table and next thing Josh knew, Stella had his hand and swung him into a pretend drunken dance.

Josh hoped they were acting. Obviously, you don't set up an ambush and then everyone gets drunk. They were convincing. One guy tripped over something and fell into another guy, who threw a punch after he steadied himself. Josh was glad he'd been warned. He took a final swig from his can. He could act, too. Josh flattened the can on his thigh and threw it into the fire just like the others were doing.

Hunger got the best of him and the sweet ginger beer on an empty stomach gave him a quick sugar buzz. He surveyed the snack table. A bag of barbeque chips yelled his name. He hadn't had those for so very long. He grabbed the bag and collapsed into a chair. The party raged on and his ears rang from the noise. He binge-ate the chip bag empty and then looked around for the cooler full of drinks. While he had his head down over the cooler, he sensed a change ripple through the crowd. They still partied, but the laughter and dancing became more subdued. Josh straightened slowly, cautiously, letting his eyes scan the faces for clues about what had changed.

He watched one woman twirl away from her dancing partner and weave drunkenly out of the light of the campfire. She approached a group of men walking towards them; five, no six men, all smiling like they were ready to party.

One stepped to the front and shook hands with the lady who had danced her way over to him and pretended she wanted him to join her. He shook his head, laughing and spoke. Josh couldn't hear what he said but watched her reaction. The woman shrugged, and then danced over to lean against George, who whispered to Josh, "This is it, stay on your toes!"

Josh hung back, as he became suspicious. Could the man in front be his Netah dad? The guy had scanned the partiers and when he saw Josh, his eyes never moved away. The guy stood taller than anyone else there and had broad shoulders like a lumberjack. He wore camouflage like everyone else. His full black beard made him look even bigger. If Josh hadn't been so afraid, he might have been impressed. His palms were damp, his heart in his throat, and his flight instincts screamed.

His stomach roiled when the guy stared at him longer than normal, confirming his suspicions. Josh knew there was no turning back. He grabbed a six-pack from the cooler and waved it towards the newcomers. George said quietly, "Let me do the talking. Good idea, the beer, I mean."

George stepped forward and held out his hand to the lead man. Josh stayed put. Two of the others left the pack and walked towards Josh, eyeing the beer. Josh remained still, letting the first guy come towards him, breaking a can out of the plastic holder. He hadn't thought to use the cans as weapons, but it could work as a distraction. *A can in the hand is worth one in the basket. That's the saying, right?* Josh snorted to himself and decided to toss the beer to the guy rather than let him get any closer. In the meantime, Josh could see movement behind the group. Men were stepping out from behind trees and walking forward with great stealth.

This is it! What do I do? What do I do?

Stella grabbed him by the hand and gently pulled him among the dancers, who absorbed him into the center of their circle. Josh could barely see over Stella's shoulder; she was taller than him and wore a big puffy coat. She draped her arms over his shoulders and moved slowly to the music, mimicking sweethearts. Josh played along, his hands on her waist, glancing at Howie. Howie winked back as he handed out beers to the newcomers, trying to keep them distracted while the others approached from behind. Josh's blood beat so loud in his ears he could barely make out what anyone said, especially with the music still blasting through the canyon. Did he hear something about a broken-down truck and borrowing a phone?

Josh saw one of the newcomers suddenly freeze in place as a thick metal collar with blinking lights was clamped on his neck. The man looked terrified. He hadn't made a sound. Behind him stood others, also frozen in place. Before the lead man noticed the others, Howie and George suddenly grabbed him by both arms and they scuffled. Between the two of them, they could not contain the man. Josh watched in horror as the man spun out of their grasp and instantly transformed into a massive elk. George and Howie transformed, as well, but their bear brawn and claws were no match for the elk's hooves.

The circle of people surrounding Josh suddenly dissolved as they transformed into various animals and joined the fray. Josh heard the growling scream of a mountain lion as it leapt onto the elk's back and sank its teeth into the elk's neck. The elk bucked and bugled, trying to toss the large cat.

Suddenly ropes sang through the air and Josh felt gentle hands pull him further away from the fight. The ropes lassoed the elk's legs and pulled them out from under him. The elk fell with a horrible thud. The lion kept its purchase until the elk stopped struggling.

"Noooo!" Josh yelled as he tried to shake off restraining hands. Stella had a hard grip on him and wouldn't let go. "They're killing him!" he screamed at her. Someone cut the music. The sudden silence was surreal.

Stella pulled Josh to face her, holding his shoulders she said, "Hush, he'll be fine." Josh strained to keep his eyes glued to the elk's face.

The elk grunted and struggled, but finally succumbed and said, "We could have done this peaceably. I only wanted to see my son." He yanked at the ropes, his chest heaving. "Remember me, Josh. I've never forgotten you."

The campground had gone ghostly quiet. Bile rose in Josh's throat. Anger and despair warred in his chest.

George said, "Okay, let's finish this. Load up the others." He made a circular motion over his head, and Josh watched as the other men were handcuffed. The collars lit their faces with an eerie green light. Josh wondered what the collars did. The men looked terrified and didn't struggle. It appeared they couldn't transform into animals. They all walked stiffly and meekly into the truck. *Did they want to be caught? Is my dad a monster and they were happy to get away from him?*

With the other men safely locked into the transport, George said, "Get up, Vehoe. You're goin' for a ride."

Vehoe? Why have I never heard his name before? Josh covered his mouth and turned away as the bag of chips threatened to make a sudden appearance on the scene.

Vehoe stood slowly and gingerly. The ropes were kept taut, several men held each. The lion remained in place, blood seeping from the wounds inflicted by its strong bite and claws. Vehoe kept his eyes on his son as they led him to the armored truck. Men opened the back end and lowered a ramp. Vehoe walked slowly up the ramp, struggling against his ropes, testing their strength. He lowered his head to walk in. At the last moment, the lion released its mouth from Vehoe's neck and jumped aside as others moved to close the door.

It all happened so fast Josh couldn't believe it. Vehoe became a man, battered and bloody, but a massive, tall, and very muscular man even so. He charged the doors with a raging roar, throwing the men who were pushing the doors closed several feet away with the force of his shoulder. He leapt to the ground and ran, turning once again into an elk, mid-leap. A shot rang out. Josh looked around frantically to find the shooter. Vehoe never hesitated. He disappeared into the trees and a loud splash made it clear he had made it to the river.

The campground erupted in chaos. Josh counted several bears, a wolf, the mountain lion, an eagle, and several otters. The eagle screeched as it veered over the trees. The otters scampered and splashed into the water. The wolf and mountain lion swept through the trees and disappeared, all racing after Vehoe. In what seemed like mere minutes, most of them returned as humans. They shook their heads. Howie approached George. "He hit the river as an elk and transformed. I didn't think he'd make it, but then he surfaced and swam away. The otters and eagle will track him."

George shook his head and looked around the scene. "I never said he was stupid. He took the only exit he could. He chose the river instead of scaling the sheer walls of this canyon. I thought he would avoid the river, swollen and frozen as it is, and this would be an effective trap, but I underestimated him."

"We all did," Howie said, clapping George on the shoulder.

"I thought I'd at least nicked him with my shot," George said as he tucked the dart gun into his vest. "At least we have his fellow escapees in custody. That's something to show for the day. Come on, let's strike camp and get out of here."

Josh slumped into a camp chair. Stella draped a blanket over him and said, "I'm sorry you had to see that, Josh."

He shrugged. "It's what I signed up for." They sat in silence, watching as people begin to disassemble the camp, collapsing tents, sloshing water over fires that erupted into columns of steam. Josh asked, "What happens now?"

Stella shook her head and sighed. "I guess we have to try again. Your dad is very smart, but our agents are smarter. He won't be able to completely disappear. We'll find him again."

"Or he'll find me again. Will I be safe in the valley? Will I put the other Netahs in danger?"

Stella tilted her head, considering this thought. "I like that your first thought is for the safety of your community." She patted his arm and said, "You ask me, you go back. You're still safest there, especially if we increase security. You'll be all right. It's not up to me, though. The council will decide."

Josh needed to move, to do something. "Hey, can I help clean this all up?"

"Sit tight a moment. I want to talk to George." Stella patted him on the knee and walked over to her brother.

"You're going to take Josh back?" she asked.

"Yep. You got this?" George indicated the packing up that was going on all around them.

"Sure, we'll be gone within an hour. You two had a long day. Why don't you take one of the trucks back? Josh looks exhausted. Plus, I think it would be safer." She raised her eyebrows, inquiring.

"Good idea," George said, pulling his sister in for a hug. "See you soon, sis." Stella handed him a set of car keys.

George walked towards a pickup, calling over his shoulder, "Come on, buckaroo. We're taking the wheels back."

Josh rolled himself out of the chair with some difficulty and then climbed into the passenger seat. The truck looked like a beater, maybe built in the 1950s, mostly rust on the outside, but a spaceship on the inside. "Whoa! This looks like Hesta's truck. Are all your trucks like this?" He reached towards a screen on the dashboard, thinking he could listen to some music.

George swiped his hand away. "Don't touch anything. That's a thingamajiggy."

Josh cracked up and pointed to another screen. "That's what, a doohickey?" he asked. "Where's the radio?"

"Like there's a signal down here? Forget it." George pushed a button and the truck shuddered but made no noise. George tapped the dim screen and steered them slowly onto a dirt two-track.

Josh heard a soft whine, but nothing more. "Is this thing electric or something?"

"Or something," George chuckled.

"Why aren't you turning on the headlights?" Josh asked, worried.

"You know what secrecy means, right?" George joked as he reached over his head and pulled down a set of night goggles from a hook. "There's another set over your head. Help yourself." As Josh fitted them over his eyes, he felt the acceleration push him into his seat as a belt whirred over his chest and lap and clicked into a lock on the seat. "Hang on, little buddy. We've got a bumpy ride for a while, then it'll be boring as he . . . eck." He sounded gleeful, and Josh saw a wide grin on his friend's face.

Bumpy ride? What an understatement! The road was a series of boulder-strewn switchbacks, steep cliffs, loose gravel washed out in deep gullies, and blind curves where the ground suddenly fell away, and it felt like they were about to go airborne. George leaned forward in deep concentration as Josh clutched the edge of his seat and a bar over the door, bouncing and tossing and breathing hard. When they finally hit a gravel road, he slumped back against the headrest.

"Bumpy? You call that bumpy?" Josh laughed with relief. "That was like the best roller coaster ride ever!"

"Yep, bumpy." George glanced over at Josh. "You okay? You didn't pee your pants or anything, did you?"

Josh snorted and took a breath, realizing he'd been holding it. His stomach felt a little woozy. "Nah, I'm fine."

"I have to admit, I put this baby through its paces, testing it. It's got several recent upgrades. Pretty impressive, right?" George nodded his approval, his eyes on the road as he relaxed against his seat.

Josh grinned and nodded slowly, taking in the scene through the truck windows. The night goggles turned the landscape an eerie green. There was no place for wildlife to hide. "How long will it take to get back?" he asked.

"Not long." George looked at his passenger. "You want to talk about anything?"

Josh thought about that and then asked, "You going to be hanging around?"

"You bet. I'm your bodyguard." George gave Josh a playful shoulder shove.

"Lucky you." Josh snorted. The wind had died, and now clouds covered the moon and stars. Even though Josh knew that the landscape was dry and scrubby, the goggles turned his view green and freaked him out. He took the goggles off. His eyelids were heavy. "In that case, it can wait," Josh said, replacing them on their hook.

"You got it," George said, and he tapped the screen to pull up some quiet flute music. Josh woke when George pulled the truck into the valley garage. They walked to the lodge in silence. The valley felt warmer and filled with a waiting stillness.

As they approached the lodge entrance, George stopped Josh. "You can't tell anyone what just happened. I should have worked this out with you before we got back here, but you fell asleep and I figured you really needed that shut-eye. We have to pretend nothing happened until we find out who he's working with on the inside. Let me do the talking and follow my lead, okay?"

CHAPTER 13

Netah Market and a Drone

George walked Josh into the lodge. Only Rodan and Haiman were in the great hall, sitting together in conversation. Rodan got up and came over. He held out his hand to George and said, "You're back? What happened? I thought you two were staying out overnight?"

Josh yawned dramatically while George answered. "We got to our spot and it was full of people having a loud party! We stayed and had a beer with them, then decided we'd never get any sleep if we stuck around. This kid needs his beauty rest! He's a growing boy!" That got a chuckle. Josh looked sheepish and enhanced his tired act by stretching dramatically.

"Well," Rodan answered, "looks like you wore Josh out. Go ahead, hit the hay, Josh. I'll walk your friend out."

Josh looked to George for affirmation. A small nod meant "go ahead" so Josh turned towards his room. Waving over his shoulder he said, "'Night, guys."

He could hear them exchange social niceties, then the lodge door shut, and the place returned to silence.

Josh didn't feel tired; in fact, he was jazzed. Maybe the nap in the truck had taken the edge off. He considered taking a nice long sauna and shower, but it might blow their story about him being so tired. Instead, he threw himself on his bed and pulled out his books. The words did not register in his brain; he set the book aside. Since an exhausted kid would have his light out by now, he pulled off his clothes and turned off the light.

He rolled onto his stomach to peer out his window and see if anything moved. He let his eyes glaze over so they could become unfocused to catch any movement. Nothing moved. Had he ever sat and looked out his window like this before? Nope. Did he know what all those shapes out there were? Nope. Did that one on the far right just move a little? Now he focused. What he thought had been a medium-sized cedar had just fallen over and begun to move across his line of vision. It had a bear shape and movements. It took up a new position on the left side of his window's view. Wow, the security detail was there and alert. They also realized his dad could be there by now. Josh relaxed.

He wished he and George had worked out signals to communicate.

Josh watched a little longer, but the lack of any movement or change finally lulled him to sleep. He curled up under his blanket and drifted off.

Before the sun came up, Josh woke to the sound of loud activity in the great hall. Josh rubbed the sleep out of his eyes as he entered the hall. "What's going on?" he asked.

He heard Tomo ask Rodan, "Do you think they're bears or Netahs? Why do you think they're here?"

Rodan frowned as he considered the possibilities. Josh knew Rodan shouldn't know about the escaped birth dad, but he did know George. Rodan answered, "You guys met George yesterday, right? Maybe these are his friends. Or maybe they're just bears."

"Should we be worried about them moving around our valley?" Esok asked. "I mean, I'm supposed to go to market this morning.

Will they be nosing around my picnic basket?" He winked at Josh, who grinned at Esok's reference to Yogi Bear.

"If they are animals, that's possible," Rodan answered.

"So that's how we'll figure it out. Anyone up to coming with me?" Esok sounded like he didn't like the idea of walking around among the bears by himself.

Josh poured himself a mug of hot water and dumped a spoonful of tea into in before asking, "Has anyone here been attacked by a bear before?" No one answered. Josh didn't know whether that meant yes and they didn't want to discuss it, or no but they were still wary. He said, "I'll go, Esok. I want to see how the market works and where it's held. Haven't been before."

They both looked to Rodan for approval, and he nodded his head. Josh took his tea over to sit next to Esok. "Okay, so tell me, do you go as humans or elk? How far is it? Do I need to bundle up?"

"Of course we go as humans." Esok rolled his eyes. "Otherwise, how are we going to carry things? It's maybe a mile away, and so yes, bundle up."

"Okay, when do we leave?"

"Sooner the better. I'll go check our surplus and see what we can use to trade. Meet me by the door in maybe ten minutes, okay?"

"Yeah, sure." That gave Josh no time for breakfast, but he was starving. He'd had nothing to eat since yesterday morning, except for that bag of chips. He grabbed an apple and broke off a chunk of bread, then returned to his room to bundle up.

As Josh bundled up in a puffy jacket, hat and gloves, Esok came down the hall carrying two large backpacks. "Here you go. Think you can carry that?" he asked Josh as he handed one over.

Josh pulled it on, grunted under the weight, but stood tall and strong, determined to be useful. "Got it," he said. They left the lodge and started walking. The sun was merely a glow on the horizon. Josh realized he rarely went outside this early. Esok's long legs left Josh behind in minutes. The effort to keep up made it impossible for Josh to talk. They didn't seem to be taking a straight path. Esok huffed and made a turn. When Josh caught up to the spot, he saw a bear curled up, asleep behind a rock at the turn. Esok's path swerved to avoid bears.

Josh caught movement out of the corner of his eyes. Other figures walked in pairs through the darkness. They were not elk or bears, but human. They all walked in the same direction. Josh followed Esok up to a thick stand of pines and disappeared. Josh followed closely and within several yards they entered a clearing. Several rows of trees created a visual wall hiding the clearing. People greeted each other as they spread out blankets in the near dark and displayed their surplus. To Josh, it didn't look like a market. It looked like what you rake up at the end of the fall from your lawn. There were bundles of dried grains, sacks of seeds, beans and dried fruits, and a wide assortment of whole dried plants, roots, tubers, and squashes.

Once they unloaded their packs, Esok and Josh walked along the line of blankets looking for things on their list. They soon had everything. Esok said, "Well, that was easy today. Sometimes it's harder, then you have to substitute. Come on, we can go sit by our stuff and wait to see if anyone else needs anything from our stash."

The way this trade commerce worked intrigued Josh. Esok had answered one of his questions. He asked, "So, if no one needs what's left, we take it back?"

"That's right," Esok said, settling down to the ground and crossing his legs to wait.

"We can't exactly leave it lying around out here. That would be wasteful."

Josh looked over what remained on their blanket and noticed that the crowd of people had thinned. "Isn't it suspicious to have all of us here in our human form?"

"Sure, but it's temporary, hidden, and that's why we do it before the sun comes up. Watch those two over by the red blanket." Esok indicated the two with his eyes.

The humans they watched were dressed the same as everyone else, in warm jackets and boots, beanies. He couldn't tell what made them different from the others. As Josh watched, they loaded their finds into two bags which they tied together. Then one turned into an elk and the human draped the bags across the elk's back like saddlebags. The two walked out of the clearing. "Now that makes sense. It has to be easier to carry things like that. Our backpacks won't work that way, though. Why don't we have saddlebags?"

"That's Ano and Eve. You met them, right?" Esok asked.

"Sure, but what does that matter?" Josh felt a little slow-headed and annoyed.

"They're not as big or strong as we are. It's a good solution for them. Pretty innovative, I think."

"Ah, okay, now I get it." Josh watched as a couple of the guys from the building lodge came over to see what they had left. He recognized Manny and Pehpe and gave them a sleepy grin.

"What ya got here, Josh?" Manny asked.

"Surplus, I guess."

Pehpe studied the blanket's contents. "Didn't we have onions on our list?"

Manny crouched next to the onions, sorting through them and picking up a couple. "These will do perfectly. How'd we miss them earlier?"

Pehpe grinned at Josh. "Hey, you coming to the site today? I can swing by and walk with you."

Josh nodded. "Yeah, that'd be great." He looked to Esok for instructions.

Esok nodded at him. "Okay, let's wrap up this stuff and head back. We all have work to do."

On the walk back Esok asked about Josh's new friends. Josh didn't mind talking about that. It distracted him from last night's thoughts about his dad. "Manny is the team leader of the guys making the clay bricks and tiles. Pehpe and I tried some designs and textures on some of the tiles. It was cool."

"What do you mean designs? How'd you make them?" Esok asked.

By the time they got to the lodge, Josh had told him everything he could remember. They carried their produce into the root cellar and put it all away. "Well, see you later, Esok," Josh said as he moved towards the door.

"Hey, thanks for coming along, Josh. I don't know why the bears freaked me out so much. Thanks for your company and help carrying stuff."

"Did something happen with you and a bear before?" Josh asked, concerned and surprised by Esok's admission.

"Well, yes, but I was just a little guy. Got a scar to show for it, see?" He pulled up his shirt and showed Josh.

Josh saw a barely noticeable pink mark. "Yep, I see it." He tried to sound impressed as they approached the entry door.

"Chuh, it's nothing. Come on, let's get out of here. Work to do!" Esok said. As they turned into elks, Josh glanced around surreptitiously to see if he could spot the bears. They were well hidden, or maybe they were off foraging for breakfast. Pehpe approached through the aspens.

At the work site, Kim met them. "Hi, fellas, you finally ready to present this morning?"

Josh and Pehpe turned into humans again and nodded.

"Okay, let's get started then." Kim led the way over to the tile area and they waited for everyone to gather. Haiman didn't come that day, and Josh remembered Haiman lived in the security lodge, not the construction one. Nohka was there.

Josh and Pehpe stood on either side of their row of decorated tiles. The others were already examining them. Manny got things started. "So, you all know that Josh joined our team last week. He and Pehpe tried some new ideas, but we never got to talk about them. I guess this is one example of why it's good to get a fresh set of eyes on a process from time to time. I'll let Josh explain."

"Thanks, Manny. Well as we were creating the tiles, I thought about where they'd go in the house. I assumed you'd glaze some for the bathroom, but most of the others would go on floors. I thought it would be safer if they had texture so they wouldn't be slippery, so I wanted to experiment with different things that could create a texture."

"How'd you make that one?" Eve asked, pointing to one.

"I rolled a pinecone across it."

Manny said, "Why don't you go down the line and tell us what you used on each."

After Josh and Pehpe got to the end of the row, the others voted on which ones they all liked the best. The one with twigs tied with the one Josh had inscribed with geometric shapes. They agreed Nohka should chose her favorites and decide where to put them in the house. That meant the decorative portion of tile work had to go on hold until she decided. Josh spent the rest of the day making and stacking the bricks that were used for interior walls.

Before he knew it, the sun approached the tops of the trees again and Pehpe came over to walk back to the lodges with him.

"Man," Josh said as they started walking. "I'm gonna spend an hour in the hot springs tonight. This job is tough. I'm sore all over!"

Pehpe laughed and nodded as they transformed into elks. They walked at a leisurely pace as a light snow began to fall. They stopped to eat whenever they found something tasty. Josh heard the buzzing fly again. He turned to Pehpe. "Is that the alarm?"

"Yep. Let's hold still and keep our eyes and ears open, in case they're nearby. Go ahead and keep eating. Wouldn't want to lead them to our lodges by accident!" The two Netahs occasionally flicked their ears to focus on other sounds. Josh picked up a motorized whirring. Quietly, he said, "I think it's a drone. Act elky in case it has a camera."

"Elky? Funny. Geez, that's just what we need. We can't hide from drones," Pehpe snorted. He lowered his body to the ground. Josh did, too. "Might as well take a load off. I'm beat. Nothing else we can do except act like tired elk."

Minutes later five elk raced past in the direction of the boundary fences. A couple of bears were moving in the same direction behind them, trying to be inconspicuous as they followed. Josh couldn't help wondering if they were chasing after his dad. He knew they expected him to show up in the valley. He couldn't say anything to Pehpe, no one was supposed to know. Then he realized if his dad were there, he wouldn't set off the sensors. He'd know how to get around them.

A drone rose above a clump of pines nearby and moved towards Pehpe and Josh. A red light blinked on it, helping it stand out against the evening sky. "Hold still!" Josh said, without moving his lips. "Pretend you don't know what it is."

"That's easy, 'cuz I don't," Pehpe snorted. "Oh, cool! Look at that!" He pointed with his nose and Josh followed his gaze. A large bird had materialized out of nowhere and circled above the drone.

"I've never seen an eagle around here before," Pehpe said.

"Whoa, what's it doing?" Josh squinted through the snow at the outline of the eagle against the sky.

"Can you see the white head?" Pehpe asked. "I think it's a bald eagle! Wait, what? What is it doing?" This was good entertainment.

The Netahs watched the eagle drop down with its legs outstretched towards the drone. With one swift movement, it grabbed one of the blades and wrenched it off. The drone dropped from the sky. The eagle dove after it and continued to dismantle the machine on the ground.

"What should we do? Is that eagle a Netah?" Josh asked, remembering the one he'd seen the night before, but playing innocent.

"I don't think so," Pehpe answered thoughtfully. "I never heard of any living around here, but you never know."

Minutes later the eagle hopped over to the Netahs. "Hi, guys," she said. "That was fun! It's okay, crisis averted. That drone's not going anywhere. I destroyed the camera, but I'm still going to take it up to about, oh I don't know," she gazed into the sky, "maybe 12,000 feet or so and drop it, just for fun. Might want to move on. I don't know how the wind will carry it, but wherever it lands, the debris field will be big! Bye, guys!" She hopped a few feet away then swung into the air, swooped over the remains of the drone, and hoisted it up with her. She caught a ride on a thermal and circled higher and higher until she was a tiny dot.

Josh asked, "You think it's safe to go to our lodges now?"

"I don't hear the alarm anymore, do you?" Pehpe asked.

"Nope."

"Then we can go. You know your way from here?" Pehpe asked.

Josh looked around and spotted their aspen grove. "It's just over there, right?"

"Yep. Okay, see ya tomorrow. Can't wait to tell the lodge what we just saw." Pehpe snorted. "That eagle is a Netah! It sounded like a girl, right? I wonder why she's here?" He took off running, kicking up little clouds of powdery snow with his hooves as he skirted the aspens and disappeared past them. Josh shook off the snow that had settled on his fur and decided a nice little jog would warm him back up and maybe help work out some of the kinks in his back from working that day. As he approached the lodge stone door, Tomo appeared. They entered together.

Tomo asked, "You know why the alarms went off?"

"Yeah, Pehpe and I saw a drone get attacked and dismantled by an eagle, a Netah eagle. We also saw like five elk running towards the boundary line and a couple of bears heading that way, too. I'm sure we'll hear about it." Josh rolled his shoulder. "I got a date with the hot springs. You coming?"

"Oh, definitely!" They hit the showers, the hot spring, then the sauna, where Tomo asked Josh about his day at the construction site. He told Josh about his own day spent dissecting a dead racoon, then they hit the showers one more time. Feeling better, they went back upstairs to wait for news.

When they returned to an empty great room, Tomo and Josh realized the others were probably still outside trying to find enough to eat. Josh had gotten used to the comfort of a hot meal three days a week, but wished it was more. Josh reluctantly left the lodge and began to search for more to eat. He'd learned to recognize most of the plants near the lodge and looked for them further away. As he munched his way down a hillside, he found others from the lodge. Since it's obviously impolite to talk while eating, it was a quiet group.

When they all entered the lodge later, Rodan reported about the alarm. "So, me and the crew," he looked meaningfully at the others who'd gone with him, "went to investigate the alarm. George and his crew joined us. We put on our conservation uniforms and drove out to the road, where we found a couple of kids standing there with a remote control in their hands, scanning the skies."

Haiman cut in, "They said they'd lost their drone, could they go find it?"

The guys laughed at that. "As if!" "Yeah, right!"

Rodan continued, "We informed them that this was a private reserve and we couldn't let them come in. We took down their names, phone numbers, addresses, and told them that if we found their drone, we'd let them know."

Esok said, "I thought to ask if their drone had a camera on it." He seemed very proud of his good idea.

"Yes." Rodan nodded approvingly. "They admitted it did."

"So then," Esok continued, "we had to inform them that we'd be confiscating it in that case. The area is protected, and therefore illegal to photograph."

Mako seemed annoyed. "That pushy girl wanted to know if this was a top-secret installation or something."

Arman added, "Right, so I said that if it was and we said so, we'd have to kill them instead of letting them go. That shut her up. They were back in their truck and speeding off in a cloud of dust before you could say jackalope!"

Josh asked, "Did anyone recognize them?"

"Not like we hang around with human kids, you know?" Arman snorted. "But they had a Colorado license plate." He turned to Rodan. "You think they were the same two kids who tried camping here a while back?"

Rodan nodded. "More than likely. I think they understand that it's not okay for them to come back, though. I don't think we'll be seeing them again."

Josh assumed it had been his friends Anton and Sarah and couldn't help but be impressed with their persistence. They were not giving up on him. And his new friend, Tomo, had kept their identity a secret. Josh realized Netahs had to be good at keeping secrets. He wondered if it would be the last he'd see of his old friends.

CHAPTER 14

Dialoguing

Anton and Sarah were not the only persistent ones in the neighborhood. The next day broke cold and clear, with a steady wind dropping the windchill into the negative digits. Haiman informed Josh that the build site would be closed because of the cold but invited him to come along on patrol. Josh agreed with some trepidation. After all, his dad was probably lurking around out there somewhere, but Haiman was a big guy, so Josh felt safe in his presence.

As the sun approached its highest point in the day, Haiman took a break to find something to eat. The two elk wandered away from each other. Josh mindlessly chewed on some seed heads when the shot rang out. At least he thought it sounded like a gun. His instincts were to freeze, but also to run. His heart raced. Within a few minutes he caught movement to his right and watched an elk approach. Josh still could barely recognize his fellow Netahs in their elk forms and he couldn't identify this one. Perhaps it was a regular elk. It didn't have Haiman's reddish coloring, and it was big.

"Hello, Josh," the elk said, obviously a Netah. Josh maybe recognized the voice? "It's me, Vehoe, your dad. Don't you recognize me?"

Josh couldn't speak. He shook his head; sure his voice would shake like his knees. *He is apparently stalking me!*

"You're not afraid of me, are you?" Vehoe asked, his voice soothing and smooth, almost oily as he continued to move towards Josh. "You heard what I said at the campground, didn't you? I told you I loved you. I-I-I would never hurt you, not ever." He ignored his own stutter.

"Okay . . . ? Then who did you just shoot? Where's Haiman?"

"Shoot?" Vehoe looked confused. "Oh tha-tha-that was just a dart gun, a tranquilizer dart. Don't worry, I wouldn't kill any of your new friends."

"Right, that makes me feel so much better," Josh jeered as he stepped back a few paces. "What do you want?"

"I want to meet you," Vehoe said, advancing still. "Once I saw you, and knew you were here, I had to come. I had to find out how you were doing and ask if I could do anything to help."

"Uh, you're a wanted man, I mean Netah. Because of you, I'm under constant suspicion already. I think you've helped enough, thanks, anyway."

"Don't be like that. You know I love your mother very much." His tone sounded friendly, conversational, like they were having a normal conversation. "Ne-ne-never stopped loving her, even when I realized I had to leave to protect her. I didn't know you were already on your way into this world."

Okay, so the excuses have already begun! Josh shouted angrily, "You didn't know Mom was pregnant? And how exactly am I supposed to know you loved her?" Josh paused, the words gathering up and pouring out like a floodgate just opened. "I never even knew you existed until a few months ago. I didn't know I would change into an elk, either, so thanks for the warning on that. Helpful." Josh decided to keep talking loudly and angrily in case anyone else lurked nearby. *Where's George when I need him?*

"No, I didn't know!" Vehoe interrupted, then almost apologetically he said, "I would never have left her."

The phrase "me thinks he protests too much" from something Shakespearean slipped through Josh's mind. As implausible as it sounded, Josh wanted what Vehoe said to be true. But Josh was too angry. With a great deal of sarcasm he said, "You would have stayed. And then what?" Josh's voice took on a taunting tone. "You'd go live somewhere in the wilderness, someplace where you could be a Netah and she could be a human, and no one from either of your worlds could find you?" Josh wanted to make the guy mad, make him lose it, make him feel the same fury.

"Um, yes." Vehoe dialed it down as Josh seethed.

"Uh," Josh raised his voice, his eyes searching frantically beyond Vehoe. "You were just going to live *happily ever after*, breaking all the Netah *rules*?" Josh wanted someone to hear them. Someone else from security must have heard the gunshot. Nothing moved nearby, not even a ground squirrel. Where were the bears? He didn't see a gun but realized Vehoe could have hidden it before approaching. Josh just wanted to get away or get this guy caught. He had to keep him talking. "You *knew* it was against the *rules*! Why is it their *number one rule?*"

His dad huffed and arched one eyebrow. "I don't know, to preserve the gene pool? To avoid creating halflings they couldn't control? It is a stupid rule."

"Oh, so it's my fault, because I'm the halfling? Not buying it. Something happened. What?" This is what they called dialoguing in the spy novels. If his dad, the bad guy, talked about himself, he wouldn't notice they were being surrounded by the cavalry. Josh struggled not to smile at that thought, even though he was kind of getting into it.

"The rule about being with humans was created centuries ago," Vehoe began. "Humans are smarter now, not as ready to believe in demons and de-de-devils. They don't label everyone who's different, or who's educated, a witch and then burn them at the stake. Nah, now we're just nerds."

Yes, he's dialoguing! Is he stuttering because he's nervous?

Vehoe turned into a human very slowly, ending with his smile.

It reminded Josh of Alice's Cheshire cat! It creeped him out. The smile went wide, toothy, and maybe a bit menacing. Josh's throat felt scratchy from yelling, so he lowered his voice. "Are you saying the Netahs were burned as witches? That doesn't make sense." Josh eased away, deciding he would remain an elk. He hoped it would give him a small advantage because he could probably run faster.

"Of course, it makes sense, especially when some of them were actually half man/half goat. It fed into people's fears just perfectly. Then there were the guys who had horns and tails." Vehoe stroked his chin thoughtfully. "Now those were the good ol' days, when we knew how to have fun, how to shake things up," he said quietly, shaking his head, like he had been there. "Where do you think people's image of the devil came from? Yeah, Netahs had a hand in it." Vehoe looked very satisfied with that as he sat on a boulder and watched Josh's reaction to this statement.

Josh noticed a stiffness in the way Vehoe held his shoulders and wondered if a dart had hit him, or maybe the mountain lion had injured him. The man's hair looked dirty and shaggy, not like the rest of the Netahs Josh knew.

Vehoe sniffed, ran his fingers through his hair, making it even more disheveled and asked, "You a student of history?"

"I guess, yeah, what they teach in school."

"Ah, yes, the schoolbook version." Vehoe shook that off. "Still, you know about Salem?"

"Uh huh, devils, witches and ghosts. Mass hysteria." Josh crossed his arms, waiting to hear the relevance, and wondering what

Vehoe would know about Halloween? How much had he lived among humans?

Vehoe said, "You want to know how we met?"

"*What?* My mom? *No!*" Josh yelled. "I do *not* want to know how you seduced my *mom.* Guh! Gross!" He shook his head and moved away as surreptitiously as possible. He couldn't keep this up much longer. Where did everyone go?

Vehoe put up his hands, placating. "Okay, okay. Don't get all squeamish on me. You don't like love stories, I get it."

"Love stories?!" Josh wanted to scream, but instead he let his voice drip with acid. "You think it's a love story when a father abandons his wife and child. That's your idea of love?"

Vehoe dropped his head and stared at his hands. Quietly he said, "I had no choice."

Josh raised his voice again, hating that he let the man get to him. "No, you *did* have a choice. You could have chosen *not* to seduce my human mother. That was the choice *you* made."

Vehoe studied Josh's face, a picture of fatherly concern with forlorn eyes, furrowed brow and all, but Josh didn't buy it. The guy reeked of fake sincerity and ulterior motives. Josh said, "You think you can weasel your way into this valley and start acting like my dad? Like you have any idea what that means?"

"It's all I've thought about since I learned of your existence!" Vehoe stood now, also angry. "Every waking hour, tending the plants, I wanted to be tending to you!" He moved towards Josh again, and Josh backed away.

"You actually think," Josh teased to distract him, "that after what you did to me and my mom, oh, and my dad, too, that I would ever be able to forgive you?" Josh snorted. "You expect us to wander off, arm in arm, into the sunset and live happily ever after? Is that how this is supposed to end?"

Vehoe kept his voice low and quiet. "Is that what you want?"

Josh laughed. "Yeah, every kid on the whole planet makes a habit of going off with a complete stranger, one who is a wanted criminal." Josh couldn't help laughing. "That's not happening. That's pathetic."

"I was locked up!" Vehoe insisted. "I couldn't come and find you and warn you about what would happen."

"Lame excuse." Josh needed an escape strategy, but his brain wasn't working that way. The longer he kept Vehoe talking, the bigger the chance someone would come along and find them. "You're a technology genius, I hear. You couldn't find a way?"

"Look." Vehoe kicked at a rock, his hands in his pockets. "That's exactly why I-I-I got locked up. I wanted to give the technology to the humans, or-or-or at least teach them some of my tricks for se-se-security." His stutter was worse. He shook his head as if that would help him form the words better. "They de-de-de . . . need it!" He got louder. "Besides, it would make us rich beyond anyone's dreams." His arms flailed as he spoke with his hands. "But no, no, no, the Netahs wouldn't let me near a computer. I fixed 'em. I played meek and contrite. I stayed alive. For you."

"You played meek?" Josh scoffed, turning his head away like he couldn't take anymore. Nothing moved near them. How was that possible? He sighed. "Well, I guess a little self-preservation is good. Not much good to me, though." He figured Vehoe wanted to appeal to his human side, that's why he'd transformed into a human. The tactic didn't work. Josh knew he could run faster as an elk than a human, although Vehoe could transform fast. He could see that Vehoe was nervous, maybe because he wasn't gaining Josh's trust. *Wait, what did he just say?* "Uh, you played meek and stayed alive for me?" He laughed at that. *Where is everyone?* "How long have you known about me?"

Vehoe had walked to the edge of a small pond. Its surface iced over in the cold. The wind had died, as if the world held its breath. Vehoe tested the edge of the ice with his boot toe and rubbed the stubble on his chin. "I've known since you went on your first family camping trip. I kept track of your mom, and then I saw you."

"How'd you know I was yours, not my dad's?" Josh demanded. He wouldn't let this guy get away with any lame assumptions.

"I could just tell. You look like me." Vehoe turned his wan smile away from the ice and aimed it at Josh.

Josh had no idea what expressions looked like on his elk face, or whether they were any facsimile to human expressions. He tried to exude boredom. He rolled his eyes and sighed, looking away. When he looked at Vehoe again, the man seemed to waver, like in a heat wave. Josh wondered if his eyes were drying out from staring. He blinked and concentrated on watching.

"You have a choice," Vehoe said with the kind of voice a man uses to reason with a child. "Come with me or stay. If you come with me, you may learn that I'm not the criminal every other Netah thinks I am. I'm a good guy. We could do great things. I could teach you everything I know. If you stay, I don't know. I might do something desperate."

"Oh, nice. I love a good threat. Yeah, that makes it easy, thanks." Josh had a plan, a cunning plan. He stared over his father's shoulder, gasped, and said, "What's that?"

The second his dad turned to look, Josh bolted. He had a full head of steam when he reached the stone door of his lodge, and nearly crashed into it, but lucky for him, Rodan had seen him coming and opened it just in time.

Josh skidded to a halt in a shower of dirt and snow, transformed, and then fell inside, but not without looking over his shoulder for a moment first.

Rodan laughed, following Josh's gaze. "What spooked you? You look like you've seen a ghost!"

"No ghost, just a guy who called himself Vehoe," Josh said quietly, panting. "My dad."

"Holy shit on a stick! Seriously?" Rodan searched the area with his eyes, his jaw clenched. Josh leaned against the wall and nodded.

Rodan dropped his arm over Josh's shoulders and steered him into the kitchen where he nudged him towards one of the counter stools. He stood there, strong and warm and comforting until Josh stopped shaking. "I'm really sorry, kid. I thought you were out there with Haiman. Where is he? He hasn't come back yet."

"Vehoe tranquilized him," Josh said.

Rodan gasped. "What? Stay here a minute. Don't move. I'll be right back." He went to the door and called out for George, who peered around a rock nearby.

"Hmm? What's up?" he asked.

"Vehoe is here. He tranked Haiman. We gotta find Haiman," Rodan said.

"He's got a tranquilizer gun?" George asked. "Okay, we need reinforcements. I'm going to Hesta first. You stay put, keep an eye on Josh. Don't let him out of your sight. If this guy's crazy enough to shoot one of us, who knows what he's capable of?" George walked away but stopped. "Lock that damned door. Don't let anyone in." Before the door closed, Josh heard him say, "Howie, Stella, you're in charge. Cover this place. I'll be back!" A corner of Josh's mouth lifted into a small smile. Where had he heard that, and with that voice? Then it dawned on him, George had said it just like the Terminator!

Rodan threw the bolt on the door and returned to Josh, who rested his head on his arms on the counter. Rodan said, "I'll get you a cup of tea. Then you can tell me what happened."

Josh could barely keep his eyes open, but the tea calmed him. They moved into the leather chairs by the windows in the great hall and Josh told him everything he could remember.

CHAPTER 15

High Tech Trouble

Josh's recounting of the conversation was interrupted by the return
of Haiman, who stood outside the windows, on the other side of
the waterfall, bugling and stomping to get their attention.

Rodan unlocked the door. Haiman entered, in his human form,
limping slightly, but otherwise appearing unhurt as he took a seat by
Josh. Rodan produced another cup of tea. Josh's eyes were heavy as he
watched Rodan in the kitchen. He thought he saw that same wavering he'd seen around Vehoe earlier but chalked it up to fatigue and
dry eyes. He blinked and rubbed his eyes when Rodan joined them.

Haiman looked exhausted and uncomfortable. "Don't start over
on my account, I saw you two talking. I assume it was a tranquilizer
dart I pulled out of my rump. Was it Vehoe? Do you know where
he is?"

Josh continued, "No. He shot you, then found me and acted like
he just wanted to talk, like he missed me, said stuff like he loved me.
Unbelievable. I lost it."

Haiman's eyes were closed and his teacup precariously tipped
towards the floor. Josh grabbed the cup just in time. "I think we
should get him to bed, right?"

Rodan nodded. Between the two of them, they were able to pry Haiman out of his chair and half carry him down the hallway to his room. They lowered him onto his bed, removed his shoes, and covered him with his blanket before tiptoeing out the door.

"You think we should call Ohma?" Josh asked.

"Look at you taking care of people." Rodan patted Josh on the shoulder. "We have a good grapevine around here. I'm sure she already knows Haiman is back. She'll come when it's safe."

"Okay." Josh settled into his chair and retrieved his tea from the side table. "So, long story short: he gave me the choice to run away with him or not, but the 'or not' came with a threat. I tricked him with the old 'What's that?' trick, made him look away, and ran for it. That's when you opened the door."

"So, Vehoe was close to the lodge?"

"Yes. Haiman and I had been eating and wandered apart. I'd gotten my bearings when I heard the shot and had plenty of time to figure out exactly where I was while he yapped. All I know is I never ran so fast in my life."

"All right. You relax. The lodge is secure. Now we wait for George's reinforcements." Rodan got up and put his mug in the sink. "You hungry?"

"Not really." He spotted a crust of bread in the bowl. "I could eat that."

Rodan handed the bread over and they parted ways.

Josh went to his room and picked up his book, hoping it would distract him. He'd found a collection of Netah tales and flipped through it before putting it down. He lay watching the shadows outside his window. Nothing moved, but the hairs on the back of his neck tingled. He rubbed his neck and rolled over, frustrated, and wide awake.

A familiar voice that sounded very close said, "How cl-cl- smart."

Josh shot up from the bed and switched on his light. He was alone. *How can Vehoe be in my room? Is it a trick? Is there a speaker somewhere?* Josh peered into corners, there was really no place to hide a camera and speaker, although who knew what Vehoe could do?

"Where are you?" Josh demanded.

"I'm here to give you a chance to reconsider your decision. Come away with me. I can help you. I need you. You're all I have."

"Show yourself!" Josh turned his initial fear into anger.

"As you wish," Vehoe responded. A low buzzing sound preceded a wavering in the air again. Josh narrowed his eyes and kept them focused on the waves. Suddenly his father appeared, sitting on Josh's chair, his hair even more wild and matted, his face dirt streaked and gaunt.

"How'd you do that?" Josh's curiosity won.

"See? I have plenty of things I can teach you." The man smiled half-heartedly.

Josh could smell the man's loneliness; it seeped out of every pore. He saw the man's eyes move to the crust of bread Josh had forgotten. "You want that?" Josh asked. "Help yourself."

"Thanks." His dad broke off a piece and crumbs tumbled to the floor as he chewed thoughtfully. "Esok hasn't lost his touch." He nodded, brushing crumbs from his beard and shirtfront.

Slightly gentler, Josh asked, "How'd you appear out of thin air?"

"It's really simple, actually."

Yes, I've got him dialoguing again. Come on, Rodan, or George, or Hesta, anybody!

"I'm listening. Teach me something."

"It's the same technology we use to hide our buildings. I just tweaked it to work on me and presto chango, I'm invisible. It's come in handy."

"I bet it has." *Keep him talking, keep talking!* "Even so, this place has been locked up tight ever since I returned."

Vehoe shook his head, as if disappointed that Josh couldn't figure it out. "I slipped inside when Haiman returned. Followed him in, really quite easy."

Although impressed, Josh asked, "How did you get your hands on something like that if you were in prison?"

"We call it an ag facility, not a prison, besides, I told you, didn't I? I fix stuff. Oh, maybe I didn't tell you. Anyway, they had to let me into the supply room for parts. I might have helped myself to a few things that were unrelated to their broken toasters, or whatever stupid stuff they brought me." Vehoe finished off the crust and wiped his hands on his grimy pants.

"You're not stuttering now. What happened?"

"Huh, you're right, I hadn't noticed." The man looked around Josh's room, as if looking for something else to talk about. "You like physical activity? I saw you working on that house. You have some artistic talents. Impressive."

With a big sigh, Josh said, "Of course you saw that. You've been watching me ever since the night at the campground?"

"I knew you were a smart kid." Vehoe smirked.

"How do you get around the alarms?"

Vehoe shrugged. "I designed them. I know how to get around them."

Vehoe picked up Josh's math book and flipped through the pages. "You having any trouble with this?"

Josh shook his head, not wanting to talk about math. He had to do something. If Vehoe could be invisible, they'd never find him. Did Josh want him found? A plan formed slowly. Maybe he could lead the others to his dad's hiding place. He said, "I have a proposal."

"Okay."

"I go with you to wherever you've been hiding. We talk."

"Yes," Vehoe agreed enthusiastically. "There's so much you don't know."

"I get to decide, though. If you convince me that you are a good guy, I go away with you. If I decide you're not, I return here and you leave, never to return. You leave me alone. I don't stop you from leaving."

Vehoe studied Josh's face and nodded. He looked more animated, color returning to his face, almost excited. "Yes. I agree." He stood and held out his hand. "Shake?"

Josh felt the prick of the needle in his father's ring but couldn't pull away. Vehoe had his hand in a tight grip. *Great. That went well.* Josh struggled, but the strength left him quickly, his voice going first.

The last thing Josh remembered was falling and being caught in the man's arms. He felt like he floated through the lodge, then the cold air hit him, and he woke a little as Vehoe unceremoniously tossed him over his shoulder and carried Josh into the night.

CHAPTER 16

History Lesson

Josh woke in a damp cave, covered by a thin blanket. He sat up and wiped the sleep out of his eyes. Spotting a small fire, he crawled towards it and held out his hands, pulling his blanket around him, even though it was worthless.

Vehoe sat on the other side of the fire, watching Josh. "Welcome back." He lifted a percolating pot of coffee off a hook over the fire. "You want some?" He waved the pot towards Josh.

"You have no idea," Josh replied, taking the tin cup. He blew across the top and took a quick sip. It was too hot, but the metal warmed his hands nicely. He sat up and looked around. "Home sweet home, eh? This where you've been hiding out?"

"Mostly. Sometimes I sneak into your lodge and help myself to one of the empty beds." He chuckled. "I bet Rodan would have a fit if he knew."

Josh did not want to talk about Rodan. He felt groggy enough that he knew running would be useless. He could see daylight in the cave mouth behind Vehoe, but had no idea where they were. He actually felt refreshed by his forced sleep. His only option was to listen to the man. "Did you really have to knock me out like that? I mean, I said I'd come with you."

"Sure, I know, but call me impatient. Besides my way meant we could both slip out together, cloaked, and no one would be the wiser until you didn't show up in the morning."

"You're not dumb," Josh admitted.

"Aw, thanks." Vehoe scratched the side of his nose. "You're not, either."

Josh took a sip of his coffee. It gave him such a caffeine rush he gasped.

"What, to-to- too hot?"

Josh shook his head. "No, but I haven't had caffeine for ages. This is strong."

"It always helps after I've been shielded."

"It messes you up?"

"You could say that." His dad slapped his knees and stood abruptly. "But enough of that." He started pacing the cave like a caged lion. "Where do we start? Ah, I know, how I met your mother." A dreamy look crossed his face. "The first time I saw her, she was walking along the Platte River. I saw her through some willows walking slowly, taking everything in, exuding such a sense of joy and happiness. She mesmerized me."

Josh gritted his teeth, sipped his coffee, felt the warmth fill him from the inside as the fuzz in his brain slowly dissipated. *Did he kidnap me just so he'd have an audience?*

"I followed her to her car, watched her drive away, and then thought I'd never see her again. Luck led me to her the second time. I'd been wandering through the woods, and she came upon me while hiking. We were up at Mount Falcon Park. You went there a lot as a little kid. Remember it?" He stopped pacing and looked at Josh expectantly.

Reluctantly, Josh said, "Yeah."

"I couldn't believe my luck." He paced again, his hands animating his words. "I turned into a human and walked towards her down the trail. She smiled and my insides turned to mush. We started talking. I told her I'd seen a mountain lion up the hill, and we should probably turn back. She believed me. I walked her back to her car."

"Very romantic," Josh interjected. "It all started with a lie, how surprising."

Vehoe stopped pacing and gave Josh an admonishing look. "Knock it off."

Josh raised one hand to placate but couldn't resist rolling his eyes.

"I tracked her down by her license plate number," Vehoe admitted, retrieving his coffee for a sip. "I had missed the opportunity the first time I saw her and wouldn't the second time."

"You stalked her!"

"Really?" Vehoe stopped at the cave mouth with his head tilting, as if he just couldn't wrap his brain around that word. "Is it still stalking if it's love?"

"You barely knew her!"

"I wanted to change that."

Josh pressed his lips together to stop the angry words from spilling out.

"Okay, maybe I stalked her." Vehoe shrugged and took a couple steps before stopping again. "It worked out, though, for a while."

"What made you leave?" Josh couldn't wait to hear what excuses Vehoe had for that.

Vehoe settled himself on the other side of the fire. "Well, I knew she'd be finishing her degree and getting a job. She'd move away. I'd be left alone."

"Why would she move? You didn't even know what job she'd take?" *This guy is so full of bull!*

"She talked about going somewhere with the peace corps."

"Oh." That sounded like his mom. "So, you left her before she could leave you?" Josh paused, then muttered, "Coward."

"No, I'm not a c-c-coward! It was . . . I knew . . . we couldn't . . . it wouldn't work!" Vehoe spit the words out, frustrated by his stutter. He panted from the effort and stood to pace on his side of the small fire again, which happened to neatly block Josh's escape route.

"Why," Josh teased, baiting him.

Josh's dad looked about the cave, rubbing the back of his neck. "I never liked all the rules. I don't see the point. All the restrictions were smothering me. I wanted to go live among the humans, to be free. I had to test that." Vehoe still looked away from Josh, avoiding his eyes.

"Free?" Josh pushed.

"Sure, and to experience human love," his dad sighed.

"Did you tell her you loved her?" Josh wanted to know if Vehoe had broken his mother's heart before he abandoned her.

"Yes."

"How did you break up?"

"I disappeared." Vehoe tried to look Josh in the eye, but Josh dropped his eyes to the fire. "Not literally, I just went away."

Keeping his eyes down as he poked the fire with a stick, Josh said, "What's the matter, you couldn't get a girl from among the Netahs?" Josh regretted his question the minute he'd said it. It sounded mean, but then again, he felt mean. This guy was bringing out the worst in him.

"Sure, it sounds cowardly, now that you mention it," Vehoe admitted. "And no, thank you for your sincere concern, I-I-I didn't find a Netah to love. But there were ex-ten-ua-ting cir-cum-stan-ces for that." He enunciated carefully to get the words out without stuttering.

"What circumstances?" Josh hated that he began to care about this story. The lame excuses just kept coming.

"My dad and brother." Vehoe walked to the cave opening and grabbed the lip of it over his head, his back to Josh. "Dad never liked me; said I was lazy, stupid, worthless. He always liked my twin brother better."

"Wait, what? You have a twin?"

"Oh yes, uh-huh. You know him, too." Vehoe paced again, shaking his head as if arguing with a voice in his head while only sharing a little of the conversation.

Josh waited, wary of Vehoe's agitation. He thought about his human father's unconditional approval and how devastating it would have been not to have that.

"It's, wait, oh, you are good!" Vehoe stopped, wagging his finger at Josh with a knowing grin on his face. "I almost said too much." Vehoe took a deep breath and blew it out. He rolled his head then looked Josh right in the eyes. "No names. That's not the point of the story. The point is my brother took away everything that should have been mine. He took my girl, he took my position in the community, my authority, my inheritance."

"Inheritance? What, were you rich?"

"What? No, we were fine, but no, money had nothing to do with it. Netahs value other things like power, and we had that. He took what was mine and pushed me away, told lies about me being crazy, that I was sick."

Josh had to carefully phrase this next question if he wanted to know who the brother was. "Why? Why would Arman do that? What did you do to him?"

Vehoe stopped in his tracks and, placing his hands on his hips, said, "Well, how kind of you to show such concern and take his side. And, Arman is not my brother. That's funny, insane, since he's . . . well he's not my brother." He shook his head as if untangling his thoughts. "You see, I'm not crazy, for starters." He paced again. "I got angry, furious that he took everything and left nuh-nuh nothing for me." He kicked at a rock and it went flying into the back of the cave. "I didn't do anything to deserve it!"

This line of questions seemed a dead end. Josh decided to change the subject. "Why did you assume my mom would leave you?"

Vehoe relaxed visibly. He sat on his blanket and then stretched out on his back, his hands behind his head, staring up at the ceiling of the cave. He crossed his ankles.

He's trying to figure out how to say what happened without sounding like a bad guy.

Vehoe said, "Well, I saw her with your dad. She was different with him. I realized she never looked at me like that."

"What did she say when you told her you loved her?" Josh demanded.

"I, well, I was biding my time, waiting for the right moment, but the moment never came. Then I saw Danny making her laugh, taking her on long walks, holding hands on the trails. It made me think about how we would have to live if I stayed with her. I never made her laugh like that. She is beautiful when she laughs."

"Yes, yes, she is." Josh agreed reluctantly. He did not want to get emotional and start feeling bad for Vehoe. On the other hand, they had both lost his mom.

Vehoe rolled onto his side and rested his head on his hand, staring at Josh through the fire. "I'm sorry. I should have thought. You miss her, too."

Josh nodded but dropped his eyes to the fire. He couldn't handle the pain he saw in Vehoe's eyes. Josh's own pain made him angry. "So you never told her? You could have just faded away into the sunset and not said anything, left her alone."

"Yes, I told her. I guess it was selfish, but I needed to see her reaction." Vehoe picked up a rock and tossed it up, caught it, did it again.

"And how did she react?" Josh prompted.

Vehoe sat up and threw the rock at the wall behind Josh. "She couldn't stop herself from laughing." He let that hang in the cave for a bit.

That didn't sound like Josh's mom. She was kind and gentle and would never laugh at a proclamation of love. "I don't believe you," he said.

"I don't care if you believe me," Vehoe said angrily.

Josh wanted to understand this, and knew it could be dangerous, but couldn't help himself. "How did you say it? I mean, were you joking around?"

"Nope." Vehoe's face became an unemotional mask.

"You're lying."

"Boy, you are one suspicious kid. You should talk to someone about that." Vehoe's voice sounded concerned, but his eyes twinkled with mischief.

"Says the Netah who knocked up my mom and left her," Josh lashed out.

"I didn't know I'd knocked her up, as you put it." Vehoe's face contorted momentarily with pain, then returned to an emotionless mask.

"What, you didn't know how human sex worked?" He couldn't believe he'd said that. *Why am I baiting this guy?* Vehoe had proven himself volatile and maybe a little unhinged. Josh picked up a stick and poked the fire again, pretending not to watch as Vehoe decided how to respond. Emotions from anger to despair to sadness contorted the man's face.

With a sigh, Vehoe said, "I knew what I was doing."

"Okay." Josh tossed the stick into the fire and sparks flew towards Vehoe. "Can we not talk about how you had sex with my mom?"

"You brought it up."

"Um, okay, whatever. New subject. What other good guy, redeeming qualities should I know you possess?" Josh asked.

"I love you," Vehoe said quietly.

"Which you demonstrated by knocking me out and kidnapping me. Next."

"I know a lot about electronics and could teach you."

"I'm told many Netahs don't trust electronics and computers. Sounds like a great way for me to get on their bad side."

"Someone has to keep the Netah security codes tight. Otherwise, all their dirty little secrets will be found out."

"I thought you said you wanted to help the humans with their security," Josh reminded him.

"Oh, sure, but that's because the Netahs don't appreciate me. They don't understand what I can do. They don't value it. I figured the humans would be grateful. I could make a fortune."

"Ah, there it is," Josh said, nodding knowingly.

"What? You think you know me? You know nothing." Vehoe fumed as he stood.

Josh explained in a singsong voice, taunting, "You want to get rich off the Netah technology. You couldn't be rich with power as a Netah, you figured you'd do it as a human, no matter what the consequences."

"You know what? I'm done," Vehoe said, crossing his arms.

Josh knew then that he had pushed the guy too far. Vehoe, though big and strong, had a chip on his shoulder the size of Manhattan. Maybe Josh should have been nicer. Maybe he should have thought about that earlier.

Vehoe took a step back, turned his side to Josh and waved him towards the opening of the cave. "You have made up your mind. I did my best. I tried to explain. You are so damned smart, you're ready to go running back to your new friends, the Netahs. Well, be my guest."

Josh leapt to his feet. As he passed Vehoe, the punch landed squarely in his stomach. His breath whooshed out and he bent double, stumbling.

Vehoe laughed at him. "Just a little something to remember me by," he said and then turned his back.

Josh didn't let himself fall but scrambled forward. In the sunshine, he paused long enough to get his bearings. *We can't be far; he couldn't carry me very far.* Spotting the line of mountains that he knew to be to the west of the valley, he transformed into an elk and galloped off to the east. As he ran, he took an inventory of landmarks. *This is the gully Anton and Sarah tried to camp in. Here's the plateau, there are the ponds, that's Hesta's rock!*

He turned into a human and, clutching his middle, he pushed the tiny red rock.

Ohma opened the door. She caught Josh before he fell to his knees and helped him into the family room.

Hesta put aside his book. "What's all this, then? The guys get a little rough with you?"

"No! Vehoe kidnapped me!" Josh collapsed into a chair. "I know where he is. George said he was coming to you about reinforcements. Are they here yet?"

CHAPTER 17

Dragnet

esta acted unconcerned about the reinforcements and their slow arrival. Josh practically yelled, "Come on, Hesta, I can lead you to him right now. What are you waiting for?"

Hesta shook his head and remained sitting on his sofa. "Calm yourself, boy. When they're here, they'll let me know. We have to be careful; Vehoe is dangerous."

Josh spun around to leave, but Ohma stopped him. "What happened to you? Let me see if you're hurt." After a little poking and prodding, she found a couple of bruised ribs, but nothing worse. Quietly, under her breath, she said, "Go to the lodge, quickly. Tell Rodan what you know. Don't wait for Hesta."

Josh nodded, shocked. Within minutes he arrived at the lodge. Rodan was addressing a crowd of burly men. Josh transformed into a human and approached them with caution. Rodan saw him and said, "Josh, where have you been? We were about to send out search parties. Are you all right?"

Josh took a deep breath, straightened his back, and lifted his chin. "I'm fine. Vehoe kidnapped me. I know where he is. He's in a cave over the plateau to the west, past the gully."

A stranger said, "I think I've noticed it before. Anyone else know it?"

Another stranger said, "Sure, I know it. Ran right past it yesterday."

George spoke, "We're almost all here. There's a squadron of Netah eagles on their way."

Crawley stood next to him. "I'll find them, and we'll meet you there." She took to the air.

George looked at Josh. "Anything else you can tell us?"

Josh searched his memory for details that could be helpful. "All I can tell you is it's to the west, towards the mountains. I ran past the gully where the hikers were a while back, over the mesa." He pointed to the mesa where he had first stood and looked into the valley. "That way."

"All right." George nodded.

"Oh, and one more thing," Josh said, "he can make himself invisible. He modified a shielding device and is using it on himself. You can almost see him, because the air around him wavers, like heat waves, but it's easy to miss."

"Huh, so that's how he's been hiding right under our noses," Rodan said. "Okay, George, this is your op. What do we do?"

"We need to surround the cave now. Wolf clan, you're the fastest runners, you lead. "Maahe." He looked at the man who knew the cave. "Position yourselves around the cave. Your vision is keen. Watch for the waves Josh described. He may also give himself away as he walks, watch the ground, feel it, listen. Now go."

As Maahe peeled away with a small group of men, they all transformed into wolves and disappeared.

George evaluated the remaining group. "Okomo, lead your pride around to the north. Spread out there to block his escape."

"Got it." Another group assembled, turned into mountain lions and padded off.

A large group of elk ran around the end of the aspen grove in their direction. They stopped in front of George and Rodan. The leader spoke. "We heard what's happening." He noticed Josh and hesitated. "Josh has returned? Do you still need us?"

Josh thought he might have recognized Manny and Pehpe from the building lodge. They were elk, though, and he couldn't be sure until Rodan spoke. "Thank you, Manny. Yes, we can use every Netah we've got. Good news is, Josh is back. Bad news is, Vehoe is hiding nearby and he has modified a shield device. He can go invisible, but the air wavers around him. Keep your eyes open." He turned to George. "Where do you want them?"

George nodded and said, "Vehoe's in a cave past the gully and plateau. You take up a position at the south end of the gully, to cover any attempt to escape in that direction."

Manny nodded. "Got it." The elk pounded off towards the gully.

George looked around him and said, "The rest of us are the proverbial cavalry. Tomo, you have the detainer?"

Only then did Josh notice Tomo in the crowd. He carried a pouch slung across his shoulder. He patted it and nodded.

George said, "Good man, you're with me, you, too, Josh. Okay, let's not waste any more time. Let's move out. Spread out to back up our friends. Stay sharp out there. We know he has a tranquilizer dart gun. Who knows what else he's willing to throw at us to escape? We can't let him escape again."

George turned into a bear, along with a half dozen of the others. All the elk from Josh's lodge transformed and followed. Josh stayed right behind Tomo and George. Tomo had the pouch slung across his elk neck, so he stood out in the crowd. The Netahs topped the mesa and spread out across the rim, leaving nothing to chance. As they moved across the terrain, small groups split off in different directions. Josh had never been part of a dragnet before, and he buzzed with the excitement.

Josh wondered why they all slowed to a cautious walk at the edge of a mesa. Then he heard something weird. It wasn't a gunshot, but it was that loud. It sounded like boulders crashing together, a loud, sharp crack. Josh studied the scene below as bears, mountain lions, and his fellow elk converged in a circle, and set up a barrier with their bodies, standing guard around whatever had made all that noise. Obviously, they had something cornered. The hill that hid the cave stood behind them, the top of the hill was dotted with wolves all watching, some snarling.

Rodan told Haiman, "You guys stay here and back up the others." George and Tomo walked down from the rim of the mesa and made their way to the outside edge of the circle, Josh and Rodan stayed close.

George turned to them as he turned into a human. "Come on, transform and follow me."

At the center of the circle, they found a space the size of a tennis court, where two enormous elk, their antlers partially grown, engaged in what looked like a fight to the death. Their eyes were rimmed with white, foam dripped from their lips, bloody gashes streaked down their sweat-shined bodies. They circled each other like prizefighters in a ring, then one turned and reared up on its hind legs to add force to its head blow. The two elk staggered but remained standing. The edge of the circle moved away from the action but did not break apart. Gasps and groans escaped from the surrounding animals in sympathy or surprise. In the circle, the larger elk lunged again, and his victim transformed into a human, obviously Vehoe, and dodged out of the way. As the charging elk recovered and turned, Vehoe transformed back into an elk and rammed the side of the other elk with his antlers. A woman screamed, and Josh saw Ohma on the edge of the circle. Blood seeped from a fresh wound on the other elk's side.

The two elk backed away from each other, became humans, and circled slowly, crouched, their hands low and outstretched for balance and their eyes glued to each other. Josh recognized the men as Hesta and Vehoe. Their human bodies were large and bloody, their shredded shirts hanging from their shoulders. Both looked exhausted; they dragged their feet, stumbled, panted for breath. Someone shouted for them to stop. Josh thought it sounded like Noomi.

"How did Hesta get here so fast?" Josh whispered to Tomo.

"You told him Vehoe was nearby," Tomo answered without moving his eyes from the fight. "Maybe he got lucky."

Josh disagreed. In fact, in his opinion Hesta knew exactly where Vehoe hid and had gone there the minute Josh left. Something else didn't make sense. "I wonder why Vehoe didn't cloak?" he said quietly to Rodan.

"Maybe Hesta caught him before he could."

Vehoe, still a man, ran towards Hesta and attempted a running, spinning kick. Hesta transformed into an elk and sprang away while the kick hit air and Vehoe crashed to the ground. Hesta stomped on Vehoe's shin. The bone cracked, Vehoe howled. Groans rose from the crowd.

It looked like it was all over. Hesta looked like he would deal a death blow to Vehoe's head, but Vehoe turned into an elk, and Hesta's leg cracked against an antler. The crowd gasped. Hesta limped away, assessing the gash in his leg. Meanwhile, Vehoe rolled unsteadily to his feet, but he crumpled back to the ground as a human clutching his obviously broken shin. Hesta also became human and slumped to the ground, as if he'd been waiting for the other to fall. He cradled his bloody leg in his hands, grimacing with pain.

Tomo tapped Rodan on the shoulder. "Time for the detainer, right?"

Tomo stepped over to Vehoe. Vehoe's chest heaved as Tomo approached. He raised an arm to ward off the inevitable, but Tomo pulled a collar, like the one they'd used in the campground, from the pouch. Vehoe only had the breath to wail, "Nooooo!" Once Tomo activated the detainer, Vehoe froze in place, a beaten, bent-over, silent man.

Tomo came back to Josh and asked, "You think he made a cloaking device, right? Maybe it's still in the cave." To Rodan he suggested, "Josh and I can go around to the cave and try to find his cloaking device."

"Good thinking," Rodan agreed.

Josh followed Tomo, impressed by his young friend, the healer who had seemed so mild mannered in the lodge, okay, other than on the mud fight day. This new side of Tomo was a courageous, quick-thinking guy with a plan. Hesta and Vehoe were completely trapped by the solid wall of Netah bodies standing guard. The two young humans squeezed past the bears and elk, and with a nod to the mountain lion at the entrance, entered the cave.

It was dim inside; the fire had been doused, and the cave smelled like damp, woody smoke. They moved into the cramped space, Josh to the left, Tomo to the right. Josh found a small ledge with some human supplies, like matches, a cloth sack of oats, nuts, dried fruits. He picked up the blanket he'd slept on the night before and shook it out, in case it was hiding something. Josh found nothing and kept moving.

"Over here!" Tomo waved Josh over. He moved towards the entrance with what looked like a watch. Josh wondered what Vehoe would need that for. Tomo tapped the face of it, peered at it a moment, then tapped again and disappeared. He reappeared and looked a little dazed but looked up at Josh triumphantly. "Got it. Come on."

The boys returned to find Ohma tending Hesta's injuries. Tomo moved to examine Vehoe's leg. "Leave him!" Ohma hissed.

"No, Ohma," Tomo said quietly. "It is not our way." Tomo tapped a button on Vehoe's collar. Vehoe relaxed and Tomo eased him to the ground. Then Tomo froze the man again before he pulled off his wool scarf and wrapped it around Vehoe's shin as gently as he could. The rest of the Netahs had begun to break up the circle and gather in small groups. The bears still stood watch.

Josh saw a couple of eagles circle overhead and land at the top of the cave opening. After a quick exchange between the eagles and wolves, the eagles took to the sky again. Josh asked George, "Are those two with us?"

"Yes." George nodded. "They'll lead the transport vehicle here."

While Ohma wrapped Hesta's thigh, Vehoe looked like a bronze statue. His eyes were glazed, and he lay stiffly, moaning inside his frozen mouth. He made sounds that alternated between pleading and raging, but he couldn't move. Josh stood behind Tomo and asked, "Did you have something to do with that device?"

Tomo nodded his head as he studied its effect on Vehoe.

Josh said, "I thought you were studying healing."

Tomo kept nodding. With a shuddering breath he turned his eyes away from Vehoe and stood up. "Sometimes we need to immobilize a patient to treat them. We need them aware but numbed. Yes, I worked on this one. It looks painful, but it's not. He's probably terrified, though. He won't get any second chances this time around."

"Will there be a trial or something?"

"Yes, but first he's going back to lockdown. They've built a special section just for him. He's going into solitary."

Ohma looked up from tucking a bandage over Hesta's head wound, and said, "Hesta will survive."

Rodan turned to the crowd, which had begun to disperse. "Okay, folks, it's over. We have Vehoe in custody and Hesta will survive." A cheer rose from the others, but it was halfhearted. Rodan continued, "Thank you for your assistance today. We can finish up here, so you

LISA KANIUT COBB

are free to go. The valley is beginning to green up, so there's plenty for everyone to eat if you're hungry. If you don't wish to travel tonight, you are welcome to stay, and we can shelter you in our lodge. I know some of you have to return to your duties and families, and we thank you for your support. We will keep you informed of the schedule for the trial, but it will probably be in about a week. Statements can be sent to me in the usual way. Any information you can give us that is pertinent to the investigation and charges will be appreciated." He looked around at their faces and nodded with satisfaction. "All right, then. Goodbye, neighbors!"

As the Netahs left the scene in small groups, a couple remained to help Ohma with Hesta. She said to Rodan, "Send someone back for the truck. We need to transport Hesta home. He won't be walking for a while." Josh saw Rodan turn to Mako and Esok. He pointed at them and nodded with his head for them to go. They turned into elk and galloped away. There remained behind a small group in human form. Josh recognized Howie and Stella. She looked up when she felt his eyes on her and gave Josh a little wave. They all stood in a circle surrounding Vehoe and spoke in hushed tones.

A low whine preceded the truck's approach, followed by the rumble of the massive vehicle Josh had seen in the canyon a few days earlier. The men slid a stretcher under Hesta and slid him into the truck bed. Ohma climbed in next to him. Then they pulled out a second stretcher for Vehoe and carried him up the ramp into the transport. He didn't twitch a muscle but did make small pleading noises. Josh watched, riveted. The solid clang of the door and its lock reassured them Vehoe couldn't escape.

Rodan walked into the cave and disappeared for a few minutes. Josh assumed he was looking for evidence, maybe pointing towards Vehoe's accomplice. Tomo and Josh turned to walk back towards their lodge. They didn't feel like becoming elk yet. When Rodan caught up with them and draped an arm over each of their shoulders, he said, "So, who's hungry?"

"Oh geez, yeah! How'd you know?" Josh hadn't noticed his own gnawing hunger. He'd been too distracted. The adrenaline still pumped in his veins.

"Netah intuition. Let's see what we can find on the way home," Rodan laughed. "We can relax tonight. It's the end of an era, the era of Vehoe. He won't get away again, we can get back to our regular lives."

Tomo said, "Right, after the trial, that is. How soon did you say it will happen?"

"Not soon enough," Rodan said. "But it takes time to gather the jurors for a trial, probably about a week. It will be a council priority to have this settled."

Josh said, "That's pretty quick. Human lawyers would take longer."

Tomo nodded. "Some of our systems are simpler than human ones. Our justice is swift. There is a permanent judiciary team that works for the council. Our communication networks are quick. The jurists are probably already gathering."

"Do you allow spectators?" Josh tried to picture how this Netah justice would work. An image of a courtroom like he'd seen on TV but filled with various animals formed in his mind. Josh decided he wanted to be able to hear the charges and defense, not just read or hear about it later. It was personal.

"Sure," Rodan answered.

"How do you make it look normal to have all the different Netahs together?" Josh asked. "I assume it won't be as quick as the council meetings I've seen."

"We make it look like a rodeo," Rodan laughed.

That picture made more sense to Josh. Rodeos could go on for days. "So, can I go?"

Rodan nodded. "Of course."

As if on cue, Josh's stomach growled loudly, and he caught a whiff of something delicious. He transformed and sniffed around for the source. New green grass shoots grew at his feet. He took a bite. Tomo and Rodan also found good grazing.

Josh lost track of time, but eventually, Tomo and Rodan returned to walk with Josh back to the lodge. Josh said, "You know, I wondered about something. How do you guys think Hesta got there before all the rest of us, and why did he fight Vehoe all by himself?"

"Hmm, I've been thinking about that, too," Rodan said. "Elk can run very fast when we need to, so that's no mystery. Why did Hesta fight him? It's probably because he's our chief. He's the biggest and strongest of us all, he figured it was his responsibility."

"Yeah, but how did he know where to find Vehoe? I tried to tell him about the cave, but Hesta didn't care. He said he'd wait for reinforcements."

Rodan stopped and stared at Josh. "Are you telling me you think Hesta knew where Vehoe was hiding? That he was in on something?"

Josh studied his hooves, thinking that through. *I can't say anything about a spy, it could be Rodan or even his second-in-command, Arman!* "I don't know, maybe it was someplace they played as kids? It's just, I wondered."

"Okay, thanks for telling me that. I'll keep it in mind when we question Vehoe." They walked in silence for a few paces, then Rodan said, "Maybe Hesta wanted you out of the way, so you didn't get hurt?" Josh had his doubts.

When they arrived at the lodge, only a few strangers milled around the great hall. Rodan turned to his youngest lodgers. "I'm going to warm up a pot of stew. Why don't you two figure out how many guests we have. We may have enough spare beds to accommodate everyone."

"Okay." Josh nodded. Tomo went to count guests, while Josh went to check on empty rooms. He decided to put fresh towels on the beds and prop the doors open in the spare rooms, so it was obvious which ones were available. He and Tomo agreed they had plenty of beds for everyone.

Back in the great room, where Rodan had brewed more tea, the Netahs settled in to visit before catching some sleep. Josh made his way over to Howie and Stella, who were peering out the windows, admiring the wavering play of evening light through the waterfall. "Hi, guys," Josh said as he approached. "You're staying the night, I understand. Where have you been sleeping while you were helping with security?"

Stella stood and wrapped Josh in a hug. "We're bears. We have nice warm coats. Look at you worrying about others. I bet you're very relieved to have this whole business behind you."

"Hiya, Josh." Howie turned and clapped Josh on the shoulder. Josh winced, his rib throbbing. "Great to see you again," Howie continued. "Our George talks about you a lot. I'm glad we have some time to get to know you tonight."

Stella said, "We live just over the pass to the south. We'll take the truck tomorrow. A bed for tonight sounds divine."

"Yeah, now it seems silly." Josh ducked his head in embarrassment. "I guess I thought you guys would all be hibernating, but it's nearly springtime now, anyway." Then he realized what Stella had just said. "Wait, was that your truck, the one George drove me back from the campground in?"

Howie chuckled, "Sure is. You like it?"

"Yeah! Where did you get it? I mean it's so tricked out and quiet. I've never seen anything like it."

"It's kind of a hobby." Howie shrugged. "I made a few small adjustments."

"Small adjustments?" George laughed as he joined them.

Josh noticed that Howie didn't laugh. "Seriously, are you an engineer or scientist then?"

"You could say that." Howie nodded. "Why, you like messing around with cars?"

"I don't know, never tried it."

Stella snorted at that. "Don't let him kid you, Josh. He's very proud of that truck. It's one-of-a-kind and very valuable. I mean, lots of Netah bears work on vehicles, but Howie has a gift."

"Huh, cool! I've been thinking about how each Netah animal might have specialties. I heard the littles are the computer builders, like they specialize in the hardware. I guess because their hands are smaller? Are you saying that vehicles are a bear specialty?"

George and his sister exchanged looks, then George answered, "Yes, we have different strengths and specialties."

"What's the specialty for elk?" Josh asked, noticing their dodge of the question and deciding not to push it.

"You haven't figured that out yet?" Howie asked.

"No, I mean, I know we build earth homes and use green energy."

"That's an adaptation to this particular landscape," Howie agreed. "What else have you observed?"

"Well, as an elk, I like to run, and can go pretty fast and far."

"Okay."

"Leave him alone, Howie," Stella said. "You sound like dad when he doesn't want to answer a question, he just keeps asking us questions instead. It's annoying. Can't you see the poor kid is exhausted?"

Howie nodded sheepishly.

George took over. "Here's an answer. Netah bears don't have to hibernate. Although our elderly members are known to slow down and take very long naps, and our pregnant ladies often sleep more than usual in the winter," he explained. He waved Josh to an armchair nearby. "Why don't you pull up a chair and tell us what else you've learned since you got here."

Josh collapsed into a chair, surprised by his sudden fatigue. *Was it power of suggestion because Stella just said he looked exhausted?* Rolling his head from side to side, he realized he was stiff with tension. Stella popped out of her chair and stood behind Josh, giving him a really good neck and shoulder rub. "Ah, that feels amazing," Josh said. "Thanks, Stella."

"You bet," she answered, kneading his neck. "You've been through the ringer the last few days, from what I hear. What do you say we talk about life as a Netah elk tomorrow? Maybe we could even arrange for you to come visit us and help Howie in his garage. I'm guessing you are more tired than any of us. Go ahead, make yourself scarce."

Josh nodded. He looked around to gauge how hard it would be to slip away. The people in the hall were all deep in conversation. "Go on, before someone notices," Stella insisted.

"Okay, thanks, Stella. Good night, guys," he said with a small wave to Howie and George.

Josh slipped down the hall to his room. He turned off his light. When he closed his eyes, the image of Vehoe's stiff form was burned into his retinas and he remembered the sounds of fear and anger that came from his frozen lips. Josh opened his eyes and watched the ceiling, where the night's clouds changed the intensity of moonlight coming into the room. That calmed him. The sounds from the great room were like the low drone of a purring cat. It reminded him of nights in his old home in the suburbs, when his parents had friends over for dinner parties that continued late into the night.

He forced thoughts of his human home and the coming trial to the back of his mind. He had no control over what happened at the trial and would not be sorry to see Vehoe punished, however the Netahs thought fit. *I'm too tired to drum up any emotional feelings for Vehoe. Maybe I want to see the end of the era of Vehoe. How else will I ever fit in and find a way to live among the Netah? I don't need Vehoe.*

Josh tossed himself onto his side, facing the wall, and pulled his blanket up over his shoulder. When he closed his eyes, all he could see was Vehoe, pacing in front of the cave, pleading his case, trying to convince Josh of his good intentions. His eyes popped open as he rolled to his back, staring into the dark recesses of his ceiling. *I wanted to believe him, but I couldn't. Why?* Was it all the suspicion he'd absorbed from the others? Was he unfair to the man? *No! He drugged Haiman, kidnapped me, and it sure looked like he was prepared to fight Hesta to the death! He never took responsibility for himself. I'm well rid of him.*

The phrase "well rid" went on repeat in his head, like an earworm. He turned it into a mantra as he regulated his breathing to its rhythm.

CHAPTER 18

Job Opportunity

For the next few days, Josh stayed at the lodge. He felt weak and fuzzy-headed after all the excitement. Rodan grilled him, trying to get all the facts lined up. Ohma visited to see how his ribs were healing. When Josh said his head hurt, she pointed out a particular plant for him to eat, saying, "That should help," like it was an aspirin or something. Josh tried it and felt only slightly better, but he kept on finding it before every meal and it eventually took the edge off his headache.

The mornings were chilly, but the sun warmed the air by midday. Clouds built up most afternoons and threatened rain most evenings, although it merely drizzled for moments then cleared, typical Colorado spring weather. The rain woke up many new plants in the valley. Josh cautiously ate only what he saw others eating.

By Friday, Rodan seemed satisfied that he could get no new information from Josh and released him to return to work. Josh needed life in the valley to go back to normal, but he noticed that his friends at the work site started to go silent the minute he got close. He knew they were talking about the upcoming trial, but not with him. Josh wanted to get mad, but then he realized maybe they were protecting his feelings.

One morning, he and Pehpe installed the tiles they had designed above the kitchen counter. Josh brought up the subject himself. "What's the latest on the trial? Do you know if it will still happen next week?"

Pehpe finished troweling and held out his hand for the next tile. "Yeah, as far as I know. Why?"

"Oh, just curious, that's all," Josh said. "Actually, I wondered if the council had run into problems or something. No one seems to want to talk to me about it. Maybe I'm being paranoid. Should I be worried?"

"Don't worry. The trial will happen. The jurors are already gathered. Are you going?" Pehpe handed him the trowel. "Here, you try doing the next one. You've seen how much mortar you need and how smooth, right?"

"Yeah, thanks." Josh took the trowel and scooped up some of the mortar, keeping his eyes on his work instead of looking Pehpe in the eye. After he placed the tile, he said, "Yes, I'm going. Do you think I'll have to testify?"

"Don't you want to? I mean, they have to hear about how he cloaked and kidnapped you."

"Yeah, I guess." Josh scooped more mortar on the wall and reached for another tile. "It's not like I remember much. I mean, we had a conversation, but it's a bit blurry." He squeezed his eyes shut tight, thinking maybe the smell of the mortar was getting to him.

"Are you okay?" Pehpe asked, concerned. "Your head still hurting?" Josh held out his hand for the next tile. "It comes and goes."

"Maybe you should go back and see Ohma," Pehpe suggested. He gently leaned against Josh's shoulder to move him out of the way and placed the tile himself. "No one knows how shielding affects a Netah. I mean Vehoe knows, but it was never designed for use on beings, only on objects. You should probably take it easy."

"I can't just lay around my room feeling sorry for myself," Josh objected. "I need to stay busy." He surrendered the trowel and mortar to Pehpe and handed him tiles as needed.

"I understand," Pehpe said, placing spacers and squaring up the tiles. "Listen, why don't you take a break from this. It could be the fumes getting to you. Go on and get some fresh air. I can finish this up."

"Thanks." Josh moved to stand in the open doorway, letting the sun warm his face. He checked their work from his new perspective and saw that only a few more tiles were needed. He liked the effects of the texture Nohka had chosen, the wavy lines he'd made with a pointed stick. He tried to picture what the finished room would look like and asked, "Why is this kitchen so small?"

"Well, it is only for two Netahs, after all."

"Unless they have kids," Josh said.

Pehpe nodded as he concentrated on the last tile placement. "Yeah, but in the deep winter when food outside gets scarce, we cook and make dinner with friends. Don't you do that in your lodge?"

Josh remembered when Rodan decided that the lodge would eat inside three nights a week. That felt like ages ago, and he'd missed the party when they'd had guests. Their menus were limited, either vegetable stew and bread or soup. "I guess you're right. We seem to be eating together inside more often these days."

"I suppose each lodge has its own traditions. Maybe the security house has fewer regular inside meals because members are often out on patrol?" Pehpe wiped off the trowel with a rag and gathered up the rest of their supplies.

Josh stepped forward to help. "Yeah, maybe that's it."

Pehpe asked, "Have you tried all the jobs at this site yet?"

"I don't know. I've made clay bricks, wheelbarrowed tons of dirt with the landscapers, tiled, but the carpentry was already done before I arrived."

"Why don't you go ahead and ask Kim? He'll tell you if there's something you missed."

"Okay, thanks. See you later." Josh wiped his hands on his jeans and followed Kim's voice. Kim stood outside the kitchen window with Haiman, discussing next steps, when Josh approached.

Haiman saw him first. "Hi, Josh, how're the tiles looking?"

"Great! We just finished up. Want to see?"

"Sure." Haiman said to Kim, "We're good?"

"You bet." Kim turned to Josh. "Hey, stick around a minute. We need to talk."

Josh nodded. "Okay, what's up?" He and Haiman exchanged nods and Haiman went inside without Josh.

"I've been watching your work and like what I see. You're not afraid of hard work and have a knack for adding an artistic touch. What do you think of your experience with us?"

"It's been fun."

". . . But? Are you ready to try something else?" Kim tilted his head and watched Josh's face closely.

Josh nodded, tucking his thumbs into his jeans pockets and studying his shoes. "Yeah, I guess I am," he admitted. He looked up. "Have I done everything around here? Are you saying it's time I tried a different field?"

"No, but the job was half done before you got here, and we're nearly done. It's only fair for you to get a chance to try other things. I'm prepared to release you to do that."

"Do you have any suggestions about what I should try next?" Josh asked hopefully, because he really had no idea what else Netah elk would do.

"How do you feel about healing? You could shadow Tomo and help him."

Josh hesitated. The thought actually made him a little nauseated. "Do I have to try everything? I mean, I'm not great around blood or wounds."

Kim laughed and nodded. "I feel the same way. No problem. How about farming and gardening? We practice a form of horticulture that is a combination of both. Want to give that a try?"

"That sounds good. When can I start?"

"Next week." He paused. "No, I mean after the trial. First, let's get everyone together for a quick wrap-up. Why don't you go and gather everyone? Tell them to meet me here in a few minutes."

"Sure thing." Josh walked inside the house and found Ano and Eve painting what might become a bedroom. Nohka and Haiman were admiring the tiles with Pehpe. Manny worked outside with a small crew on landscaping and blending the site into its surroundings. They had bushes and grasses placed and ready to be planted. Boulders, rocks, and soil had been placed in random patches that appeared completely natural. Josh was impressed as he returned to wait with Kim, and asked, "What other fields can I try as an apprentice?"

"Well, let's see. There's the security team, of course, you're in their lodge. There's the diplomatic corps. You might like that. You already have friends among other Netah groups. There's our judicial branch. We also have groups working in engineering, sound, and light research."

"What would I have to know before I could work in research?"

"We would test your basic knowledge and then supplement it with books if necessary. You'd start as a lab assistant and learn as you go like you've done with us."

Once the crew had assembled, Kim drew them into a circle, keeping Josh at his side. Kim fixed his gaze on two guys who seemed deep in conversation and waited for them to finish. Then he said, "Thanks for coming together, team. I wanted you to have a chance to see our visitor before he moves on to his next field." He put his arm over Josh's shoulder and said, "Josh has been a great addition to our team. He worked well with all of you, worked hard, didn't balk at any task given him and offered new ideas. That's the kind of guy or gal we're looking for, but since this was his first assignment, we have to let him see what else is out there."

There were nods of agreement and approval around the circle. Josh glanced at Ano, sorry he'd see less of her. She caught his eye and smiled encouragingly.

Kim continued. "Let's call it a day. I have a thermos of tea if anybody wants some before you head home. Take a moment to wish Josh well." Kim stepped back out of the circle and poured himself a small mug of tea, watching his crew mill around, waiting for their turn to talk with Josh.

Haiman and Nohka came over first. "Hey, Josh," Nohka said. "It was great meeting you. Thank you for the beautiful tiles. I love them!"

Haiman nodded his agreement. "You need me to walk with you back to the lodge?"

"Oh, no, thanks. I think I can find my way by now."

"Good job," Haiman said, giving him a friendly pat on the back and walking away with Nohka.

Pehpe walked over and said, "Want some company on your way back? Let me know when you're ready, okay?"

"Yeah, that'd be great, thanks," Josh said.

Eve and Ano overheard, so Eve said, "We'll join you, too, if that's okay?" Ano's eyes were wide with hope.

"Sure!" Josh and Pehpe said at the same time.

"Okay," Eve said, then with a nod to Ano, said, "We need a few more minutes to finish painting the bedroom. Can you wait twenty minutes?"

"Yeah, unless, you need help?" Josh asked.

"No, we only have the two rollers. You could help us clean up, though. Give us fifteen minutes and then come find us inside, okay?"

"Sure." Josh tucked his hands in his pockets and wondered how he would know fifteen minutes had passed. Time was fluid among the Netahs.

Manny came up next. "Nice job with the tiles, Josh. You're very creative, and I liked how you worked with Pehpe, letting him join you and try his own ideas. That shows good leadership skills. What will you try next?"

"Sounds like I should go to the horticulture group. Kim suggested it. I wondered, did they help with the plantings here?"

"Sure did. In fact, let me introduce you to our horticultural consultant. She designed it all." Manny looked for his person and catching her eye, waved her over.

A tall blond with a pixie haircut walked up and held out her hand, then pulled back when she realized it was caked with dirt. "Hi, Josh. I'm Posie. Sorry about the dirt." She brushed her hands together to remove some. "Nice to meet you."

"Hi," Josh said, a little taken aback that she knew him.

Manny said, "Posie, you finished up here today, right? Josh says he wants to try horticulture next. Can I ask you to swing by his lodge on Monday and take him with you on your next assignment?"

"That would be my pleasure," she said with a quiet smile. Her chin tilted down in a deferential way when Manny spoke to her, but when she spoke to Josh, she raised her chin and looked him right in the eye. She asked, "Can you be ready to go at sunrise?"

Josh's eyebrows flew up, but he straightened his face and replied as calmly as possible, "Uh, sure. Do you always start so early?" *This could be a deal breaker.*

"No, but my project next week is at the other end of the valley. We're mending a riverbed and stand of willows." Manny watched this exchange and then nodded approvingly as he waited for Josh to respond.

Josh relaxed and said, "Okay, I'll be outside my lodge at sunrise then. Thanks, Posie."

"Not a problem," she said, moving away to speak with one of the others. Josh heard her say, "Do you have any questions about finishing up?" They walked up the hill of the site, talking, pointing, nodding.

Manny clapped him on the back and said, "Well, this is goodbye then, Josh. Nice working with you, and I hope we see you again."

"Thanks, Manny. Bye." Josh beamed at the praise as Manny turned and walked away.

Josh watched Posie. It looked like she knew what she was doing. He wondered how long it would take for him to know plants like that. His experience potting geraniums with his mom in their front porch planters would probably not go very far out here. He felt eyes on him and turned to see Eve, Ano, and Pehpe standing behind him in their elk forms.

Pehpe laughed, "I saw you watching Posie. Did you just set up to meet on Monday? Look at you, making new friends already!"

Eve said, "She seems nice. Not as nice as we are, but nice enough."

Ano grinned mischievously. "Don't let her break your heart, Josh."

Josh blushed but grinned back at Ano. With a sigh he said, "Yeah, right. You guys hungry? I think I saw a fresh patch of clover on my way over this morning. Come on, I'll show you."

"Ooh, clover . . . a taste of spring!" Eve giggled as she walked next to Pehpe.

Josh turned into an elk. Ano walked up next to him and said quietly, "Just because you're moving on to another field doesn't mean you have to be a stranger. Want to meet me tomorrow and go for a nice long walk?"

He nodded to Ano. "That sounds great. Tomorrow is Saturday, right? Shall we meet around mid-morning? I can meet you at your lodge."

Ano looked flustered. "But you've never been there, you'll get lost. Besides, we're well hidden." She turned into an elk and continued. "I'll come by your lodge to pick you up, and later, I'll give you a tour of our place."

Pehpe wandered over to stand next to Josh as they watched the females walk along the edge of the aspen grove. They lingered, waiting for Pehpe. A thought occurred to Josh. "Hey, Ano was flirting with me, right?"

"Huh?" Pehpe hadn't been paying attention. He chewed thoughtfully and glanced after the females. "Maybe, I don't know, probably."

"You'd tell me if you knew she liked me, wouldn't you?" Josh asked quietly.

"Yup, uh-huh, definitely." Pehpe nodded.

Josh wondered if Pehpe was as clueless as Josh felt. Which reminded him. "Hey, do you know when the trial is set to begin? I thought it would be within a week."

"That's right. It starts Monday."

"Shit!" Josh spit out the word angrily.

"What?" Pehpe asked in alarm.

"I just promised to go with Posie on Monday, but I have to go to the trial." Josh hung his head. "I hate breaking promises."

Pehpe smiled a grass-filled, toothy elk grin. "You're worried she won't like you if you break your date?"

Josh sighed, "Maybe, I mean, no, it's not a date!" He suspected she'd probably understand if she knew anything about him at all. "No, not worried," he said. "But I do have to get word to her. I'll go find her. I'll be right back." Moments later Josh returned.

Josh looked from Pehpe to Ano. Could elk shrug their shoulders? That's what it looked like Pehpe did before he said, "Problem solved. I'm still hungry. How about you?"

"Yep."

Josh realized he hadn't really worked out any details for their walk the next day. He nibbled his way next to Ano and pretended to accidentally brush against her side. Not knowing his way around Netah elk niceties, he figured it would be nonthreatening. Ano stepped away in alarm.

"I'm sorry, I didn't mean to scare you," he said.

She huffed. "Scared? I'm not scared of you."

"No, I mean, I'm sorry I bumped into you," Josh said, wondering what made her angry this time. He waited and watched her reaction.

Ano cocked her head at him, then the ends of her mouth quirked up, and she moved closer to nudge up against him as he had just done. "Apology accepted," she said.

Josh grinned. "Good, I'm looking forward to our walk tomorrow."

"Me, too," Ano agreed.

"I mean, a walk with someone new," Josh corrected himself.

"I'm not new, you've known me for ages," Ano snorted in a very unladylike and elkish way.

Josh looked her straight in the eye now, trying to see if she laughed out of humor or sarcasm. The twinkle in her eye said humor and teasing. He took on a professorial tone as he answered, "Yes, a new female, of a certain species, a species with which I have recently become acquainted." He paused to judge the effect of his tone. The amusement remained on her face, so he continued, "A species and female of said species with whom I would like to become better acquainted." He gave her a very toothy and probably grassy grin.

Ano transformed into a human and gave him a royal curtsy, a lovely smile softening her features.

Josh transformed immediately and responded with an elegant bow. When he straightened, he held out his hand to take hers and asked, "What time shall I expect your visit, milady?"

She offered her hand, and Josh kissed it. She giggled and said, "If it's not too early, milord, I shall arrive when the sun has reached the yardarm and you have broken your fast."

"As you wish, milady." Josh bowed again. Then he studied her a moment before asking her with a grin, "Are you a student of Shakespeare?"

"He's been dead a long time, so not precisely, but who isn't?" she said.

"Are we going to continue to talk like this tomorrow?" Josh laughed silently.

"As the mood requires," she said in a royal tone as she turned back into an elk and wandered off looking for more to eat.

Josh nodded and thought twice about bowing again. He had always loved Shakespeare and had suddenly found a fellow admirer, of Shakespeare, that is. "Hey," he said, "What's a yardarm, anyway?"

"A piece of a sailing ship, I think," Ano said over her shoulder.

"Huh," Josh said, as he, too, turned back into an elk to look for one last bite to eat.

Pehpe showed up at exactly the right moment and said, "I'm stuffed. Ready to go?"

Josh nodded.

Pehpe paused. "Everything okay? What did Ano want?"

Josh shook his head. "Yeah, I'm fine." Leaning towards his friend he said quietly, "She's definitely flirting, so yes, she likes me, just so you know."

Pehpe squinted as if that would help him figure it out, then with a nod he said, "Yeah, she likes you, I could tell."

"How?" Josh had to know what he'd missed.

"Well," Pehpe said. "How about the way she chooses to talk to you when she gives the rest of the builders the cold shoulder?"

"Dude," Josh sighed. "I have a lot to learn about Netah girl signals."

"You'll get the hang of it. Don't rush it." Pehpe grinned.

Eve and Ano had found each other and walked away. Ano stopped and looked back at Josh. "Bye, Josh. See you tomorrow!" She gave Eve a sly grin as they walked away. Then they took off on their lovely elk legs.

Pehpe nudged Josh as they followed and said quietly, "You sly dog!" They were simply elk, innocently walking across the valley, and there were no innuendoes hanging in the air at all.

CHAPTER 19

High Altitude Date

The next morning, Josh woke up early and paced the great room, peering out the window at every pass. He had no idea what time the sun would be past the yardarm. He really wished he could look it up online, but of course, he couldn't. Having no watch or phone or computer to check for the time left Josh a bit disoriented, it was an adjustment. He hadn't yet learned how to listen and talk through the Netah undernet. That seemed more for messages, not getting information from a search engine. Frustrated at the lack of resources for getting information, he finally went outside to get breakfast, figuring Ano would appear soon, and he could eat while he waited.

Ano finally appeared and Josh walked over to meet her.

"Well met," she said with a little smile.

Having spent what felt like the whole morning waiting, Josh wasn't in the mood for more Elizabethan role-playing. "Yep. Where are we heading?" he asked.

With a sigh of disappointment Ano answered, "Everything okay?"

"Sure, sure, sorry. I'm fine. It's just," he hesitated, then decided to be honest. "I had no idea what you meant by 'sun over the yardarm' and so I've been watching and waiting for hours. Stupid, huh?" He tried to laugh at himself so he wouldn't sound whiney.

Ano nodded. "I get it. You're still trying to figure out how to live as a Netah, and we treat time differently from humans."

"Yeah, there're no clocks, but we all seem to sleep and wake at the same time. I sleep really well, usually, but it's really different not working on a time schedule," he said.

"I guess that's our animal parts, our biological clocks, right?" Ano asked.

"Right. I don't think humans pay much attention to theirs."

"I never thought about it like that," she said. Josh was grateful that she understood his difficulty.

Ano said, "I thought we'd go to a beautiful lake hidden up a mountain valley. Do you feel up to a climb?"

"Sure, but can we start off slowly? I just ate," Josh admitted.

"That works for me, I just ate, too."

"Okay, which way?"

Ano led the way towards the mountains and a place where a river came tumbling over rocks into the valley. They climbed steadily as the morning air warmed, or maybe they were warmed by the effort of the climb. They paused at the stream under some cottonwoods that had lacey green buds just forming on their branches, and they took a sip. They had only exchanged a few words so far. Having caught their breath and taken a drink, Josh wanted to talk. "Hey, can we rest here for a bit? I need to catch my breath."

"Sure, no problem." They settled on the ground on a patch of soft buffalo grass and gazed out over the valley.

Josh asked, "Have you had a chance to try other fields already? Did you try horticulture?"

"Yes, we all start working at different things when we're kids. I tried horticulture years ago. I hated it." She shrugged and laughed at herself. "I'm not sure why. Maybe I'm not patient enough to wait for things to grow. I need instant gratification. With construction, you see progress every day."

"Hmm, that makes sense. Do you ever wish you could use bull-dozers to make it easier?" Josh asked.

"Easy is not the point. Our way is traditional, it's organic, and we've been perfecting our methods and designs for centuries," she said. "Besides, it would be very obvious there are humans out here if we suddenly had bulldozers kicking up dust."

Josh could see her point and liked that she had opinions and was proud of her work. "Are there books that describe the building process? I mean are there Netah textbooks?"

"Yep," Ano said. "My grandfather actually wrote one of the most popular books about building design. He studied with a very famous human architect. You might have heard of him, Frank Lloyd Wright?"

Josh's head snapped up, his muzzle dropping open. "You're kidding me. How could he do that?"

"Simple, he studied at Taliesin West," she said with a very matter-of-fact tone and maybe a hint of bragging. "He had to stay human the whole time, of course, but everyone does that. He wrote his book afterwards when he returned to us. He learned to take long walks alone so he could transform for a while where no one could see him and recover a little, then return to the site. You know the apprentices all lived and worked together in the same place. Grandpa said it was grueling but worth it. I have a copy of his book, if you want to see it."

"I'd like that," Josh said. "Did he inspire you to go into building?"

"Probably, and I also prefer the design end of things. I have a lot of designs, but no one has bought one."

"That's amazing. Can I see them?"

"I'll show you when we get back."

Josh asked, "How many other Netahs live among humans like that? Is it always so they can learn something?"

"Hmm, they really don't tell you much in your lodge, do they? You must feel so lost all the time. I don't mean spatially, but about how things work here."

"The guys are not very chatty," Josh admitted. He'd gotten used to not knowing what to expect or even what to ask.

Ano had paused.

Josh said, "Yeah, yeah, I know. You're not sure how much I'm supposed to know."

Ano frowned and said, "Screw that. You should know. I think it sucks that no one talks about this stuff with you. It's not all a big dark secret. We must remain hidden, yes, but why shouldn't you know how we live? It's like they expect you to just absorb from the air what we learn from birth."

Josh nodded. "Yeah, that's for sure."

"Well, I'm just gonna tell you, because I'm your friend. Every Netah spends a year living as a human. We can choose when and where. It can be school; it can be at a job. We all go before we're twenty years old, that's the only hard and fast rule."

I have time to figure out what I want to do, I'm only fifteen. He asked, "Have you done your human year yet?"

"No, I'm still deciding." She got to her feet and gazed uphill.

"You know," Josh said, also getting up. "It sounds like how humans who go to college do a study abroad year. It's supposed to broaden our horizons and give us new perspectives."

"That's exactly right." She nodded. "So, you understand that it's important. Come on, we should get moving. I'm not sure how long the weather will hold. See those puffy clouds peeking over the mountain? There could be just a couple more, or another thicker and darker cloud right behind it. We might lose our opportunity to see the lake." She started walking along the stream.

Josh followed, thinking about all she'd just told him. He asked, "If it's so hard to be human 24/7, how do you get through it?"

"Hah, that's the real test, isn't it? Sure, we may be at a job, or school, but we have to figure out how to get back to our Netah forms and stay hidden. It's part of the process." She stepped up her pace and broke out into an easy trot.

"So, what if you fail at that?" Josh called after her, thinking it would be so easy to slip up, especially if you were pretending to be a college kid, and there were parties and stuff. He didn't think she heard him, because she didn't answer. Instead, she broke into a gallop. The hill grew steeper, and he struggled to keep up. They only slowed when they entered a clearing surrounded by pines. Ano stopped to sniff the air. "Do you smell that?"

Josh sniffed but didn't know what she had sensed. "What is it?"

"Well." She paused. "There's obviously the pines, and wet rocks, but I hear something else, and can smell it, too."

Josh stood very still and paid better attention to what his nose picked up. He smelled pine and the sweet plants along the mineral-laden stream, and he heard a low rumble. "Is that rumble from a waterfall?"

"Well," Ano agreed. "There is a waterfall, actually a series of them, but they are small. It's more than that. I can't quite make it out."

Josh stuck out his tongue and tasted it. "There's a rainstorm somewhere nearby. Maybe you're hearing thunder from that?"

Ano stuck out her tongue, as well, uncomfortably close to Josh's mouth. She nodded. "That's it! Good job. Hey, try this." She put her nose to the ground and bit into a plant at her feet without chewing or biting it off.

Josh tried it. It made his lips tickle, so he let go. Ano stayed still and closed her eyes. Josh moved closer, thinking maybe she wanted him to taste that specific plant. He put his lips on the same plant. A vibration came through the leaves. He opened his eyes to see Ano watching him. She had not moved away but had released her mouth.

Josh released the plant, not liking the look she gave him. *Is she waiting for a kiss or something?* "Uh, what are we doing?" he asked.

"I wondered if you'd be able to feel the vibration. It's our undernet, our communication network."

Josh heard her words, factual words, but he suspected he missed something. He really wished he could figure out Netah body language. "Wait, what? You feel word vibrations?"

"Well, kind of." Ano beamed. She started walking again, and Josh walked beside her. "We learn how to understand and send infrasound vibrations through plant roots. I wondered if you could, since you're a halfling and didn't grow up learning that."

"You're wondering what else I can or cannot do?" This was familiar territory, unless she referred to Netah relationships, dating, or something else physical, which he really did not want to have to think about at this exact moment.

"I guess." She hesitated. "Sorry. Maybe I'm being insensitive."

He chuckled. *Oh good, she doesn't want to talk about that stuff, either!* He said, "I couldn't begin to tell you what I don't know." Maybe he could change the subject. "Can you teach me how to understand the undernet?"

"I'm not sure." Ano thought about that a minute. "Maybe Tomo would be better, he's a healer. He understands how our bodies work better than most. Maybe he can teach you how to interpret what you hear or feel. It'll probably be like learning a new language."

"I'll ask him." The tension eased, subject change number two: "Do you know where the trial will be?"

"Sure, I just got that message, too. I'm on the jury. You know the other Netah elk, as well. The council chose me, Nohka, Kim, Esok, and Rodan." She paused and remembered something. "Oh, and to answer your question, it's at the southern edge of our valley, near a stand of old growth firs."

"Huh," Josh responded. The whole idea of the trial had seemed unreal, like it would never actually happen. Suddenly it became real. "Is there anything else you can tell me about the trial?"

"Not really. I think you know it will look like a rodeo. I believe Lorna will be the judge and the jury will have other animal Netahs. Usually there is a small group of peers, and then other Netahs who have special abilities or senses. I'm curious to see who else will be on the jury."

"The charges are serious, right? Will Vehoe be killed this time?"

"We don't do capital punishment."

"Oh, right. I knew that." Josh fell silent. They'd been having such a nice morning, walking, running, sipping cool refreshing stream water. "You know what? It's such a beautiful day, let's not let the trial spoil it. Do you mind?"

Ano raised her eyebrows then nodded. "You're right, let's worry about the trial when we have to, not now."

Josh asked, "Do you think we should still go to the lake like you planned? I mean it smells like the weather is changing."

She studied the clouds, then said, "I think we'll be fine; the clouds are blowing over. Besides, it's not like we melt in the rain, our coats keep us warm and dry. If you're still up to it, I am."

"Okay, let's go," Josh laughed.

Ano led them through the underbrush. There was no trail to follow, so he fell in behind her. At first, they walked easily into the woods, but their route became steeper, through thicker underbrush, then the boulders got bigger, and the trees spread out and became stunted. Josh remembered that these high-altitude trees were probably bristlecone pines. *Okay, so I know two plants already, geraniums and bristlecone pines. Oh, and dandelions.* The air cooled off as the clouds continued to pour over the top of the mountain and a stiff breeze stirred leaves off the ground.

By the summit, they had left the tree line behind, and Josh felt like he was at the top of the world. The wind whistled through spaces between boulders. They could see for miles in every direction. Gusts stirred the surface of a lake just below them, making it sparkle in the patches of sunlight. Josh heard the little squeaks of picas among the rocks and watched a chipmunk scamper and disappear a few feet away.

Josh heard a loud crack and his heart skipped a beat. He turned to see Ano's reaction. She grinned, shrugged, and led the way gingerly towards the lake and a grassy knoll surrounded by thick bushes that protected them from the wind. They settled down to rest and watch the clouds rush overhead.

Josh sensed vibrations through the ground. He rested his nose on a soft cushiony tuft of grass and tried to see if he could make any sense out of the vibrations. He detected a definite pattern. He made a low rumble in his throat and felt it translate through the grasses into the ground.

"Hey!" Ano yelped. "Did you do that?"

"I, uh, maybe?" Josh grinned.

"Do it again!" She kept her head up but seemed to concentrate on where her body touched the ground.

"Why?"

"I don't know, it felt funny."

"What did I say?"

"What did you try to say?"

"Nothing, just a hum."

Ano laughed silently. "Yeah, that's right. The hum was so strong, though, that I felt it through my tummy!"

"Huh." Josh tried to concentrate and see if he could feel anything else from the ground. "Is that the wind making the sound, or communications from someone?" Josh asked.

Ano lowered her muzzle to the ground and checked. "Wind."

"Ah." Josh felt the tingle of the ozone in his teeth. "Are we safe up here?" he asked, hoping not to sound worried.

Ano watched the clouds a moment, their color deepening towards gray. "I'm not afraid of a little rain, but that cloud," she indicated with her nose, "looks ominous. Look at my back, the fur is bristling, right?"

"Is that static?" Josh asked.

"I think so. We heard thunder, but no lightening so far. This might just all blow right over."

"You want to wait it out up here?" Josh asked incredulously.

"Sure."

Josh lowered his head to the ground to create less of a target for lightening and tried to pretend he was as calm as Ano appeared to be.

Her composure broke when a bolt of lightning struck on the other side of the lake and was immediately followed by a thunderclap that rattled their bones. She leapt to her feet and yelled, "Come on, let's get out of here!"

Tearing down the mountain after Ano was scary and exhilarating. They crashed through the brush, leaped over boulders, slid down scree fields. At the cottonwoods, they paused long enough to take another drink, then continued running across a mesa, a sheet of rain hot on their heels.

As they came off the mesa into the valley, a light drizzle caught up with them, washing the dust out of the air and their coats. Ano slowed just as the rain turned into a deluge. Laughing, she transformed and then leaned against a pink boulder streaked with white quartz. The boulder slid inward silently, revealing her lodge. Josh transformed as they stepped inside. Eve approached with towels. "That was close," she said. "You guys okay?"

Josh wiped his face and toweled his hair, then draped the towel around his shoulders. "I wondered if we could transform into dry humans. I guess not, eh?" he laughed.

"Doesn't work that way," Ano giggled. "Come on, we can dry by the fire." Ano led Josh into a great room. A wall of windows tucked under an overhanging rock ledge, looked like his own lodge, with a similar smooth, red stone floor. The stucco walls were stained a warm yellow. A firepit filled the center of the room, with a cone-like chimney suspended above it and disappearing into the ceiling. The chimney looked like red clay pottery. Low flames rose from a bed of sand-colored gravel, surrounded by a river rock ledge. They settled onto purple and green floor cushions.

"How did you know we were coming?" Josh asked Eve. "Thanks for the towels."

Eve looked at Ano and said with a smirk, "A little bird told me."

"Or a Netah elk?" Josh asked.

"Yeah, or that."

Josh held his hands to the warmth of the flames and found himself wondering what created the heat under the rocks.

As if reading his mind, Eve said, "There's a flammable gel underneath. It's odorless and smokeless. Our all-things-environmental expert, Noomi, didn't object. Cool, huh?" She turned to Ano. "How far did you get?"

"We made it to the lake, but then the storm blew in and we tore out of there. We ran all the way back," Ano said.

"Nice workout!" Eve sounded impressed.

"Yeah, I'll probably pay for it tomorrow." Ano grinned.

"That's okay, you have a whole day to rest before we're back to work. I was just going to warm up a pot of soup for the evening. How does that sound?" Eve asked Ano.

Ano looked at Josh. "We have plenty. Will you stay?"

"That sounds great, thanks. Meantime, can I have a tour?"

Ano nodded and they all rose to their feet. As they passed down a skylit hallway, Ano pointed out features, like a shower and bath space, a yoga studio, a room filled with drafting tables and shelves, and their own private hot springs bubbling up into a stone pool and spilling through a floor drain at the end of the hall. "That's our in-floor heat. Lucky us, right?" Ano said.

"Nice," Josh agreed.

Eve placed a kettle full of soup on a trivet over the flames in the fireplace and then they all relaxed on the floor pillows and watched the rain pelt the ground outside.

Josh remembered Ano's designs. "Is this a good time to show me your designs?"

Ano startled, then moved to her feet with enthusiasm. "You bet. I'll be right back."

As soon as Ano left, Eve said, "You two seem to be getting along."

"Yeah, I guess." He shrugged. *Nosy much? If she's looking for gossip, she won't get it from me!*

Eve frowned. "That's great."

"Uh-huh. We had a nice walk." *On the other hand, maybe Eve is just being friendly? Is that why she frowned at me, because I'm not being friendly? I should lighten up.*

"Good." Eve got up and wiped the kitchen counter before disappearing down the hall.

Josh had missed his opportunity to be friendly with Eve. He hoped he'd get another chance. He didn't know why she rubbed him wrong, but realized it would be a bad idea to antagonize her if he wanted to get closer to Ano. They were roommates, after all.

Ano returned and Josh studied each drawing for long moments, pointing out things he thought were interesting. Ano seemed pleased. She moved closer and looked over his shoulder at the drawings with him. Josh could feel the heat radiating from her body, almost tasted it. Actually, it tasted like fresh green grass.

Ano noticed. "You like it? It's my new scent, Verde." She held up her wrist for him.

Josh nodded. "It's really nice," he said. "It's like springtime in a meadow full of wildflowers."

"That's what I thought!" Ano exclaimed, beaming. She rested her head on his shoulder with a contented sigh as he finished flipping through the pages.

Josh set the notebook aside and rolled onto his back, his hands under his head. He opened his mouth to say thanks for a great day, when he felt her hand slip into his. He sniffed and realized that Verde wasn't the only scent in the room. His own exposed armpits were ripe as they'd ever been. He lowered his arms and sat up quickly, keeping her hand in his and turning to her. He looked into her soft brown eyes and nearly melted where he sat. She was pretty. He looked down at her hand and ran his finger through the tiny hairs on her arm.

"Ano, today has been one of the nicest days I've had since I became a Netah. Thank you, and thank you for everything you told me about Netah life. You are a good friend."

Ano gazed into his eyes. Josh squirmed. She said, "You know I'd like us to be more than friends, right?"

Josh simply nodded, fighting the urge to look away. "I don't know how to be more than a Netah friend," he admitted.

Ano's smile grew, and she pressed her lips together as if to control it. "I'll be gentle."

Josh laughed and smiled affectionately at Ano. "Gentle is the least of my worries." He gathered his thoughts while studying her delicate hands. "I've never had a girlfriend, even as a human, but now? I don't know where to begin."

"I will teach you," she murmured.

His eyes drifted to the dancing flames. "What if I step over a line that I don't know about? What are we allowed to do? What are the rules of dating for Netahs?" Josh stopped there. He could barely speak, and he felt his voice begin to waver. *What's going on here? I'm terrified!*

Ano gently let go of Josh's hand and gazed into the fire, as well. They sat in silence for several minutes as they both got their feelings under control. Finally, Ano said, "What if we ask permission before we do anything?"

"What, from Hesta or something?"

"No, silly, from each other!" She leaned towards him. "Like this. May I kiss you?"

With a sigh of contentment, Josh nodded and met her halfway. Their lips met and lingered. Ano put her hand on his cheek and moved her lips to the side of his mouth, his cheek, his chin.

Josh felt heat rise from his core. It was scary and exciting. He wanted more, but also didn't. He pulled back and stared into her eyes, searching. He saw affection, excitement, and a little disappointment. He had to do something about that.

"I like you, too," he said quietly. "That was nice, no not nice, wonderful!"

Ano's smile widened and she leaned in again.

"But." She pulled away. "But let's stop there. Let's talk and get to know each other. Tell me how dating works among Netahs, so I know and can relax. Okay?" He saw the little lines gather between her eyebrows. "Please?"

Ano tilted her head to the side and said, "Okay."

With a sigh of relief that Josh hoped Ano wouldn't misinterpret, he got to his feet and stepped towards the door. "I should go."

"What, no dinner?" Eve said, coming back into the room as if on cue.

"No, thanks, though. It smells really good." Josh got to the door and then turned back. "Will I see you at the trial?"

"Sure," they both answered.

Josh nodded and pulled the door open. "Good, thanks for a wonderful day."

"You're welcome!" they both answered. Josh heard them giggle as he gently shut the door.

The rain had stopped, but water still dripped off an overhang and down the back of his neck. Josh stepped away and skirted puddles that were quickly being absorbed by the soil. The edge of the setting sun disappeared over the mountains as he watched.

Josh gulped in the cool fresh air and got his bearings as he turned into an elk. He walked slowly, nibbling his way across the landscape. *Hesta told me the girls aren't shy, but I'm not ready for this.* He noticed landmarks in the valley. *I like Ano, a lot, but . . . I don't know anything!* He knew where the lodge was from where he stood. *Maybe I need some guy advice, but who can I ask?*

Stepping inside his own lodge, he spotted Tomo sitting by the windows, gazing out, his mind obviously miles away. Josh sat next to him. Tomo blinked and turned to Josh. "How was your day?"

"Very nice." Josh nodded. "Ano took me to a beautiful mountain lake."

"Did you avoid the storm?"

"Just barely, but yeah." Josh grinned. "What did you do today?"

"Not much." Tomo shook his head, running his hand through his dark floppy hair. "I guess I had a lot to process from the last few days. How are you holding up?"

"You mean about my dad?" Josh asked, grateful Tomo wouldn't pry for details about his day. *Talk about a lot to process!* On the other hand, he had so many questions, and he trusted Tomo not to make fun of his cluelessness.

"Yeah, that and how's your head? You worried about the trial?"

"I wouldn't say worried." Josh rubbed the back of his neck. "Maybe relieved is the word. I want to hear his excuses in front of a jury. I know what he told me, but I got to a point where I couldn't believe a word he said."

"I'm sorry," Tomo said. "That must have been hard."

"Confusing, annoying, maddening." *Just like me trying to figure out how to talk to Netah girls! I do not have time for that now.* He sat back and relaxed. "I think it's weird that I didn't really fear him, even after he kidnapped me. I felt angry. Maybe I wasn't fair to him," Josh said.

"Fairness is not usually a concept that comes up in a kidnapping," Tomo said. "Escape, maybe."

"He didn't seem strong. He seemed frail."

"He carried you out of here in broad daylight, so not that frail," Tomo laughed.

Josh realized that was true. "Yeah, I guess. Hey, enough of this! What time do we leave for the trial?"

"You have another whole day before it starts. I think most of us will be there."

"Right. Tomorrow may feel like the longest day of my life." Josh dropped his head between his hands.

"Hey, leave it to me. I have an idea."

"Thanks, Tomo. You're a good friend."

Tomo shook his head. "It's nothing." He stood up. "So, I understand you had a conversation with Ano about our undernet. Want to do some experiments on that? I can teach you a few things, at least, get you started. I mean, we all kind of learn it as we grow up around here, but I think I can help you."

"That would be awesome!" He almost said "Dude!" but stopped. He hadn't heard anyone use that expression for so long. It sounded so human. It felt wrong. *Wait, how did Tomo know about his conversation with Ano? The undernet? Is there no privacy on it? Weird!*

CHAPTER 20

Last Goodbye

The next day Josh and Tomo sauntered out the door well after the sun passed the yardarm. At least Josh had slept well. They made their way at a leisurely pace towards the eastern side of the valley, which Josh had not yet explored. Willows, whose branches turned red as they woke in the warm air, filled a marshy area. He spotted a beaver lodge in one pond. The pale blue sky felt enormous and endless. A cool breeze swept off a river filled with ice melt. They crossed it in two leaps through the shallows, then followed a gorge between two peaks, clothed in dense evergreens.

Josh called out to Tomo, who had moved ahead, "I know you want this to be a big mystery, but how far are we going? I mean, I did a big hike yesterday with Ano, and am a little sore from that."

Tomo stopped and waited for Josh to catch up. "We can rest here for a bit if you want. There's a really nice view just over that ridge, which was my destination. Can you make that?" He indicated the direction with a wave of his big head. Josh suddenly noticed that Tomo had grown new antlers. Josh wondered if his were growing, as well. He couldn't exactly reach up a hand to find out.

"Okay, yeah, probably," Josh agreed. "Hey, nice antlers."

Tomo looked puzzled. "What? Oh, right. Yeah, they always start growing this time of year. Yours are coming in, too, you know."

Josh had wondered if his would grow in the usual springtime schedule, since they had appeared in the fall originally. Their reappearance now felt like a good sign.

Tomo started off again and then abruptly froze and said, "Shh!" Josh froze in place. They picked up the sound of human voices. They moved into a dense stand of pines for cover and focused on the voices.

Josh whispered, "Do you recognize who that is?"

Tomo tilted his head and listened intently. "They sound familiar," he whispered, too. "Let's listen."

Josh didn't move a muscle except to scan with his eyes for movement. The voices were approaching, getting louder. He heard a male and a female. They could be anyone from the village, but for some reason Josh didn't think these were locals. He couldn't pick out words until he heard the phrase: high school. That settled it, they were not locals. Netahs didn't go to high school!

Tomo settled quietly to the ground, his ears still perked up. Josh did the same. Then, Josh recognized the laughter. It was Anton and Sarah. *Again!?*

He could see them sit on a log, digging into a pack. A few minutes later they resumed their hike.

After they'd passed, Josh asked Tomo, "We're no longer on our Netah land, right? I mean, we passed the wires a long time ago. Where are we?"

Tomo answered, "We're on Bureau of Land Management land. Those two are probably day-hiking. I mean they're not carrying large packs, right?"

"We going to follow them?" Josh asked.

"Up to you." Tomo shrugged.

"I'm dying to know why they're back here. Do you mind?"

"Okay, but let's keep our distance." Tomo led the way through the woods, pausing as needed to remain unnoticed. The two humans reached a pond and rested again. Josh got closer so he could hear.

Sarah sighed and asked, "Do you still think we saw Josh that day?"

Anton pulled at the dry grasses in front of him. "It sure looked like him."

Sarah reached over and put her hand on top of his. "You have to let him go, Anton. He's gone. He's not coming back."

Anton shook his head, pressing his eyes with the heel of his hands.

Josh gasped, but he kept his eyes on his old friend while his ears strained to catch every word.

Anton squeezed his lips together with determination, then dropped his hands to the grass and yanked up a handful to sort through. He picked out a long wide piece and held it to his lips. He made a buzzing sound, blowing against it. His shoulders shook with quiet laughter. Sarah giggled and scrambled to watch him do it again. Anton played the grass like it was a kazoo and managed to produce a tune that sounded like taps. Josh had had enough; he moved away and found his friend Tomo.

Tomo said, "They used to be your friends, right? They were the campers and the kids with the drone. Did you expect them to come back?"

Josh snorted. "No, never. I don't know why they keep showing up. I think Sarah's parents have a place in the mountains, maybe it's close."

"He really seemed to miss you," Tomo said.

Josh realized Tomo had heard that part. "Yeah, I'm glad they have each other." Josh considered what they'd said. "I think he's been searching for me, like he thought he'd seen me."

"When could that have happened?"

"Maybe . . ." Josh tried to remember the series of events. "I was camping with Rose before Hesta came. Anton could have spotted me with a drone. Maybe his drone woke us up! We turned into animals, and Rose sprayed the site, so the humans we heard approaching turned around and ran. I had forgotten about that."

"Where were you?" Tomo sounded alarmed.

"I have no idea, except it took Hesta and me two days to get here later. He thought we'd gone at least eighty miles." The two Netahs considered the facts for a moment.

Tomo spoke. "Yeah, no way Anton could have followed you here. It must be a coincidence."

"You think? I wonder." Josh sighed. He and Tomo glanced in the direction of his friends. Josh said, "It makes sense that they're together. Sarah is very empathetic. They've known each other forever.

"How does that make you feel?" Tomo asked.

Josh stared into the treetops, scanned the horizon through the tree trunks, studied the wildflowers pushing their way up through the leaf humus at his feet, and listened to the chickadees singing in the bare trees. He bit off a tiny dried strawberry hiding at his feet. Swallowing, he said, "Life goes on. We change. I have a good friend, too." He looked Tomo in the eye. "I've changed! I mean look at me!" They both laughed and nodded in agreement. Josh turned to continue their walk up the hill. "Besides, look where I live. It's amazing. It's fantastic. So, where are we going? Views, caves, waterfalls? What?"

"I had a view in mind."

"All right, lead on. The therapy session has ended!"

The two friends climbed until the sun blazed directly overhead. They walked to a saddle between two peaks. Several yards away the ground suddenly dropped off in a sheer cliff. The horizon held misty layers of distant mountains and they spotted several mountain goats just below them.

"Wow!" Josh said. "Where are we?"

"You don't know?" Tomo asked.

"Not really, I mean, Colorado still, probably?"

"Yes."

"But you can't tell me any more than that, right?" Josh asked.

"Yeah, for now. But don't worry. I think that once the trial is over and your father is taken care of, you won't have to keep proving yourself anymore, at least not any more than the rest of us."

Tomo and Josh sniffed the lichen and gave it a taste. Josh said, "I'm okay, you know."

"Yeah," Tomo responded. "But just so you know, if you need a friend to talk to, of course, you can call on me. I'm here."

"Yeah, I know," Josh said. "Thanks." He breathed in the cool mountain air with all its tastes and smells: sweet, musky, minerals, and plants. "I wouldn't go back even if I could."

"Really?" They started back down the mountain.

"Yeah, I mean, school was okay and all, but also high stress combined with massive amounts of boredom. At least here I can read what I want, work where I want, eat whenever I want. How could I ever go back? How could I ever give up this freedom?"

"I see."

"I'll tell you another thing," Josh said. "I don't miss all the stress around girls. The girls here seem so normal, they're not all gooey inside and boy crazy. They feel more like equals. And the guys, there's no one I can name who seems all sex starved or anything. It's almost as if no one even thinks about it. Am I right?" Josh didn't want to admit how Ano had made him feel. He hadn't been ready for that.

"Sure," Tomo agreed, "but that's only because you have not yet experienced the rut."

"Huh." Josh bit his lip as he reviewed in his mind what he knew about that. The males bugled, they fought each other, they decorated their antlers with vegetation to get the attention of the females. The females lived in harems. The strongest elk won his choice of female and then guarded the harem. That was what he'd learned on Wikipedia before he left home and his computer.

Tomo spoke. "As a healer, I know the chemical changes that take place in our brains and bodies. As a Netah, I have grown up watching the mature ones go through it. It's completely natural and unavoidable."

"Do we have to talk about this now?" Josh asked.

"No, of course not, it's just that I have experience that may help you know what to expect." Tomo paused. "It may be different for you as a halfling. I think that if you know what might happen and are prepared, it won't be as disturbing."

"Disturbing? Have you gone through the rut already?"

"Yes." Tomo seemed to be holding something back.

Josh became alarmed. "It was disturbing?"

Tomo glanced at Josh. "Let me explain."

"Okay," Josh agreed. "Go ahead, I'm listening."

On the way downhill Tomo described how the chemical changes felt. They were strong and consuming. Anyone who fought the feelings only felt worse. He said it was best to roll with it, not judge, and not hold back.

"You mean about the fighting part?" Josh asked. He didn't want to discuss the chemical attraction part, not yet.

"Yes. Listen, I'll have your back. You might want to try to stay out of it and just observe, but I think that will be harder on you, traumatizing. I've spoken with other healers about it, and no one knows what will happen to you. You're the first Netah anyone knows about who hit puberty before transforming and becoming fully Netah."

"So, am I like your senior project? You'll be studying and reporting on my progress while keeping me out of trouble?"

"I don't know what a senior project is, but as a friend and a healer, yes, you are my project." Tomo bit off some fresh green buds at shoulder height and chewed a moment before saying, "I want to help, and I will not judge. I know this is all new to you. Will you let me help?"

"Will I let you?" he said to Tomo. "Duh, yeah, and thanks! I mean, I'll have your back, too, if you need me."

"That's reassuring." Tomo teased but then seemed to reconsider his sarcasm. "Judging by the size of your antlers, you will be formidable."

"What? Really? I can't even feel them," Josh said. He tossed his head around as if testing for their weight.

"Yeah, they're at least a foot long with two branches already. Plus, since you arrived at the lodge, you've grown taller. Didn't you notice that?"

"Ha!" Josh laughed. "It's not like there's a mirror."

Tomo laughed as he transformed and entered the security lodge, Josh close on his heels.

"Heyo! They've returned!" Rodan greeted them from the far side of the great room.

"What, you thought we'd skip out before the big trial?" Josh laughed.

Arman chortled. "Wouldn't put it past you, halfling."

Rodan raised one eyebrow at Arman. Josh rolled his eyes. "Have a little faith! I wouldn't miss this rodeo for the world. When do we leave?"

"I'm driving the truck in the morning," Arman said. "It's not far, but no one wants to hold up the trial waiting for you to get your beauty sleep." He turned to Rodan. "You're riding with me, right? The children can climb in back." He snorted at his own sarcasm. "Meet us at sunrise out front."

"You got it," Tomo responded, ignoring Arman's snide remarks.

Rodan pointed to the counter by the kitchen. "Posie dropped off some reading material for you, Josh."

Josh found a stack of thick landscape and horticultural books. "Well, I guess I'd better get to it." He gathered them up and walked back to his room, his curiosity piqued.

He flipped through illustrations of prairie, mountain, forest and wetland plants, shrubs and trees. They were beautiful watercolor renderings, and he admired the artistry as much as the detail. His eyes grew heavy before he got to the end of the first book, so he stacked them all next to his bed and turned out his light. He knew he'd have plenty of time to study later. Tomorrow he had to be up early, and he wanted a clear head for the trial.

CHAPTER 21

Rodeo

Josh climbed into the back of the truck with Tomo. He held up his fist for a bump. Tomo looked blankly at him. "Hold yours up like this," Josh instructed. With a shrug of his shoulders, Tomo complied, and Josh bumped his fist and finished with an exploding flourish, including the sound effects. Tomo checked his knuckles. Josh laughed. "Come on, it's a signal between friends. In this case, it means 'let's do this!'"

Tomo grinned and held his fist back up. They bumped and he copied the flourish and then nodded. "Curious, amusing, and strangely companionable."

"You sound like Spock," Josh laughed. He braced a foot against the wheel well when Arman started the truck and wished they had a cushion to sit on.

"Who's Spock," Tomo asked. He rolled the spare tire behind the truck cabin and sat on it, grabbing the side to brace himself. He left room for Josh.

With an exaggerated sigh, Josh said, "Never mind." He moved to sit on the tire.

"Suit yourself." Tomo shook his head.

"I can see what you're thinking and no, I have not lost my marbles." Josh held tight.

"You can't see my thoughts. That's crazy," retorted Tomo. "And what are marbles?"

"Okay, so now we have something," Josh laughed. "You teach me about girls, and I'll teach you all the really cool things about humans that you don't know. Deal?"

"Deal," Tomo snorted, pleased and mollified.

Rodan spoke through the open back window of the cab. "Someone's feeling better this morning."

"Yeah, I feel great," Josh shouted over his shoulder. "I don't think I even rolled over last night, I slept so hard."

Tomo asked, "And your head is better?"

"Yep, no complaints."

Everyone fell silent for a moment. Josh broke the silence. "So, how long do trials like this take?"

Rodan turned in his seat and answered, "It's hard to say. The charges against Vehoe are serious. They will be read, the proof provided, then Vehoe will have a chance to defend himself."

"Vehoe won't have a lawyer to speak for him?"

"No, we eliminate the middle man," Rodan answered. "There are some among us who have special abilities beyond those of ordinary Netahs. They almost always make up the four others that are not from the community of the accused. Since this trial is a big deal, I'm sure they will be there."

"What kinds of abilities?"

Arman let out a huff of disgust. He turned to Rodan and said, "Does that kid ever stop asking stupid questions?" He shook his head and stared out the windshield.

Rodan answered, "Give the kid a break. How is he supposed to learn if he doesn't ask questions?" Josh was glad Rodan had his back.

Arman muttered, "It's like having a freakin' toddler around all the time."

Rodan paused then said, "As if you know anything about toddlers." To Josh he said, "We defend ourselves, because a couple of the jurors can detect lies."

"Huh," Josh turned to watch the dust billow out behind the truck as he remembered that Lorna, the lynx who was council president, had sat in his lap the first time they met and that contact had been like a lie detector, while her purring relaxed him. He noticed several small groups of elk moving in the same direction they were going. The truck followed a twin track barely visible as dirt ruts. He asked one last question when he realized they were slowing and probably almost there. "Will I have to testify?"

No one answered as the truck pulled up to a small corral with a set of bleachers on one side under a metal roof. They parked next to several other pickups, including the one Josh knew belonged to Howie and Stella. *Okay, there's someone I know.*

Everyone got out of the truck. Arman waited for Josh, tossed him a cowboy hat while he placed his own squarely on his head. Josh realized it fit the ruse that this was a human rodeo, not a Netah trial. Arman said, "Quit worrying. Rodan has your statement. He recorded the facts. It's Vehoe's trial, not yours. Everything does not revolve around you." He moved to walk away and then turned back. "However, if you are asked questions, be honest, no matter what."

"No matter what?" Josh squeaked. Arman was not helping his nerves.

"Yeah, because they'll know if you're telling the truth." Arman grinned. Josh didn't like that sneer. Arman started to walk away, but paused again and said, "It's not like you have anything to hide, right?" As he followed Rodan and Tomo, he said over his shoulder, "Come on, don't dawdle."

Josh watched as a small group of elk approached the corral. Barely pausing in their steps, they all transformed into humans wearing western-style clothes and climbed the steps to seats under the awning. Josh and Tomo took seats Pehpe had saved for them. As they sat down, Josh looked around at the sea of faces behind them in the stands and spread out around the corral. He recognized not only his new elk friends from other lodges, but also several other familiar faces. Fern sat with her parents, Crawley sat next to Atlas and Thomas, and George chatted with his sister and Howie at the railing.

Voices hushed and all eyes turned to a slender woman wearing a white cowboy hat and shirt. She stepped into the arena. At her signal several people pulled away from chatting in the stands and headed down to the arena. Voices grew hushed. Josh watched Crawley's brothers, Atlas and Thomas; Fern's mom, Julia; George's sister, Stella; and a pretty young woman, a stranger, all walking into the arena. From among his elk friends, Kim, Nohka, Ano, Esok, and Rodan rose to their feet and followed the others.

The jurors picked up folding chairs and set them down in a semicircle in front of a small enclosure made of wire fencing. Vehoe sat inside the enclosure, a blinking collar at his neck, his hands manacled in his lap. The jurors faced the stands.

The woman in white raised her fist and silence fell on the crowd. The woman spoke into a microphone like she was the announcer at a rodeo. "Ladies and gentle Netahs, thank you for your attention. Today we will hear charges against Vehoe. I ask all in attendance to please remain silent and alert. We have assembled our jurors." She looked around at those seated in the ring. "We will begin with the charges. Atlas, you have our attention." She held out the microphone, and they waited as Atlas stood and took up the mike with righteous dignity.

The smoky smooth voice of the woman obviously belonged to Lorna. Josh studied the other jurors and leaned over to Tomo. "Who's the girl? I don't recognize her."

Tomo shrugged. "I'm not sure. She's pretty, though, right?"

"Yeah, but there's something about her eyes." Josh stared at the girl, who looked up with a mischievous grin, and gave him a small wave before she could stop herself. "Is it possible? Is she the eagle that broke the drone?"

Tomo laughed quietly. "Wouldn't that be cool. Did we get her name?"

"Nope." Josh raised his hand to wave back, then glanced over at Ano, who had seen the whole exchange and glared at Josh, her arms folded across her chest, her lips a thin line. Josh realized she was acting jealous. *Good to know, tread lightly!*

Atlas cleared his throat and tapped the mike, his ten-gallon black hat shading his eyes, while his large silver belt buckle glinted in the sun. Lorna sat down. Atlas began, "Thank you, madame president." He paused long enough to perch a small pair of reading glasses on the end of his nose and then read the charges from a notebook.

Josh remembered Atlas's imperious manner from the last time they'd met. Josh looked around and caught Crawley's eye. She winked at him when their eyes met and then returned her gaze to her brother. Atlas flipped a couple of pages and adjusted his glasses. "To the charge of relations with a human, I present proof in the person of Josh, a halfling Netah elk who only became full Netah within the last few months, as his human body reached puberty. Josh, please stand." Atlas raised his chin to search for Josh in the stands.

Josh stood a few moments with his head down, his hands in his pockets, then sat back down. Tomo patted his back.

"Josh's human mother did not know that his father was Netah, which mitigates the circumstances, as no knowledge of our secret society was divulged. However, because her only son had to leave unexpectedly and with no explanation, of which there could be none, she suffered great mental anguish. Her recovery is slow but assured, as we have a very talented mental health expert overseeing her care." He paused and looked up from his notes. "Are there any questions?"

Yeah, who's the mental health expert? Josh did not, however, ask his question. He considered the possibilities and wondered if it was Fern's mom? Or maybe her dad was the psychologist? Josh couldn't remember. He also didn't want to slow down the proceedings with questions that were off topic. It helped to know his mom was being looked after.

A stranger raised his hand and Atlas pointed to him and nodded. "How do we know Vehoe is the father? What proof do we have?"

"Samples have been analyzed from both Vehoe and Josh. It has been confirmed and is incontrovertible."

Josh's mouth dropped open. *When had they taken a sample?* His mind raced until he remembered his injuries when he arrived at Hesta's house, which were treated by Ohma. She could have kept the bandages for testing.

Atlas continued, checking his notes. His voice droned and Josh couldn't concentrate. Instead, he watched the faces in the stands, noting their reactions. When Atlas paused for questions, no one moved. However, low voices rose from around Josh as people murmured things like, "The guy is a real nutcase!" and "Why am I not surprised?" Others visibly squirmed in their seats. Many glanced surreptitiously at Josh. Josh studied his hands. He chewed on a hangnail, and tried to listen, grateful for the cover his hat brim provided.

Atlas continued. "The accused then approached his son, but the boy was able to talk his way out."

Josh coughed and mumbled, "Approached? That's what you call a kidnapping?"

"Way to go, Josh," Pehpe patted him on the back, as Tomo snorted at Josh's comment.

Atlas looked up from his notes and gave Pehpe a withering look before he continued. He described the cloaking and kidnapping, and final parting punch.

Gasps and groans rose from the stands and the people standing around the corral. Josh looked over at Rodan, who nodded back. Josh knew that Rodan was the source of this information. Many people around the corral began talking angrily and gesturing wildly, obviously upset by this story. One guy kicked the post he stood next to, which didn't look like a good idea, as he limped back to his position along the railings. Josh thought Atlas was laying it on a bit thick, calling him a boy, drumming up sympathy from the stands. No one had called him a boy for a while.

Atlas had paused and looked up, waiting for questions. None came. The only sound was the whine of protests coming from Vehoe's frozen mouth. People sat forward to listen as Atlas described the manhunt.

The tone of the voices in the stands changed to jubilation as people all around Josh congratulated each other, clapped each other on backs, whooped and hollered like they were at a real rodeo and this was the excitement they had come for. Atlas turned his back to the stands and faced Vehoe. "How does the accused plead?"

A tense hush settled on the people and all eyes turned to the prisoner. Thomas stood from his seat, looked at Vehoe, and tapped a small device he held in his hand.

"Nnnuummph!" Vehoe responded. Thomas frowned and tapped his device again, apparently allowing Vehoe to speak more clearly. "Not guilty." With another tap, the young man silenced Vehoe again. In the meantime, laughter erupted from the crowd, followed by boos and insults aimed at Vehoe. Josh almost felt bad for the guy. No one seemed to be on his side. This did not feel like justice. Who would defend Vehoe?

LISA KANIUT COBB

Lorna took the microphone from Atlas. She turned to Vehoe and said, "Vehoe, you may now plead your case." She did not hand him the microphone but placed it in a stand next to the enclosure. Then she picked up her chair and moved it away, turning it so she faced Vehoe. The others in the arena did the same. Lorna nodded to Thomas; he tapped his device.

Vehoe looked at the jurors sitting in front of him, then up into the stands. He seemed to be gauging his audience.

Josh whispered to Tomo, "He has to defend himself, no lawyer?"

"Right. Simplifies things."

"Doesn't seem fair. How do they detect lies?"

Tomo looked at Josh and explained in a low voice, "Stella watches for physical ticks that show lies, Julia can see changes in his magnetic field, Thomas can smell emotional reactions like Lorna, I don't know what the other girl does."

Josh nodded, impressed.

Vehoe's voice rose to fill the stands with a high, childlike whine "It's not my fault. It's all my brother's fault!"

The stands erupted with boos and hisses. Several people even threw rotten vegetables at Vehoe.

"You don't have a brother!" someone yelled from the railing of the corral. "Spineless! Unbelievable! Figures!" were some other shouts.

"Yes I duh-duh- do!" Vehoe's voice boomed defiantly. "M-m-m-a my twin is Hesta." A collective gasp rose from the stands. Vehoe shouted. "He stole everything from me. As the oldest, I should have been in charge. I should have had Ohma, bu-bu- but Hesta stole her. He convinced my father I was wu-wu- weak and unfit to lead. My father puh-puh- pushed me aside." He hung his head and took a breath. Josh had heard the man stutter before and thought how frustrating it must have been for Vehoe.

More quietly Vehoe said, "I fell in love. She didn't judge me." He paused, a picture of pure dejection. "I didn't know the muh-muh- meat was tainted. I needed money. I thought I was heh-heh- helping thuh-thuh- that school. I di-di- didn't know!" Now he whined. Josh squirmed in his seat. This was difficult to watch.

"I-I-I had to escape and find Ja-Ja- Josh. I had to explain. I thought he'd understand. No-no- nope. That tha- that little shit . . ." he spit that word out like it tasted bad, "turned away, too!"

A roar rose from the stands as people jumped to their feet and yelled. Some stomped their feet to drown him out. Lorna stood, turned a very stern face to the crowd, and raised her open hand, then closed it into a fist. It was very effective. People sat and hushed.

Tomo put his arm over Josh's shoulder. "It's okay," he whispered. "It'll be over soon."

Vehoe raised his chin and waited a moment. "Technology." His voice became steady and low, and he spoke very slowly, enunciating. "We have so much to offer. I-I-I-." He paused as if the stuttering would stop that way. "I wanted to help the humans."

Shouts from the stands objected. "Not your decision!"

"What about us?"

"Who do you think you are?"

"You're a fraud! A dirty rotten liar!"

"You only care about yourself!"

Josh listened in horror. This didn't feel right. How could they just convict him like this? It felt like mob justice. Why didn't anyone take his side? Why didn't anybody believe him? Josh couldn't turn away, but he felt his insides doing flips. A bad taste rose into his mouth.

Lorna once again stood and raised her arm for silence. Atlas stood beside her as if his bulk would help give her some authority and security. His face grew stern, angry. Lorna's face remained inscrutable. People must have respected her a great deal, because the minute her hand went up, a hush descended on the arena. She picked up the microphone and nodded to Thomas, who tapped his device again. Vehoe was silenced, frozen in place, his eyes wide with fear.

Lorna handed the microphone to Atlas. With a small nod, he said, "We will now hear evidence that is pertinent to this case from community members and experts." He handed the mike to Thomas.

Thomas stood and flipped through his notes while he waited for people to settle down. Finally, he tapped the mike and said, "Thank you, Atlas."

Thomas addressed the arena. "I have had a week to examine Vehoe and run some tests. It appears that he has done grave damage to his own brain by using the shielding device on himself. He used it multiple times over a period of several months. The result is that he is losing his ability to form words and sentences, the stutter is an obvious symptom. His neural networks are breaking down rapidly. I do not expect him to survive the summer."

Murmurs rose from the stands as Thomas turned and handed the microphone to Julia. She had no notes. She stepped forward and spoke with authority. "I concur with Thomas that the device has damaged Vehoe's mental capacity. My examinations and discussions with Vehoe revealed that he suffers from several states of mental collapse, from paranoia to forgetfulness to bouts of violent rage and deep depression. He is a danger to himself and others. I recommend that he be placed in a secure retreat and cared for with as much compassion and kindness as is possible, in spite of his past transgressions. He is a dying Netah and does not have long to live." She lowered the mike and her head, and then returned to her seat.

Josh looked over at Vehoe and couldn't help seeing the rim of white around his eyes. He looked terrified. *Was his condition news to Vehoe?*

The arena had erupted in turmoil as people yelled at each other, at Vehoe, and at Julia. They didn't like what she'd said, like it was just an excuse for him to get away with something. They didn't agree he needed compassion and kindness. Lorna listened to the people. She looked at Julia sympathetically and nodded her approval.

Stella took the microphone from Julia and looked up at the stands. She waited for people to settle back down, then began. "Under the circumstances, the crimes would warrant erasure and banishment. It appears the defendant has already started the process on himself, unaware of the effects." Murmurs of agreement and a little derision rose from the arena.

Stella continued, "I detected no lies, however, I agree that he is a danger to himself and others, particularly in a retreat for the mentally ill. I recommend he be returned to detention. In addition, Hesta must be questioned as to the veracity of the accusations made by Vehoe. If Hesta is found culpable, then Hesta must be held accountable. The accusations do not add up to a crime, but would be a serious stain on his judgment and character. We must assess the accusations and then reconvene and determine Hesta's place in his community."

Gasps and exclamations rose all over the arena. Josh looked at Noomi and Ohma. Noomi had her face buried in her mother's shoulder, obviously crying. Ohma hid her face in Noomi's hair. *Did they not know Hesta's relationship to Vehoe? They must have! Someone had to know!*

Stella asked Thomas, "Can you tell me Hesta's condition? I do not see him here today."

Thomas answered from his seat, needing no amplification to say, "Hesta is recovering slowly from his injuries. His leg will need at least another month before he can put weight on it."

Lorna stood. She turned to the last person sitting before her. "Netse, do you have any further recommendations or comments?"

The delicate young woman rose from her seat. Her cropped white hair shifted as she took the microphone and paced in front of the others, her head down, as if gathering her thoughts. Then, she raised her chin and took the microphone from its stand. "We have learned many new things today, including accusations against a respected member of our society. We may have learned motives for at least some of Vehoe's crimes. That does not excuse them." She paced, her eyes scowling at the dry ground then lifting to squint into the stands. "By our laws, the body of evidence is strongly against the accused. He has shown a blatant disregard for our laws and our community. He committed murder. I understand Julia's plea for kindness, but agree with Stella that the retreat house is not appropriate. I recommend that he be returned to detention and be allowed to live out his days there, under close supervision and competent mental and physical care, as we would treat our elderly and infirm. We are not monsters." She gazed sternly at the crowd before she attached the mike to its stand and returned to her seat. The people in the stands fidgeted and grumbled, perhaps unconvinced that they were not monsters.

Atlas retrieved the mike and announced, "Jury members will now discuss what has transpired. Netahs you are released to move around and speak with each other as you see fit." The people in the center of the arena drew their chairs into a closed circle and spoke with soft voices to each other.

People quietly left the stands and gathered around the corral. Some watched the jurors, looking for signs of assent or dissent. Others treated the trial as an excuse to catch up with friends. George and Howie could be heard laughing from the back of the corral. Josh saw Ohma and Noomi huddled together in a top corner of the stands, their faces stony. He started up the steps towards them. When Noomi saw him, she scowled and shook her head emphatically, so Josh turned away. *Is she mad at me that Hesta is injured? Does she blame me?* He wanted to believe her feelings would change once she realized none of that was his fault.

Crawley appeared out of nowhere, which was not unusual for her. She pulled Josh into a hug and said, "How are you holding up, boyfriend?"

That made Josh smile. It seemed like years ago that they had pretended to be dating at the school dance. As he pulled away from her hug, he planted a kiss on her cheek. "Jeez. We had fun that night, right?"

"You can say that again." She held up her pointer finger. "But don't," she said with a wink.

"You are so literal!"

"You are so big!" Crawley stretched to put her hands on his shoulders, and she looked him up and down. "Did I shrink, or have you grown?" she laughed. "What have they been feeding you?" She shook her head. "Whatever, keep it up." She ran her finger over his upper lip and fought to control a big smile.

"Oh, you know, the usual." Josh pretended nonchalance. "Vegetables, seeds, fresh air, and Rodan's special tea."

Crawley laughed, "I bet it's the tea!"

Josh said, "Yeah, it's the tea. Hey, I didn't know your brother, Thomas, would be one of the special jurors, and Atlas is what, the prosecutor?"

"More like the court jester." She rolled her eyes.

"No, he seems very competent."

"Yeah, for a blockhead, he can be useful. People don't want to argue with him. He's very protective of Lorna. He's kind of like an oversized body guard." Crawley shook her head and focused on the center of the arena. Josh turned to see the jury move their chairs back into a semicircle facing the stands while Netse took the microphone. With no further prodding, everyone gave her their attention. Josh and Crawley sat together.

Netse's high, sharp voice came clearly through the sound system. "Ladies and gentle Netahs, the jury has decided. Vehoe is judged guilty of murder and traitorous sedition." She turned and handed the mike to Lorna.

Lorna said, "Thank you, members of the jury, for your service to your community. I release you from further duty. Our judicial experts will investigate the accusations made by Vehoe with regard to Hesta's involvement. We have appointed Netse as our Special Investigator into the matter. Vehoe will be returned to the detention center and kept under close watch, as we believe he is a suicide risk and a danger to others. That is the recommendation of the court." Lorna paused to sip a glass of water, while murmurs died down in the stands. Finally, she announced, "It is time to hear from the community. Please raise your hand if you wish to voice objections or have questions. We will begin with our peer jury members."

People shifted in their seats. Josh leaned in to whisper to Tomo, "I thought she was a lawyer, but she's an investigator! Maybe she's both."

Tomo nodded then asked, "Do you have any questions for Vehoe?"

Josh was grateful he hadn't said "your dad." He shook his head. "No. I just want this to be over and behind me."

They scanned the faces in the stands, and it soon became clear that no one seemed interested in further questions. Lorna announced, "If there is no further discussion, we will vote. Anyone against following the recommendations of our head juror raise your hand." Lorna patiently searched for a raised hand. The crowd sat motionless. "The Netahs have decided unanimously then. Thank you. This court is adjourned."

CHAPTER 22

A Bear, a Raven, and a Fox

Some people milled around, others instantly transformed and left. Crawley patted Josh's arm, then swooped over the heads of the crowd to land near her mother. Josh and Tomo were delighted when Netse transformed into an eagle and circled once over their heads, then gave a loud eagle cry before flying away. Tomo asked, "You want to walk back with me? I could use the exercise."

Josh nodded. "Give me a minute, though, okay? I want to say goodbye to some people." Before he could get far a commotion down in the center of the ring drew everyone's attention. Vehoe had been allowed to stand, to prepare for transportation. During the brief moment he could talk again he called out over the crowd. "Arman, I'm sorry!"

A collective gasp rose over the arena, and everyone stopped in their tracks. Then a roar of voices turned the quiet rodeo arena into chaos. Lorna motioned for the jury to return. Atlas moved to her side and they exchanged a few private words. Moments later, with a nod from the jury, Atlas took the mike and said, "Arman, report to the ring, immediately."

Everyone looked for him, but Arman seemed to have disappeared into thin air. Josh watched as the security bachelors formed up and moved through the subdued crowds, searching for Arman. Five minutes later, Rodan reported back to Lorna. Atlas once again took the mike and this time he announced, "Arman appears to have left the proceedings. Anyone with information as to his whereabouts, please report to the council. Thank you for your assistance. You are free to go."

After a few moments, the crowds began to disperse again. Josh watched as Tomo approached Ohma and Noomi. Josh wished he'd stayed with Tomo and could hear what they said. He assumed it had to do with healing Hesta, since Tomo studied with Ohma.

Josh found the bear siblings as they got to their pickup truck. "Hey, you two, are you leaving the valley now?"

"Josh!" Howie sounded happy to see him. Stella moved in for a hug. "Well, that went well. I wonder why Vehoe apologized to Arman, though. Weird, huh?"

Josh made a pained face. "Did they ever figure out if Vehoe had an inside man?"

Stella and Howie frowned and then shrugged. She said, "Looks like he just named his spy, right?"

Howie said, "It's for the council to decide. They still have to talk with Hesta and decide his role. I guess Arman will be included in their inquiries, if they can find the guy. Vehoe's fate has been decided. That must be a relief to you, eh, Josh?"

"Definitely." Josh removed his borrowed cowboy hat and scratched his head. "Did you know Vehoe was Hesta's twin?"

Howie and Stella frowned, looking at each other for confirmation. "Uh, no," they both said, shaking their heads.

"Me, either. I can't believe no one here knew about it. I mean, how could that even happen?"

The siblings studied the toes of their cowboy boots.

Josh frowned. "There has to be someone here who knew their parents, knew them when they were growing up?" He waited, angry that this secret could be kept in such a small community.

Just then Lorna nudged the back of his knees in her lynx form. She looked up at them and nodded a greeting before she transformed into her human self. "I couldn't help but overhear your question, Josh," she said. "I wondered why no one raised it during the trial."

Howie and Stella shrugged. Lorna continued, "Since no one asked, I assumed everyone knew. It is possible that there is no one left in the valley who knew Hesta and Vehoe as boys. Their parents are long gone." Lorna focused her golden eyes on Josh and said, "You should be aware, Josh, that this valley has known troubled times. A leadership battle many years ago became famously contentious."

"Between Hesta and Vehoe?" Josh asked.

With a sigh, Lorna explained. "There were two factions. I did not know of their familial ties, only the rivalry, but those things tend to be kept within a community. They prefer not to air their dirty laundry; I think the expression is." She looked pleased at her little joke then glanced over at Stella and Howie. "If you two don't mind, I would like to talk with Josh a moment before he returns to his community."

"Sure, no problem." Howie nodded. "We'll keep in touch, Josh!" They opened their truck and climbed aboard.

Stella opened her window and said, "You will be close to us this summer. Don't be a stranger!"

Howie leaned over and spoke through Stella's window, "Maybe you can help me with the truck!"

"That sounds amazing, thanks, guys." Josh felt Lorna slip her hand under his elbow and steer him away from the milling Netahs.

She said, "You know, there are some things about the way Netahs live that you still have to learn. For instance, how many older men have you met in the valley?"

Josh thought about that. "Mako seems the oldest in the lodge. Are you suggesting that there are no other older Netahs? Is that what Hesta meant when he said he could use some help in the valley?"

"Perhaps," Lorna said. "You will learn a lot about life as a Netah elk this summer, when they go to their summer grounds. Then you will experience your first Netah rut season. I do not wish to ruin it for you or give you any preconceptions. Let me just say, for some it is wonderful, for others it is not. Who knows how you will fare?"

"Huh, I've been hearing comments about summer games. Is that what you mean?"

Lorna dipped her head in assent. Josh patted her hand on his arm. They had arrived at the corral fence, and he rested his arms on the top rail. He fingered the brim of his cowboy hat as he nodded at people's greetings. Lorna leaned against a post and crossed her ankles and arms, watching Josh with a twinkle in her eyes. "I like you, Josh. You can cope with just about anything. You embrace change, which is very smart, because you cannot avoid it. I hope you can keep your curious and sunny manner." Josh snorted and grinned to himself. *If only she knew!* "You will be challenged," Lorna continued. "There may be ill-feelings harbored within the valley from old conflicts. I almost want to move you away to avoid the possible trouble. Would you want that?"

"Huh? What? Move away from trouble?" Josh laughed, turning to her. They had only met a few times before, but Lorna treated him like a friendly aunt who looked out for him. She had a quiet air of authority that no one questioned, and Josh liked that about her. "That wouldn't help." He shook his head slowly, then joked. "Trouble seems to follow me like a dark cloud."

Lorna raised her eyebrows, and said with a sigh, "Be aware that your friends will never be far away. Go visit the bears if you need a break."

"Okay." Josh squinted at her, as if trying to make sense of something in his head. "I'll keep my nose clean, don't worry. You say my friends will be nearby? Are you talking about Fern, Rose, Crawley, and George? If that's true, wow, that will be awesome! Thank you." He searched the faces around them. "Speaking of which, have you seen George?"

George had been talking with a group of his bear friends nearby. He stepped away from them and approached. "Did I just hear my name?"

Rodan walked past and asked, "You need a ride back, Josh?"

Josh shook his head. "No thanks, I'm walking with Tomo." Rodan nodded and opened his truck door to climb inside.

Meanwhile, Josh squirmed in George's bear hug, laughing. He gasped when he was released, then coughing for dramatic effect, he said, "I understand that you live close to our summer grounds? You live near Howie and Stella?"

Laughing, Lorna patted Josh's arm and said, "I'll leave you two. Stay safe, Josh. Goodbye."

"Thanks, bye." Josh nodded.

"Nearby? It's all relative." George squinted. "But yeah. You planning a visit?"

"Definitely. How will I find you?" Josh asked.

George considered that and said, "We don't usually mingle with you elk in the summer, so I can't think of anyone here who knows where we are! Wait, no, I know. Crawley is always around. Or maybe one of the others would be willing to lead you to us."

"You mean like Fern or Rose?" Josh asked, excited.

"Sure." George nodded. "I'll set it up. Say, you haven't started learning how to communicate with our undernet yet, have you? I mean, that would make it easy."

"Tomo said something about that, yeah, and said he'd try to explain it and teach me," Josh said.

"You talking about me?" Tomo wandered over. "Hi, George!"

"Hi, Tomo, is it? Nice to see you. Like that detainer thingy you made. Worked great," George said.

"Yeah, thanks. What did I say I'd try to explain?" Tomo asked.

"The undernet, remember?" Josh asked.

"Oh sure. We've kind of been a little distracted, but sure. We can work on it all summer long."

"Oh great, summer school," Josh grumbled. He noticed Tomo's look of disappointment and laughed. "Kidding." He held up his fist and Tomo remembered what to do.

"Whoa! What's that, like a secret handshake or something?" George exclaimed. He held up his fist and Tomo demonstrated again. George loved it. "Hey, Josh, have you seen Stella and Howie? I was supposed to hitch a ride with them."

"Oops, I think they already left."

"Those little boogers!" George growled. "No problem, I'll ride with one of these other ranch hands. See you later." He hailed a couple of cowboys and walked away with them.

Tomo asked, "Did you talk to everyone you wanted to?"

"Aw, man! No, I missed Fern."

Tomo grinned from ear to ear as he watched a fluffy fox rub against Josh's ankles like a cat.

"Fern!" Josh stepped away, and she transformed and threw herself into his arms.

"You didn't really think I'd let you get away without a hug, did you?" she asked, then turned to Tomo and gave him the ol' fluttering eyelash treatment. "Who's this handsome guy? A friend of yours?"

"Fern, Tomo. Tomo, Fern."

With a newfound cowboy drawl, Tomo touched his brim and said, "Pleased to meet you, ma'am."

Fern's eyebrows rose and she gave him a coy smile. Meanwhile, Josh checked out her outfit, complete with a short white skirt, red cowboy shirt and boots, and white cowboy hat. She looked like a Texas cheerleader. She turned her eyes back to Josh and appraised him top to bottom. "You been working out?"

"A little." Josh grinned at Tomo, his sparring partner. "Also, a bit of construction work." He bent his arm and made a fist for her, a big grin on his face.

"He's wimpy, check mine!" Tomo said, making a fist, too.

"Oh my!" Fern said, squeezing Tomo's arm. With a flip of her long red ponytail, she slipped her hand into the crook of each guy's arm. "Come on, guys, let's take a walk."

"Which way you goin'?" Tomo asked.

"Whichever way you're going," Fern replied with a flirty giggle.

Josh felt like he was in an old western, walking off into the sunset, except it wasn't that late yet, and most cowboys rode horses or pickup trucks.

"Seriously, Fern," Josh said. "Where are your folks? Don't you need to go with them?"

Fern stopped in her tracks and frowned at him, crossing her arms. "Josh the killjoy! You know, a girl doesn't get many chances to enjoy the attention of two handsome boys like you. Couldn't you let me enjoy it a little longer?"

Tomo gave Josh a shove on the arm and said with a sly grin, "Yeah, Josh. You're no fun!"

Josh laughed, held up his hands, and said, "Is there something you two want to tell me?"

Tomo laughed. Fern turned to go find her folks, but not before giving Josh a swat on the behind. "Ow!" she complained, shaking her hand like it hurt. She transformed and bounced away through the sagebrush.

Tomo was still laughing. "I like her!"

"Yeah, I think everyone does," Josh groaned. "Come on, let's get out of here." He could see that they were among the last people standing around. It appeared the stands would remain, abandoned until the next time they were needed for a trial. Josh transformed and took off. Tomo caught up and they raced all the way back to the lodge. They were a good match, one minute one led, then the other passed.

CHAPTER 23

Messy Family

The trial only took a day. Josh couldn't believe that it was over already. As they approached the lodge, he found himself feeling at loose ends. His friends had all left town and who knew when he would see them again. He could look forward to working with Posie, but how could he get word to her that he could work now?

"Hey, Tomo?" Josh asked.

"Mmm?" Tomo paused at the lodge door.

"Can you communicate with Posie for me?" Tomo nodded. "I need to let her know I'm available. Maybe she can swing by for me in the morning?"

Tomo nodded. "Sure. On it." He lowered his head and put his lips around a large bunch of grasses in the water. He didn't bite, he hummed. Josh waited as Tomo kept his head down, no longer humming, apparently listening. Tomo raised his head. "She's far away. Not returning soon. She'll stop by after."

"Huh, that means I'm sitting around waiting with nothing to do!"

"Don't you have some books to go through?" Tomo reminded him. "It might be good to have a little downtime, right?"

"Oh, right. I could do some prep reading." They transformed and walked inside. Before Tomo could duck into his own room, Josh asked, "Say, are you helping Ohma with Hesta? How's he doing?"

"He'll recover, but it will be slow."

"Will you be there when they question Hesta?"

"Yeah." Tomo screwed his eyes shut and bit his lower lip. "That's going to be hard on Noomi and Mesenova, not to mention Ohma."

"Yeah," Josh agreed, leaning against his bedroom door. "Do you think I should go see if there's anything I can do?" Josh asked hopefully. He had been very surprised and a little hurt when Noomi waved him away.

Tomo said, "Why don't you let me assess things tomorrow. I'll let you know if I think a visit would be welcome."

"I'll bet Mesenova would be happy for a break. I could take him out for a game of hide-and-seck. It's his favorite." Josh remembered the little boy fondly. Then something suddenly occurred to him. "Tomo, if Hesta and Vehoe are brothers, that makes me Hesta's nephew, right?"

Tomo snorted, "Uh-huh."

Josh continued slowly, "Noomi and Mesenova are my cousins, my family."

Tomo cocked his head. "You're absolutely right." His face clouded. "Not that you have any choice, but you may want to distance yourself a little. I mean, Hesta's our chief, for now, but that also means there are loads of bucks looking to topple him. That puts you in his shadow, but with a small status elevation."

"Status? I never noticed anyone paying attention to that sort of thing before. What does that even mean?"

Tomo paused before answering, as if searching for words that would be kind or at least clear. Finally, he explained, "Status is earned, during the summer games, but once a winner, always a winner in our eyes. That's status."

"And it applies to family, as well?" Josh asked.

"Right, so you are now a bigger target."

"It sounds like war, but I'm only a nephew, and a halfling at that. How can I be a threat to anyone?" Josh felt like pounding something, but his door looked very solid. "That reminds me, do you know how Vehoe is doing?"

Tomo leaned his back against his door and studied his fingernails before saying, "Word is that he will recover, at least from his physical injuries. The big question is how long will his brain function? That's a big unknown because that kind of brain damage has never been seen before."

"Maybe . . ." Josh considered how to put his next question. He now understood how reputations followed family. He asked, "Do you think I would be allowed to visit Vehoe? I kind of felt bad that no one spoke for his side at the trial. Who's looking after him? Besides, I may not have much time left to talk to him."

Tomo softened. "Are you sure you want to? I mean, hasn't he put you through enough already?"

"Yeah, definitely, but he is my father. Maybe he'll tell me more about our family."

"I am talking with him as part of his care team," Tomo said. "Do you have specific questions?"

"I want to know about the power struggle, who was involved? Also, are there more relatives?"

Tomo nodded. "I can ask around discreetly for you. Do you know that while Hesta is injured, a council of elders is in charge? I can ask them who might have more information for you."

Josh nodded. "Okay, thanks." He pushed his hair out of his eyes. "Do I know these elders?"

"Well, sure. Mako is one, so is Manny. I think they both like you, so don't sweat it." Tomo grinned and scratched his head. "This is going to be one heck of a summer."

CHAPTER 24

Romance in the Air

The next day, Tomo was already gone when Josh appeared in the great hall. Josh threw himself into his floor mopping chore. Then he settled into the library with the books Posie had left for him, studying the drawings, learning the differences among the many grasses that grew in their valley. That first evening, Tomo returned to the lodge early with Ano and Eve in attendance. They invited Josh to go for a walk with them. He jumped at the chance to get outside with his friends and stretch his elk muscles.

The girls took off with no warning and Josh and Tomo had to race to catch up. Josh felt the tension from his neck and shoulders fall away as they ran. They found seats on a large red rock formation and settled down to digest and talk. The ongoing investigation into Hesta and Vehoe's history came up immediately. Tomo said, "Hesta says that he won his place as the chief of this valley in a leadership challenge ten years ago. It had nothing to do with their father, although he admits their dad had been hard on Vehoe."

"Is that always the way leadership is determined? With a fight?" Josh asked.

Ano answered, "We prefer to call it a challenge rather than a fight, except that, yeah, it can turn violent."

Eve said, "Of course it helped that Ohma chose Hesta, as well. I mean she is the old chief's daughter and therefore very high ranking."

Josh said, "Ranking?" He turned to Tomo. "Like the status we were talking about yesterday?"

Tomo nodded, and Ano said, "Yeah, but our status has nothing to do with wealth or anything. It's about character, family, and reputation."

Tomo agreed, "Right, and it seems Vehoe's character was always under attack, from his father and his brother."

"Are you saying they used character assassination against Vehoe to turn others away from him?" Josh asked. "Sounds like nasty politics."

"That's a good simile, Josh," Tomo said. "At any rate, Vehoe made it easy for people to believe the stories, because he had always been rebellious, according to Hesta."

"Were you guys around when this was happening?" Josh asked, looking around at all three of his friends.

Eve took a breath before answering, as if gathering courage. "We were all too young to pay any attention to those kinds of things."

"Huh." Josh realized he had not taken politics seriously until recently, either. He wouldn't be able to vote for several more years as a human, so politics hadn't really seemed important. "I guess that explains why no one knew they were brothers. Although Mako should have known, and Haiman. I mean they're old."

Tomo shook his head in disagreement. "I think there's an unspoken rule that the winner takes all and the losers keep their mouths shut. We can't have our strongest men fighting among themselves all the time. It has to wait until the rut season. Then challenges happen and our females make their choices. Meantime, we have to live and work together."

Tomo stood and they walked towards the lodge, the girls veering off towards their own lodge. Josh followed Tomo at a distance, lost in his own thoughts about simmering grudges, and how females had a lot of power to keep the peace in this society.

The next day dawned gloriously warm. Tomo left early, and Josh ran laundry. These domestic tasks were mindless and easy, and Josh lost himself in them, then buried himself in his textbooks that afternoon. Once again Tomo invited him outside at the end of the day, while the sun hung high enough over the western mountains that they'd have light for several more hours. Ano and Eve appeared as if they had all agreed the night before to meet again. Josh realized that they were getting together to keep Josh informed.

After eating, they sprawled beside a stream bank carpeted with soft new grass, capturing the last warm rays of the sun on their tawny fur coats. Netse was staying in Ano and Eve's lodge. She had talked the night before with the girls. Ano said, "Netse thinks there will be no criminal charges against Hesta. He broke no laws. It appears Vehoe was the problem. He never accepted the results of the challenge or Ohma's choice."

Josh said, "Arman has not returned to the security lodge. Has anyone seen him?"

"Nope." Tomo shook his head.

"So what happens with him? I mean, didn't Vehoe imply Arman was involved when he apologized to him at the trial?"

Tomo sighed and nodded to the girls. "I'll field this one. I guess that until he shows up, we'll never know his connection, but he will remain under suspicion. My guess is he won't show up. He'll move to another herd and settle in, probably changing his name and never mentioning anything about it."

"Would he get turned in if he was found out?"

"Yes, in most places, but there are places a Netah can disappear and no one asks questions."

"What about the guys that broke out of the ag facility with Vehoe, wouldn't one of them know who their inside man was?" Josh asked.

Eve grinned. "You'd make a good detective, Josh."

Tomo nodded. "Do you want to be involved in the inquiry, Josh?"

"Probably a conflict of interest." Josh frowned.

"Well, at any rate," Tomo said. "I'll pass along your questions to Netse. She'll know who should follow up on that. As for Hesta, his injuries are serious, but will heal. He will have to retire as chief, however. He will not be able to withstand a physical challenge."

Josh asked, "Is the chief always challenged, every year?"

"Yes," Ano said. "That's how we ensure that our biggest and strongest male is in charge."

"What if the biggest and strongest," Josh hesitated, then continued, "is a bully or just plain stupid?" He didn't intend to imply that Vehoe fit that description, but the comparison couldn't be avoided.

"If the biggest is a brute," Eve answered, "we have ways of ensuring that he doesn't win contests. There are disqualifying behaviors that knock them out of competition. We have ways to ensure that only males of high moral character and standards win. Our creative competitions play a large part."

Tomo agreed. "It helps that the females choose the winners in many contests."

Josh took that in then asked, "Will Hesta have to leave his home?" Josh thought about their cozy dwelling.

"No," Eve said. "It is theirs, they built it."

"Who would be the next female to choose if Ohma and Hesta retire from leadership? Noomi?" Josh asked.

"Could be, or maybe it will be me!" Eve said proudly.

Ano and Tomo nodded knowingly, while Josh's mouth fell open. "Are you Noomi's age?" he asked.

"No, but I am old enough to choose soon, if I can decide." Eve looked sideways at Tomo, and Josh wondered if she'd already made her choice. Josh wondered if Tomo even knew Eve liked him.

"Tomorrow," Tomo began, "I will volunteer to care for Vehoe until his death. I want to document his condition and will try to make him as comfortable as possible, mentally and physically."

"It won't be easy," Ano said. "I'm impressed, Tomo. I hope the elders agree to that."

Josh couldn't imagine spending the summer without Tomo at his side to help him figure out how to navigate the summer contests. He'd counted on Tomo. On the other hand, he admired his friend's curiosity and compassion. "I guess you'll have a different study subject then." He grinned mischievously. "I'm not half as interesting as a Netah with mental and physical health injuries."

Tomo sighed and rolled his eyes. "Nope, you're just a halfling, who survived childhood, poisoning, kidnapping, and being torn from his family. You're boring."

The others laughed. Ano leaned closer to Josh and batted her long dark eyelashes at him. "I think you're interesting!"

Josh looked her in the eye. Her face seemed very close, and he could smell the grass on her breath. He surprised her with a quick kiss right on the lips. In response, she did not move away, and her eyes studied him, taking in his growing antlers with a wry grin.

"Oh, get a room!" Eve groaned as she rose to her feet, laughing.

The next day Tomo left for the ag facility with a pouch full of herbs and instructions from Ohma. The Netahs all seemed restless, spending as much time as possible outside as elk. Finally, Pehpe appeared at the lodge one evening and asked for Josh.

"Hey, Josh, how are you?" Pehpe shifted on his feet. "Missed you at the construction site. We finished today."

"That's great!" Josh said. "Does that mean Haiman and Nohka will be married soon?"

"Yeah, who told you?"

"No one." Josh grinned. "It seemed logical."

"Right, well, the ceremony happens tomorrow. Are you coming?"

"Oh geez, no one told me! I don't have a gift or anything."

"Don't worry, we go as elk. How would you carry a gift? Besides, they don't want things. Friends are more important. Haven't you figured that out yet?"

"Uh, okay." Josh nodded. "So, where, when?"

"Don't worry, everybody is going. Just follow the guys from the lodge. I'll see you there."

"Yeah," Josh said. "Hey, thanks for telling me. I might have woken up to an empty lodge and had no idea where everybody went! These guys are not the best at communicating."

"Maybe it's because they're in security, you know, secrets and stuff?"

Josh snorted. "Yeah, maybe."

The morning fog and dew quickly burned off as the sun rose. Josh followed the Netahs to a site near the biggest river in the valley. It rushed with snowmelt, splashing and sparkling in the sunlight. Swifts dove over the river, snatching insects for their breakfast. Nohka and Haiman were there already standing in front of some fragrant green willows near a quieter section of river. Nohka wore a crown of blue and white wildflowers that looked beautiful against her tawny fur. Haiman looked like he'd combed his head and face fur, and he already sported an impressive set of antlers. They were lost in quiet conversation as the community gathered around them. A chorus of birdsong rang out from the willows and Josh could identify magpies, a red-winged blackbird, chickadees, and a meadowlark, accompanied by the deep-throated croaks of frogs. Josh couldn't help grinning as he found a space between Pehpe and Ano.

A truck arrived in a cloud of dust. Hesta opened the door, and a few Netahs wandered over to talk with him. He eased his broken leg out the door and, pulled himself to his feet, leaning on the car door. Ohma rushed around to him with a set of crutches, and they walked together to the front of the crowd as Netahs made room for them. They exchanged quiet greetings, then hushed. They were the only humans in the area.

Netse flew onto a branch behind Haiman and Nohka. It wasn't quite sturdy enough and swayed precariously for several moments. The birds ceased their songs and a hush settled over the Netahs. Netse said, "Thank you for coming out on this glorious morning to witness one of our most important and happy ceremonies, the joining of two Netahs, Haiman and Nohka." She waited for the applause, in the form of foot stomping, to quiet and began again. "Hesta and Nohka, do you pledge to love and honor each other in sickness and health, as Netahs in your elk and human forms, for as long as you both shall live?"

"We do," they answered together. They were gazing fondly into each other's eyes.

"Do you have a symbol of this pledge you wish to share with each other?" Netse waited.

Nohka lowered her head to the ground and picked up a flat disk of wood with her lips. She held it out for Haiman to take and then said, "Haiman, as a tree forms rings every year with new growth, so will I embrace every year that I am able to grow with you." He nodded and reverently placed the disk on the ground between them. Nohka waited expectantly.

Haiman licked his lips and glanced into the faces of his friends, gathering his composure. Then he picked up a smooth, red, polished rock from the ground. He placed it on top of the disk of wood. "Nohka, as a river rock sits in a streambed, and is smoothed over time by the force of the running water and the gentle motion among the rocks, so will I strive to become smooth and well formed by my closeness to you and your gentle influence." He kissed her on the lips.

The clearing erupted with bugles, birdsong, and frog croaks as Netahs pushed forward to congratulate the new couple and offer them words of encouragement.

Josh stayed back from the crush as he drank in the signs of friendship, compassion, and love among these Netahs. He felt a warm body nuzzle close to his right side, and he looked over to see Ano, happy tears trickling down her cheek from her big brown eyes. He placed his head against her neck, smiling. His heart felt ready to burst as he thought of his own lost family and friends. Ano's warmth reminded him that he had friends here. Another body brushed against his left side, and Josh turned to see Noomi smiling up at him. She pressed her cheek against his for a moment then said, "Welcome to the family, cousin." Josh gave a huge trembling sigh as he realized, he could be happy among these Netah.

AUTHOR'S NOTE

Netaheva'o'tse is a Cheyenne word that means "to change quickly." *Netaheva'e* means "to be different." The Cheyenne nation has a very good online dictionary at cdkc.edu where I found these words. I borrowed the first part of these words to name my creatures, the Netahs, for several reasons. I wanted my secret society to have been on the American continent from the very beginning of humans walking there, so a Native American influenced name made sense. It is also common among various Native American tribes to tell stories about people who change into animals or have special relationships with particular animals. One of the most famous characters is Kokopelli, the trickster flute player, who can transform into lots of different animals. Finally, I wanted to embrace and promote Native American attitudes towards caring for the land and animals. My characters are not based on any specific legends or people and are completely fictional.

Research Links

Hebrew name information
https://www.behindthename.com/name/joshua
https://www.urbandictionary.com/define.php?term=Josh

Renewable energy
https://www.energy.gov › energysaver › types-homes
for information about energy efficiency, efficient earth shel-
tered homes.
https://www.betterbuildingssolutioncenter.energy.gov/
search?field_technology

Character names
http://cdkc.edu/cheyennedictionary/lexicon/main.htm
http://www.cheyennelanguage.org/names/namesaudio.pdf
for information about Cheyenne names, their meanings, and to
hear their pronunciation in the original Cheyenne.

Facts about Elk, by Alina Bradford
https://www.livescience.com/54313-elk-facts.html

How to Make Pine Pitch, by Jamie L. Burleigh
https://www.primitiveways.com/pine_pitch_stick.html

Characters

Netah elk

Ano	flirty apprentice builder
Arman	grumpy second in command, security lodge
Esok	security bachelor
Eve	crabby builder apprentice
Haiman	redheaded security bachelor, fiancé of Nohka
Hesta	valley chief
Josh	main character, half human, half Netah
Kim	construction crew chief
Mako	oldest security bachelor
Manny	tile chief
Mesenova	Hesta's son
Nohka	Haiman's fiancée
Noomi	Hesta's daughter
Ohma	Hesta's wife, healer
Pehpe	apprentice builder
Posie	horticulture consultant
Rodan	security lodge captain
Tomo	bachelor healer intern

Humans

Anton	Josh's best high school friend
Danny	Josh's adoptive dad
Maureen	Josh's mom
Sarah	Anton and Josh's high school friend

Others

Atlas	raven, Crawley's brother, trial prosecutor
Crawley	raven, council person from book 1
Fern	fox, Josh's friend from book 1

George	bear, from book 1
Howie	bear, George's brother-in-law
Julia	fox Fern's mom, psychologist
Lorna	lynx, council president
Maahe	wolf leader at dragnet
Netse	eagle juror
Okomo	mountain lion leader at dragnet
Rose	skunk, pretend foster sister from book 1
Stella	bear, George's sister
Thomas	raven, Crawley's brother, healer and juror
Vehoe	Josh's birth dad

ACKNOWLEDGEMENTS

I have been very lucky to have had several beta readers, especially Katie and Jackie, who gave me enthusiastic encouragement, spent time brainstorming with me, and helped me find places where I may have gone a bit off-topic. Then came the editors at Friesen Press who performed several rounds of suggestions to help steer my edits. This is all after I thought I had the work pretty darned cleaned up. It's a humbling process, but at every step I heard that the story was good and knew each edit could only bring improvement. Thank you, Cam, for helping to walk my book through the process at Friesens Press.

My patient and kind husband has been on my team for over 40 years. Wes has been yet another reader, and has spent many a night listening as I kvetch about whatever story element or character I'm struggling with at the time. Thank you for sharing the good and bad days with me, and betting on me every time.

Thank you, Deb, Donna, and Julie, and all my other fans who have so patiently waited for me to finish book 2. Here it is! Also, hold onto your seats…book 3 is underway.

Thank you to my friends and colleagues at SCBWI, who share and understand the writing life, ups and down, and everything in between. I love meeting fellow authors and I'm really looking forward to working together. Thank you to the local bookstores who carry my books for me. I've found my people.

Thank you to my enthusiastic reviewers, especially Fleur who kicked off the reviews campaign for this book.

Thank you to Reading the West for recognizing the first Netahs book on your long list, and NIEA for making the first Netahs a finalist for your indie excellence award. I hope you'll love this book even more!

LISA KANIUT COBB is the author of *The Netahs, Into the Wilderness,* the first book in the Netah series, which won recognition on the Reading the West long list, and as a finalist for the NIEA award. Book 3 in the series is in progress. She also wrote the writing resource book *Literary Ideas and Scripts for Young Playwrights,* a book that uses various sources from poems to myths to inspire creativity, observation and problem-solving skills while creating scripts. Her short story *Something Fishy* was included in the anthology titled *The Offices of Supernatural Being.* Lisa is an active volunteer with the Society of Children's Book Writers and Illustrators, the Authors Guild, and the Colorado Independent Publishers Association. She lives and writes in Colorado.

www.lisakaniutcobb.com
Facebook: lisakaniutcobb
Twitter: @Netahmom
Instagram: @lisakaniutcobb
LinkedIn: lisakaniutcobb
GoodReads: lisakaniutcobb

ALSO BY LISA KANIUT COBB

Fiction

THE NETAHS
INTO THE WILDERNESS
BOOK I

(Available on Amazon)

Non-Fiction

LITERARY IDEAS AND SCRIPTS
FOR YOUNG PLAYWRIGHTS

(Available on Amazon)

READ ON FOR AN EXCERPT FROM

THE NETAHS
INTO THE WILDERNESS

the first book in the Netah series

LISA KANIUT COBB

PROLOGUE

The Netah council would move the team in closer. The kid was getting to a dangerous age, an unpredictable one. He'd been watched since birth, and so far, there were no signs that he could change, but they had to be certain. The new recruits checked in with their controller. Chief Crawley paced back and forth on a branch, her black wings twitching. She tried to exude authority on her first assignment for the council.

Fern waited with absolute stillness as only foxes can, even though her graceful body practically trembled with excitement. "What's the boy like, sir?"

Chief Crawley reported with an even voice, "Josh is a bright kid. He's likeable and on the quiet side, maybe because he's an only child. You might be able to get close to him through one of his friends."

"Okay, but if he starts to change, what do I do?"

"Get him outside and away from humans immediately. Don't mess around. Secrecy is number one. But meanwhile, relax. You're not alone in there," Crawley reassured her.

"Should I pretend to like him?" If she'd been her human self, she would have been blushing, not having much experience with guys and certainly none with humans.

"Your call. You did the training, even if it was a little rushed. "Good luck." Crawley nodded at Fern in dismissal.

"Thank you, sir!" Fern disappeared into the high grasses. Her little, red-furred body briefly reappeared as she leaped over a fence with a swish of her bushy, white-tipped tail. Chief Crawley liked the kid; she was spunky and not afraid to think outside the box, even if she was a little green at the job.

Chief Crawley turned to George, who towered over her. She leaped up a few branches higher. "News?"

Scratching his head and then his hindquarters, the bear seemed to gather his thoughts. Winter was fast approaching, and he was already feeling a bit sluggish and ready for a good long sleep. He reported, "Nothing much. Except he either has a scalp problem, or something is happening on his head. He scratches it all the time. That could be our first sign."

Chief Crawley cawed as she hopped onto a lower pine branch. "You mean he scratches his head like you? Maybe you both have fleas." She cackled at her own joke, flapped her black raven wings into place, and searched their surroundings. "George, are you sure no one saw you come down here?"

"No, never, sir!" He raised his chin and straightened his back - military style. "I was just a kid climbing down into a gully. Who'd care?"

"Good job." Crawley studied her friend from the academy, her head tilting to one side and then the other. "Can you believe we got this assignment together? How you doing? I know it's hard to be human all day."

"I know, right?" The bear relaxed his military posture and sat down. "I'm beat, but at the end of the day, I sleep like a bear. Pun intended."

"How long did you work on that one?" She smirked, appreciating the effort. "Anything else?"

"Yes. When is Rose coming on board? We need someone on the inside—in his home. That's definitely a security weakness."

"She'll be there tonight. It's all arranged. If that's all, we'd better split up. I'll go first. Give me five minutes before you climb back up to the trail. Okay?"

"Roger."

"Who's Roger?"

"Just an expression I picked up. It means yes."

Chief Crawley shook her head at the strange ways of humans as she took off. George watched her bank to the east and then circle as she surveyed the area. When she was a tiny black dot over the mountains, George took a deep breath and shook himself into action. The scent of fallen leaves underfoot followed him as he left. Being a Netah agent had always been his dream, and he was not going to let his people down.